Praise for *Second Time Around*

"Nancy Moser takes my breath away with plots that sizzle with excitement, unexpected turns, and characters who are fun to spend time with. You can't go wrong with *Second Time Around*."

—Hannah Alexander,
author of *The Crystal Cavern* and
the Christy Award–winning *Hideaway*

"Though time travel has fascinated novelists from Mark Twain to Audrey Niffenegger, no one writes time-stream fiction like Nancy Moser. First with *Time Lottery* and now with *Second Time Around*, she shows us that time travel isn't just about the fourth dimension. It's about the *human* dimension: love, faith, forgiveness, and healing. The story is memorable, the characters are real, and the journey through time is strange and wonderful. Don't miss it!"

—Jim Denney,
author of the Timebenders series
and *Answers to Satisfy the Soul*

"This hope-filled story will draw you in from the first page. You'll meet characters you admire and ones you love to hate. Yet through it all is woven the thread of G... ...gnty turning human choices into Hi... ...miss this tale!"

...er,
auth... ...age,"
...g in *A Bride for a Bit*

D1042577

PROPERTY OF
BEAVERTON CHURCH OF
THE NAZARENE LIBRARY

SECOND TIME AROUND

Nancy Moser

© 2004 by Nancy Moser

ISBN 1-59310-478-2

All rights reserved. No part of this publication may be reproduced or transmitted in any form or by any means without written permission of the publisher.

Scripture quotations are taken from the HOLY BIBLE, NEW INTERNATIONAL VERSION®. NIV®. Copyright © 1973, 1978, 1984 by International Bible Society. Used by permission of Zondervan. All rights reserved.

Cover Image © Lookout Design

This book is a work of fiction. Names, characters, places, and incidents are either products of the author's imagination or used fictitiously. Any similarity to actual people, organizations, and/or events is purely coincidental.

Published by Barbour Publishing, Inc., P.O. Box 719, Uhrichsville, Ohio 44683, www.barbourbooks.com

Our mission is to publish and distribute inspirational products offering exceptional value and biblical encouragement to the masses.

Printed in the United States of America
5 4 3 2 1

To my dear parents through marriage:
to Beverly and in loving memory of Bill.
Nothing made me happier than becoming a Moser.
Twenty-nine years and counting. . .

Whatever is has already been,
and what will be has been before;
and God will call the past to account.
ECCLESIASTES 3:15

Bangor, Maine

The car plunged off the cliff.

"No!"

David Stancowsky catapulted from sleep in time to hear the final echo of his cry fall away in his empty bedroom. In his empty house.

He gave himself the requisite ten seconds to allow his breathing to return to normal. There was no need to turn on a light, because he slept with one on. He grabbed the hand towel, which he placed on the bedside table every night, and rubbed his face roughly, then wiped his balding head. Would he ever be free of this nightmare?

Millie. Her car flying off the cliff. His fiancée dead.

Over the past forty-six years he'd come up with many scenarios as to how and why it had happened. Bad brakes, speed, she'd fallen asleep. . . One police officer had even broached the idea of suicide, but David had cut him off. How dare anyone even suggest. . . Their life together had been perfect, their wedding imminent. They had their entire lives in front of them.

If the crash had happened today, modern forensic technologies would have been able to show him exactly what had happened. But in 1958, a car that crashed into the ocean was lost, and a splintered guardrail told all the story that could be told.

Or that would be told.

David burrowed back into the covers, arranging his two body pillows on either side of him, remaking the moat that he nightly created in the middle of the king-size bed. Once settled, he adjusted the pillow for his head around his ears.

Drowning out the silence.

If only. . .

Atlanta, Georgia

They'd buried her mother a week ago.

Vanessa Caldwell sat in the lawyer's office with her husband, Dudley, ready to hear the will of a mother she hadn't had contact with in thirty-four years.

The lawyer had his back to them as he fiddled with a VCR.

"Can we please get this over with?" Vanessa asked. "I have things to do."

Dudley put a calming hand on her knee and gave her a *behave yourself* look.

Vanessa didn't feel like behaving herself. She wanted this over. At her father's request, she'd skipped the funeral. Gladly. She wasn't in the mood to play the grieving daughter before a crowd. What little grief she did have was a one-act show that would be played out best here, as a way to expedite this last necessary step before she left the whole incident behind. And if she didn't have to act at all? That would be even better. She'd play it by ear.

Actually, she was interested in the will more for curiosity's sake than a desire to get anything. Whatever pittance her mother might have left her meant nothing. Materially, she and Dudley were more than well off, so a few extra dollars would merely be added to their bank account. And from a sentimental point of view? There was no sentiment left. At age sixteen, when her parents divorced, Vanessa had chosen to live with her banker father rather than her independent, hippie mother. She had no regrets. Until Vanessa's marriage to Dudley, her father had provided the material requisites of life, while in return, Vanessa had filled the void caused by her mother's absence. The truth was, her father was a weak man. He would have fallen apart if it hadn't been for her capable presence. They'd been a good team, the dependent and the dependable.

Bottom line: He was Daddy. This woman who'd died was Mother.

"There," the lawyer said, finally facing them. "Sorry for the delay. These machines make me all thumbs. Are you ready?"

"Sure." *Whatever.*

He pushed the PLAY button and moved out of the way. Vanessa could only assume the old woman who came on the screen was her mother. She looked like an aged flower child, her white hair long and unruly, the design on her East Indian top punctuated with beads. Vanessa would not have been surprised if she'd flashed a peace sign.

Yet when the woman started speaking, when she said,

"Hello, Nessa," the voice spiked a connection, a memory to Vanessa's childhood before her mother had abandoned them. Vanessa felt the faintest hint of warmth, startling her with the knowledge that such an emotion *had* existed between them. Once.

"I hope you appreciate how this old free spirit is resorting to something very establishment by making this video for you, Nessa. But I see no other way to talk to you, to tell you what's on my mind and my heart. I hesitate to leave you anything because that's where your father excelled. I never could compete with that, nor could I compete with—or condone—the heady manipulation of people and events that is the hallmark of your father's life. There is no peace in such an attitude. No peace with the world, with God, or with oneself. We both know that what Yardley Pruitt wants he gets one way or another. But you need to know that I wanted you, Nessa. I fought for you in the courts. You remember that, don't you? I fought for you, but since your father could always make justice sing his own tune, I lost. I lost everything. I lost you, then lost sight of you. . . Are you married? Do I have grandchildren?"

The woman on the video sniffed then rearranged the flow of her broomstick skirt. "Life is often difficult, Nessa, but I've found it's best to 'rejoice in our sufferings, because we know that suffering produces perseverance; perseverance, character; and character, hope.' " She smiled at the camera. "Wise words. If only we'd listen."

She gave her head the slightest shake and continued. "But I mustn't digress. The message I want to leave you with, dear daughter, is one of regret. My deep regret, and my desire to relieve you of your own. The truth is, I don't know how your life turned out. Are you happy? Are you fulfilled? Through the years I've seen a few clippings of your father's life—bank PR stuff—but never any mention of you. Your father's penchant for manipulating every breath of those in his domain under the guise of need cannot have been to your advantage. It grieves me to think about how many chances you may have missed to find your true character just by the fact that you are your father's daughter."

Her mother sighed deeply. "I would have given you those chances, Nessa, by letting you blossom out of your own dreams and desires, instead of letting your father maneuver your life and emotions by playing the guilt card. I would even have let you fail, face consequences, and earn things on your own merit—not by having the right connections. This is a lesson I've learned in my own life. It's one I cherish. But every instinct, every fiber of my being doubts that you've ever been afforded the opportunity to grow in yourself, your faith, or your character. From the moment you chose your precious daddy—"

"That's enough!" Vanessa said. "Turn it off."

The lawyer hit the PAUSE button, and Dorian Pruitt's face froze oddly on the screen. "You really need to let her finish, Ms. Caldwell," the lawyer said.

Vanessa stood, gathering her purse. "I see no reason to listen to my mother now, when she didn't have the decency to contact me in decades. You heard her. She doesn't even know my married name. She knows nothing about me. I'm going to be fifty this year. I am past the age of needing to listen to my mother. Especially an odd, estranged one."

Dudley pulled her arm. "Come on, Vanessa. Just a few more minutes. What can it hurt?"

She was weary of the whole thing. "It hurts plenty when

she says Daddy has ruined my character by being kind to me, nice to me, needing me, loving me. That's absurd. He's a wonderful man."

Dudley cleared his throat.

She glared at him and clipped each word. "Don't start."

He adjusted himself in the leather armchair. "You know I won't, but maybe I should. What your mother says makes sense. You have to admit he does push our guilt buttons a lot."

"We don't help him out of a feeling of guilt, we help him out of love. I am no one's pawn."

He shrugged and pointed at the screen. "I like her. I wish I'd known her."

"You can't like her." *I won't allow it.*

He sighed. "I'm not your enemy, Vanessa. And if you'd stop being so defensive and finish listening to the video, you might discover your mother isn't either."

It was not like Dudley to confront her. Theirs was a flat-line relationship. Any deviation above or below that line was quickly dealt with in the fervent pursuit of the status quo. "How can you be on her side? My father and I are the ones who were left behind when she ran out on us."

The lawyer stepped between them. "Ms. Caldwell. Please listen to the rest of the video. It was your mother's wish that you see it."

"So she can belittle my father and me?"

He patted the back of her chair. "Please."

It was evident they were not going to let her leave until this was finished. So be it. She returned to her seat.

The lawyer messed with the remote. "How do I back this thing up a few seconds?"

"Here," Dudley said, reaching for it. "Let me do it."

He relinquished the control, and Dudley made the picture dance backward before hitting PLAY.

Vanessa's mother continued. ". . .the moment you chose your precious daddy. . .you don't realize it, Nessa, but your entire life changed at that moment. What could you have become, what kind of person might you be now, if we'd been allowed to keep our mother-daughter relationship alive?"

What was this "allowed" business? Her mother was the one who'd made the choice never to see her again.

Her mother put a hand to her chest. "I know my life would have been richer for it. And maybe all my worries about your father's influence are moot. Maybe your life is full of joy and purpose and all good things. The tragedy is, I don't know. And so I must go on what I suspect. Forgive me if I'm wrong, but my greatest hope for you stems out of my greatest fear."

Vanessa crossed her arms. Joy? Purpose? Good things? She'd like to shove those blessings in her mother's face. It was disconcerting how correct this woman was about how Vanessa's life *had* turned out, as well as her father's continued presence. And yet, it was also annoying. Her mother was acting as if it was inevitable that her life was less than perfect, full of weakness, and void of meaning. Vanessa knew exactly what she was doing. And if anyone was controlling things, it was she. Not her father.

". . .giving you all my possessions—such as they are. And I want you to know that I've been very fulfilled being a second-grade teacher. It has not brought me your father's kind of riches, but it has made me rich. Find that kind of wealth, Nessa. Find the wealth that comes from having faith, from trying your best, and from doing good out of love, not out of guilt or as a power play. I love you, flower-baby. Always have. Always will."

The tape mercifully came to an end. Dudley shut off the machine as the lawyer returned to his desk. “Here are the keys to your mother’s house. It, and the contents, are yours to do with as you please. She was a nice woman, your mother. An interesting woman who knew her own mind. I liked her very much.”

Good for you.

Vanessa stood to leave and Dudley followed. Once in the parking lot, he asked, “Where to?”

“My mother’s house. I want this done with. Over.”

He opened her car door. “Hasn’t this got you thinking, Vanessa? Don’t you wonder how your life would have been dif—?”

Vanessa shook her head vehemently. “I will not deal with ‘if onlys.’ I won’t.”

Malibu, California

Lane Holloway sat on her deck overlooking the Pacific, sipping a hazelnut mocha. Joggers teased the edge of the waves as they sped past, flipping up sand behind them. Seagulls dive-bombed fish and crustaceans in the shallows. In her lap was a script—*the* script for *the* movie that would finally win her an Oscar. Although she knew it wasn’t a sure thing, she had a feeling about it. Her agent concurred. This was one of those special parts that would test her mettle as an actress and provide her with a vehicle to either shine or flop. It was up to her.

Her agent currently was negotiating the price. She was happy to let him deal with such things. What was a few million one way or the other? Just give her the chance to do it. She’d earn their money back. She was box-office gold.

The french doors to the deck opened behind her, and her personal assistant and old high-school chum, Brandy Lopez, came out. "You're up early," Brandy said, putting away her keys.

"You know I don't sleep well alone."

Brandy set her notebook on the table. "Can I get you another mocha?"

"I'm fine. But help yourself."

She disappeared inside. Lane book-marked the page in the script and tried to turn her thoughts to the other to-dos of the day. Brandy liked to keep busy, and Lane was glad to oblige. She was in awe of people who actually liked to serve others. Lane much preferred being the serve-ee.

Brandy returned with her mocha and took a seat across the table. Lane waited for her to ready her notebook and pen as she did every weekday morning. But this time Brandy just sat there grinning.

"Uh-oh. What's that smile for?" Lane asked.

"I have a present for you."

"You've got to quit doing that, Brand. You're constantly buying me—"

"Trinkets. Hey, who knows you better than me? Besides, they're just little things. Nothing big. Nothing expensive. You know that."

"I do like that raspberry tea you found."

"See? I know what you like and I like to get it for you. It gives me pleasure, and if you don't let me do it, I'll pout. And you don't want to see me pout, do you?"

Lane laughed. No indeed, she did not want to witness a Brandy-pout. Her friend, not attractive to begin with, turned positively menacing when her brows dipped and her lip popped into prominence. Brandy had perfected pouting since their high-school days. "So, what did you get me this time?"

With a flourish, Brandy pulled an envelope from the inside of her notebook. "For you."

There was nothing on the envelope but Lane's name written in Brandy's cursive. It was not sealed. Inside she found a ticket. "What's this?"

"It's a lottery ticket. But not just any lottery. A Time Lottery ticket."

The ticket had a printed number on it, the Time Travel Corporation—the TTC—logo, and a space where Brandy had written Lane's name.

"See?" Brandy said, pointing at the ticket. "It's yours and yours alone. You can't give it to anyone else. I bought it for you."

Lane set the ticket on the table between them. "But the Time Lottery is for people who want to go back into their lives and relive something, change a choice they made. I'm very content with my life here. There's nothing I want to change."

Brandy crossed her arms.

"There isn't."

Brandy's glare was second only to her pout in the negative effect it had on her looks.

Lane stood and moved to the railing that overlooked the Malibu beach. "You seem to forget that I'm living the American dream. I'm a movie star. I've kissed the hunks of my day: Johnny Depp, Mel Gibson, Brad Pitt. . ."

"You are the envy of hot-blooded women everywhere."

"Exactly."

"Unfortunately, your off-screen romances haven't been so successful."

"I got rid of Klaus."

Brandy shuddered. "Yuck. Good riddance."

Lane crossed her arms and looked toward the horizon. "It's hard to find true love when you're famous."

"*Au contraire*, Laney-girl. Enter the Time Lottery." Brandy joined her at the railing and ran a hand over the back of her shoulders. "I'm just looking after you. I know it's ironic that plain ol' Brandy found herself a wonderful husband and has four great kids, while Lane, the movie-star stunner has nada. I've asked God to explain, but He's keeping mum."

Actually, Lane had come to the conclusion that God was keeping score, and since she'd already received a myriad of blessings, He wasn't about to give her more.

Brandy left her side to stick her finger in the soil of a potted geranium nearby. "Forget loser-Klaus; I thought you might like to explore what would have happened if you hadn't dumped Joseph."

Joseph Brannerman was two men ago. "I think you liked Joseph more than I did."

Brandy moved on to check the ferns. "These need water. . . . I liked him only because he was perfect for you."

"So you've said. Repeatedly."

Brandy turned her attention away from the plants. "So I *know* as fact. You're way too picky. Good men don't grow on trees. Take my Randy."

"I thought you wanted me to take Joseph."

She joined Lane back at the railing, her voice low. "Promise you won't tell?"

"Sure."

"I also bought a ticket for myself."

Lane played the *aghast* emotion to perfection. "Have you been holding out on me all these years? Was there a Romeo in your past you want to explore more deeply?"

"Randy is Romeo enough for me. But I have always wondered what would have happened if I hadn't followed you out to Hollywood—if I'd stayed in Minnesota."

Lane put away her teasing. "You'd go back to Dawson?"

"Maybe I could have helped my mom more."

Lane put an arm around her shoulders and pulled her close. Brandy's mother had been an abusive alcoholic, and leaving her had been the hardest—yet best—thing her friend had ever done. They watched the tide a few minutes. Then Lane turned around and swept a hand to encompass her home. "Enough of this talk. I'd be stupid to go back. Look at what I have: this home, one in Montana, an apartment in New York. . ." She spotted the script on the table. "And what about my acting? That script will win me an Academy Award. I know it."

Brandy shook her head.

"Don't shake your head. It's a good part. It will let me explore new sides to my—"

Brandy snickered. "That's one way to put it. Your backside, front side. . .yes, sirree, the world will see all sides of Lane Holloway."

"Nudity doesn't have the stigma it once had. All the big actresses are doing it."

"Well, alrighty then."

Lane had discussed it with her agent, and they'd decided the nudity was a necessary risk. Besides, she was in good shape for nearly thirty-five. She had nothing to hide. And much to gain.

"Have you gotten around to reading that book I want you to make into a movie?" Brandy asked.

"I started it." She hadn't.

“Baloney. It’s probably still sitting on your bedside table.” She took a step toward the french doors leading inside.

“No,” Lane said, stopping her. “I haven’t. But I will.”

Brandy pointed at her. “Making a movie out of that book may not win you an Oscar, but it would be a good vehicle for you. Great parts all around. A gripping, life-changing story. The young mother Merry loses her son and husband in a plane crash and comes to realize that her selfish discontent caused them to be on the plane in the first—”

Lane raised a hand, stopping her. “I’ll read it. I promise.”

“Yes, yes, so you say.” Brandy returned to her seat at the table and opened her notebook, readying for the daily errands. “As far as winning the Time Lottery? Never fear, Laney-girl. The chances of either one of us winning are slim. After the success of last year’s drawing, I’m sure they’ll sell a ton of tickets. So don’t worry about it. I just thought it would be fun to think about.”

Lane acquiesced and gave her a hug from behind. “And I thank you for your continued thoughtfulness.” And it *would* make her think.

If only. . .

Kansas City

Alexander MacMillan opened his front door, only to have Cheryl Nickolby burst past him, slam the door shut, and press herself against it like a woman on the run. “Phew! I made it!”

He crossed his arms and rolled his eyes. “What are you doing?”

She relaxed her stance, smoothed her brown pants and

sweater, then yanked him close with such force that he expelled a puff of air. After a hello kiss that left him even more breathless, she stepped back and answered his question. "I'm only following your directions. You've stressed the need for discretion and emphasized the necessity to never, ever, ever let anyone from the media know that you, the Time Lottery Czar, are dating me, Mistress of the first lottery and doctor extraordinaire." She clapped her hands to her chest dramatically. "Heaven forbid the world know we have the hots for each other."

Mac looked behind him, checking for six-year-old ears. "We care about each other."

"Same thing." She breezed past him. "Now, where's the real man in my life? Andrew? Olly olly oxen free!"

Andrew came running from upstairs, jumped from the third step, and barreled into her, wrapping his arms around her waist.

"Whoa, bud! Nice to see you, too."

He let her loose. "I made the garlic bread, but I spilled spaghetti sauce on my shirt, so I had to change."

"If you were making the bread, how did you spill sauce—?"

Mac rumpled his son's hair. "Long story. Let's eat."

During dinner, Mac found himself watching Cheryl as she teased Andrew and told them about her new job at a local hospital. For her to leave Boulder, Colorado, and move to Kansas City to be near the two of them still left him stunned. Actually, everything about Cheryl left him stunned. She was a stunning woman. For Mac to have found two women in his lifetime, first Holly, and now Cheryl. . .

The women were two ends of a spectrum. Where dear Holly had been ten years younger than he, petite, dark-haired, sweet, and domestic, Cheryl was ten years older—nearly forty-eight—tall, blond, vivacious, and a brilliant surgeon. It didn't make sense that such diverse women would fit into his life. Fit with him. And yet they did. Each in their time.

Ha. Time. The unrelenting taskmaster.

And yet. . .the whole Time Lottery phenomenon still astounded him. For the winners to be able to go back in time, into their own lives and change something, explore their Alternate Reality—their Alternity—was miracle enough. But to be offered the option to stay there and live out that new choice or come back to this one was mind-boggling. Mac was beyond glad that Cheryl had chosen to come back to the present. To be here. In his life.

Actually, as incentive to take the job as the public relations liaison for the TTC, Mac had been offered a chance to go back into *his* life, to the time before Holly was murdered by an intruder, to change her death to life. In spite of the temptation, he'd refused. To go back and live a life with Holly in his Alternity would be to leave their son here, alone. It was something he could not do.

"Can I be excused?" Andrew asked.

"*May* I. And yes, you may."

Mac and Cheryl sat in silence until voices from the family-room TV drifted into the kitchen. Then Cheryl put a hand on Mac's. "I saw you deep in thought. About what?"

He smiled and kissed her hand.

She got out of her chair, and he gladly made room on his lap. "I'm finding this secrecy very hard, you know. I'm not a secretive person. What you see is what you get."

"An attribute."

"I've already heard the buzz about me moving to Kansas City. A reporter asked me about it."

"What did you say?"

"That I'd fallen in love with the town when I'd come here to participate in the Time Lottery. And after my experience in the past, I felt the need for a fresh start. Plus, I said I'd befriended the most amazing, sexy man who has the ability to make my epidermis tingle in a most delightful way."

He leaned his head against her neck. "You saved me, you know. My decision not to go back—"

"Shh." She began to rock, and he joined in the rhythm.

"I want to tell the world about us, Cheryl. I do."

"I know."

"We just need to get through the next lottery. Then the attention will be on the new winners, and we can be free to be you and me."

"Free to be *us.*"

He closed his eyes and was comforted by the beat of her heart.

If only. . .

No one whose hope is in you will ever be put to shame,
but they will be put to shame who are
treacherous without excuse.
PSALM 25:3

Bangor

David Stancowsky sat in his office on the top floor overlooking the Penobscot River. Snow fell and occasionally attacked the windowpane, dying against its warmth. David smiled at the victory. The cold couldn't get to him. It wouldn't dare. He was safe in this world of his creation.

But was he happy?

It was not a question he pondered often. Yet ever since buying a Time Lottery ticket. . . He leaned back in his leather chair, holding the ticket between his hands. He'd made no secret of the fact he'd bought one, but *had* couched his purchase by buying a ticket for every employee of Mariner Construction. If he could have bought a hundred for himself, he would have done so. But the Time Lottery people had set it up so there could be only one entry per person. Most likely they didn't want some wealthy eccentric buying up a million tickets, skewing the balance between rich and poor. An annoying concession in this age when political correctness ruled.

He forced himself to take a deep breath and let such inequities go. He had one chance, and if God was good and merciful He would let David win. After all, didn't he deserve it? After Millie's death he'd never married. Though he couldn't say he'd been completely faithful to her memory, she was never far from his thoughts. And he hadn't abandoned his promise to Millie's father, either. Ray Reynolds was the founder of Mariner Construction, and upon Millie and David's wedding engagement in 1958, Ray had named his soon-to-be son-in-law his successor. When Millie died, David had stayed on and had even taken over when Ray retired. Now it was David who paid for Ray's care in the nursing home a few miles north of town. David had suffered great loss with dignity and loyalty. And he'd done his duty.

Not that his life had been wasted. He'd had a good life, a successful career. He was well liked and well feared—a powerful combination in the business world. But the bottom line was that he deserved to win the lottery, to do it all over again with Millie by his side. Millie and children.

Was it his old age talking? Probably. At seventy-four, with more aches and pains than he mentioned to anyone, David was ripe for another shot at age twenty-eight, at making a good life better.

His secretary's voice sounded on the intercom: "Earl Degan, line one. He's checking on the delivery of the drywall."

Drywall. Who cared about drywall when the drawing for the Time Lottery was tomorrow?

David picked up the phone.

And life went on—for now.

SECOND TIME AROUND

Decatur, Georgia

Vanessa Caldwell stood at the front door and took a deep breath.

"You want me to do it?" Dudley asked.

She glared at him, mad at herself for hinting at any weakness. "I'm fine."

Dudley took the key ring away. "Sure you are. Though I must say I *am* a bit surprised by your reaction. Your mother's dead; it's not like you're going to have to talk to her."

But to enter her world. . .

He pushed the door open and stepped aside, forcing Vanessa to go first. She stood on the threshold and peered in. Sunlight streamed in the windows, and she could visualize the entire floor plan from her position. The tiny living room was to the left, the kitchen could be seen beyond a beaded doorway straight ahead, and a small hall led to the back, to what certainly would be a bedroom and bath. The depth and breadth of her mother's world consisted of four rooms. Vanessa's master-bedroom suite consisted of four rooms. Her closet could have swallowed this living room whole.

Dudley peeked past her at the eclectic mix of antiques and homespun. "A blast from the past, isn't it? Hippie city."

Once a hippie always a hippie? Vanessa went inside and picked up a "World's Best Teacher" picture frame that showcased her mother with a gaggle of smiling kids. Tie-dyed curtains framed windows that held a parade of African violets. A quilt hung above the fireplace, and a ratty pair of clogs sat next to an oak rocker close by. An odd mix, yet the home had an unusual charm, more than Vanessa had expected—or wanted. She'd always pictured her mother living in a hovel, dressed in hand-me-downs. Barely getting by. Paying dearly for leaving and causing the divorce.

There was a knock on the opened front door. "Hello?" An elderly woman stepped inside, then stopped. "I'm so sorry to bother you, but when I saw the car. . ." She carried a stack of mail held together by large rubber bands and extended her free hand toward Dudley. "I'm Mildred Crown. Dorian and I have been neighbors forever. And you are. . . ?"

Dudley pointed to Vanessa. "You want the daughter. She's the daughter."

Being deemed "the daughter" was an odd experience. Vanessa shook Mrs. Crown's hand. "It's nice to meet you."

Mildred stared at her, obviously studying her. "My, my. To finally meet. . ." She shook the rest of the sentence away. "I was so sorry when Dorian passed. And sorry that I couldn't be at the service. My arthritis makes it hard for me to get around much. Yet when I saw your fancy car in the drive. . .I just had to come see, knowing it probably would be you."

Knowing?

She took a step toward the door. "I'll leave you be. I'm sure you want to take some time going through the trimmings of your mother's life. She was an amazing woman. A wonderful woman." Mildred glanced at the mail. "The postman left these with me since Dorian's mailbox was full. I took the liberty of opening a few. Sympathy cards. Many from former students telling how your mother changed their lives. Dorian did love being a teacher. Almost as much as she loved you. And in turn, she was loved by so many." Her hand found her chin. "Loved by *you*, I hope? Finally loved by *you*?"

Dudley stepped toward her, showing her out. "Thanks for stopping by, Mrs. Crown." He closed the door with a gentle *click*. "Well, then. . ."

Vanessa found herself rooted in the middle of the room, the mail clutched to her chest. She was appalled to feel the sting of tears and squeezed her eyes shut against them.

Dudley did not venture to touch her. He seemed to know better. "It will be all right, Vanessa."

Yes, yes. Of course it will. Everything always came out all right. She would make it so.

Yet it unnerved her that her next thought was to call Daddy. With difficulty, she shooed the thought away.

Her whole life had been a lie.

After going through various cupboards and closets, after having her mother's life descend on her like a smothering shroud, Vanessa sent Dudley away to get lunch. She needed time alone to face her past. Her mother's past. And try to find a future.

She sat on the quilted bedspread, the evidence of the lies spread before her. Near the footboard were forty-eight sympathy cards from friends and past students lauding Dorian Pruitt's effect on their lives. Her mother had lived a significant life. She didn't have riches or power or fame. But she'd lived well and touched others.

Vanessa's father had lied. Her mother was not miserable and of no use to anyone; a pathetic nobody who had no purpose in the world. And yet that was not the worst lie. The evidence of that deception lay directly in front of her and revealed itself in the form of a second set of letters.

She'd found them in a box, in the drawer of the bedside table. Dozens and dozens of letters addressed to Vanessa and marked "Return to Sender." Postmarks from her teen years to the present, with the latest marked last Christmas. All sent to her father's house, trusting him to forward them on.

But he hadn't. Not one letter had made its way into Vanessa's hands.

Initially, after she read the letters, Vanessa's anger had spread from her father to her mother. In the later years why hadn't Dorian sent the letters to Vanessa's home?

Then she remembered the video. Her mother hadn't even known her married name—there was no reason she would know. In college, after following her father's instructions to have an abortion, Vanessa had flunked out of school. She'd been an emotional and mental mess. When she met stable and kind Dudley Caldwell, without meaning to, or even wanting to, Vanessa fell in love—or at least intense like. When Dudley proposed, she'd agreed, and in an act of defiance against her father had foregone the fancy, society wedding and eloped. It was a decision that still elicited anger from Yardley Pruitt. But because of that one act, there were no society clippings for her mother to peruse, clip out, and save. In the fall of 1976 Vanessa Pruitt had quietly become Vanessa Caldwell and had slipped into the Georgia night. Forty miles from her mother, yet a lifetime away.

That was then; this was now. Vanessa looked over the final Christmas letter.

> *I love you, dear Nessa. May you find the true meaning in the celebration of our Savior's birth. I pray you come to know Him as I have. I pray you find your true purpose in Him. . . . Remember what I've always said: "Just because you can, doesn't mean you should." I've tried to live that motto, and by doing so I've found great happiness. Only*

your absence kept it from being complete. Yet I'm afraid that through your father's possessive tutelage you may have lived out too many opportunities because you could, not thinking about whether you should. It's never too late to change that, dear girl. Toward that end. . .please call me. Just one phone call. I have a gift for you that could change everything, something I thought of the other day and bought for you. I want you to have it, because I want you to have every chance to live a life of fulfillment and joy.

She lowered the letter into her lap. How many times had Vanessa heard her mother say that line: "Just because you can, doesn't mean you should?" Yet had Vanessa ever applied it to real life? The trouble with being Yardley Pruitt's daughter, Dudley Caldwell's wife, Rachel Caldwell's mother, and a professional and acclaimed volunteer and fund-raiser was that the air was heavy with things she *could* do. Which made her remember her father's motto: "Those who can, should."

As if she'd been slapped, she realized her parents' viewpoints were diametrically opposed. No wonder she'd been forced to create her own counsel. The question was, which parent was right?

Vanessa looked back to the letter. A gift? What could her mother offer her? Vanessa needed nothing.

The memory of Daddy pressing a hundred-dollar bill into her hands popped front and center. It was not a single memory but a collective one in her post-mother years. "Go buy something," he'd say. "Then come back and show me what you've bought. You do so much for me, Vanessa. I don't know what I'd do without you helping this poor, old, lonely man."

Annoyed at first, she'd come to accept and even foster the

fact that he needed her. Though Yardley Pruitt managed to appear strong in his role as the president of Fidelity Mutual Bank—by hiring strong people around him—in his personal life he was rather pathetic. Vanessa enjoyed the position of power she earned by making him depend on her, one loyal daughter helping the needy man. Eventually she'd discovered that the power surge she gained by giving could be extended past her father's domain. Anyone who knew Vanessa Caldwell commented on her altruistic nature. She hadn't received three volunteer-of-the-year awards for nothing—even though her thank-you speeches suggested otherwise: "Thank you for this award and your kind words about my work. It was really nothing. . . ."

Yes, indeed, Vanessa had created a life around the art of being a professional giver, an organizer extraordinaire. In return, all she asked from the recipients was a little respect, recognition, and gratitude. Until a half hour ago, she'd thought she'd received those sentiments from her father, but then the letters proved he'd been playing her. Duping her. Lying to her. It was unacceptable.

She shook her head, forcing his image away. She ran a hand over letter after letter that showcased her mother's loving words and prayers. Words of faith that God would take care of them both and loved them both. To think that Dorian Pruitt had never given up trying to contact her daughter even when she'd received constant rejection. To think that her father had intercepted every one of those letters and sent them back.

"It wasn't my doing!"

Her words quickly soaked into the rag rug, making her wonder if she'd even said them aloud.

No matter. She'd felt them and ached with the anguish and confusion behind them. Her unassuming, needy father had placed himself as a mighty guard between mother and daughter. A pit bull where she'd believed him to be a cuddly lapdog. He'd lied and said her mother didn't love her anymore and wouldn't have been able to take care of her if she did. He'd called Dorian Pruitt a loser, a woman who hadn't appreciated what she had when she'd had it. A mean woman who'd made the two of them suffer with loss. Yes, indeed, Yardley Pruitt had spent his life making Vanessa think she'd chosen correctly by staying with him. Who needed a mother, anyway?

I did.

Vanessa pulled the packet of letters to her chest and fell sideways onto the bed, pulling her knees close. How would things have been if she'd chosen to be a part of her mother's free-spirited existence instead of burrowing into the safety of her father's intractable life of black and white with no room or tolerance for gray? Her heart throbbed with a sorrow and uncertainty she hadn't experienced in. . . .in thirty-four. . .

This was ridiculous. She forced herself to sit and reached for a tissue on the bedside table. Wallowing in the could-have-beens was a waste of time. It was too late. Her mother was gone.

As she blew her nose, she noticed a ticket on the bedside table. She picked it up. It was a Time Lottery ticket. Had her mother bought one for herself, hoping to go back and live another life? Were the regrets she'd mentioned in her video so strong that she'd longed for another chance?

Vanessa made note of the date. The choosing of the three Time Lottery winners was tomorrow. Irony of ironies. Wouldn't it be horrible if her mother was one of the winners? Talk about too late. . .

Vanessa placed the ticket with the letters when she noticed the name handwritten on it: *Vanessa Pruitt.*

Not Dorian Pruitt.

Vanessa.

"Me?"

She stared at her name, then grabbed up the Christmas letter.

> *Please call me. Just one phone call. I have a gift for you that could change everything, something I thought of the other day and bought. . . . I want you to have it, because I want you to have every chance to live a life of fulfillment and joy.*

Chance.

A chance to change everything.

The Time Lottery.

Vanessa's heart beat double time. She'd never considered buying a ticket. To do so would be to admit her life wasn't perfect. But now. To know that her mother had wanted her to have the opportunity of a second chance. . .

"Oh, Mother."

The drawing was tomorrow. As she calmed her breathing, she realized she could finally allow herself to consider the words Dudley had wanted her to think about:

If only. . .

Malibu

As soon as Brandy left for the day, Lane rushed into her living room and turned on her Bose stereo system. There were speakers in many rooms, and within seconds she surrounded herself with Fauré's "Dolly" Suite. Though she could tolerate silence in the daytime hours, she had trouble dealing with it in the dark. And dark was descending quickly.

How laughable. Lane Holloway. Mega movie star. Leading a glamorous life of premiers, beaded gowns, and Harry Winston jewelry. Yeah, right. If the world only knew how many evenings she spent alone with nothing to do, no place to go, and worse yet, nowhere she was *able* to go without getting pounced on by paparazzi. She couldn't even take a walk with the assurance she'd have privacy. She was a prisoner in her home. So in order to dispel the power of the four walls, she kept them filled with light and sound.

To keep away the boogeyman. At the thought, she moved to the kitchen and flipped on the lights. When was the last time she'd thought of that phrase? High school? She and her boyfriend Toby had loved to watch scary movies, though Toby *had* confided that his motivation stemmed more from her need to cuddle close through the scary parts rather than any great story line or fascination he had for blood and guts.

She smiled at the thought of him. She'd been thinking about him often lately. Memories of Toby had surfaced when she'd gone through the rather public breakup with Klaus (actors—can't live with them; can't live with them).

Toby and his dimples. His shy way of looking over his long lashes, sticking his hands in the pockets of his jeans. And his kisses. . . Tomorrow was the Time Lottery drawing. Brandy had bought her a ticket, wanting her to give her life with Joseph Brannerman a second chance. She leaned on the breakfast bar and thought of the lovely Joseph with his perfect *GQ* persona, perfect manners, perfect life.

Too perfect. Lane wasn't surprised that Brandy liked him. To the outsider, Joseph was everything the celebrity Lane

Holloway could ever want or need. He was comfortable with her fame, earned a six-figure salary as a stock analyst, and could converse with Steven Spielberg and Tom Hanks as easily as most people chatted with their mailman.

What no one realized was that Joseph was high maintenance. Mt. Everest-need-oxygen high. After he'd moved in with her, she'd never felt at ease, never felt like she could bum around in sweats and no makeup, eating crackers and Easy Cheese for dinner if the mood hit. Joseph looked exquisite at all times. Even lounging around on Sunday morning he looked like an ad for the good life.

He was too much work. And so she'd let him go, hooking up with Stefan Embers for a quick go-round (what *was* she thinking?) before living, most recently, with Klaus. *He* was not high maintenance. Low maintenance. No maintenance. No self-maintenance. Klaus was an easy-going, lazy slob. Where was her medium-man, her man in the middle of high and low maintenance? A man who had balance in his life and could help her balance hers?

Toby Bjornson.

She laughed at the thought. Toby? No way. And yet. . .

She opened the refrigerator. Brandy had stocked it with all sorts of healthy things bent on maintaining Lane's size-two figure. As a teenager, she'd been able to eat whatever she wanted. If Lane never ate another salad. . .

An impulse formed and she moved to the pantry. Yes! She took out the bag of chocolate chips and read the back. The Toll House recipe promised her satisfaction amid the dark and lonely night.

Within seconds she had the mixer out and the ingredients ready. She didn't have any nuts but would make do with double the chocolate chips. Using the remote, she shut off the classical music and turned on the kitchen TV. She flipped channels until she found a program to match her mood. *Dirty Dancing* was showing on a movie channel. Perfect. Memories flooded back of making cookies with Toby in her parents' kitchen while the sound track played. . . .

Cooking to a beat had always been her specialty.

Kansas City

John Wriggens, the chief administrator of TTC, leaned back in his chair, forming a pencil bridge between his hands. "So, Mac. Tomorrow is the day. Is everything set? Are we ready to welcome three more guinea pigs into the winner's circle?"

Mac clenched his jaw in a way that had become too familiar. After catching Wriggens taking a bribe from the husband of one of last year's winners, Mac had wanted to get an investigation going into Wriggens's suitability to oversee the program. And yet, he couldn't. On a whim, he'd agreed to overlook Wriggens's breach by securing his own job as the public relations liaison for the Time Lottery. He had the job for as long as he wanted it. But in return, he had to deal with the moral and administrative ambiguity of John Wriggens. It was a price that alternated between doable and deplorable.

Today was the latter. Wriggens was acting as if the lottery was his baby, when in truth—as far as Mac could see—he did little to earn his six-figure salary. But Mac would endure. For the good of the cause.

He realized Wriggens had not waited for his answer but had continued to talk. He was reiterating logistical details of tomorrow's drawing as if *he* had set things up and not Mac.

Mac resorted to a tried-and-true method to get out of Wriggens's office as quickly as possible: He sat back and let the man ramble. He hoped he'd finish soon because he had a lunch date with Cheryl and did not want to keep the lady waiting. She was such a joy, such a burst of energy into his life as a widower. He didn't know what he'd do without her.

Suddenly, Mac noticed silence. Wriggens was grinning at him.

Oh dear.

Wriggens leaned forward on his desk, his voice low. "Who is she, Mac?"

Mac felt the heat in his face. "She?"

"The woman who's preventing you from fully listening to me."

Not listening wasn't *all* Cheryl's fault. Mac looked at his watch. "Forgive me if I seem distracted. My mind is swimming with details." He stood. "I really need to check to see if all the lottery tickets have arrived. We've ordered some extra security to oversee them being placed in the sphere for the drawing. It's best not to risk any hint of impropriety."

The smallest of snickers escaped Wriggens's mouth. "My thoughts exactly, right, Mac?"

As Mac left, the back of his neck tingled.

What did Wriggens know?

Cheryl started to hand Mac a sandwich across the center console of his car, then pulled it back and offered her face for a kiss. He was glad to oblige.

She sighed extravagantly, then whispered, "We've got to

stop meeting like this."

He opened the Thermos of coffee and poured. "I thought you, of all people, would be energized by the intrigue. Not many couples get to picnic in a car—in the far corner of a parking lot of an abandoned park."

She took a bite of a sandwich, then held it out for him to taste. "The park is abandoned because it's January and Siberian out here."

He exchanged hot coffee for a sandwich. "Just a few more days. Once we get through the latest drawing and send-off, I'll take you somewhere special."

"Oh, this is special," she said. "We've done special. How about public?"

He'd actually been thinking of finding an obscure little restaurant in an obscure little town where people might not be up on their latest celebrities, because both Cheryl and Phoebe Thurgood—the other Time Lottery winner to return a year ago—were *known* and had been featured periodically in updates on their post-lottery life. A photo from Phoebe's marriage to Peter Greenfield had even been on the cover of *People*, but they'd wisely gone underground since then. Mac hoped they were finding a little wedded bliss.

With Phoebe out of commission, Cheryl was the only past winner whom the press would interview before the drawing tomorrow. Yet Mac had to smile. He remembered last year's press conference before the winners were sent on their journeys. Cheryl had revealed a star quality. She was a natural in front of the camera and had no trouble putting the media in their place. It was a trait that might come in handy.

"Do you ever wonder how Leon's doing?" Cheryl asked.

The question took him by surprise, though he realized it

shouldn't have. Leon Burke was the one winner who'd decided to stay behind in his Alternity, in 1962 Tennessee. There was no way anyone could know whether he was thriving or in misery. Yet any life had to be better than the life of a homeless, murdering transient Leon had lived in the present. He'd been so desperate to go back in time that he'd actually killed the legitimate winner, Roosevelt Haven, and had taken his place. Such horrible complications were possible the first year, but no more. A more stringent ID process had been set in place.

The murder of Roosevelt could have been the end of the entire Time Lottery program if it weren't for the insatiable fascination people had with the concept of getting a second chance to do things right. Or at least better.

". . .wearing a bikini and a diamond tiara for my interview tomorrow. What do you think?"

Mac blinked. "What did you say?"

"*Tsk, tsk,* Alexander. You weren't listening."

"Sorry."

She set her sandwich in her lap, took his hand, and kissed it. "It'll be all right, Mac. I know it will. Relax. God's got it covered. Plus, I'll be there."

God and Cheryl Nickolby. It *was* covered. How could he fail?

The race is not to the swift or the battle to the strong,
nor does food come to the wise or wealth
to the brilliant or favor to the learned;
but time and chance happen to them all.
ECCLESIASTES 9:11

Kansas City

Mac put a hand on the back of Cheryl's neck. "You ready to face the lions?"

"Ah, think again, bucko. The better question is, are they ready for me?"

He laughed, then snuck a kiss to her cheek before heading onstage to introduce her. The applause was immediate. The Time Lottery auditorium was filled to capacity. Many of the seats were taken by media and those who'd been invited. But the line for general admission had been two blocks long.

The VIPs looked very important in their front-row seats. Yet they had no advantage over the cameraman in the back or the janitor who would sweep up afterward. Let them feel important now. The great equalizer was the swirling Plexiglas model of the world that contained the gyrating tickets of all the entrants. Buy one ticket, get one chance. Simple.

Yet not so simple. The intricacies of the Time Lottery experience reinforced Mac's belief in an all-wise, loving God who delighted in handling amazing details. How else could it be explained that last year's winners had each met each other in their pasts? Phoebe had met Leon in 1962, Cheryl had met Phoebe in 1969, and had met Leon in 1973. As a man of faith, Mac knew better than to condone the excuse of "coincidence" in regard to such miracles. Added to this unexpected phenomenon was the fact that both Phoebe and Cheryl had come through the experience with a heightened faith and a deeper sense of purpose. Free will prevailed, but that didn't mean there wasn't a plan, a perfect plan that people messed up repeatedly. The Time Lottery was a chance to get it right.

Mac moved to the edge of the stage and waited until the applause faded. He crossed his hands in front and smiled. "We meet again." He accepted their laughter. "I welcome you to the second annual Time Lottery drawing. Before we leave here today, we will choose three new winners to participate in this scientific marvel of marvels, giving them a chance to travel back into their own lives to change something. However. . . utilizing the full extent of our marketing know-how, we are going to let you wait just a bit longer and—"

There was a communal moan. He raised a hand, playfully fending off their objections. It was all part of the game, and in truth, they knew that as much as he. "Milk the moment" was an established right—nay, duty—of every person or organization in the public eye.

"To aid you in your wait, I would like to introduce one of last year's winners, Dr. Cheryl Nickolby, who will have the honor of picking the winning tickets."

Cheryl burst from the wings, hands waving like an Olympic gold medalist come home. They exchanged a proper hug and as the applause continued, Cheryl offered a curtsy and a by-your-leave sweep of her hand. "Keep it up and I'm apt to forgive you for all the meddling you've done in my life this last year."

"You love it!" yelled a man in the third row.

Cheryl smoothed her long black jacket over her very short skirt. She had wonderful legs. . . . "Let's say I've accepted it as a necessary evil." She winked at them. "You are evil, you know."

"We try!" yelled one reporter.

"You ain't seen nothing yet," added another.

"Watch it, bucko," Cheryl said.

Once again, Mac was amazed at her affinity for banter. Even during such an auspicious occasion, she drew shouts from the audience. It was impossible not to feel at ease in her presence. No wonder she was such a successful doctor.

But if he didn't step in, Cheryl would banter them into the next hour. "Are there any questions for Dr. Nickolby?"

"Do you wish you were going again?"

The shake of her head was vehement. "Been there, done that. I am very happy with my current state of affairs, thank you."

"You mention affairs. How is your love life?"

She shook a finger at them. "I walked into that one, didn't I?" She glanced at Mac but revealed nothing. "To bring you up to date, for those of you who've been covering such insignificant news as terrorism or the lack of world peace, you should know that I have recently taken a position at St. Agnes Hospital here in Kansas City and am enjoying my job immensely. There is currently no Mr. Wonderful in my life, so keep those cards, resumes, and expensive gifts coming."

"When are we going to read a book about your Time

Lottery travels?" a reporter asked.

Mac knew both Cheryl and Phoebe Thurgood—the other winner who'd returned—had been offered huge sums to share their stories. Neither had succumbed.

Cheryl answered by putting her hands on her hips like an exasperated mother. "Oh, that would be smart, wouldn't it? Letting you in on *more* of my life? I think not. I need to keep a few secrets to myself."

"That's not fair!"

"Chicken."

Cheryl waved their comments away, then took a step closer to the edge of the stage and waited for their silence. "Seriously, ladies and gentlemen, what I will tell you is that this phenomenon, this Time Lottery, is a scientific wonder bordering on miracle. It deserves the utmost support and respect of all. I ask you, I beg you, to do nothing to undermine the good it's doing. Cherish this opportunity and this organization. Because if you don't, you'll have me to contend with."

"Promise?"

She took a deep breath and looked at Mac. "With my threat properly in place, I now pass the ball back to Mr. MacMillan, who will take us one step closer to the all-important moment we've been waiting for."

She moved aside, offering him center stage. He began his spiel. "The Time Lottery is the culmination of twenty-two years of scientific research spurred by the ageless questions of *what if?* Before the inception of the Time Lottery, humankind traveled through life making mistakes, having regrets, leaving hopes unrealized. But then a miracle. The discovery of the Loop and a way to tap into an alternate reality—the Alternity."

It was a wonderful word. . . .

"You've all experienced it. Those memories and dreams that seem real enough to grasp and hold on to. Moments. Fleeting instants visited but then lost when the sights and sounds of the present push them away. In just a moment, three lucky people will be chosen to embark on a new adventure, to receive the gift of a second chance. Three explorers will travel back into their pasts, confronting a few of the what-if questions that plague us all, discovering the possibilities of chances not taken and choices ignored. They will visit what could have been, their minds fresh and unburdened by what has happened since that moment, each one free to explore a new choice."

Mac closed his eyes. "Think back. Remember that argument that cost you your job? Remember letting the love of your life slip away? You've often wondered what could have happened, haven't you? How would your life have been different if, at one critical juncture, you would have said yes? Or no? Or said nothing. Now is your chance to find out.

"Let me share with you in layman's terms how this opportunity to travel to the past has come to be. First off, we must ask the question, what is reality? All I know of my world is what I experience from my own point of view, my own perceptions. We each interpret this moment, in this room, in a unique way. And within that part of the brain we've termed the 'Loop,' all the real and perceived moments of your life are interwoven into a unique perception of what was, what is, and what could be.

"When you are asleep, your dreams are your reality. You know nothing of your waking life; you *care* nothing about your waking life. Likewise, when you concentrate on a memory, *that* seems to take on a reality, just for a moment. The science of time travel taps into this fascinating interweaving of dreams and memories.

"Despite what you've been taught by science fiction movies, the past is an *individual* phenomenon, and there are as many timelines as there are people. A new timeline branches off every time you make a decision. Each of us spins off thousands of alternate streams of time every day. Quantum physics has taught us that those timelines have real existence.

"What the technology behind the Time Lottery does is allow the traveler to hop over to one of those other time streams, into a timeline of his or her choice. The body stays here, acting like a kind of tether to the traveler while he's off in the other reality. If he decides to stay in the new timeline—in his past—eventually his consciousness makes the switch permanently. The tether is severed and his body here dies. But in the other timeline, he has a real body and can live out a normal lifespan.

"When we send a person back in time, we place their physical body into a carefully monitored, medically induced coma. Once we've done so, the mind—which went to sleep concentrating on the time and choice it wants to explore—will be free to choose the new timeline extracted from the Loop, that place where the memories of a lifetime are stored."

He glanced at Cheryl. She gave him a smile that spurred him on.

"After a person has experienced his or her Alternity for seven days—a measure of seven days in the present, but an undetermined number of days in the past—TTC doctors will introduce a gentle electric burst to the Loop, and a strange phenomenon we call 'Dual Consciousness' will kick in. At this point, our time traveler will finally be able to see both lives—the past and the present. It's like waking up from a dream and remembering it with total clarity, seeing both realities at the same time. At that point he or she will make a decision. Stay? Or come back? The choice will be up to each person.

"Those who choose to stay in the past will continue on with life in their own Alternity. *That* will become their new reality. After they make their choice, the Dual Consciousness will quickly fade. And within a day, their body here in the present will die."

It was a frightening thought and he hurried on, not wanting the audience to wallow in it.

"But please note, during the state of Dual Consciousness, the traveler can easily choose to leave the past behind and come back to this present time. The traveler merely has to focus his thoughts on something unique in this life in the future, and the power of the mind will draw him back here, into his own sleeping body. But unlike a person emerging from a normal coma, our Time Lottery winners will be able to remember what happened, and anything they've learned will come back with them."

He took a final breath, as eager to move on as the audience seemed to be.

"One more thing before we draw names. You need to know that nothing the person does in the past will affect things in our present. If someone goes back and decides not to have children in her Alternity, her children in the here and now will not suddenly disappear. So don't worry. Each Alternity is separate and distinct, a world within itself."

Mac surveyed the room. They were ready. "And so the time has come." He looked to Cheryl and offered his arm. Together they walked toward the revolving globe. He loved having her there to share this moment that was so important to him. That had been so important to *them*.

Once at the Sphere, he pushed a button and the globe stopped its roll, causing the paper snowstorm inside to wind down. A small door stopped at Cheryl's eye level, the pieces of paper plastered to its side. He opened it only enough for her to extract three tickets. She held them protectively against her chest.

"May I?" she asked.

He extended a hand, giving his permission. They moved to the edge of the stage, where she began.

Bangor

More than anything in the world, David Stancowsky hated being late. It had taken all his self-control not to hang up on the electrician who'd called him at the office just as he was going out the door. Once he left, he drove way over the speed limit—which was not a good idea on the snow-packed roads of Maine in January. But he had to be on time. Ha. *Time waits for no man. . . .*

He'd made arrangements to watch the Time Lottery drawing with Ray Reynolds, the man who should have been his father-in-law. He thought it would be appropriate. If David won, he would be going back to save the life of Ray's daughter. He and Ray had stayed close all these years but Millie's mother Rhonda was another story. After Millie's death, she'd suffered a distressing surge of independence, and had suddenly decided she wanted to be on her own. It made no sense. Ray had done everything for her and as thanks she divorced him? David had heard that she'd remarried, but it was a sore subject that he didn't bring up in Ray's presence.

David listened to the Time Lottery coverage on the radio. As he parked at the Woodside Retirement Home, he listened to a man telling about the history of the Time Lottery, how it had come about due to twenty-two years of research. It wouldn't be long before they'd have the drawing. He had to get into Ray's room, turn on the set. . .

With a quick wave, David hurried past the receptionist and raced down Corridor B to Ray's room. The door was open and he knocked on the jamb. Ray was napping in his recliner. The TV was off. David was torn between politeness and expediency.

He flipped on the set, then shook Ray to waking. "Ray?"

David's attention was drawn to the television. The same man he'd heard on the radio was talking. "After a person has experienced his or her Alternity for seven days—a measure of seven days in the present, but an undetermined number of days in the past—TTC doctors will introduce a gentle electric burst to the Loop, and a strange phenomenon we call 'Dual Consciousness' will kick in."

Good. They hadn't got to the drawing yet.

With a groan, Ray sat straighter in the chair. "Oh. David." He noticed the TV. "Is it that time already?"

David pulled up a chair. "Just." He found his Time Lottery ticket in his pocket and held it front and center.

The man on TV continued: "One more thing before we draw names. You need to know that nothing the person does in the past will affect things in our present. If someone goes back and decides not to have children in her Alternity, her children in the here and now will not suddenly disappear. So don't worry. Each Alternity is separate and distinct, a world within itself."

Ray shook his head. "I still don't understand how that works. How can something in the past not affect the future?"

David did *not* want to discuss it now. It was hard not to shush the older man. Instead he put a hand on Ray's knee. "They're going to draw the names now."

Ray patted his hand. "Good luck, David."

"Thanks."

The man on TV led a stunning blond back to the revolving globe, which was twice their height. When the globe stopped its spin, David felt his heart stop, too. This was it. His one chance to find happiness in the arms of his true love. His Millie.

A small door was at the woman's eye level, the pieces of paper plastered to the globe's interior. The man opened it only enough for her to extract three tickets. She held them protectively against her chest.

"May I?" she asked.

The man extended a hand, giving his permission. Together they moved to the edge of the stage.

David forced himself to breathe.

"Ouch!" Ray said.

David realized he'd squeezed the old man's hand too tightly. He released it and let his hand do damage to its mate against his chest.

The blond smiled at the cameras and took a breath. "The first winner of the Time Lottery is. . .David Stancowsky, number 285937840."

David stared at the ticket. Had he heard—?

Ray slapped him on the back. "That's you, David! Will you look at that, you won!"

David began to sob.

Peachtree City, Georgia

"Hand me the seam cutter," Vanessa said from the ladder. "I think it's on the floor next to the water tray."

Dudley complied and Vanessa trimmed the wallpaper at the ceiling, then climbed down and surveyed the dining room. "I hope I have enough paper. If only I hadn't made that mistake above the door. I really would like to finish before Daddy comes to dinner Friday. He never has liked our old wallpaper so I'm hoping he likes—"

Dudley stood directly in front of her and made a time-out T with his hands. "Break time."

Vanessa picked up a roll of paper. "I can't. If we stop, it won't get done and—"

Dudley tossed his arms in the air. "You are a piece of work, Vanessa Caldwell. I've played along, taking an extra day off work because I thought you might need me to help you deal with your mother's will and the letters. But I did not want to spend the time wallpapering a room that was perfectly fine simply because you feel some need to be an overachiever."

"The wallpaper was eight years old. It was time for a change."

He sighed, dismissing her lie for what it was. "Actually, I stayed home because of something else that's happening today." He checked his watch. "Happening now, in fact."

Vanessa found the tape measure under a pile of scraps. "Was the measurement for a full strip ninety-six or ninety-eight?"

"Who cares?" Dudley drilled a finger on his watch. "The Time Lottery announcement is on. Don't tell me you didn't know that, didn't remember—" He watched her a moment, then nodded. "Ah, you *did* know. You *did* remember. You're chicken."

If the shoe fits. . . "I don't see any reason to watch when the chances of me winning are worse than the chances of me being crowned Miss America."

He took the tape measure from her. "Suit yourself. I was just thinking of you."

As usual. Dudley was good at thinking about Vanessa, being the essence of polite, doing all the right things. Suddenly, she thought of something. "Are you happy, Dudley?"

"What?"

"Are you completely satisfied with your life? Our life?"

He snapped the metal tape measure into its holder, pulled it out, and let it snap back again. "We have a good life. Sure, there are things I'd like to change, but—"

"Did you buy a Time Lottery ticket?"

He set the tape measure on the table and went into the family room.

She hurried after him. "You *did* buy a ticket?"

He used the remote to turn on the TV. "You had one. I figured I should, too."

Dudley never complained, always acted as if everything was fine. Funny how the word *fine* suddenly made her skin crawl. She took a seat at the other end of the couch. "What choice would you like to change in your past?"

He shrugged.

She angled toward him. "Don't give me that. You must have thought about it or you wouldn't have bought a ticket."

He pointed to the screen. "Shh. They're announcing it right now."

A classy woman whom Vanessa recognized but couldn't place moved to the edge of the stage. She held three tickets.

Vanessa was just forming the thought, *This is ridiculous*,

when the woman on TV began.

"The first winner of the Time Lottery is. . .David Stancowsky, number 285937840." There was applause.

"One down. . . ," Dudley said.

"Two to—"

"The second winner of the Time Lottery is Vanessa Pruitt, number 583920589."

It was as if the applause on the TV was in the room with them. Vanessa looked at Dudley. His jaw was in a gawk mode. As was hers.

"You won," he said quietly.

She nodded, then shook her head. This couldn't be happening.

But it was.

She ran to the bathroom.

Malibu

Lane perched at the edge of the couch cushions as her agent droned on and on about negotiations for her dream part in her dream movie. She was only half listening. Her attention was on the television and on the Time Lottery ticket on the coffee table. The handsome emcee and that woman doctor-winner from last year walked toward the globe.

It was time for the drawing.

"They love you, Lane. They want you for this part and—"

"Sol? Can I put you on hold just a minute?"

"Hold? Well. . .I suppose."

"Thanks." *Click.* She didn't feel *too* bad. Sol had put her on hold dozens of times. Besides, it would be for just a few seconds until the winners were announced. When her name wasn't called, she'd get back on the line and he would never know that for this brief moment she had let herself contemplate being somewhere else, living some other life than the one she lived. She was glad she'd refused Brandy's offer to watch it together. She needed to do this alone.

After picking three tickets, the doctor moved to the edge of the stage. Lane turned up the volume. "The first winner of the Time Lottery is. . .David Stancowsky, number 285937840."

As the cameras panned the audience as it applauded, Lane found herself praying, *Please, please, please. . .*

The woman continued, "The second winner of the Time Lottery is Vanessa Pruitt, number 583920589."

Only one left. Lane almost shut the television off. The odds were astronomical before, but now, down to one person in the entire nation. . .

Then an odd thing happened. As the blond who was last year's winner looked at the final ticket, she got the oddest look on her face, as if the name before her was familiar. Yet it was more than that. As a master of created emotions, Lane read hers. The confidence the woman had shown up until now was gone. She was confused. And even afraid. What would make her afraid? Whose name would cause such a reaction?

The emcee didn't speak but obviously wanted to know what was wrong. The woman showed him the ticket. His expression mirrored hers.

You couldn't write a more suspenseful movie scene if you tried. Lane yelled at the TV. "Just read it!"

The man seemed to hear her because at that moment he told the doctor the same: "Read it."

She cleared her throat. "The third and final winner of the

Time Lottery is Lane Holloway, number 173092983."

Lane gasped, put her hands to her chest, and was shocked to feel the pulse of her heart already pumping triple time. "Me? Me!" She jumped off the couch and did a victory dance, then realized she still had the phone in her hand.

"Sol!" She got him back on the line and vaguely heard him talking to someone else in the background. "Sol!"

"Whoa, Lane. Take it down a notch. I'm here."

Lane watched as the TV showed pandemonium in the auditorium. Some people were standing, some cheering, and some looked appalled. She pitied the two people on stage who were unsuccessfully trying to calm the crowd. "Sorry, Sol, but I. . .I. . ."

Suddenly Lane realized that the chaos in the Time Lottery auditorium was not merely a celebration for the winners, but the public's reaction to *her* name being called.

She let the network announcer's voice interrupt her thoughts: "We can tell by the audience's reaction that not everyone is pleased Lane Holloway's name was called. Already I'm hearing rumblings: How can a woman who has the world in her hands win this chance? How can that be fair? We'll put a call in to Ms. Holloway and get her reaction."

Lane snapped to attention. How could they be so mean? "Sol? I'll call you later."

As soon as she hung up, the phone rang. She tossed it on the couch as if it were poison. The sounds from the television were an affront and she flipped it off, letting the remote keep the phone company.

She looked around her living room. The colors, the lights seemed more intense than before. Nothing seemed real. It was as if this moment were happening to someone else, as if she were acting in a movie and this was a set and the scene that had just played out was carefully staged.

She waited for the director to yell, "Cut!"

But the moment continued. And it scared her to death. She sank onto the couch and wrapped an afghan close.

Kansas City

Mac left the stage with Cheryl at his heels. As soon as he was out of the sight line of the audience, he raised his hands and looked heavenward. "Why? Why?"

Cheryl put a hand on his shoulder and leaned close. "Mac. Shh. It will be fine."

He swung toward her, his eyes wild. "It will not be fine!"

Her glance around them made him aware of other ears. "Come on," she said. "Let's go in the greenroom so you can collect your thoughts."

He nodded and led the way. Once inside, with the door closed, he paced in front of the seating area. "This is a disaster. We can't have a movie star win."

"Why not? If she bought a ticket like everyone else, then she has a right to win."

He stopped pacing. "Of course she has a right, but the media is going to go crazy, even more crazy than usual."

"Calm down. With your Hollywood Image-Maker background, with all the experience you had pre-Time Lottery, working the media to obtain the results you wanted for your clients. . .this will be old hat for you."

Suddenly, the door opened and Wriggens appeared. *Not* who they needed to see.

"Well, Mac," he said, closing the door. "I'd say congratulations are in order."

Mac wasn't sure if he was serious or not.

Wriggens crossed the room and took hold of Mac's upper arms. "You are either the most brilliant man in the world, or the luckiest." He shook his head incredulously. "Lane Holloway? It's perfect. Absolutely perfect."

Mac stepped back. And away.

For the first time, Wriggens seemed to notice he wasn't pleased. "Why the glum face? We have ourselves a movie star! Talk about marketing. And media attention? It's a gold mine of free publicity. I couldn't have planned it better myself."

Mac had a bad feeling. "John, you didn't—"

"No, no. I didn't rig anything. I wouldn't do that."

And yet, according to his actions during the last lottery, he *would* take a bribe. If Mac hadn't caught him. . .

Wriggens suddenly seemed eager to leave. He put his hand on the doorknob. "We don't have time for your lofty reservations about someone of Lane Holloway's stature winning the lottery. The fact is, she did. And the other fact is, you have to deal with it. Now. The media is waiting in the auditorium for a statement."

"You talk to them," Mac said.

Wriggens pointed a finger. "This is your job, Mac. It's why we pay you the big bucks. Now get out there, act excited, and do what you can to make sure the Time Lottery is front-page news for many days to come."

Wriggens opened the door and waited for Mac to pass through. Cheryl followed and slipped her arm through his. "It'll be all right."

His head shook in a perpetual no.

She offered no argument to counter it.

⊶

"Mr. MacMillan, what is your response to those who will cry 'Unfair'?"

That it is unfair. Mac cleared his throat and addressed the press. "I can assure you that the safeguards to protect the Time Lottery from bias are extensive. Ms. Holloway had as much or as little chance as the rest of the entrants who had a ticket in that globe." He wished he felt as sure as he sounded. But ever since seeing Wriggens's face when Mac had said, "John, you didn't—" Mac had seen the slightest hint of guilt there. Wriggens had looked away. Innocent people did not look away.

Another reporter stood. "But doesn't this make the lottery a bit anticlimactic? I mean, there's no way a star like Lane Holloway would ever stay in her Alternity and give up what she has now. So isn't it kind of a waste? The essence of the lottery is the chance to stay behind."

Mac had thought of the same thing. "We should not presume we know what Ms. Holloway will do. Though she is a celebrity and much of her life is a known commodity, this will be her private exploration of her private past."

"So we won't be privy to what year she's going to visit? Last year the winners told—"

"And they will share again—as much as they feel comfortable sharing." He gave them a steady glare. "You might keep in mind that the more gracious you are to the winners, the more willing they'll be about sharing information."

Another reporter: "Do you think Ms. Holloway will choose to relive her first love in Hollywood, her first costar, Guy Evans, and pursue—"

Mac cut her off with a raised hand. "Please do not speculate. The three winners leave in one week. Three winners. Please remember that. Ms. Holloway is not the only one to have received this honor. But please give all the winners the utmost consideration as they make their decisions and prepare for this great adventure. Now I have work to do."

God help us all.

Hope deferred makes the heart sick,
but a longing fulfilled is a tree of life.
PROVERBS 13:12

Bangor

If it had been possible to fly, David Stancowsky would have spread wings and glided back to his office. Yet even if his body was grounded, his soul soared. He was going to see Millie! He was going to hold her and kiss her and. . .

His memories collided with fantasy. They'd become dangerously intertwined these past forty-six years, and he often had trouble distinguishing between their actual relationship and the one he'd gone on to create without her. The truth is, they'd never been physical beyond the moral restrictions of 1958. Millie was a good girl, a fact David had admired, but also one that had caused him great frustration. Their wedding couldn't come too soon. Then Millie would be totally his.

Back in 1958, with the blessings of Millie's father, David had started to plan a glorious affair in the biggest church in Bangor. Millie had been unreasonable when she'd asked for a small gathering with little to-do. He'd overridden her ridiculous notion. The daughter of the president of Mariner Construction, the wife-to-be of his successor, needed to be married in a style befitting their social status. Or at least the social status they hoped to attain. You become what you pretend to be. At any rate, a caterer had been chosen, the florist was flying in David's favorite flower—calla lilies—and three hundred invitations would be sent out. And Millie's dress. . .

David had found a dressmaker who was ready to sew up a lovely copy of Jackie Kennedy's 1953 wedding gown. The Stancowskys would create their own Camelot in a home on a lovely wooded lot. He'd had an appointment to show Millie the dress, but she died the day before. . . . The stage had been set for a perfect day.

Until the argument. Until an angry Millie drove away in the rain, lost control on a curve, and plunged into the ocean.

David shuddered and turned into the parking lot of his office. It was not his fault. He'd meant no harm bringing Millie to Bar Harbor for a day trip. Sure, he would have loved to stay in a single room at the bed-and-breakfast there, but Millie had overreacted, and their argument had escalated to her wanting to call off the wedding. He didn't want that. He couldn't allow that.

He pulled into his CEO parking spot near the front door of Mariner Construction and shut off the car. His breathing was heavy. He closed his eyes and willed himself to calm down. All those regrets, all those mistakes. . .now that he'd won the Time Lottery, he would finally break free from them. And Millie would be his once more.

He looked at his reflection in the rearview mirror and adjusted his features until they looked triumphant and in control. Now, only now, could he enter the building and greet his people and accept their congratulations. Proof that David Stancowsky was once again victorious over all that stood in his way.

He knew something was up when he spotted his secretary, Dina Edmonds, peeking out the front door. Why wasn't she up on the fourth floor guarding his inner sanctum? Knowing Dina, she'd probably arranged for some sort of celebration. Dina was like that. She'd been his secretary since the very beginning, always taking care of him and the interests of the business. Sometimes David wondered if he wasn't more expendable to the company than Dina was.

He saw flutterings of people through the glass front of the building but looked down, pretending not to see. Let them have their celebration. He would accept it graciously.

As he opened the door and stepped inside, the silence was broken by, "Surprise!" The lobby was full of his employees. Dina moved close, giving him an awkward peck on the check. "Congratulations, Mr. Stancowsky."

Linda, his head estimator, stepped forward. "We watched the drawing on TV. We all heard your name."

David put his hands on his hips and feigned anger. "You watched on company time?" As expected, no one responded, heightening the positive effect when David smiled. "I'd be mad if you hadn't watched. We all had something at stake today. We each had a ticket." *Thanks to me.*

"Mr. Stancowsky, come this way," Dina said, pointing to a long table against the windows. "We got you a cake to celebrate."

A full sheet cake with yellow frosting roses anchored one end of the table, while a bowl of orange punch balanced the other end. Paper cups, napkins, plates, and forks filled in the middle.

David put a hand around Dina's shoulders. "Surely you didn't plan this ahead—?"

"Since you were so generous giving all fifty-two of us a ticket, I was hoping one of us would win. And if not, we still could eat cake and commiserate our loss." She glanced up at him, then down again. "But to have you be the winner, Mr. Stancowsky. . . No one deserves it more."

"You are the gem in the Mariner crown, Dina, and I want to thank you for putting together this celebration. I'm just sorry we all couldn't win."

"What year are you going to visit?" Linda asked.

David stepped toward the cake. "1958."

"That's before I was born," said a deliveryman.

"That's before a lot of you were born."

"Wasn't that the year after you joined the company?" Linda asked.

"Yes, it was. But it was also the year a dear woman was killed. Millie was the love of my life and I've never forgotten her. We were going to be married when her car went off a cliff."

There were the expected gasps. This was not common knowledge. "That's horrible."

"How tragic!"

Then Dina's soft voice. "And you've. . .you've loved her ever since."

David realized she was the only one who knew the whole story—because she'd been there. "Ever since."

She nodded, then moved to the cake table and took up the knife. She turned to him, her smile shaky. "Would you like to do the honors, Mr. Stancowsky?"

Peachtree City

Dudley paced up and back in front of her. "I don't know about this, Vanessa. Maybe you should think about turning it down."

She was thinking all right, but not about that option. "You bought a ticket, too."

"But I never thought either of us would win. The whole thing is an interesting concept, but—"

"It's a miraculous scientific achievement."

"That plays into the disillusionment of the American public." He stopped pacing. "When will people realize they need to be content where they are? With who they are?"

"So we shouldn't strive to be better? To be more? To do more?"

He sidestepped around the coffee table to sit beside her. "I've spent twenty-seven years of my life trying to make you happy. And now. . .what year are you going to visit?"

She wished she knew. Should she visit her mother in the past? Go back before the divorce even happened? Or what about her decision to be a professional volunteer? Though it was rewarding, being the supergiver of her time, talents, and treasures could be exhausting. . . . Yet what would she do instead?

"It's the baby, isn't it?"

"What?"

"I know we don't ever talk about it. But I'm sure you've thought about the baby you aborted in college. How could you not think of it?"

He was right. "My father had me abort that baby."

Dudley's sigh was weary. "I won't argue with you. I came

into the picture a few months after the fact. But let's say you do go back to have your baby. That would mean you may or may not hook up with me. Which means you may or may not have Rachel. You'd give up one child for another?"

I've given up plenty. "It wouldn't be like that."

"It most certainly would." He stood. "You know what I want to change?"

"What?"

"You ever finding that stupid lottery ticket." He left her.

Just as she soon would be leaving him.

⁂

"Vanessa Rae! Why haven't you returned my calls?"

She prepared an excuse her father might find feasible and left the truth for another time. "The phone's been ringing constantly since I won, Daddy. I had to let the machine take the calls. I couldn't—"

"But my calls. . .certainly you have time enough to talk to me."

Time enough? Hmm.

"And it's not just today. Where have you been the past few days? Even before the lottery I called and called and no one was home. You know how nervous I get when I can't get ahold of you."

"Dudley and I had some business to attend to."

"I didn't want to talk to Dudley."

I was going through my mother's things. I was finding out the truth about how you kept us apart. There was so much to say, yet a lifetime of old patterns to rip apart before any of it could be said. And she didn't feel up to it.

"Hello? Are you even there?"

"I have a lot on my mind, Daddy. I have a big decision to make."

"Which is why I'm calling. I know the perfect time for you to visit."

Imagine that. "When?"

"The year you married Dudley. Your decision to marry Dudley."

This was old news. Although her father and Dudley had found a measure of mutual respect over the years, in Yardley Pruitt's eyes, Dudley still wasn't good enough for his only daughter. Yet the biggest strike Dudley had against him was that he and Vanessa had met, courted, and married without thought to Yardley's wishes or input. For that one all-encompassing sin, Yardley balanced a twenty-seven-year-old chip on his shoulder. "Don't start, Daddy."

"Don't act like you're so happy. I know you're not."

"Leave it alone, please."

"Don't take that tone, young lady."

Vanessa hated when he called her that. At forty-nine she wasn't young in any sense of the word and was feeling older all the time.

He was waiting. She gave him what he wanted. "Sorry, Daddy."

"As you should be. Now, back to the issue of Dudley. Though I will admit he was better than some of those losers you dated, we both know you could have done better. Your college rebellion pained me greatly, Vanessa, and I handled it the best I could."

Compared to the rebellious battles of many of her 1970s classmates, hers had been a skirmish. As far as doing better than Dudley? To be fair, he'd been a good catch. There was no one more stable, more constant than Dudley Caldwell. Yet there'd never been a spark between them, and certainly no fire. Their life was comfortable and contained. And though she'd had multiple moments during their marriage when she'd fantasized about a real romance, complete with real passion, she'd refused to let it pull her away from what she had.

"You know I'm right, Vanessa. You know your Dudley-decision would be the best choice to explore. Truthfully, sometimes I find him a bit too needy."

Vanessa stifled a laugh. "He's very kind to you, Daddy," she said. "To me, too."

"Yes, yes. But back to your decision."

"I don't know what I'm going to do. That's the purpose of this week between the drawing and the leaving, to figure it out. Now, I really have to go."

"You call me later and we'll discuss this more. Or maybe drive over. This house gets pretty lonely, you know."

So he said. Repeatedly. But seek him out for *this* decision? Seek advice from the man who'd lied to her all these years?

"Vanessa?"

"Later, Daddy."

"I'll be waiting to hear from you. Don't let me down. I'm the only one who knows what's best for you. You know that."

The only thing she knew was that the rock upon which she'd based her life was crumbling.

Malibu

Lane slammed the door to her bathroom. "No more!" she yelled.

Her agent, Sol, answered from his side of the door. "Do not be angry at me, Lane. I'm the one who should be mad. What were you thinking buying a lottery ticket at the same moment I'm negotiating my tush off, trying to get you the part of your career?"

"I didn't buy it. Brandy gave it to me." It seemed a moot point.

"Then don't accept the prize."

"Too late. I've already called the Time Lottery people and accepted. It's done."

"Call them back. You can undo it. That's the only answer that makes any—"

She opened the door to face him. "Are you nuts?"

"Sometimes. Often, working for you."

She pushed past him toward the living room, towering six inches over his five-foot-three frame. The phone was ringing. Again.

Brandy stood at the breakfast bar. "Do you want me to get it?" She pointed toward the front door. "And the driveway is full of reporters."

Sol's cell phone rang. Lane pointed at it. "Don't you dare."

"You're going to have to deal with them, Lane. If you won't give back the prize, it's your only alternative."

"It's all my fault." Brandy sat.

"Don't blame yourself. It was a wonderful gesture, a—"

"Gesture?" Sol said, laughing. "Oh, that it would have stayed a gesture."

Lane fell onto a bar stool next to her friend, resting her head in her hands. "If only they'd leave me alone for this one week. Then I'll do the time-travel thing and be free of them."

"They'll be in your past, too. You haven't been free of the

press since you were eighteen." He moved across from her, into the kitchen. He poked her arm, making her look up. "By the way, what year are you going to visit? What choice could you possibly regret?"

She hated the condemnation in his eyes. The mocking. She glanced at Brandy—who expected her to revisit her Joseph connection. They'd never understand her wanting to go back to see Dawson, Minnesota, much less Toby.

The phone and the doorbell rang at the same time. The press was getting restless. And bold. She half expected to see them on her back deck, hands cupping their faces to the window for a peek at the great Lane Holloway.

Then suddenly, another choice presented itself like a prize behind door number two. And when she realized Toby could be a part of this choice, too, she smiled.

"I'm waiting, Lane. What year?"

She stood, taking the power position. Yes, this seemed right. This seemed perfect. "I'm going back to 1987."

"Your first movie came out in eighty-eight."

She nodded.

"You still lived in Lawson, Mawson—"

"Dawson."

Brandy slid off her stool. "But Joseph wasn't in Dawson."

"I know."

"Nothing's in Dawson."

"You were in Dawson—with me."

"Yeah, but. . ." Lane could see her friend go through a memory scan. Suddenly Brandy put a hand to her head. "Eighty-seven was the year we graduated. The year you won the audition and brought me with you here, to—" Her fingers danced on the counter and her head started shaking. "Oh my, Lane. . .no. . ."

Sol looked between them. "Enough old home week. Tell me what's going on."

Brandy did it for her. "She's going back before the tryout, before the tryout that gave her the part of Bess!"

"Bess made her a star." He whipped around toward Lane. "You can't be serious."

"I am."

He let out a huff. "That would be like Lana Turner never going into Schwab's Drugstore to be discovered."

"That didn't happen. It's just legend."

"And your point is. . . ?"

It was all so clear. To find Toby again, to rid herself of the pressures of stardom. All in one amazing shot. She moved to get a bottle of water. "I want to see what normal would have been like."

As she passed him, Sol rolled his eyes. "Oh, please. The entire world reeks of normal and would give anything to be in your movie-star shoes. And you want to join them, wallowing in mediocrity?"

She unscrewed the cap on the water bottle. "I had a good life in Dawson."

"Then why did you want to leave?"

She took her drink and moved to the window to face the ocean view. She saw a reporter tiptoe onto the deck, as if on cue, camera already snapping. She calmly closed the blinds. Soon the whole world would see what Lane looked like pulling blinds. Pitiful. She set the water down and fell onto the couch, pulling her feet beneath her.

Sol took a seat on the ottoman. "Why don't you go back to a time within the framework of your current life? Maybe explore what would have happened if you would have gotten the starring role in *When Harry Met Sally*? I'd like to know that one."

It wasn't good enough. It wasn't extreme enough. It wasn't far enough back. Lane had come to recognize the roles she'd gotten—or not gotten—as for the best. Even her few clunkers had been learning experiences. Besides, what good did it do to live in angst about a choice that was beyond her control, a choice that often was determined by obscure factors having nothing to do with her acting ability?

The doorbell rang a second time and they all looked in its direction. "Brave little buggers, aren't they?" Sol said.

"Maybe I should talk to them and get it over with."

"I could arrange it. I could tell them you want to give a statement."

Lane looked at Brandy, who stood nearby, gripping the back of the loveseat. Her eyes were flitting wildly, but she was smiling.

"What are you thinking, Brand?"

"I'm thinking that this is cool. To go that far back? And I'll be there with you, I mean, not me as me now, but me as the eighteen-year-old me. We'll have a blast—or as much of a blast as was possible in Dawson." She smiled broadly. "I'm impressed by your gumption, Laney-girl."

Sol shoved the ottoman back a foot. "This is crazy. Go have a fling with some what-if moment if you want, but don't do something so drastic. Don't risk everything."

"It won't affect you, Sol," Lane said. "What I do in my past will not affect you here. I'm exploring *my* Alternity. It's parallel. The timelines don't intersect." She felt dumb saying all this, as if she understood the science of it. But it *was* the truth, at least as she understood it. "If I go back and—"

Sol stood. “If you go back before the audition, if you attain that precious ‘normal’ you’re after, you’ll end up staying in Dawson, marrying some Swedish farm boy, having too many kids too, too fast, and blending into oblivion, never to be heard of again.”

Lane’s stomach grabbed, but she said, “What’s so bad about that?”

“What about me?” Sol said. “Once you dig your domestic roots and don’t come back, I’m out my biggest client.”

She couldn’t argue with his basic point. “Maybe the movies I’ve already made will have a resurgence. You get a percentage of all those. . . .”

“Until the novelty wears off and your audience moves on to stars who are producing new movies, better movies. Eventually you’ll be lucky to find DVDs of your movies two for ten dollars at Wal-Mart.”

“Wow,” Brandy said, plopping down on the loveseat. “You’re quite the doomsayer, aren’t you?”

“I’m a realist. And hey, if I’m out of a job, so are you.”

Brandy shrugged. “You’ve known Lane a few years; I’ve known her my whole life. She’s my best friend and I love her. I’ve got the most to lose, so if I’m willing to let her do this thing so she can have a shot at something even better than she has now, then so can you.”

Sol snickered. “Dawson, Minnesota? Better?”

“Don’t knock it,” Brandy said.

He squinted at her. “Didn’t you have a drunk mother back in Dawson? Didn’t you come out here with Lane as a means to escape her backhand?”

Brandy raised her chin and pulled a pillow into her lap. “Yeah, well. . .what’s past is past.”

Sol laughed. "Not anymore. Not since the Time Lottery!"

"You're just jealous," Brandy said.

"Hardly."

While the two of them bantered and bickered, Lane lay her head against the couch pillows. These two important people in her life could argue over the color of the sky. Finally, she'd had enough. "Come on, you two. Time-out. I'm tired. Really, really tired."

Brandy popped out of her seat. "That's our cue. Everybody out."

Sol gathered his briefcase. "Might as well. I'm not needed here. Or there. Bye, Lane. Let me know if and when you want to be an actress again."

"Had to get one last dig in, didn't you, Sol?" Brandy said.

"Sue me."

Brandy gathered her things and took an exaggerated breath as they all congregated at the front door. "Ready to meet the enemy?"

Sol sighed. "Just open it."

In one sweeping movement Brandy opened the door to the crowd of reporters and pushed her way through to her car. Sol followed. It was chaos.

"Lane! Lane! Tell us—"

"Who's that?"

"Go after her; maybe she knows something."

"That's the agent. Mr. Epstein, what year is Lane going to visit?"

"No comment."

Lane shut the door. Locked it. And sank to the floor. The Spanish tiles were cold.

Kansas City

Cheryl snuggled deeper against Mac's shoulder. "You're not here."

At her words, Mac blinked and realized she was right. He hadn't been concentrating on the here and now; the fact that he had this lovely, vibrant woman in his arms; soft music playing on the stereo; the smells of dinner still lingering from the kitchen. He kissed the top of her head. "Sorry."

"Another group's been chosen, Mac. Step one is done. For the most part, the technicians and scientists take over from here."

"I know." It wasn't that.

"Are you thinking about *your* chance to go back? Are you thinking about Holly?"

Bingo.

She sat up. "Do you regret not taking the chance Wriggens gave you? I know your reason was Andrew—and a fine reason he is, but—"

"No, no."

"I don't believe you."

He laughed. "Would you please stop being so insightful, intuitive, in—"

"Incapable of accepting bunkum as the truth?" She traced his left eyebrow with a finger. "It's okay to be human. And it doesn't hurt me one bit to know you'd like to go back and stop your wife from being murdered. You loved her deeply. That's a good thing. I'm not threatened by that love. I'm inspired by it."

"I can't imagine you being threatened by anything."

She stopped tracing and looked to the ceiling. "Hmm. You're probably right about that."

"I am in awe of your confidence."

She faced forward, putting her feet next to his on the coffee table. "Don't be. I'm too arrogant and egotistical to be threatened by anything. But if I were truly a nice, wise older woman, well then. . .I suppose I *could* offer you a list of fears and foibles."

He squeezed her shoulders. "You are a nice woman, often wise, and I've told you our age difference means nothing to me."

"I *have* aged well."

It was an understatement. No one would ever guess Cheryl was in her late forties. As Mac got older himself, he'd come to realize how little age meant. It was a state of mind. And Cheryl's mind put most twenty-year-olds to shame.

He continued his compliments, meaning every word. "You're a wonderful woman. An amazing woman. An astounding woman."

She reclaimed her spot, snuggling against his chest. "You spoil me."

"It's my joy."

They breathed in unison a few minutes. Then she said, "I really should be going. In fact I'm leaving right now." She did not move.

He smiled against her hair and held her tighter.

"Oh, Mac," she whispered. "I'm having a tough time leaving." She kissed a button on his shirt. "I wish I could stay."

Oh yes. He wanted her to. "I'd like nothing better."

"See?"

"We've talked about this, Cheryl. We both want to do this right. What God is bringing together—"

She slapped his chest and sat up. "Let no hormonal people put asunder. I know. I know. I hope He appreciates our sacrifice."

Mac stroked her hair behind her ear. "He does. And He'll bless it when the time comes." He caught himself. "I mean *if* the time—"

She wagged a finger at him. "Uh-uh, Alexander MacMillan. You said *when.* Is that a proposal?"

It was. In a way.

"I'm waiting."

He kissed her cheek. "When it's a proposal, you'll know it's a proposal."

"Promise?"

"There will be no question."

5

"With man this is impossible, but not with God; all things are possible with God."
MARK 10:27

Kansas City

Alexander MacMillan stepped into the limo, his cell phone to his ear. Dealing with Chief Administrator Wriggens was arguably the hardest part of his job. The man needed constant reassurance—and monitoring.

The driver closed the door and Mac settled in for the ride that would collect the winners for their final press conference. Earlier today he'd picked them up from the airport—David Stancowsky flying in from Bangor, Vanessa Caldwell flying in from Atlanta, and Lane Holloway flying in from Malibu. All were safely ensconced in the Regency Crown Center, a lovely hotel that went out of its way to cater to these Time Lottery elite.

The limo pulled into traffic. A light snow was falling. "Things are progressing, John," he said into the phone. "So far, so good."

"You call this good?" Wriggens said. "Last week, when the

press initially pounced on the winners, I had high hopes for some extraordinary publicity, not just exterior shots of their homes or the incessant third-person rehash of their past accomplishments—or lack thereof. I wanted interviews with *them,* not segments of *This Is Your Life* or insipid speculation as to what year they'll choose to visit."

Mac closed his eyes. "It's our own doing. We beg the press to leave the winners alone during this week between the drawing and the departure so they can finalize the specific choices they want to change and make arrangements to be gone—perhaps forever. I can't believe you're complaining that the media is cooperating."

"Get off it, Mac. I don't want cooperation. I want exploitation. We have only this one time each year. We have to make the most of it."

The man had no shame. More, more, more. He was never satisfied and had the capability to focus like a laser beam: The bottom line was Wriggens's god. He wasn't choosy about how he worshipped it and wouldn't waste a moment if a commandment or two were broken in the process. The ends always justified the means.

Although Mac knew applying logic would be unsuccessful, he gave it a shot. "You know the no-interview request is for the good of the winners."

"Yes, yes, but I bet if we took a poll, most people have their choice figured out before they even buy a ticket. This week-long interim. . .you're wasting everyone's time, Mac. Time that could best be used to promote and nourish the program. Sometimes I wonder about your loyalty and your priorities."

And I yours. Mac slumped in the soft leather of the limo's seat and closed his eyes. He still had a hard evening ahead of him. “Fine. I’ll take a poll of one right now. What would you change?”

“Me?”

“Sure. Pin it down to one moment, one decision, one past choice.”

“I’m not eligible to buy a ticket.”

“But surely you’ve thought about it. Surely you’ve done some mighty soul-searching.”

There was the slightest of pauses. “I’ve got another call. I’ll see you at the press conference.”

Lurking in the back, no doubt.

The limo pulled in front of the hotel. The driver went around and opened the door. As soon as Mac exited, a bevy of cameras converged, following Lane Holloway as she sprinted from the hotel entrance to the car.

“They’re out in force today, Mr. MacMillan,” she said as she stepped inside the vehicle. David Stancowsky led Vanessa Caldwell into the fray, with the cameras clicking wildly.

As Vanessa got in, David winked at Mac. “No turning back now, is there, Mr. MacMillan?”

“None at all.”

David and Mac took seats across from the two women. Once they pulled away, they each took a deep breath, smiling at their unison.

“I apologize for the cameras during your exit,” Mac said. “Have they been hounding you all day?”

“I’m afraid it’s my fault,” Lane said. “I bring out the worst in people.”

“Nonsense,” Mac said. “We’re thrilled to have you here.”

“I will say it’s quite exciting sitting next to Lane Holloway,” Vanessa said.

"I've got the better view," David said from his facing seat. "You're every bit as lovely in person as you are on the screen."

If Mac hadn't had time to get to know Lane after picking her up at the airport, he would have been surprised by her blush. But after talking to her and finding out she was delightfully unassuming. . .

"Please," Lane said. "Can we forget the movie-star title for the rest of this? At least between us? We're all winners. We're all in this together, right?"

"I'm in," Vanessa said.

"Absolutely," David said.

Mac beamed. He retrieved a note card from the inner pocket of his suit. Such lists were essential during these stressful two days. "While we're gathered I thought I'd go over a few details. Time tends to go too quickly these last eighteen to twenty-four hours."

"Time. Amusing," David said.

"Tonight we will take you before the press one at a time. You may make a statement or just answer questions, but you obviously know that the press—the world—wants to know the year you are going to explore and something about the whys behind it. It will be short, and I will be there to cut things off when I think it's appropriate. We want to make this as painless as possible."

Vanessa sighed. "I'll do whatever it takes, Mr. MacMillan. Please know that."

Mac looked at her. He'd done research on her life. She was the recipient of many awards for volunteerism. Definitely a giver. He foresaw no problems with her at all.

"Big groups don't bother me," David said. He winked at

Lane. "And you've obviously got that one down."

She smiled. A good sign. Mac continued. "Now, as for your actual journey tomorrow. Once again, we will pick you up at the hotel, then deposit you into individual waiting rooms at the TTC building, where you will change into scrubs so you're comfortable during your journey. Your family can be with you as you wait so you can say your good-byes."

"I'm going solo," David said. "How about you ladies?"

Lane answered first. "Me, too." Her face looked a bit sad.

Vanessa looked worried. "My father, my husband, and my daughter are going to be there. If you'd rather they not be. . ."

"They are very welcome."

She seemed to relax. Mac continued. "When it's your time to go, I will take you into the Sphere—"

"It's rare to see an actual geodesic dome," David said. "I would have liked the contract on that one."

"The Sphere houses the working area of the Time Lottery," Mac said. "Inside are a team of doctors, technicians, and a few dignitaries looking on. You will lie down, and we will attach some life-support monitors, IVs, a catheter, etc."

"Fun," Lane said.

"Essential," Mac said. "Once you are settled, our medical staff will position an fMRI device around your head, pinpoint the Loop portion of your brain that holds your memories, and give you a dose of the Serum in the form of a shot. The Serum acts as a magnifier for your thoughts."

David made a face. "Work on making the Serum in pill form, eh, Mr. MacMillan?"

"Next you will be asked to think of the time you wish to visit and the choice you'd like to make differently. You will fall into a deep sleep, similar to being put under anesthesia, except your mind will be wonderfully awake as you enter the past. Your consciousness will quickly adjust, and you will experience your Alternate Reality—your Alternity—totally innocent of the future, of how things were the first time around."

"But we'll make a different choice," Lane said.

"You will. As you're traveling into your Alternity, you'll be concentrating on the choice you want to make differently. With the help of the Serum, when the moment of choice comes, you will feel strongly urged to take one path over another. That's when the power of the mind, the power of suggestion, takes over. After that, you will be free to live out the consequences of your new choice."

"And you can't intervene?" David asked.

It was an odd question. "No, we can't. You are alone. You are human. You are vulnerable to all the laws of nature." He shook a finger at them. "So risk wisely. If you die in your Alternity, you die there."

"But would we die here in the present?" David asked.

"No, but your second chance *will* die."

Vanessa raised her hand. "You say 'risk wisely'. . .isn't this whole thing a risk? I mean, time travel. . ."

"The risk is minimal. Since your body isn't going anywhere, since we have medical personnel monitoring you every moment, and since you are experiencing all this within your mind—we are merely enhancing and directing your own thoughts—there's not much to go wrong."

"Famous last words," David said.

Mac could have used fewer comments. "After seven days in your Alternity, we will initiate an electrical charge to the Loop portion of the brain. It will give you the ability to regain your 'real' memories. We call it 'Dual Consciousness.' It lasts only about an hour, but it's plenty of time for you to choose to stay in your Alternity or return to us here. If you stay in the past, all memory of your life in the future will fade and will seem like a dream. As your body here dies a peaceful death in the Sphere, any family you have in this time—or charity of your choice—will receive the benefits of the $250,000 insurance policy provided by TTC."

"I prefer not to think about that part," Vanessa said.

Lane patted her hand. "It'll be all right. I know it. We're very lucky."

"I agree. But it goes deeper than luck. You are blessed," Mac said. He leaned toward them. "Though the TTC is a secular corporation, I happen to believe God is behind you three being chosen. Everyone has a unique purpose, and for whatever reason, God has chosen you to get this second chance. I only ask that you don't waste it."

They all nodded. The Sphere loomed at the end of the block.

⁂

The three winners settled into the greenroom to wait for the press conference. Vanessa approached the coffeepot. "Coffee, anyone?"

"Sure," David said. "Black as you can make it."

Lane lifted a hand. "No thanks."

As Vanessa poured, Lane pulled Mac aside. "Can I talk to you a moment?" She glanced at Vanessa and David chatting by the coffeepot. "In private?"

"Of course." He led her back into the hallway. "Is there a problem?"

"Not exactly. But there is something I have to tell you."

His mind filled with a thousand things that could go wrong.

"You know how I have to tell you what change I want to make in the past?"

"Yes. You have made a decision, haven't you?"

"Two decisions."

"I know it can be hard to choose, but you—"

"No, no, you don't understand. I am perfectly willing to tell *you* my real decision, but I want to tell the press—the world—something different."

"Why is that?"

The right side of her mouth pulled up crookedly in a coy smile he'd seen on-screen a hundred times. "Come on, Mr. MacMillan. You're a marketing whiz. You were a part of Hollywood before the Time Lottery got ahold of you. Image-Maker. . .wasn't that your title?"

He shrugged.

"Modesty becomes you." She swept a hand through her hair and it fell into place as if it knew exactly where it would be most stunning. "The point is, you're very familiar with spin."

He used to be the master. "You're in need of some spin?"

"I am. I want to tell the world I plan to visit 1987 in order to explore a relationship with my high-school sweetheart."

"They'll love that. Everybody loves a love story."

"Including me. And I do look forward to seeing Toby again."

"But?"

"The choice I really want to explore is in regard to the audition I had at age eighteen. The one that got me the part of—"

"Bess! The one that ignited your career. Everyone knows that story."

She shrugged. "But my real decision—the change I want to explore—has to do with *not* attending that audition."

Mac drew back his head. "But that was your big break. If you hadn't won that audition, who knows whether—" He stopped. "You might not have become a star."

"Exactly. I am the first to admit that timing is everything, breaks are a blessing, and talent often does nothing but keep the ball rolling. There are a lot of very talented actors out there who never succeed."

"But people think you have the perfect life. They won't understand your willingness to give that up."

"I know." She started to bite a fingernail, then folded it under and put it behind her back. "If the public knows the truth—that I might be willing to give up fame and all that comes with it—they'll think I'm ungrateful. . .not satisfied with what I have. . .with the life *they* helped create. If I stay in the past, the legacy of my work will suffer. That's bad enough, but if I come back to reclaim my life here, who knows what effect that kind of bad press will have on my future? Yet if love is involved. . .I think they'll be more forgiving."

Mac nodded with understanding. "I see your dilemma."

"So will you help me? Be my coconspirator?"

If Wriggens found out about this, if the press heard about this. . . But Lane's logic was sound. If she was to fully benefit from her Time Lottery experience, a little subterfuge would be necessary. Actually, it might be kind of exciting.

He held out his hand. "You've got a deal."

She shook his hand but used it to pull herself close enough to kiss his cheek. "I owe you one."

Montebello, California

Toby Bjornson set his beer on the TV tray, slumped into his recliner, flipped on the TV, and opened the bag of taco-flavored Doritos. Dinner. He didn't have time for more. Though his boss had wanted him to work late on the house they were trimming out, he'd told him no. He had things to do. If it got him fired, so what? He was tempted to explain when they'd asked but didn't. Couldn't. He used to brag about being Lane Holloway's ex-boyfriend but had stopped when people gave him too much guff about falling so low when she'd risen so high.

And now that she'd won the Time Lottery? Life wasn't fair. Why hadn't he won? *He* needed a second chance. A third and fourth chance.

He flipped through the shopping channels until he found the Time Lottery press conference. He'd come this far. He couldn't stop watching now. He'd bought the newspaper for an entire week since the drawing, and he'd watched more news than he had in two years. But ever since hearing the press mention Dawson. . .he had to know her plans. Laney. His Laney. Was she going back to see *him*?

That's what he would have done. If she wanted the same thing. . .that was fate. He'd always felt they were supposed to be together. If it weren't for that stupid audition, they would have married and raised a passel of Tobys. He even might have gone to college. She'd wanted him to, even though she'd had no such plans herself. Ever since he'd met Laney in fifth grade she'd been obsessed with Hollywood. Their first outing alone was when she made him sneak into a movie theater to see *The French Lieutenant's Woman* because she simply had to watch everything Meryl Streep was in. All those weird accents. Couldn't the woman speak regular English? After Lane left Dawson, Toby wouldn't watch a Streep movie. He couldn't.

If only he could have kept her from going to that audition, strapped her down to a chair, if need be. He'd make her happy. He'd show her life could be good, even in small-town Minnesota.

On television, a *GQ* type with blond hair strolled out on the stage. Toby recognized him from the drawing. Mac-something. The guy took a seat at a table that had two mikes on it. Toby turned up the volume.

"Good evening, ladies and gentlemen. I want to welcome you to your final chance to speak to our three Time Lottery winners. As you can imagine, they've had an interesting week pinpointing the decisions they wish to change. In a few moments they will have the chance to share their decisions with you. The number of details they share are at their own discretion. Please respect that. Obviously, most of us would want to go back and change a negative into a positive. And such negatives are often embarrassing."

A reporter jumped the gun and asked a question. "But doesn't the TTC need to know the details?"

"Yes, *we* do. And the winners will be interviewed by a few choice personnel and their decisions noted. But the wonderful aspect of the entire time-travel phenomenon is that it is not dependent on the TTC understanding the moment in question, but relies on the winner's own thoughts, their own brainpower, and their own Loop to bring them back into their own lives to the right point in time. It's quite miraculous."

"But what—?"

The Mac-guy raised a hand. "Let's introduce one of the winners, shall we?"

"Yeah," Toby said to the TV. "Now would be good."

"Without further ado, I would like to introduce to you a woman who has earned herself a place in the hearts of an entire nation. A woman who is as charming in person as she is on-screen. May I present to you Lane Holloway."

Toby applauded with the audience. "Yay, Laney! Go get 'em!"

Laney looked gorgeous in a long brown skirt, long-sleeved blouse, jacket, and boots. Classy, classy lady. And those golden-brown eyes when she looked in the camera. . .

"Good evening, everyone," she said. "I'd like to make a statement, and then I'll answer a few questions. First off, I am very honored to have been chosen one of the Time Lottery winners, and I want to assure everyone that I will not waste this chance. Much of my life is an open book, and I've heard complaints that I shouldn't be greedy, that I already have so much, have attained so much."

She looked down, and Toby recognized a glimmer of the insecure girl he once knew. "There is no defense for me winning such a chance, and frankly, I am peeved by those who believe I need to create one. The Time Lottery is just that. A lottery *of* chance that's all *about* chance. A second chance." She took a deep breath. "I plan on returning to my hometown of Dawson, Minnesota, to the year 1987, to my high-school years."

Toby jumped from the chair, sending the chips flying. "Yes! She loves me! She still loves me!"

He forced himself to sit down because she wasn't done. "As you all know, though I may have been successful in my career, my love life has been less satisfying. And so I am going back to take another shot at a past love."

Dozens of hands were raised with questions, which could be summed up into one: "What's his name?"

She looked to the man beside her. "I'd really rather not say."

He leaned close and said something.

As the press waited for her answer, Toby grabbed the sides of the TV. "Say it! Tell them it's me!"

Laney looked at the camera. "His name was Toby. That's all I'll say."

It was enough.

He kissed her face on the screen. She still loved him! That's all that mattered.

Kansas City

Mac paid the babysitter, went into the family room, and shut off the television she'd left on. He emptied her half-full can of Dr. Pepper into the sink, the pop and sizzle marking its descent down the drain. The room smelled of microwave popcorn, and he found its source on the counter. He took the bowl to the kitchen table, sat, and absently pinched the last few kernels from the bottom. The press conferences were over. They were a success. Even Wriggens was satisfied. No small feat.

Mac had seen the three winners safely to their rooms at the Regency and had spent the last of his energy reassuring them that everything would be fine. Lottery jitters were inevitable. For tomorrow was D-Day. Departure day. The lives of David, Vanessa, and Lane would be changed forever. Whether they stayed in their Alternity or came back, the experience was significant and indelible. This memory they would not forget.

Mac shoved aside the popcorn bowl and got up to shut off the lights. Though he longed to talk to Cheryl, he knew it was best she wasn't with him right now. For many reasons, not the least of which was the fact that she'd been called to the hospital for emergency surgery on an accident victim. Though her presence would have been a balm, it also would have been a distraction to a mind already fragmented and weary.

He entered the foyer to lock the front door and, as happened every time he completed this mundane chore, was reminded of the one time when the door hadn't been locked. When evil had entered this house, killed his wife, and hurled his tiny son across the room. If only. . .

He shook his head against the daily—if not hourly—mantra and headed up the stairs. He'd had his chance to go back. He'd refused, because to live in the past with Holly would be to leave his son here alone. He would not do that to Andrew. He could not. No matter what his pain.

He walked softly into Andrew's room. The boy lay sprawled on his bed, covers askew. Mac tucked in arms and legs and smoothed the blankets on top. *Safe as a bug in a rug.*

Andrew stirred and opened his eyes. "Daddy. . ."

Mac stroked his head, smiling down at him. "Son."

What else could be said?

Even youths grow tired and weary,
and young men stumble and fall; but
those who hope in the LORD *will renew their strength.*
They will soar on wings like eagles;
they will run and not grow weary,
they will walk and not be faint.
ISAIAH 40:30–31

Kansas City

Vanessa Caldwell felt guilty. Here she was, in the waiting room, moments away from being taken into the Sphere to be hurtled back in time, and her overriding desire was to be alone.

But she wasn't alone. Her loving family had gathered to see her off. As her father argued with Dudley about why there was air, and as her twenty-one-year-old daughter, Rachel, cowered on a chair like a wallflower afraid of social contamination, Vanessa envied the other winners' decisions to do it alone, to not have anyone see them off. If only she'd been so brave.

As if she'd had a choice.

During the last week, Dudley had come to terms with her

choice to revisit her twenty-first year, her pre-Dudley life. He'd come around when she'd begun to stress her desire to explore life with her mother rather than the life she'd have had with her aborted baby.

It had been the same in regard to Rachel. In fact, Vanessa had decided not even to mention the baby-detail to her daughter. Rachel had enough self-esteem issues. Rachel Frances Caldwell had often been teased by her grandfather that the *F* initial of her name stood for Frumpy. Though cruel, it *was* an apt description. Vanessa had hoped going to an Ivy-League school would help Rachel find a style. Any style would do. But the girl was decidedly blah and boring. Brilliant. But boring.

Not that Vanessa couldn't have benefited by a makeover herself. She'd been pretty once. But in the last few years, her skin had lost its glow and was being betrayed by wrinkles; her thick, blond locks had darkened and thinned into the short layered style she wore now, whose only attribute was that it was easy to take care of; and her dark eyes had paled, reminding her of the bleached-out eyes of her Tiny Tears doll after she'd given her too many baths with Bab-O.

Dudley, Rachel. . .which left her father. Yardley Pruitt had not come to terms with her choice. It didn't matter if she focused on the aborted baby or her desire to spend time with the woman Yardley had divorced. Neither option was acceptable to this man who had placed himself in the center of her life in so many ways. Too many ways.

In his defense, it wasn't that Daddy was controlling. Vanessa liked to help him and felt most in control when she was doing so. She found her identity in being capable, organized, and dependable. She liked nothing better than to have someone comment on one of her good deeds, and fed on their awe and gushing gratitude, knowing that her offerings lifted her above the lowly recipients who wouldn't know what to do without her. Only one person refused to play the game by needing her or paying homage: Rachel. Ever since she was old enough to form her own opinions, Vanessa's daughter had rejected her mother's favors, advice, and help with a cold, nearly disdainful scorn. Which is why Vanessa spent as much time as possible away from home. She'd be the first to admit she was a mediocre mother. And in psychobabble terms, perhaps she hadn't tried too hard out of spite for her own mother's abandonment.

Only now she knew it wasn't an abandonment. *Ostracism* was a better word. Her mother had been banished from her life by a vengeful father.

She stole another look at Rachel. The girl returned a faint smile, then looked down. Vanessa had wanted to have a talk with her before leaving, confess all the mistakes she'd made, and tell her the truth about her grandmother, but she'd chickened out, supposing it was ridiculous to think she could develop a maternal backbone *and* a close mother-daughter relationship in a week.

What she *had* done was leave her mother's letters on the dresser in Rachel's room. Her mother was much more eloquent than she; let Dorian Pruitt Cleese tell Rachel the truth. The letters had changed Vanessa's life; she only hoped Rachel would let them change hers, because Rachel was indeed the product of a too-busy father and mother. It would have taken a miracle for their progeny to develop any other way. And miracles had been decidedly absent in their lives.

Until now.

Vanessa hugged herself. Any moment now Mr. MacMillan would come in to get her. Any moment now she'd be rushing back in time—or rather, her mind would take the trip while her body stayed here. It was unfathomable and she shook her head, not willing to ponder the idea long. She was more than willing to accept and enjoy the perks of technology as long as she wasn't expected to figure out how they worked.

Suddenly, the door opened and thought became reality. Mr. MacMillan came in, smiling at her. "Are you ready?"

She put a hand to her stomach and nodded. At least she thought she nodded.

Dudley came to her side. "This is it?"

"This is it," Mr. MacMillan said. "Time to say your farewells."

Vanessa turned to Rachel first. The girl had stood but did not step forward, forcing Vanessa to go to her. She held her daughter's face in her hands. "I love you, honey."

She waited for Rachel to break down, tear up, offer some hint of emotion. But Rachel merely nodded and accepted Vanessa's hug before reclaiming her chair.

Her father held out his arms. "Vanessa. Dear girl. I don't know what I'll do without you." She let herself be enveloped by his protective force. Oddly, the Elvis Presley song "Make the World Go Away" sang in her head. That's what Daddy counted on Vanessa to do—make his world easy and snug. The term *enabler* came to mind, but now was not the time to entertain such psychoanalysis. Besides, that reality meant little right now when another kind of reality screamed in her ear, one she was going to have to face alone. Not just reality, but her Alternate Reality: Alternity.

She shivered, but the movement was absorbed within her father's arms. Then he kissed her head and let her go.

It was Dudley's turn. When she turned to her husband, it was as if she were seeing him for the first time. He was not a handsome man. Never had been. She'd married him soon after the abortion to escape her pain. To be needed amidst her own need. Ardor had never been a part of their lives. They were pros at nice-ing each other to death.

As they did now. Dudley gave her a quick hug, kissed her cheek, and said the right words. One, two, three, and she'd be on her way. . . .

She suddenly found herself all out of politeness. The need to be alone returned, and she stepped toward the door with such purpose she made Mr. MacMillan scramble after her. Out in the hall she hesitated. "Which way?"

"To your right, Ms. Caldwell. Down to the last door on the left."

She captured the hall with her stride, causing Mr. MacMillan to pull up on her arm, slowing her. He brought her to a stop. "It's all right, Ms. Caldwell. Families mean well, but they don't always help."

She looked back at the door, then slapped a hand to her mouth, hating the emotion that had suddenly welled up inside. "I may never see them again! I need to go back. If only—"

With a firm hand, Mr. MacMillan stopped her from bolting. He nodded toward the door at the end of the hall. "The 'if onlys' are addressed in this direction."

The door leading to the Sphere beckoned. Forget the new choice she was planning to make in the past; she had the biggest choice of her life to make right now.

She looked at Mr. MacMillan. He raised an eyebrow and offered her his arm. "Shall we?"

Lane sat in the waiting room. She bit a fingernail, made herself stop, then resumed biting. Her nails were a small sacrifice at the moment.

I should have let Brandy come.

But no. Though Brandy might have made her laugh or held her hand (saving her manicure), the final good-byes said here, just moments before *it* happened, would be too much. It was better they'd said good-bye back in California.

The sad thing was, there was nobody else she could have asked. No boyfriend, no friend-friend, no family. Her parents had died a few years earlier—her father of a heart attack and her mother of cancer—and she had no siblings. She was alone in the world.

How ironic to be recognized by millions, loved by millions, yet known by so few. The cost of fame was high indeed.

Help me. Please help me.

When she realized she'd just prayed, she nearly took it back. Surely God didn't appreciate people like her who called on Him only when they were in deep need. Indeed, hers was a foul-weather faith. *Help me! Fix it! Make it all better!* When was the last time she'd called on the Almighty with good news? Happy prayers?

Sorry. I owe You so much. I'll try to be better. Just get me through this. . . .

The door opened and Mr. MacMillan entered. "Are you ready?"

Lane's butterflies dive-bombed her toes but she nodded and found the strength to stand. "It's showtime."

It didn't surprise David that his first reaction to the inside of the Sphere was business related. As soon as he was through the door, he stopped and stared. It was like walking into the inside of a globe, except all the surfaces were painted sky blue. "Exquisite."

Mac laughed. "Glad you like it."

David did a three-sixty. "But one observation. . .there are thousands of wasted cubic feet. The TTC has money to burn?"

"We have a message to send. A square room with eight-foot ceilings may provide function, but it would not portray the dream properly, nor excite the senses."

David snickered. "You excite the senses of your victims before putting them in a medically induced coma?"

Mac put a hand on David's back and pointed to the people in the balcony encircling the room. He whispered, "I'm afraid it's more for them than you."

"Ah. VIPs. Can't budget without them."

"I see you understand."

"I haven't been in construction for nearly fifty years without understanding what's what. What scares me is putting my life into the hands of the lowest bidder."

Mac laughed. He extended an arm toward a team of employees in lab coats who were seated before a bank of computers and other machines. "These are the people who will make sure your trip is safe. As you so aptly deduced, the building has nothing to do with your trip. These people are the key."

David gave them a salute. "Bonuses for everyone!"

They laughed, and a doctor and nurse stepped forward from one of the hospital beds, which took up positions at nine, twelve, and three o'clock. For the first time, David allowed himself to notice that two of the beds were full. Vanessa Caldwell and Lane Holloway lay in the beds at nine and twelve, a white, curved machine wrapped across their foreheads. An IV drip and monitors did their life-sustaining work.

"Remember, I dislike needles," he said.

Mac motioned to the doctor standing nearby. "We are now entering your realm, Dr. Rodriguez. If you will please put the patient at ease?"

The doctor came forward and shook David's hand. His eyes were kind, but he looked way too young to know much of anything about anything. Then he stepped back to display the equipment surrounding the bed. "I'm afraid there *will* be a few uncomfortable moments as we attach life-support tubes: an IV, a catheter, and sensors at vital points."

"I define the most vital point as keeping me alive."

"Exactly. And I assure you, there is little danger."

"I'll have to take your word on that."

"Actually," Dr. Rodriguez smiled, "yes, you will."

The pretty nurse cut in. "Let me assure you, I am an expert at pricking and probing."

He winked at her. "I'm sure you are, Nurse. . . ?"

"Connor."

"First name?"

"Doris."

David sat on the bed. "With Doris by my side, I'm ready for anything." *I just want to get this over with.*

But Dr. Rodriguez wasn't through showing off the tools of his trade. He moved to the curved machine that would soon wrap around David's head. "The roots of this machine are in the fMRI—the Functional Magnetic Resonance Imaging—that is used to map the body. Since we are only interested in the brain, we have minimized the size. To be even more specific, we have perfected a technique for pinpointing the neurocircuitry enabling system called the Loop—that part of the brain that's activated by the stimulus of memory. Through this machine, we will continuously monitor the brainwave signature of the patient as the Loop uncoils."

He patted the machine. "It works the same as a traditional MRI, through the use of nonionizing radiation. We tap into the Loop through the use of the MRI's magnet and radio waves and then go a step further and map your unique brainwave signature."

It sounded good. And normally David would have enjoyed the tech-speak. But not today. Not now.

Doris touched his shoulder. "Would you like to lie down so we can get started?"

"Now you're talking."

Mac stepped away and they pulled a curtain around the bed. Nurse Connor was right. She was good at pricking and prodding. She also smelled wonderful. Like honeysuckle. When she was done she smiled down at him. "How are you doing?"

"Don't leave me."

She took his hand. "I won't."

Dr. Rodriguez pulled back the curtain, letting Mac back in. Then they positioned the MRI machine around David's head. David was glad his eyes weren't covered. It would have been unbearable not to see.

Mac came into view. "This is it, Mr. Stancowsky. Would you like to say anything?"

"Don't screw this up, okay?"

He felt Doris squeeze his hand. It would be all right. In a few moments he'd be seeing his Millie again. That was worth any risk.

Dr. Rodriguez stepped beside him. "I'm going to give you a shot now. All you have to do is relax and think of the time you want to visit and the new choice you'd like to make. Don't worry if nothing happens right away. The Serum will take effect within minutes and help you hold on to the memories. Bon voyage, Mr. Stancowsky."

David felt the prick of a needle, then a warmth. He closed his eyes and concentrated on the past—his new present. *I live in Bangor, Maine. The year is 1958. My fiancée, Millie, and I are on a prewedding weekend trip to Bar Harbor. We're staying at the Rocky Ledge bed-and-break—*

He was flying, weightless. Soaring through his thoughts until suddenly, the color of David's memories intensified, as if a light had been turned on. He smelled the combination of salt air and cinnamon. He heard a scratchy record playing "Mona Lisa." And there, standing next to a porch swing, was his lovely Millie. She turned and looked at him.

His body had weight again. He had substance. He smiled and moved toward her.

The VIPs had left and Mac stood alone on the balcony of the Sphere. He looked over his charges: Vanessa, Lane, and David. They appeared serene. Sleeping. But he knew their minds were busy, working hard in their Alternity, living out a choice that would take them to places undiscovered. It used to be said that space was the last frontier. Perhaps. But a frontier that was just as unfathomable, just as exciting, just as limitless, was the human brain. These ordinary people lying before him were explorers, every bit as brave and adventurous as Lewis and Clark or any astronaut.

He watched the technicians at the computer terminals, manned twenty-four hours a day. He saw Dr. Rodriguez make a notation on Lane's chart, look up, and see Mac. He took a few steps toward the balcony, speaking softly, as if sound could disturb their sleep. "They'll be fine, Mac. I promise. Go home."

Mac nodded. He could leave now. The winners didn't need him. And they were not alone.

Father, take care of them.

Never alone.

The fear of the LORD *is the beginning of knowledge,*
but fools despise wisdom and discipline.
PROVERBS 1:7

Athens, Georgia—1976

Vanessa stood at the curb and let the swarm of college students swell around her and past her. Their spring jackets were a rainbow above the common denim of their jeans. They all had somewhere to go.

So did she. If only she could remember where it was.

Her mind was blank.

She looked around the University of Georgia campus, trying to get her bearings. What day was it? She looked at her watch, but it didn't help with anything but the time. 10:20. If it was Monday, Wednesday, or Friday she should be heading to Russian History. But if it was Tuesday or Thursday, she should be heading back to the dorm after Business Fundamentals. The trouble was, she wasn't on the right corner for either. And her arms were empty of books.

Suddenly queasy, she put a hand to her stomach. Then she knew. Then she remembered.

She was pregnant. The building in the next block was the clinic where she'd take care of it, make it all go away. In the purse on her shoulder was cash from Daddy, tearfully obtained, but obtained nonetheless. *"How could you do this to me, young lady? You must take care of it immediately."*

Which is what she was about to do. No thanks to Bruce. The creep. She'd never speak to him again. Not that she wanted to.

A lie.

She heard a new wave of students coming up behind her to cross the street. She'd cross with them. She'd let them sweep her up in their wave and move her toward her destiny.

Don't do it.

She turned around, looking for the voice. At the edge of the sidewalk a girl argued with her boyfriend. No one was speaking to Vanessa. Yet the voice had *seemed* real and had been accompanied by the oddest flash.

She let her own voice sound—and was surprised to find it amazingly strong. "I don't have to do this."

Then, without permission, her legs moved. Walked. Away from the intersection. To stop would be to argue with herself, so she let her feet take her away, let them lead her to a grassy spot under a tree. There they gave out and she sat. If it wouldn't have caused a scene, she would have tipped onto her side and pulled herself into a fetal curl.

Fetal. Ha.

Instead she leaned against the trunk, closed her eyes, and rubbed her abdomen, hoping the confusion would pass with the morning sickness.

"Oh. . .my. . .goodness! Nessa!"

Vanessa's eyes shot open. No. It couldn't be.

It was.

Her mother.

Dorian Pruitt skipped over the grass, her granny dress dancing around her legs. In one final motion, she fell to her knees and scooped Vanessa into a hug. "My dear, dear daughter. I barely recognized you! How are you?"

She was better when she was free of the embrace. Her mother was the one who was unrecognizable. Vanessa hadn't seen her for five years, and *that* mother figure had not been the wild-and-free woman before her. Always a bit different, but never this far-out. "What are you doing here, Mother?"

Dorian sat on the grass cross-legged, arranging her dress. "I've come back to get my master's. The grade school gives me Tuesday and Thursday mornings off. My teaching assistant takes over."

"You're still teaching?"

"Of course. I don't dare let a year of munchkins slip by without the pleasure of my company."

"Since when do you need a master's degree to teach second grade?"

"Since I want to be the best teacher I can be." She swatted Vanessa on the knee. "Learning for the joy of learning. . .you should try it sometime." She didn't wait for her daughter to defend herself—not that Vanessa could. She'd never been a good student. "I've missed you so much."

Vanessa didn't believe that one. If her mother missed her, wouldn't she have tried to contact her? Not a card. Not a phone call.

Her mother plucked a blade of grass and twirled it between her thumb and forefinger. She audibly let out one breath before taking another. "So. Are you happy, Nessa?"

"Sure."

" 'Sure' is the answer of the uncommitted."

You want me to jump up and down? These last five years alone with her father had been busy ones, taking care of him. They'd been okay. Fine.

Okay and *fine.* Two more words of the uncommitted?

A reply was needed. Vanessa drew her knees closer to her chest, a barrier between her heart and this woman. "College is awesome." It was a huge exaggeration but definitely not an uncommitted word.

Her mother squinted. "Hmm. What's wrong?"

At first, all she could do was stare. She wasn't used to someone reading her. Vanessa could be crying and her father wouldn't ask that question. Someone else's emotions were always an imposition to Daddy, so Vanessa had learned to keep them in check. Yet suddenly, crying was a reality. The tears flowed and she bowed her head into her knees.

Her mother stroked her hair. "Oh my. Oh dear. I see it was no coincidence I passed this way and found you here."

Vanessa looked up. "But it was! I didn't plan to be here. I was heading—"

Her mother hooked Vanessa's hair behind an ear. "Heading where?"

Vanessa got to her feet. "Nowhere. I need to go home."

"Oh no, you don't." Dorian pushed herself to standing, her feet getting caught in the long skirt of her dress. "I'm not letting you loose just yet. We're going to lunch."

"I can't. I don't have time. And it's not even eleven."

"Oh pooh. You *are* your father's daughter. Or you were. But today you're mine, and my philosophy is to eat when there's reason to eat, not when it's scheduled or proper. As far as time?"

She linked her arm with Vanessa's. "This is a time of celebration. I'm getting to spend time with my daughter, and nobody, not even your father, can interfere."

What's that supposed to mean? But how could she object? She had nothing better to do.

Something to do, but certainly not something better.

Frankie's Café sat directly across from the arches on the edge of campus, catching students—and their dollars—as soon as they hit Broad Street. Vanessa had been there only once because close proximity was all it had to offer. The floor was sticky, the food greasy, and the tables were stained aqua Formica with chrome legs that wobbled. Once had been more than enough.

And now, entering the student hangout with her mother dressed like an over-the-hill hippie. . . Vanessa was proud of the clean lines of her own wide pants and belted tunic, her long, straight hair compared to her mother's frizz-bomb.

Yet when they walked in the door, the cashier beamed and raised his hand for a high five. "Dorian, baby. The day isn't complete without your shining face."

Her mother smacked his hand, then interlaced her fingers with his and squeezed. "Flattery will get you anywhere, Frankie." She yanked Vanessa close, claiming her. "I would like you to meet my daughter, Vanessa."

Frankie gave her the once-over. "Well, well. This is her, huh?"

"In the flesh. Isn't she lovely?"

"Almost as lovely as you, babe." He shook Vanessa's hand. "I'm glad you finally came to your senses and contacted this fine lady, because she—"

Mother led her away. "Let's sit." Over her shoulder she called out, "Two Frescas, Frankie. Lots of ice."

Vanessa detested Fresca but didn't say anything. She was too busy thinking about Frankie's comment. Her mother had discussed their relationship—or lack thereof—with this stranger?

They opened their menus as a waitress who was old enough to be Frankie's mother brought the drinks. "The lunch special is a cheese frenchee with fries," she said.

Mother slipped her menu into the space by the salt and pepper shakers. "Oooh. That's for me. How about you?"

Vanessa had no idea what a cheese frenchee was and didn't care to find out. "Do you have a chef's salad?"

The waitress let out a burst of air. "You want rabbit food, go to the Green Earth at Five Points." Then she pointed to the left-hand side of the menu. "The BLT has a bit of lettuce on it."

"Fine. No fries."

"Chips?"

"No chips."

The waitress raised an eyebrow and looked at Vanessa's mother. Dorian laughed and said, "Don't blame me. You know *I'm* your best customer. I may like natural threads, but I abhor bean sprouts. I like a little grease with my food."

"We're going to name the new griddle after you."

"Much obliged."

As soon as the waitress left, Dorian reached across the table and took Vanessa's hands in hers. "So. Under the tree. The tears. What can I do to help?"

Vanessa was dumbstruck. For five years Daddy had been stressing that her mother didn't care about her and wanted nothing to do with her. Yet here, in the span of a few minutes, she'd heard evidence to the contrary.

She pulled her hands away, setting them safely in her lap. "What did that man mean when he said it was about time I came to my senses and contacted you?"

"You'll have to forgive Frankie. He's as subtle as a whack by a two-by-four. I know you didn't contact me on purpose today, but I'm thrilled with the contact just the same. I have to admit I've lived on the edge of endurable having all my letters returned, all my phone calls intercepted."

"What are you talking about? What letters? What calls?"

Her mother's back found the chair. "I was afraid of this."

"You've been trying to contact me?"

The flat of her mother's hand hit the table, making the ice jiggle. "I knew it! That louse! How dare he keep us apart." She leaned forward. "For a while, when the letters were returned, I thought *you* were avoiding me, but then when I drove to Buckhead and stopped by the house and got the runaround. . .I got the picture. Daddy dear would stop at nothing to keep us apart."

"You came to the house?"

"More than once. But either Yardley answered and said you weren't home or no one answered."

"Daddy always told me never to answer the door when I was home alone unless I was expecting someone."

"There you go. Premeditated, calculated ostracism. He certainly thought of everything. It's bad enough he skewed the facts against me in court, getting them to grant him full custody when he didn't deserve it any more than—"

"But *you* left *us*, Mother."

Her jaw dropped. "Is that what he told you?"

Suddenly, the thought of eating anything was impossible. "He said you didn't love us anymore, that you didn't appreciate any of the wonderful things he worked so hard to provide. He said you wanted to go live like a hippie, in a commune." She lowered her voice. "Have sex all the time. Free love and all that."

Her mother made two fists and shook them over the table. "I could just strangle that man! How dare he lie like that?" Her hands dropped. "Though I should have expected it. I was naïve not to expect it, knowing him as I do."

This didn't make sense. Daddy was a good man. Daddy loved Vanessa. He wouldn't lie—

She felt her mother's hand on her arm. "I don't mean to blow your world apart, honey. Yet, apparently it needs blowing."

Vanessa looked at the door. If only she could rewind the last half hour, she'd find herself standing on the corner near the clinic and. . .

And what? Would she walk across the street and get the abortion? While she'd been sitting under that tree, hadn't she felt the slightest bit of relief that she *hadn't* done it?

But now, for her mother to come along and further complicate her life. . .she didn't need this. Not now. Not ever.

Mother was talking and she wasn't listening. "I'm sorry if this hurts, Nessa. But you don't want to spend your entire life based on a lie, do you? Depending on a liar? The truth may be painful now, but I guarantee it would hurt a lot more later."

Vanessa shoved her glass away, making it spill over the edge. "Why does it ever have to hurt?"

She recognized the look her mother gave her, and for a moment old memories melded with the present. "Certainly you're not that naïve?"

Vanessa didn't want to hear it, though she had heard it from others like Bruce and her friends: "You've got to stop letting your father use you. He shouldn't be calling the shots—you should."

It was perfectly natural for Daddy to need her and depend on her. Since the divorce all they had was each other. They were still working things through, but it was getting better. Vanessa was feeling stronger, and every once in a while she actually found herself in control. She liked the feeling.

Yet you also love being needed. It makes you feel important. Admit it.

But what about the lies? What about her father keeping her mother away?

The waitress brought their sandwiches. Mother poured a huge amount of ketchup on her plate and dragged the tip of her fried sandwich through it. Wary of her own choice, Vanessa lifted up the bread to inspect the BLT, yet felt little like eating.

"I don't mean to make waves, Nessa. That's not how I envisioned our first chat, but you're twenty-one. You're a big girl. Life is full of hard knocks and hard truths. Your father has been doing a number on you—on both of us—by keeping us apart. And living under such hype doesn't do anybody any—"

"I'm pregnant."

The cheese frenchee plopped into the lake of ketchup.

Vanessa scanned the café, suddenly afraid everyone had heard her shame, but no one looked her way. "Less than an hour ago, I was heading to the clinic to get an abortion."

"But you didn't."

She shook her head. "I ended up under the tree. Then you found me."

Her mother laughed. "No-sirreeny. God found you! And then He let us find each other. This is wonderful."

Vanessa stared at her, incredulous. "Hardly. It's a disaster."

Her mother lifted a hand. "We're talking about two different things, honey. Back to your pregnancy. . ."

"Don't say it so loud."

She lowered her voice. "Do you love the father?"

I thought I did. "He doesn't love me. He's gone. Out of the picture."

"I'm so sorry."

That was *not* what her father had said.

"Who suggested the abortion?"

Vanessa rearranged the triangles of her sandwich. "Daddy."

"He disgusts me."

"It seemed like the right thing to do."

"The easy thing. The quick thing. Not right. Not by any means right."

"But it's okay. It's done all the time now. My friend had one."

"Then I pity your friend."

"Pity?"

Her mother took a deep breath along with another bite. "Just because you can doesn't mean you should. I'm not going to preach at you, Nessa. But I am going to tell you there are other alternatives."

"I can't keep it. I'd make a horrible mother."

"Now, now. We'll work through this thing together. I promise." Her mother pointed to Vanessa's sandwich. "But for the moment, eat up." She raised a hand and called for the waitress. "Agnes? Could you please bring us a large milk over here?" She looked at Vanessa. "You're eating for two, you know."

Two. One more than herself.

Vanessa drank every drop.

As soon as Vanessa entered her dorm room, her roommate, Connie, jumped off the bed. "So? Did you do it?"

It took Vanessa a moment to remember what "it" was. "No." She sprawled on her stomach, pulling her pillow into her cheek.

Connie stood over her. "You chickened out?"

"Not exactly."

"You changed your mind?"

"Not exactly."

Connie shoved her over and sat. "Then what happened?"

"I ran into my mother."

"You're kidding. After all this time?"

Vanessa told her all about it. Connie moved to her own bed, resting her arms on her knees. "Your dad's been lying?"

"It appears so."

"Bummer."

Vanessa snickered.

Connie sat erect and aimed an imaginary gun. "Want me to go with you to confront him? I could be your backup. 'I am woman, hear me roar!' "

"You've been watching too much *Starsky and Hutch*."

"I prefer *The Avengers*. Sure do miss Emma Peel." Connie did an Emma-jab with her leg and put the "gun" down. "You gotta know, Vanessa, Yardley Pruitt is not going down easy. He owns you."

"Don't exaggerate."

"Who pays for your tuition and dorm room?"

"A lot of parents pay. Unless a student is smart like you and gets a scholarship."

"But I doubt most people have a daddy who gives them fifty bucks a week to blow on clothes and booze."

"If he didn't give me spending money. . . I don't have a job."

Connie scooted back and pulled her legs beneath her.

"Maybe the question is, why not? I work. Bruce works. All our friends work."

"Daddy says I need to concentrate on my studies—not that it does much good."

"That's not why he doesn't want you to have a job. Where do you go every weekend?"

"You know Daddy lives less than an hour away. It's not that big a deal one way or the other."

"Then don't go. This weekend, don't go."

It wasn't that simple. "He needs me. And Saturday he has a dinner party he wants me to help with. He doesn't have a wife. I have to take her place."

Connie raised a hand. "I wouldn't touch that one. . . ."

"You have a dirty mind."

"Hey, I only go with what you tell me."

Vanessa flipped off her shoes. "Daddy says I'm a big help. He says—"

"Daddy says, Daddy says. . ." Connie rolled her eyes. "Like *I* said, he owns you. You are bought and paid for. One slave running to her master."

"It's not like that."

"Of course it is. You've been selling out for years. Your mom just proved he's done a number on you. He's kept the two of you apart. Isn't it time you called him on it?"

Vanessa didn't say anything. The idea was tempting but also scary. She'd never talked back to her father, much less called him a liar. Besides, she needed *him* right now. She was failing two classes, and she needed him to pull a few strings. . . .

"You're afraid he'll cut you off, aren't you?"

Her teeth clicked shut. "He could. He probably would."

"Maybe your mother could take over and give you some bread."

"She's a second-grade teacher. She doesn't have any money."

"But maybe this is about something more important than money." Connie got up to leave. "I have class. Hang in there, Vanessa."

She'd give it a shot.

"Vanessa Rae! Why haven't you called?"

She shut her textbook. She couldn't remember a thing she'd read the last half hour anyway. "I've been busy, Daddy."

"Today wasn't a day to be busy, it was a day for the. . .you know."

He couldn't even say it, yet he expected her to do it? "I didn't go through with the abortion."

"Why not?"

"I'm having second thoughts."

"You're not planning on marrying the bum, are you? Because don't expect me to spring for any have-to-get-married wedding. You told me he dumped you."

"He did."

"Good."

Thanks a lot.

"So what's the problem? We agreed this was best."

A flood of words put pressure on the gate holding them back. *I saw Mother. She told me you've kept us apart. So many lies, Daddy. How can I ever trust you again?*

"I'm waiting."

"I don't want to rush into it. This is a big decision."

"Not at all. You're unmarried. You got yourself pregnant.

You're in school, *trying* to get a degree."

She didn't like how he emphasized the word "trying."

"Certainly you can't be thinking of keeping it."

Her mind hadn't gotten that far. "I don't know, Daddy."

"I can't have an illegitimate grandchild. I won't. . . . I gave you money—"

It was always about money, always about him. "I'll return the money."

"That's not the point. We made a decision and I expect you to follow through. You're weak in that department, Vanessa. You have a tendency to fall short, to bow out of the final goal. 'He who hesitates is lost.' "

Lost. It was exactly how she felt. " 'Night, Daddy."

"But we're not finished. I need you to—"

"I'll call you tomorrow."

"But—"

She hung up on him. And felt a surge of power.

Interesting.

Dawson, Minnesota—1987

"Miss Holloway? Are you with us?"

Lane looked up at the teacher. All eyes were on her. "Sorry. What did you say?"

"Obviously nothing that you heard." Mrs. Williams took up residence beside her desk. Too late, Lane covered the bright yellow flyer. The teacher pulled it free. "Hmm. It seems our own Lane Hollo*way* wants to take Holly*wood* by storm."

There were laughs all around.

Mrs. Williams handed the flyer back.

Jamie Calfield grabbed it away and read it, made a disgusted face, and shoved it to the edge of his desk, where it slid to the floor. "Do you actually think an audition that's held in Minnesota will make you famous? Get real."

Mrs. Williams retrieved the flyer and put it back on Lane's desk. "Lane is allowed to have dreams, Jamie. You might try having a few yourself." Then she gave Lane a pointed look. "But not during my class."

Lane glanced at her boyfriend, Toby Bjornson, seated the next row over. He shrugged. He didn't believe in the audition either.

Mrs. Williams moved to the front of the room. "Now, back to Gorbachev. What effect do you think his new policies of glasnost and perestroika will have on US-Soviet relations?"

Lane wanted to scream, "Who cares?" Gorbachev, Reagan, Khadafy, Oliver North. . .what did any of them have to with life in Dawson, Minnesota?

And what does you becoming a movie star have to do with life in Dawson, Minnesota?

Lane put a protective hand on the flyer. Grandma Nellie had given it to her last week, and she'd been carrying it around ever since. *"You go, child. You take this chance to let your star shine."* Her star? Sure, she liked to perform. Sure, she always got the lead in the school plays. Sure, she loved acting more than anything. But acting in Dawson was far different than acting in Hollywood. At the audition, she would be up against the hopes of every wannabe in the nation. The nationwide search for Bess in the new movie *Empty Promises* was the most exciting actor event since the search for Scarlett O'Hara in the thirties. Their audition appointment was for seven this evening in Minneapolis.

Lane caught Toby glancing back at her. He smiled and offered a wink. He was the main reason she *wouldn't* go through with it. They were engaged to be engaged, a condition they'd been holding onto since fifth grade when he'd first taken her hand in the coatroom at recess. But what would happen to the *us* of "Toby and Lane" if she went off to Hollywood?

It was a reasonable question but one that sent her into an Excedrin headache No. 78. She couldn't think about it anymore. She was leaving for Minneapolis in a few minutes, as soon as class got out. She was. Grandma was taking her. There was no turning back.

The bell rang and Lane's stomach stirred up more butterflies than she'd gotten watching Cher accept the Oscar for *Moonstruck*. Her family laughed at how involved she got with the awards. Nervous. "You'd think you were the one up for the award," her father had said.

Someday. . . Hey, if Cher could win, so could she.

Toby scooped up her books and they headed for the hall, where he draped his arm across her shoulders.

"Don't look so smug," she said.

"What?"

"I saw the look on your face when Jamie made fun of the audition."

They stopped at her locker for her coat. "Hey, he spoke the truth. He told you exactly what I've been telling you—"

Lane slammed the locker shut. People looked in her direction so she yanked Toby toward the exit. "I don't need everyone telling me it's a long shot. I know that. But I promised Grandma I'd go."

Toby pulled her head close and gave it a kiss. "I just don't want you to get hurt. Is that such a bad thing?"

"I don't want to get hurt either, Tobe, but I'm afraid if I don't try, it will hurt even more."

Once outside, Lane scanned the waiting cars for Grandma's red Rabbit. "There she is."

But as she turned to give Toby a good-bye kiss, he dropped their books and took hold of her upper arms. "Don't go, Laney. Don't go."

"But I promised—"

Grandma moved her car forward in line until she was centered on Lane. She beeped the horn. When Lane looked her way, she tapped her watch. *I know. I know.* Lane turned back to Toby. "I have to go."

"No. No, you don't. You have to stay here with me."

Suddenly, an image flashed in Lane's mind. She was wearing a red blouse, crying in front of a table where three people sat. Three judges. Judges at an audition? Was she crying after making a fool of herself?

Toby was talking. ". . .put yourself through that?" He pulled her into his arms. His safe, warm arms. "I love you, Laney. I'm only trying to protect you."

She closed her eyes, resting her head against his shoulder. In his arms her butterflies landed. He was right. Why should she put herself through such pain? The image of crying in front of the judges returned. Who needed such humiliation?

Not her. Not her.

She pushed back in order to see his face. "I. . .I won't go. You're right. I don't need to put myself through this. I don't have a chance anyway."

He hugged her even closer now that she was truly his again.

"I have to tell Grandma."

He stood aside, sliding his hands in his pockets. Grandma Nellie was leaning over the gearshift, watching. She rolled down the passenger window and called out, "Don't just stand there. Destiny calls, child."

Oh dear. As Lane walked closer, Grandma flipped the door handle, making it pop open. Inviting her in.

She opened the door but knelt beside it. How could she tell her most avid supporter she wasn't going? Couldn't go. Because she was chicken. She couldn't look at the older woman.

Grandma sighed deeply. "Uh-oh. What's going on?"

She had to say the words. "I can't go."

"It's normal to be afraid."

Lane put a hand on the seat, steadying herself. "I don't like the feeling."

Grandma laughed, but softly. "No one does. Fear is a part of life, child. You can't let it win. A body has to push through it." She reached across the seat and put her hand on Lane's. "I don't have any special knowing if you'll get this part or not. I just want you to try. No regrets, remember?"

Lane smiled. "No regrets" was Grandma's battle cry.

But was it hers?

"Hey, Lane? Where's your limo?" It was Jamie. Jamie smacked Toby on the shoulder. "What are you going to do after she gets rich and famous? Be her chauffeur?"

The hurt in Toby's eyes clinched it. Lane didn't want to experience pain by going to the audition, and she didn't want to cause it either. She looked at her grandma. "I'm sorry, Grandma. I really am."

She stood, shut the door, and walked toward Toby.

Her grandma called after her. "Lane!"

It was hard to keep walking.

"So?" Toby asked.

She leaned her forehead against his cheek and lowered her voice so Jamie wouldn't hear. "I'm not going."

"You're—?"

"Can we get out of here?"

He gathered their books, pulled her under his arm, and they walked away.

"Hey, hey, Lane," Jamie said. "What'd you do, chicken out?"

She could take heckling. But what she found harder to handle was the sound of her grandma gunning the engine as she drove away.

She couldn't win. She just couldn't win.

They walked along their special place, across the walking bridge that spanned the Lac qui Parle River. The sound of their feet on the old wooden slats was reassuring, a connection with other days spent running over the bridge, pretending to be pirates or pioneers. They stopped halfway across and looked over the water. Lane zipped up her jacket and snuggled against Toby's shoulder. "Hold me. Just hold me."

He held her tight and she heard his heart beating. The sound gave her comfort—the beat of the heart of the boy who loved her. What could be better than that?

She'd expected his question, had even braced herself for his question, but when it came, she found she still wasn't ready with an answer.

"Why did you change your mind?" he asked.

She thought of where she and Grandma would have been at this moment: on the highway to Minneapolis, Grandma pumping her up with big talk of big plans for her talent. "I don't want to talk about it."

"But you were so set, so sure. I'm glad, but—"

She pushed away from him. "Don't give me a hard time, Toby Bjornson. Ever since I heard about the audition you've been after me *not* to go."

"Your parents didn't want you to go either."

"My parents have trouble believing Hollywood is a real place. They're meat-and-potatoes people. They like things they can wrap their hands around, not dreams."

He stroked the edge of her cheek. "You *are* talented. I've always said that."

Talented enough for Dawson—population fifteen hundred. She turned her face so his hand fell away.

His voice took on its normal tone. "So, just to know. . . what did I say that made you change your mind?"

Truthfully? Nothing. She thought back to the image of a failed audition, wearing a red blouse, crying. . .

Suddenly, she looked down. She wasn't wearing a red blouse. She was wearing her lucky blouse that she'd worn when she got the part of Eliza in *My Fair Lady* at school last year. It was blue.

Toby repeated himself. "What did I say to change your mind?"

She sidled close again. "Just hold me."

Bar Harbor, Maine—1958

David set their suitcases beside the porch swing of the Rocky Ledge Bed-and-Breakfast and watched his Millie as she strolled its length. He loved the way her slim skirt hugged her legs. If only the plaid jacket didn't cover up the best of his view. He'd asked her not to wear it. It was too. . .northwoods. "So. You approve of this place for our honeymoon?" he asked.

She looked away from him, out over the front yard that was dotted with red and gold mums. "It's very nice."

His eyes were drawn to the gravel parking lot where his pride and joy was parked: a 1958 Pontiac Bonneville Sport Coupe. He really should ask the proprietor for a cloth to wipe it off. Odd how it suddenly seemed as if he were looking at it for the first time. He'd had it for three months. A litany of facts ticker-taped across his brain: *The exterior is a two-tone Calypso and Burma green with chrome to the highest standards; power windows, steering, and brakes; a "Wonderbar" a.m. radio; a sliding Plexiglas sun visor; a "Memo-Matic" power memory seat; Rochester "TriPower" triple, two-barrel carbure—*

"Maybe I should leave you and your car alone?"

He realized he'd been staring at it. "Can't a man be proud of his possessions?"

She didn't answer.

"Millie?"

She gripped the railing. "Possessions. Yes, David. You are the proud owner and conqueror of all you survey."

What was that supposed to mean?

This was not the first time she'd made such an odd comment. He passed it off as a stress-induced result of planning a wedding.

And yet. . .he studied her a moment. Her eyes were sad. There was no reason for her to feel that way. He'd planned a marvelous weekend. Everything would be perfect—if she cooperated. He moved to her side, pulling her under his arm. "Aren't you glad you decided to stop being difficult and come?"

"Yes, David."

He picked up the suitcases and headed to the front door. When she didn't follow right away, he had to clear his throat. Why did she make him do that?

An antique check-in desk stood in the middle of the foyer. A silver-haired woman wearing a froufrou apron over an aqua dress came out of the back. "Welcome, welcome!"

David removed his hat and shook her hand. "I'm David Stancowsky. I have a reservation."

She moved behind the desk, readying a check-in book. "Yes, indeed, Mr. Stancowsky. My name is Mrs. Stephens. We have your room ready. If you'll just—"

Millie pulled on the sleeve of his suit. "David? You said we'd have two rooms." She looked at Mrs. Stephens. "We're not married yet. We're just checking out the accommodations to see if we'd like it for our honeymoon."

David couldn't believe she contradicted him. This woman didn't need to know the details of their lives.

Mrs. Stephens put a hand to her mouth. "Oh. I see. Well, yes, we do have two rooms available." She led him through the paperwork and handed him two keys. "Dinner's at six-thirty. Will you be joining us?"

"That would be nice," Millie said.

David palmed the keys. "Actually, no. We can't. We have other plans."

"What other plans?" Millie asked.

He picked up their luggage. "Let's go see the rooms." He accentuated the plural *s* just a bit, hoping she'd notice.

"Mrs. Stephens?" Millie asked. "I'd love to have a tour of the home. It's absolutely lovely. And I adore antiques."

Since when? David wanted to be alone with her, not

eyeballing some out-of-date dresser.

The old woman looked at him, then back at Millie.

"Please?"

"Of course, Miss. . . ?"

"Millie Reynolds. Call me Millie." She turned to David. "Go on up, darling. Get settled in your room. I'll be up shortly." Then she walked into the parlor, exclaiming to Mrs. Stephens about some rocker.

What had gotten into her? As the two ladies moved on with their tour, he had no choice but to take the suitcases upstairs or stand like a lackey in the hall.

He'd deal with her later.

David had already unpacked their suitcases—in their respective rooms. He glanced at his watch. He would wait five more minutes before seeking her out, strongly suggesting that she get upstairs, with him, where she belonged. He was just putting his wallet and keys on the dresser when he heard a tap on the door.

"Come in."

Millie opened it, peering in. "Oh, there you are. I wasn't sure which room you'd be in." She buzzed inside, commenting on the antiques in the room, giving a running commentary of all Mrs. Stephens had told her.

He said nothing but sat in the wing chair before the fireplace, his hands clasped.

She fingered a vase painted with flowers. "Did you know the china Mrs. Stephens uses for the meals was her great-great-grandmother's? It was brought here on an immigrant ship, all the way from England."

She finally glanced at him. Then away. He tightened his jaw even more. "Where are the suitcases?" she asked. "I'll unpack."

"I've already done that."

"Oh." She wiped her palms on her skirt. "So. Is this your room or mine?"

He spoke again but didn't move. "It was supposed to be *our* room."

She sidled past him to the window, pulling aside the lace curtain. "We agreed, David. No hanky-panky before the wedding." She suddenly smiled. "It's starting to rain!"

He got out of the chair to look. "Why do you sound happy about it?"

"Oh. I'm—I'm not." She watched the rain, yet her face *did* look oddly happy. "I bet these roads get really slick in the rain. Dangerous."

"Not if you know what you're doing. And what do you care? I'm the one who drives."

She shrugged. "I told Mrs. Stephens we'd be here for dinner. We might as well take full advantage of the place."

"But I told you—and her—no. I have other plans for us."

She sighed deeply and took in another breath. "Frankly, David. . ." She shook her head. "I'm sick of your plans."

A response stuck in his throat.

She took a few steps away from him, her arms crossed. "In fact, I think this would be a good time to clear up some of the plans *you've* made for our wedding."

"What are you talking about? There's little to discuss. I'm taking care of everything."

"*You're* taking care. Not we. Always you."

"I'm just trying to do things right. I have connections. And your father has given me free reign—"

"My father sees you as the son he never had—and always wanted."

"That's a bad thing?"

"It is if you're the invisible daughter."

A headache loomed. "Your father is laying down big bucks to give us the kind of wedding we want."

"*You* want. You've never asked me."

"Are you picking a fight with me?"

She took a step toward him. "What are you going to do? Hit me?"

What? "Millie. You don't want to do this." He'd never hit her. Ever. He wouldn't hit a woman.

He saw a flicker of doubt on her face before she raised her chin defiantly. "I'm tired of this conspiracy between you and my father, trying to control me."

She'd never objected before. In fact, Millie's agreeable nature was one of the things David loved about her. She was a good woman, and an obedient daughter. She was a woman who knew where she belonged in the scheme of things. She'd make the perfect wife.

She continued her ranting, not needing him to goad her on. "I am sick of you acting as if you know me, taking care of every detail. You're loving me to death. You're smothering me, David. I have opinions. I have dreams. And if we're going to get married—"

The "if" got his attention. "What do you mean, 'if'?"

She crossed to the door. "I'm not sure marriage is a good idea. For me to go directly from my parents' home to yours. . ."

"But where else would you go?"

"I could get my own apartment. Live alone awhile."

"Don't be ridiculous. Besides, your father and I have an agreement."

Her laugh was bitter. "A business agreement. He wants you to take over his construction business as the son he never had. I'm merely part of the benefits package."

"That's not true." *Not completely true.* He moved toward her, his arms outstretched. "I love you, Millie. I adore you."

She spoke under her breath. "You want to possess me."

He stopped short of touching her. "You're exaggerating again."

She glared at him. It was a look he'd never seen before. And it scared him.

How had they gotten to this point? He tried to backtrack. "Millie, dear, let's calm down. Don't ruin the weekend I planned."

"You planned! You planned! Where was I in this planning?"

"Right where you should be. By my side."

She laughed again. "Or two steps behind you." She opened the door. "I have to get some air. Alone."

She slammed the door, leaving David staring at it. How dare she say these things after all he'd done for her? If it wasn't for him planning the wedding—showing some good taste—they'd be having a tacky affair that would not speak well of his business. Her *father's* business. Mariner Construction's image. She was a sweet girl, but it really would behoove her to realize his talent in such things.

He turned around and looked at the chair by the fireplace. He would settle in and wait for her. It wouldn't take her long to realize what a fool she'd been.

He took a step toward the chair when suddenly, the flash of an image invaded his mind and stopped him cold. The image of a car hurling off a cliff. A two-tone Calypso and Burma green car.

Ridiculous.

Or was it?

He whipped around to the dresser. His keys were gone!

He ran downstairs, burst through the front door, and down the porch steps. Millie was in the car, but she'd flooded it. He ran toward her through the rain. She saw him and her face contorted in panic. She fumbled for the lock, but he got to the door and yanked it open.

"Leave me alone, David! Let me go!"

Rain pelted them, as well as the car's interior. He reached across, pushed her hand aside, and took the keys. She stared at her empty hand. Her shoulders dropped. She let out a breath. Good. She'd realized her foolishness.

He pulled her from the car, relieved to be able to close the door against the rain. Logic said they should run, but David sensed Millie had no run left in her. He practically had to carry her up the front walk. "Now, now. I don't know why you got yourself so worked up. Enough of this nonsense. Where were you going to drive anyway? As you said, it's raining. It's dangerous. You have no business being on the road. You could have been killed."

Her voice was a whisper. "I could have hurt your precious car."

As they reached the steps, Millie raised her face to the rain, forcing them to stop. What *was* she doing? "Come on, Millie. Don't be stupid. You'll catch your death."

She looked at him as if he'd said something profound, then lowered her head and let him lead her inside.

"There. All cozy warm." David gave Millie's covers one final tuck. He placed his arms as posts on either side of her and leaned close. "I don't know what's gotten into you. People don't get cold feet seven months before the wedding."

Her eyes sparked. "So there's a rule for that, too?"

He let it go. He didn't want to upset her again. "If you're a good girl and go right to sleep, I won't even tell your father."

She turned on her side, ruining all his hard tucking-in work. "Good night, David. Make sure the door's locked on your way out."

He retrieved an afghan from the foot of the bed and moved to a chair by the window. "I'm not going 'out.' "

She bolted upright. "What?"

He sat, draping the afghan around his legs. "I'll sleep here tonight."

"No! I mean, there's no need."

"I want you to feel safe and secure."

She hesitated, then managed a smile. "I'm. . .I'm fine. You paid for two rooms. It would be a waste of money for you to stay here."

"Don't worry about that."

She looked toward the door, then back at him. "But people will talk."

He conceded the point. "Yes, they might. But you know what they'll say?"

"No."

"They'll say that David Stancowsky is a good fiancé who is willing to sacrifice his own comfort to be near his dear Millie. To make sure she feels loved."

She stared at the space between them a few moments, then fell back into the covers, pulling them to her chin.

He stood. “Would you like me to tuck you in again?”

She shook her head.

He sat back in the chair. Her wish was his command.

No temptation has seized you
except what is common to man.
1 CORINTHIANS 10:13

Present-Day Montebello

Toby Bjornson's hand shook as he dialed the number. He hadn't slept well for two nights. The first night was spent making a decision. The next morning he'd called in sick and spent most of that day as well as the night hustling up enough nerve to go through with it.

He couldn't wait any longer. Laney was only going to be gone a week on that Time Lottery thing. He had a lot to do before she came back.

A woman answered, "WKRB, your leading news station. How may I help you?"

"I. . ." He cleared his throat. "I need to speak to Diane Madison."

"Pertaining to what, please?"

"Laney. . .Lane Holloway. I have information."

Her voice changed, sounding wary. "Ms. Madison is in a meeting. May I take a message?"

"I need to talk to her. Now. She'll want to talk to me."

"And why is that?"

He took a fresh breath. "Because I'm Toby. Lane Holloway's Toby."

A pause. Then, "Hold, please."

Toby laughed. This was going to be great.

Atlanta

Reporters and more reporters, all wanting to talk to *him,* Yardley Pruitt. It was very flattering, even if they only wanted to talk to him because his daughter was a Time Lottery winner. Why not take advantage of it? There should be some perk for being her father. He hadn't talked to any of them yet but had spent last evening working up a statement, a press release that detailed their strong father-daughter relationship and explained how he, as a single father, had been the driving force in Vanessa's life. He'd even managed to insert a mention of his business, Fidelity Mutual Bank.

Ready to leave for work, he pulled the living-room curtain to the side and scoped out the front of the house. There were four reporters gathered near the row of oak trees that lined the street, or rather, three reporters and a TV cameraman. Yardley could easily go into the garage, get in his car, and back out without speaking to them. Or. . .he could exit through the front door and walk *around* to the garage. *"Mr. Pruitt! Mr. Pruitt! Can we ask you a few questions?"*

Then, as the essence of graciousness, he would slip in his statement as if he was always this eloquent first thing in the morning. Perfect. He hadn't gotten where he was without learning how to commandeer a moment. He was a master commander.

He straightened his tie, took up his briefcase and keys, and exited the house through the front. Once outside, he turned his back to the street in order to lock the dead bolt, giving the reporters time to reach him. Photos against the majesty of his home would be ideal.

The reporters did not disappoint but ran close, shouting their questions. "Mr. Pruitt! Mr. Pruitt! Can we ask you a few questions?" Had he pegged it, or what?

He turned around and feigned a surprised look, then let it change to one of dignified cooperation. "Of course. I suppose I can spare a few minutes."

A pretty blond spoke into a microphone. "Your daughter went back to 1976 in order to spend time with your ex-wife, Dorian Pruitt Cleese. She must have been quite an amazing woman for Vanessa to use her one chance at the Time Lottery to visit her. Can you tell us about her and why your daughter did not have contact with her all these years?"

Yardley found himself tongue-tied. They wanted to talk about Dorian?

When he didn't answer, another reporter asked, "Records indicate that your ex-wife recently passed away. And she'd remarried years ago—though her second husband is no longer living. Did you go to the funeral?"

"No comment." He turned his back on them, fumbled the key in the lock, and escaped inside the house.

This was not what he had in mind. Not at all.

It was all Vanessa's fault.

Kansas City

Mac watched Toby Bjornson on the small TV in his office. This was not good. Not good at all. It was a blessing when they went to commercial.

A moment later, Wriggens stormed in. He pointed at the TV. "You saw?"

"I saw."

"What hole did he crawl out of?"

"When Lane said his name at the press conference, I knew this was a possibility."

"Which is another point I'd like to talk to you about. I really would have liked to be consulted about her telling the press one decision while telling us something different."

"It was a last-minute request. I didn't have time to consult you."

"You didn't make time."

And your point is. . . ? Mac returned the subject to the issue at hand. He turned his back on the TV, facing Wriggens head-on. "Toby's coming forward could be a plus if—"

Wriggens's laugh was not kind. "He's a loser. He's a construction peon. Probably makes five bucks an hour, and face it, clean shirt or no clean shirt, he's a prime candidate for a makeover on one of those TV shows. Dirt-bucket was the description that came to mind."

It was apt.

Wriggens began to pace in front of Mac's desk. "The man's an opportunist, plain and simple, grabbing his fifteen minutes of fame at the expense of our good image."

"We had those types last year," Mac said. "Phoebe's husband, Cheryl's mother. . ."

Wriggens handily ignored him. "This moron is trouble. Professing his undying love for his 'Laney,' offering all sorts of juicy details about their life back in Minnesota? I expect her lawyers to call any minute."

"You're overreacting."

"Yeah? He says they were engaged."

Mac shook his head. "I don't believe that's true. I think Lane would have mentioned that. He's got to be lying."

"Big surprise. But the trouble is, with Lane gone, he has free reign with her life. He can do and say what he wants."

"Oh dear."

"I had a more explosive way of expressing my concern, but yes, 'oh dear.' He could cause major damage in a week."

Mac rocked in his chair, trying to think. "Yet maybe. . . since it's so obvious he's a cretin. . .no one will believe anything he says. They'll see him for what he is."

"And love him for it. Mac, face it. The American dream has evolved into every person having a right to bring others down to their level. He's a working man, an everyday Joe—below an everyday Joe, if you ask me—but I'm not sure the public will make the distinction. He's a man who once was in love with a megastar. She rose to high heights and he was left behind. Woe is he."

That *was* how Toby was playing it: Lane left him behind; he got the shaft.

"And it was all Hollywood's fault." Wriggens raised a finger. "Never take the blame for anything, Mac. It's always someone else's fault. Personal accountability has become a four-letter word."

"Playing the blame game *has* become a national pastime."

"On that we do agree. And I especially like the part where

he said he will be making himself available to Lane if she comes back. She went into the past to rekindle their love, and if she comes back, he's ready, willing, and able to throw himself at her feet. Or in her bed."

"But she didn't go back to be with him. She went back to skip the audition."

"The press doesn't know that. Toby doesn't know that."

Mac didn't know what to say.

Wriggens stopped pacing. "Fix it, Mac. ASAP."

"How? The damage is done."

"Find Toby. Get him to lay low and shut up."

"I repeat, how?"

Wriggens turned toward the door. "Make him an offer he can't refuse."

Where was Don Corleone when he needed him?

Malibu

"What the—?"

Brandy couldn't believe the throng of reporters that was camped in Lane's driveway.

Her husband hesitated at the street. "You want me to pull in?"

She wasn't sure. "Why are they here? Lane's gone for a week. Why are they staking out her house?"

"You're asking me to explain the workings of the media mind?" He pointed. "They've seen us. Do we take the defensive or offensive?"

"What do you think?"

"Well. . .I've always wanted to be offensive."

"Oh you. Go for it."

He revved the engine, making her feel as if their car were a bull getting ready to charge. "Here we go!" He pulled into the driveway and the reporters scattered, making room while craning to see who they were.

Randy turned off the car. "Let me get out first and come around to get you."

"Gladly."

As soon as he exited, they pummeled him with questions. He said nothing but helped her out, placing her under his protective wing.

"What are you doing here?"

"What relation are you to Lane?"

"Who are you?"

That last question was repeated at least a dozen times. As soon as Randy had the front door unlocked, as soon as Brandy's means of escape was secure, she turned to the reporters. "Who am I? I'm your worst nightmare if you do anything to harm the property or the reputation of Lane Holloway."

She closed the door on them, her heart pumping.

Randy clapped. "You didn't need me."

"I always need you. And never forget it."

Randy looked around and she realized it had been awhile since he'd been here. "Which bedroom are we painting?" he asked.

"Hers." Brandy led the way to the back of the house. "She's had the paint and supplies for months, but getting a contractor in here who isn't overly gaga, or one who doesn't capitalize on the fact they worked on Lane Holloway's home, is impossible."

"Who's saying I won't capitalize on it? Maybe I want to grab the spotlight like that Toby guy."

"I never did like Toby. Not really. He may have been slightly cute in 1987, but he was also an annoying little ferret." In Lane's bedroom, Brandy moved to open the blinds on the french doors leading to the balcony but, remembering the press, thought better of it. She flipped on all the lamps.

"Not much light to work," Randy said.

"But enough?"

He shrugged. "Where's the paint?"

She'd get to that. First, Brandy wrapped her arms around his neck. "Giving up your day for me. . .have I told you how much I adore you?"

"Not today." He accepted her kiss and gave her a few extra in return.

Reluctantly, she let go and surveyed the room. "Lane will be so surprised."

"Only if she comes back. She might not, you know."

Brandy nodded and got the two cans of Sunshine Yellow paint from the closet. She couldn't think about that. She couldn't.

Bangor

Dina Edmonds hated having a clean desk—yet strove for it. As Mr. Stancowsky's personal secretary for forty-six years, she prided herself on being the essence of organization. Hence, a clean desk was proof of her abilities. Yet now, with David gone, a clean desk was a gaping testament to the fact that she had little to do. Without his presence, her life was empty. Boring.

But he'll be back. He'll come back to me.

She shook her head adamantly and whispered under her

breath. "Stop it, Dina. He will not be back. He's with Millie. She wins."

Again. Millie would win again.

Though Dina had loved David from the first moment she'd met him in 1958, he'd never returned the emotion. Not that she hadn't tried to change his mind. She still felt shame at her reaction to Millie's death. At the time, she'd thought of it as an opening. Surely it was fortune smiling down upon her. After all, the poor widower would need comfort as he found a way to go on with his life.

The trouble was, David never "went on." Not emotionally, anyway. Career-wise, he lucked out when Millie's father allowed him to continue his transition to become head of Mariner Construction. Ray Reynolds had accepted David as the beloved son-in-law he would never have. Yet, set for life in his career, David had poured his attention in that direction and had politely refused Dina's overtures toward sharing a more personal part of their lives. He'd been polite enough but was unyielding, until she'd finally realized (it had been a Tuesday, May 12, 1964) that she had a choice: She could be in David's life as his secretary or not at all. It hadn't been that hard of a decision. She knew she wasn't a pretty woman, and her talent with men was limited to her ability to organize and be efficient. Since there never had been a string of suitors in her life, since she'd come to grips early on with the possibility that marriage might not be a reality—ever, with anyone—Dina made the choice to be David's right-hand man. Woman.

Now, at age seventy-four, her life *had* contained moments of satisfaction. She'd taken quite a few business trips with David. All on the up-and-up, of course. She never would forget the time they'd celebrated a huge contract in New Orleans by going to dinner at a top-floor restaurant that revolved and offered an amazing view of the city. It could have been a romantic evening. . . .

Day to day, she took her pleasure in small things. In David's "Well done, Dina" and the vase of flowers he always had delivered on her birthday. And she liked nothing better than to stand beside him as he gave her instructions, drinking in the marvelous, woodsy smell of his aftershave.

Monetarily, her compensation was more than fair. In fact, she knew she was overpaid for her position, but also knew he could afford it. And wasn't loyalty worth something? Forty-six years at one job was nothing to sneeze at. In truth, she had more money than she needed and had used a chunk of it to purchase a lovely home that offered a magnificent view of the Maine woods. It wasn't showy, but it was hers.

David had never seen it.

She rearranged her stapler a half inch to the left, making it parallel with her in-box. She could have retired years ago, but as long as David kept working. . . Actually, it was imperative they both continue to work. How else would she get to see him?

She had saved enough to go on a world cruise, but what fun was such a trip alone? Her most avid hope was that one of these days she'd have the nerve to ask him to join her. Platonically. As a dear, lifelong friend. She'd been on the verge of asking right before Christmas but had chickened out.

And now it was too late. He was gone. And he wasn't coming back. Why should he? Millie was in the past. Only old age was here in the future.

She jumped when the phone rang. "Mariner Construction, David Stancowsky's office."

"This is Bonnie Brown from *USA Today*. We were wanting

some more information about this woman Mr. Stancowsky is visiting in the past. We've found clippings about her tragic death, but we were wondering if there was anyone there who knew her who could tell us about their relationship?"

For once in her life she abandoned rationale. She found herself saying, "I can talk to you."

"And you are. . . ?"

I'm the woman David should have loved. "I'm Mr. Stancowsky's secretary. I've worked for him the last forty-six years."

"Really? Tell me more."

"You said Millie was unappreciative in regard to the wedding?" Bonnie Brown asked. "Can you give me an example?"

If Dina had been in a court of law, an attorney would have jumped out of his chair and yelled, "Objection! Hearsay!" regarding what she was about to say. Yet, since there was no one to object, no one at all. . . "I witnessed Mr. Stancowsky's detailed preparations for their wedding." She remembered seeing the sketches and swatches for the dress after the fact. "He was involved in every detail. He cared immensely. They were just beginning to plan things when she died, but from his level of discouragement, I got the impression she wasn't cooperating."

"In what way?"

Speculation, Dina. This is all speculation. "She didn't appreciate his amazing attention and eye for detail, his interest. Most grooms want minimal involvement in wedding plans—especially back in 1958. But not Mr. Stancowsky. He did everything for his Millie. I know her stubborn disinterest and willfulness hurt him."

"She sounds a bit immature. Was she younger than he was?"

"Six years younger." A thought came to her. "In fact, I think her immaturity had a lot to do with her death."

"Oh?"

It was as if someone else were in control of her mouth. Dina knew she should stop saying such negative things but couldn't stop herself. The dam of silence had been breached, and decades of bitterness streamed out unstoppable.

"Mr. Stancowsky took Millie for a weekend trip to a bed-and-breakfast. All very proper, I assure you. He just wanted to show her this particular place because he planned to go there for their honeymoon. It was a lovely place. I saw a brochure."

"This was close to the location where she crashed?"

Dina nodded, though Bonnie couldn't see her. "Yes. Mr. Stancowsky told me later that they'd gotten into an argument and Millie had driven off—in his prized Pontiac Bonneville. A beautiful car. Sage green. She drove off in the rain, showing no concern for him or the weather. She had a tantrum and died for it."

"That's a strong statement."

Dina clamped a hand over her mouth. *Too strong!* This was not what she wanted people to focus on. If David were here, he would be appalled at her words. In his absence, she was his advocate. She needed to let the world know what a wonderful man he was. She had to turn the attention away from Millie and onto David's good works. "If you don't mind, Ms. Brown, I know Mr. Stancowsky would rather you focus on his public life. Did you know he has received twenty-four awards for his business acumen? Mariner Construction, which started as a small Bangor company, has now completed projects in forty states and two countries. It is a multibillion-dollar business."

"Billion you say?"

Money always was an attention-getter.

Montebello

Toby skipped work. Again. After his interview on the morning show, he'd hurried home to wait for other calls. From other reporters on other TV stations. He wasn't dumb. He knew how this worked. If the weekly loser on one of those reality shows could get a gig on national talk shows, so could he. After all, he wasn't a loser. He was the true love of a Time Lottery winner and a movie star. Double bonus points.

By the time he got home, he had three calls on his answering machine, the most exciting from a network morning show in New York City. They wanted him. Tomorrow. They were sending a car for him in an hour. A plane ticket would be on the computers at the airport. Then a limo ride and a couple of nights at a ritzy hotel. Meals included, of course.

Finally, he was going to get a feel for what Lane enjoyed every day of her life. It was his turn now, and he wasn't going to waste a moment of it.

He shoved a pair of khakis into his duffle bag. The phone rang and he cleared his throat, preparing for another interview request. Maybe he should charge a fee. . . .

"Mr. Bjornson?"

"Yes?"

"This is Alexander MacMillan from the TTC."

"The what?"

"The Time Travel Corporation. The Time Lottery people."

Uh-oh. This couldn't be good. "I can't talk now. I'm just

heading out the door."

"We really need to talk, Mr. Bjornson."

"I told you, I don't have time." He thought about bragging and decided, *why not?* "I have to get to the airport. I'm going to be on TV tomorrow. Network, national TV."

"I. . .I don't think that's wise, Mr. Bjornson."

"Hey, people think I'm interesting. And they have a right to know me. I'm the man Laney went back to see. I'm important in her life. Giving me up was her biggest regret."

"But you weren't engaged, were you?"

How did he know that? "We were engaged to be engaged. If Laney hadn't gone to that stupid audition, we would have been."

"You shouldn't say you were engaged."

"I can say anything I want to."

"You shouldn't lie, Mr. Bjornson. It will whip around to bite you. Lies always do."

"I don't need a morality lesson from you, Mr. Whatever-your-name-is. Now, if you'll excuse me, I have a plane to catch."

Toby hung up hard. Nobody was going to stop him. Nobody.

Kansas City

Mac sat with his hand on the receiver. Toby was on a roll, and there was nothing anyone could do to stop him without bringing the guy even more attention. He just hoped Toby's fifteen minutes would fade before Lane's week was up.

He turned toward his credenza and flipped the TV back on. *Please, Lord. No more bad press.* When he saw a teaser that showed a picture of Vanessa's father, his stomach dropped. He caught only the tail end of the promo and heard ". . .what is Vanessa Caldwell's father covering up? Exclusive footage, right after the break."

Mac had met the man only once in the Time Lottery waiting room, but in that short time Yardley Pruitt had revealed himself to have an ego. He was a man used to getting his own way. But what did the reporter mean about "covering up"?

Mac wanted to go home. He ran his hands over his face, waiting for the commercials to be over. He tried not to think of possible scenarios with Mr. Pruitt. Why borrow trouble?

Speaking of. . .

Wriggens came in. "You're watching?"

"I'm watching."

Wriggens sat in a guest chair, moving it for the best view of the television. "What do you think he's covering up?"

"I prefer not to speculate."

"Mmm. Did you take care of the Toby situation?"

Might as well come out with it. "He won't talk to us. He's having the time of his life. He's going to be on a national morning show tomorrow."

"Why didn't you stop him?"

"And how should I have done that?"

"Offer him money. Anything."

Mac knew the limits of the Time Lottery budget. A couple hundred bucks wouldn't stop Toby Bjornson. "It's not about money. It's about fame. Getting attention. Nothing can stop him until Lane comes back."

"Great. Until then, who knows what libelous thing he might say? Her lawyers will be at our throats."

"Hopefully not our throats. His. We're not saying anything."

"But Toby's been let loose because of us. Lawsuits always

trickle down. We'll get sued." Wriggens hesitated. "Unless. . ."

"Unless what?"

He shook his head, then pointed at the TV. "It's on."

They watched the Yardley Pruitt interview—which was not much of an interview at all. The man only said two words: "No comment." But that didn't stop the anchor. "Since that interview with Mr. Pruitt, we have done some research into the life of the late Dorian Pruitt Cleese and have found that she was an exemplary teacher, winning many awards and the accolades of her peers. Here is Sue Benning, the principal of Ms. Cleese's school."

The report went on to interview the principal and two other teachers. Now Mac knew why Vanessa wanted to go back and explore life with her mother. She was a fascinating woman. He wondered what had happened that had kept them apart for over thirty years.

He bet Yardley Pruitt had something to do with it.

Cheryl tossed the lettuce salad. "I still don't understand why you're so upset about Toby. He's really kind of pitiful. And people aren't dumb. They'll see he's no love match for Lane." She sprinkled the lettuce with Romano. "Actually, I can't understand why she ever was interested in him—especially enough to go back to rekindle some teenage passion." She forced a shiver. "Yuck. I think you and Wriggens are overreacting. Take a breath, Mac. Let it die on its own."

Mac checked on the meat loaf. If only he could tell her what Lane was really doing in the past.

He felt her eyes on his back and turned toward her. "What?"

"There's something you're not telling me, isn't there?"

"No." He turned back to the oven.

She slid between him and the appliance. "Uh-uh. Does not compute. Lucky for me you are a horrible liar. Fess up."

He couldn't meet her eyes. "I can't."

She traced his jawline and smiled her amazing smile. "Of course you can."

"I can't. I promised."

She abandoned the seductive approach and thrust her hands onto her hips. "Promised who?"

He risked a glance. "Lane."

Her eyebrows rose. "Oh, so it's Lane now, is it? You two are on a first-name basis?"

"Cheryl. . ."

"We made a deal, Mac. No secrets. I'm too old to deal with secrets in a relationship; besides, it's against my nature. My life's an open book to you. And yours supposedly is to me."

"And it is." He'd told her more about his life with Holly than he'd ever told anyone. "But this is business."

She removed her apron and drilled it into the counter. "You know what? I'm sick of secrets. You insist on keeping our relationship a secret and now you're keeping a secret from me. It's a pattern I can't condone. It makes me weary and drives me crazy. I'm going home." She strode to the entry, where her coat hung over the banister.

Mac hurried after her. "I would tell you if I could, but it's imperative nobody knows—until Lane chooses to tell."

"She's not here!"

"Exactly. So I can't speak of it without her permission."

She shoved her arms in the coat and refused his attempts to help. "You don't trust me."

"I. . ." Actually, Cheryl did have a penchant for speaking first and thinking later.

"Fine. On this note of distrust, I hereby declare this evening over." She yanked open the door.

"But—" Mac stopped when a group of reporters ran toward the door.

"Shut it!" he yelled.

She started to, but with a cock of her head, opened it wide and stepped out onto the stoop.

"Dr. Nickolby. . ." said one of the reporters. "What are you doing here?"

"Ask him." She nodded toward Mac. "Ask my boyfriend." She went to her car.

Let the wise listen and add to their learning,
and let the discerning get guidance.
PROVERBS 1:5

Athens—1976

He's doing it on purpose!

Vanessa tried not to stare at Bruce as he blatantly flirted with Amanda Jones in their Accounting Principles class. Tried not to even look at him. But it was impossible with him sitting one row over and two seats up. The seats weren't assigned, so she knew he'd placed himself directly in her sight line to bug her and flaunt his status as a free man in spite of her pregnancy. In spite of all they'd shared.

And exactly what did *we share?*

She pretended to study her textbook and hoped the teacher would make his entrance soon. If she heard Amanda giggle one more time. . .

The thought returned: *What* did *you and Bruce share—besides sex?* They'd spent two months together. They'd met at a kegger right after they'd returned from Christmas break. He'd been drunk. She'd been drunk. And they'd ended up curled together on the stairs, lips locked, bodies wanting more. They hadn't had sex that night. But when he'd called the next day, she'd gone out with him, knowing where it was heading. Two people didn't backtrack easily from a lip-lock like the one they'd shared—though they had managed to hold off until the third date.

It wasn't that Vanessa was promiscuous. She wasn't. Not really. But as her college years progressed, and as she saw more and more of her girlfriends succumbing to the pleasures—or pressures—of sex, she'd decided to take the plunge herself. There had been only two before Bruce. And they hadn't lasted long. Thank goodness.

She'd thought Bruce was different. Two months was respectable (a new world record). They'd even talked about a life together after graduation. Vanessa had mentioned marriage but Bruce had leaned toward living together. She'd been skeptical of what Daddy would have said to that one, but figured since she was twenty-one he couldn't do much. *Except make my life miserable. Except cut off my allowance.*

She shut her textbook with a slap, causing Bruce to look back at her. Money and guilt. It always came down to those two factors with Daddy. He held her captive with her need for money and his need for her. What was that line from a song in *Cabaret*? "Money makes the world go around. . . ."

She found herself doodling. The word *Mother* curved around a heart. A heart? Symbolizing love? And her mother? She scratched out the picture. Yes, her mother had suddenly reappeared in her life. Yes, she seemed to genuinely care for her. But love?

What was love? Did her father love her?

She looked at Bruce. He winked at her and she looked away. Bruce certainly didn't love her.

No one did.

The teacher came in. Time to think about facts and figures. That was fine with her. Those things were tangible. Measurable. They offered a right or wrong answer.

Unlike love.

⊶

Vanessa heard the phone ringing from the hall. She ran into her dorm room and caught it. "Hello?"

"You're out of breath. Are you all right?" It was her mother.

She sat on the bed. "I was fine until I sprinted for the phone."

"Sorry. Next time I'll wait until you're home."

If nothing else, her mother could make her smile.

"Actually, you wouldn't want to miss this call because I'm issuing an invitation. To my house. Tonight."

But it's Friday. I have to go home. Daddy's expecting me.

"Don't answer until I give you the whole scoop. I have good reasons that could trail up a chalkboard and down a wall. Just listen. Promise?"

Vanessa fell back onto her pillow. "I'm listening."

"Number one, you and I have five years of bonding to make up for. Number two, I would like you to see my pad."

"Your *pad*?"

"Hey, if *The Dating Game* can talk about bachelor and bachelorette pads, so can I. I'm single, you know."

I know.

"On to reason number three. I make great fondue. Just got a new pot with all those little forkie-dealies."

"Forkie-dealies?" Her mother's vocabulary was making her a parrot.

"Reason number four is that I'm also inviting two lovely

friends. I'd really like you to meet some of the people who populate my life."

Whoopee. Gangs of fun. "Anything else?"

"Actually, yes. We need a fourth for Pitch."

"Aha. The real reason comes out."

"I left it for last."

Vanessa laughed. It was a foreign experience. That fact made her say, "Yes. I'll be there."

She'd go see Daddy tomorrow.

Dawson—1987

Lane didn't want to go home for dinner. She didn't want to face her parents, and especially not Grandma Nellie's disappointment. She'd snuck out of the house before. If only she could sneak in.

Toby pulled up front. "You want me to go in with you?"

"Instead of me would be good," she said.

"You shouldn't be afraid of your grandma. She's just a bitty thing."

Lane snickered. "Bitty with a bark. You've heard her."

He nodded. Anyone who spent much time at the Holloway house had heard Grandma go off on one thing or another. Not that she wasn't usually right, but she did have a way of stopping the world and making it listen.

The front door opened and Grandma came outside. She stood on the stoop, her arms crossed.

"Uh-oh," Toby said.

Lane took a deep breath and got out.

"I'll wait."

"You'd better not." She shut the door and headed up the walk. Toby drove away.

"He'd *better* drive away," Grandma said. "How dare he talk you out of fulfilling your God-given destiny."

Lane tried to brush past her, but Grandma barred the door—all four-foot-ten of her. "I made the decision, Grandma. Not Toby."

She pointed in the direction Toby had driven. "When are you going to see he's not the man—and I use the term loosely—for you?"

Lane scuffed her toe on the stoop. "I love him. My future's here. With him. This is my home."

Grandma stepped aside. "Then go on in, Miss Dawson, USA. Go eat your lefse, lutefisk, and spritz cookies; marry your childhood sweetheart; and play the lead in the high-school plays with their cardboard sets and hand-me-down costumes. But don't come crying to me when that dream of yours takes over your gut and makes you ache with maybes. You make many decisions like you did today and you'll wind up without any maybes. Just could-a-beens."

Grandma went in first, leaving Lane on the edge of the threshold. On this side sat the world, weaving its cords around her, teasing her, ready to pull her away into the unknown. The exciting unknown? On the other side was home and everything she knew. Inviting. Welcoming. Sure. Constant.

Her mother appeared. "There you are. Come in. Dinner's ready."

Lane stepped inside.

"Mother Nellie, if you bang your glass any harder on the table, it's going to break into a hundred pieces."

Grandma Nellie glared at her daughter-in-law. "Then we'll just have to buy another jar of jelly, won't we?"

Lane's dad slapped a hand on the tablecloth. "Mother, that's enough. We know you're mad at Lane, but that's no reason to insult Joyce."

Grandma pointed her fork at him. "It's partly your fault she didn't go to the audition."

"My fault?"

"Grandma, don't. . ." Lane hated when they fought.

As usual, Grandma ignored her. "You and Joyce are so intent on sticking around Dawson—no matter what—that you can't see that others need to get out. Escape."

Lane's mom laughed nervously. "You make Dawson sound like a prison."

"A prison of dreams. That's what it is."

"You're exaggerating, Mother. Dawson is a wonderful place to live. Sure, it's going through tough times now because of farm prices, but we'll get through this depression like we got through the last one. And you should talk. You've lived here your entire life."

Grandma sat back in her chair. "The prison bars are high."

Lane's dad threw his napkin down. The corner of it dipped into his gravy. "Are you saying you have regrets about living here?"

Grandma looked across the table at Lane. "Plenty."

Lane was shocked. She'd always thought Grandma was so hip on her "No regrets" line because she had none. To find out the opposite. . .

Her mother pointed at the soiled napkin. "John, your napkin."

He picked it up and wadded the soiled spot to the inside.

"Life has enough hurts without searching them out. Talent or no talent, I"—he looked at his wife— "*we* think Lane made a good decision by not going to the audition. It was a huge gamble. One she couldn't win."

Couldn't? Lane's heart dropped. Wouldn't maybe, but couldn't?

Grandma came to her defense. "Don't you dare tell this darlin' child 'couldn't.' I will not have you stifling Lane's prospects like you've done your own."

He pushed his chair back. "You don't approve of what I've done with our life here?"

Grandma crossed her arms and huffed.

Lane's father's face reddened. "You think I wanted to sell the family farm? You think I wanted to move to town? I had no choice. . . ."

When the shouting continued, Lane ran from the table and up the stairs, slamming her bedroom door behind her.

At the tap on the door, Lane pulled her face out of her pillow. "Go away."

"It's me. Brandy."

Lane let her best friend in, then locked the door behind her and sat on the bed, pulling a teddy bear into her lap. Brandy took up residence at the foot. "Toby told me you didn't go to the audition."

"Did he call you?"

She shook her head. "He came to Burgers-to-Go."

"Great. Then I suppose everybody knows."

"Pretty much. But why didn't you tell me you'd changed your mind?"

"I didn't plan on not going, it just happened. Grandma was there waiting to drive me, but then Toby was there and. . .I chose Toby."

She shook her head. "You're crazy. You shouldn't give up your dream for anyone, especially a guy."

"But. . .you wouldn't understand."

"Thanks a lot."

Oops. "I'm sorry, I didn't mean—"

"No, you're right. I've never had a boyfriend, so how could I possibly understand sacrificing my entire life for one? Wasting my talent to make some boy happy?"

"We love each other."

"Hmm."

"We do."

"As you said, I wouldn't understand."

"Brandy, don't."

Her friend grabbed a *Seventeen* magazine and flipped through it. "What you don't seem to get is that no one wants you to be a movie star, much less believes you can do it. No one except me and your grandma."

She suddenly felt sick to her stomach. "I should have gone."

"If it makes you feel better, you could zero in on the fact that it was a huge long shot."

"Double huge." Lane tossed the bear aside and went to the window. Some kids were riding their Big Wheels on the sidewalk.

"You *have* been schizo about it, wanting to go one minute, being scared the next. Maybe that proves you're not ready to make it in Hollywood."

"Stars get nervous, too."

Brandy wrapped a strand of black hair around a finger. "I can't imagine Sigourney Weaver or Sissy Spacek being nervous. Ever." She grinned. "If Sigourney was scared, she wouldn't be able to blast all the aliens."

Lane's drama teacher had told her nerves were a part of acting. No one became someone else without being nervous. And if you learned how to use it right, it could actually help a performance.

Brandy came to the window and put her hand on Lane's shoulder. "Don't sweat it. *That* audition's over. Move on. Meanwhile, want to go to a movie in Canby? I hear they're showing *The Living Daylights*. Timothy Dalton is the new Bond."

Sure. What else did she have to do?

Later that night, after watching James Bond save the world from the KGB, Lane finished her algebra homework. Or tried to finish it. Her mind was busy with what-ifs, and the audition flyer kept making its way to the top of her papers.

This would have been the night *after* her audition. Would she have been home, giddy because she'd done well, or curled in a ball in bed because she'd blown it? Either way, she wouldn't be doing algebra.

She shoved her binder off her desk. Who needed algebra anyway?

You might. If you don't become an actress.

She laughed. If she didn't become an actress, if she stuck around Dawson, there was still a chance she'd never need algebra. Especially if she kept her job at the dime store.

The thought of being forty and cutting fabric swatches for old ladies wanting to match some ancient sweater to a piece of gabardine, or stocking shelves with fuchsia silk flowers and Cover Girl lipstick made her cringe.

I want a family. I'll be a mom. My parents expect it. Everyone expects it.

She flipped off the reading light and gathered the papers that had come out of her fallen notebook. A green piece caught her eye, and before she even turned it over she remembered what it was. *Romeo and Juliet* auditions. Wednesday, March fourth.

Her heart flipped. March fourth was tomorrow. Up until a week ago she'd planned to try out, but when Grandma had convinced her to go to the Hollywood audition she'd set the notion aside.

She smoothed the paper on her desk. If she couldn't be a little fish in a big pond, she'd be a big fish in Dawson.

Bar Harbor—1958

David dabbed his mouth with a napkin. "You're a lucky man, Mr. Stephens."

The elderly gentleman sipped his coffee. "And why do you say that, Mr. Stancowsky?"

"Your wife has outdone herself." He turned to Mrs. Stephens. "I believe this was the best breakfast casserole I've ever had. You'll have to give Millie the recipe." He nodded at Millie, who'd been rudely quiet. "You'd like that, wouldn't you, Millie?"

She nodded.

She still wasn't acting normal. She'd tossed and turned all night—not that he'd slept well in the chair. And she'd barely said three words during breakfast.

Oh well, once they were on the road heading home, she'd snap out of it. And he had a wonderful surprise planned for the afternoon. The seamstress David had hired was expecting them to come to her home to see the designs and fabric selection for the wedding dress. David had spent a lot of time coordinating with the woman, making sure the dress would be perfect. Millie would be so surprised.

Mrs. Stephens stood to clear. "You let me know if there's anything else I can do for you before you check out," she said.

"Thank you. We will."

David rose and pulled out Millie's chair. "Let's get our things together and we'll be on our way."

Mrs. Stephens paused at the door to the kitchen. "Oh. I nearly forgot. There was a message left for Miss Reynolds last night. You were already in. . .indisposed, so I didn't want to disturb you."

Millie's eyes lit up. "Where is it?"

Mrs. Stephens set the dirty dishes back on the table. "I'll get it for you."

"I'll come with you."

David started to follow the women when Mr. Stephens said, "I sure have enjoyed talking with you, Mr. Stancowsky. To think that we both fought for our country. Me in Germany and you in Korea."

Yes, yes, they'd been through this. "I really need to go with Millie—"

The old man patted the table near David's chair. "My wife will take care of her. My, my, you are an attentive one, aren't you? I promise she'll be all right out of your sight for five minutes. Now sit."

Though David didn't like the man's insinuating tone, he had no choice but to comply. If only Mr. Stephens's voice weren't so horribly loud, he might be able to hear what the women were saying in the check-in area. As it was, he could see only a smidgen of Millie's back as she stood at the counter.

"What was your unit again?"

In the silence of the pause, David heard Mrs. Stephens say, "A handsome man with curly red hair. Midtwenties."

"Oh," Millie said. "Thank—"

"Your unit, Mr. Stancowsky?"

David heard the sound of paper being torn. He popped up from his chair, nearly toppling it. "We really have to be going." He hurried to the entry in time to see Millie press some torn paper into Mrs. Stephens's palm.

"Millie!"

She swung around, then headed up the stairs. "Let's get our things together, David."

David watched as Mrs. Stephens retreated to the kitchen. He wanted to run after her, grab the note, and read it. But Millie backtracked down the stairs and slipped her arm through his. She gave him her first smile of the morning. "David darling? Come on. Don't we need to go? You said you had a surprise for me."

They headed upstairs. "What was the note?"

"Oh, nothing," she said. "I lost an earring at that cute gift shop yesterday and the proprietor dropped it by with a note. See?" She opened the palm of her hand, revealing a gold earring. The other one was on her ear. He hadn't noticed she was wearing only one earring at breakfast. And why would she wear only one earring to breakfast?

"You asked Mrs. Stephens what he looked like."

They reached the hallway upstairs. "I hadn't paid any attention to the names of the stores. I wanted to know—"

"Handsome with red curly hair, midtwenties. I don't remember any clerk looking like that."

He felt the slightest hesitation in her walk. They'd reached her room. "Neither do I. Maybe it was the owner's son." She kissed his cheek. "Let's get going."

Something wasn't right.

Seamstress and wedding-dress designer Lydia Peters had asked to meet with David and Millie at her lake house on Lake Wassookeag, forty minutes west of Bangor. The fall leaves were past their prime and the rain had forced many of them off their branches. The cabin was painted gray, and window boxes accented the exterior. The lake sparkled thirty feet out the back.

"This is charming, David," Millie said. "But why are we here?"

"My surprise, dear one." He opened her car door and took her hand, helping her out.

Mrs. Peters met them at the door. "Come in, come in. Thank you for coming out here. We're just closing things up for the winter."

Inside, the house was paneled in wood. A fire in a potbelly stove created the much-needed heat. "Oh, this is lovely," Millie said, as Lydia moved them into the main room. "If this were my place I doubt I would ever leave."

"We have no choice," Lydia said. "It was only built as a summer camp. The pipes will freeze."

Millie smiled and did a three-sixty, stopping with her eyes on David. "So. . . ?"

David nodded to Lydia. "Go get it." To Millie he said, "Sit. Sit here."

Lydia went into a bedroom and returned with a big artist's sketch pad and fabric draped over her arm. She stood before Millie and flipped the cover of the pad, revealing a rendering of the dress. "It's a replica of Jackie Kennedy's dress. You know the dress she wore when she and Senator Kennedy married five years ago? Notice the portrait neckline and the bouffant skirt that's decorated with the interwoven bands of tucking. We could do wax flowers like she did, but that would add considerably to the cost." She looked at David.

He loved being able to wave a hand, giving his consent. "Do it. My Millie deserves to have a dress every bit as nice as a socialite senator's wife."

Millie's eyebrows dipped. "This is your surprise?"

David leaned over and kissed the top of her head. "It's all yours, dear one. I've spared no expense."

Lydia set the drawing down and draped the silky fabric across Millie's lap. "Feel the lusciousness of the silk organza."

Millie pushed it away and stood. "I don't want it! I don't even like it!"

Lydia stepped back. David stepped between them. "Millie. Don't be silly. This is Jackie Kennedy's gown. It's—"

"It's her gown. Not mine. I don't want someone else's gown." She was crying. "I want to choose my own wedding dress. It's not your place, David. It's not your place!" She ran out the lakeside door, running toward the dock.

David was mortified. How dare she embarrass him like this?

Lydia bit a fingernail. "What do you want me to do, Mr. Stancowsky?"

He pointed to a chair. "Sit. I'll be right back."

He marched out the door and down to the dock. Millie stood at the farthest point, her back to him, arms crossed. He was surprised when she turned around to face him. "You've hurt Mrs. Peters's feelings, Millie. You need to go apologize."

Millie's jaw dropped. "Me? Me apologize?"

"You certainly don't think it's her fault. She's gone to a lot of work to create—"

She pressed a hand to her forehead. "David, you have to stop doing this."

"Doing what?"

"Planning everything without me. Taking charge."

"Someone has to."

Her face crumpled into its pre-cry mode. "That's not fair. You haven't given me a chance to make any decisions. Just because I don't know exactly what I want. . . It's still seven months before the wedding. This is supposed to be a special experience. When the time comes, my mother and I are supposed to work together to create a wonderful wedding."

He snickered. "Well, there's your problem. Your mother couldn't decide to have cream or sugar in her coffee. If I waited until the two of you made a decision, we wouldn't get married until 1960. But maybe that's what you're striving for. . . . Is that it? Or are you getting cold feet?"

She didn't say anything and once again showed him her back.

He felt a sudden swell of panic. Did she have doubts? Was she wanting out of the engagement? This couldn't happen. His—their—entire future depended on this marriage. All his plans would be ruined. . . .

He slowly approached and put his hands on her upper arms. He placed his mouth near her ear. "Don't do this, Millie.

Don't throw away what we have. Our future is bright. Your father is grooming me to take over Mariner. It's a good move. We'll be very well off. Don't ruin everything by giving in to childish doubts."

She swung around so violently he nearly lost his balance, coming within inches of falling off the dock. "It's all about Mariner, isn't it? You don't love me. You love the business—which you can only get by marrying me."

"That's not true."

She laughed and pushed past him, walking toward the house. When she didn't go inside but started walking around the side toward his car, Mrs. Peters opened the back door. "What about the dress?"

Millie didn't stop walking. "It's officially on hold." Then, suddenly, she backtracked to the door. "It seems I'm in need of a ride back to Bangor. Can you take me, Mrs. Peters? I'll pay you for your time."

Mrs. Peters looked to David. "I. . .I suppose I could."

"I appreciate it." She turned to David. "I'll see you tomorrow."

"Tomorrow?"

She stood her ground by the door. "I don't want to talk to you anymore today, David. I don't want to be with you."

His heart pounded against his chest. "You don't want to talk to me? You don't *want*?"

She turned to the older woman. "May I come inside for a few minutes before we leave, Mrs. Peters?"

The woman looked as if she'd been asked to strip naked. And no wonder. She was forced to choose between this emotional woman or the man who was paying the bills for her hard work. It was no contest, but David regretted the fact she'd been put in this position.

But then, suddenly, she opened the door fully and stepped aside so Millie could go in.

"Mrs. Peters!"

She gave him a look of regret. "I'm sorry, Mr. Stancowsky." She closed the door.

David was left standing in the yard. Surely this was a dream. It had to be a dream. The past few days were like someone else's life. Up to now, he'd had everything carefully planned. Every detail. Why had Millie suddenly changed from his charming, agreeable fiancée to this woman who found fault in everything he did?

He saw a curtain being pulled aside. Millie peeked out, then stepped back.

He got in the car and drove home. She'd come to her senses.

David was not expected back at work that day. He'd taken time off to finalize the wedding dress.

His secretary, Dina Edmonds, looked up from the filing. "Mr. Stancowsky." She glanced at a clock. "Did everything go all right?"

David handed her his coat and hat and nodded to the opposite side of the office. "Is he in?"

"Yes. Of course." She took a step toward the intercom. "Let me tell him you're—"

"No need." He headed to Ray's office.

Millie's father stood at a drawing board, leaning over a set of blueprints. "What are you doing back so soon?" he asked.

David had spent the entire trip back stewing over Millie's disturbing new attitude, plus planning what he would say to her father. Although he and Ray had a good relationship, nothing could be taken for granted. His position as CEO-in-waiting was directly linked to his marrying the boss's daughter. And there was nothing David wanted more than to be the head of Mariner Construction. Under his tutelage, it could move from a fledgling company into a Northeastern powerhouse. He had big plans and he couldn't let something as minor as a domestic spat sabotage them.

The question was how to approach Ray Reynolds about his daughter's wedding mutiny. The father-daughter relationship seemed complicated. Millie was Ray's only child, yet as far as David could see she was not a daddy's girl. Ray was not subject to her every whim. If anything, just the opposite. Millie went out of her way to please her father. . .the obedient child. It bode well for her being an obedient wife.

At least that had been the plan. Until now.

The two alternative tacks were to tell Ray exactly what was going on and seek his advice—in which case, Ray might think less of David for letting things get out of control. Or David could state the facts plainly, but assure Ray things were still under his control—which all in all might be more advantageous.

David motioned to the desk. "Can we sit? I have something to discuss with you." *Discuss* was a good word. A sharing of the power.

Ray moved to his executive chair. "This sounds serious."

"It's a concern, but under control." David waited until Ray was seated, then sat across the desk from him. "I need to inform you that I may have to take some fairly strong action regarding the wedding. Millie is not cooperating with the plans."

"In what way?"

"No need to bother yourself with the details. But it's

imperative we stay on schedule for the May date. With the push of the construction season starting in June, it's a necessity for things to continue on schedule. I've promised you I would be back from the honeymoon in time to dig into our summer work, and I will not break that promise."

Ray sat back, making a tent with his fingers. He nodded. "Anything I can do to get Millie in line?"

Here was the clincher, the ace in the hole that would bond father-in-law and son-in-law. "Millie mentioned a desire to involve your wife in the wedding plans, but I have a concern. . . ." *Tread delicately, David.*

"Your concern is valid. If Rhonda gets involved. . ." He sat forward. "Let's just say I, above anyone else, am aware of my wife's lack of decision-making capabilities. She is a follower and needs a stern and steady hand to make it through life. In truth, I fear Millie is much the same."

He couldn't have said it better himself. "I knew you'd understand. So I'll take care of Millie."

"And I'll let Rhonda know what's what." He stood. "Don't worry, David. Between you and me, this wedding will come off as planned. On schedule."

One last soothing of the ego. . . "I knew I could count on you." David cocked his head toward the blueprint. "Is that the new elementary school?"

Since the plan for the women in their lives was firmly in place, they moved to the drawing board.

David did not call Millie that night. He'd let her *think* she was in control. She'd know the truth soon enough.

The end of a matter is better than its beginning,
and patience is better than pride.
ECCLESIASTES 7:8

Decatur—1976

"Welcome, welcome! Come in!"

Vanessa was wrapped in a hug. When her mother let go, she spotted one of the other guests. He was an overweight man her mother's age, wearing a Hawaiian shirt adorned with yellow hibiscuses. He held out his arms. Vanessa braced herself for another hug.

"So this is Dorian's little Nessa. Not so little anymore, are you?"

As Vanessa was captured by the man's arms, Dorian laughed. "Nessa, meet Harry Cleese."

The man let her go and winked. "Cleese. No relation to John."

She didn't get it. "John?"

"John Cleese? *Monty Python and the Holy Grail*?"

Ah. "Nice to meet you."

"Harry teaches sixth grade at my school."

"Dorian breaks them in and I shove them along their way."

"Nudge is a better word, Harry. You nudge them."

The man's laugh was loud and boisterous, making the hibiscuses shake. "No, I shove. Both hands sometimes. What's with kids today, anyway?"

"Ah, the question of every generation." The other guest stepped forward and Vanessa was taken aback. He was a gorgeous black man with a wide smile and kind eyes. He held out his hand, yet oddly, Vanessa found herself disappointed that he wasn't a hugger like the others. "Lewis O'Neal. No relation to Ryan—or Tatum. Nice to meet you."

Mother put her hand on his shoulder. "The three of us go to the same church. Lewis is the maintenance man there."

Vanessa wondered if "maintenance man" was a fancy name for janitor.

"You should hear our Lewis sing," her mother said. "Man, what a voice. Praise the Lord!"

Praise the Lord? This was not the Pruitt style. Church was a place to be seen, to make business contacts.

Her mother must have seen her confusion. "This is not the type of churchgoing we used to do, Nessa. This is real."

She felt a wave of defensiveness. "Ours was real. Is real."

"That's what I thought, too, but let me tell you, the faith your father and I had was as deep as a wading pool." She smiled at Lewis. "But now. . .I've taken the plunge and have jumped into the deep end!"

Harry raised a fist. "Off the high board!"

Lewis laughed. "Splashing all the way."

"Dog paddling for the Lord!"

No. It couldn't be. Her mother was a Jesus-freak?

Dorian suddenly stopped laughing and made a curlicue in

front of Vanessa's eyes. "Uh-uh. Don't give me that look. I'm right about this God stuff and your father's wrong. Together, we were wrong in how we brought you up in the church—sitting *in* the church but never being *of* the church, never being people of faith."

Harry pulled her under his arm. "I'm the one who invited her to come with us. She's been there ever since. Jesus got a good one when He captured your mother's heart."

Captured her heart?

Her mother's voice softened. "While I was going through the divorce, I realized I needed something more than myself to get through the hard times. You should know that being kicked out of your life was the worst time in *my* life, Nessa." She turned to her friends. "Yardley has been telling her *I* was the one who left *them*."

Harry shook his head vehemently. "No sirree, little lady. Dorian was the hurt one. Your father didn't think she was good enough for his climb up the ladder to be one of Atlanta's elite. He called her an embarrassment because she'd gained a social conscience that looked beyond the establishment. Plus, she was just a lowly teacher."

Her mother shrugged. "And I *did* refuse to wear that awful orange knit dress to a fancy dinner." She made a clutching motion at her bosom. "It was pulled together right here with a yellow daisy pin. Awful. Just awful. Not me at all."

Harry laughed and stepped aside, showcasing her current caftan made from scarves. "So speaks Miss Couturière 1976."

"Oh pooh. The clothes were just part of it," Mother said. "Though Yardley and I started out on the same page when we were married, he was blind to the changes in the world, the things that *needed* changing. All he cared about was his stupid bank. I became an activist and he didn't like it. He wanted me to turn back into something I wasn't anymore, something I could never be again." She found Vanessa's eyes. "And when I couldn't—and wouldn't—he dumped me. After twenty years of marriage, he dumped me like an old shirt in the giveaway pile. And then, as the cherry on the cake, he took you away from me—physically, mentally, and emotionally."

Vanessa's throat was dry. What could she say? "I didn't know."

Her mother nodded and squeezed her arm. "Enough of this. Let me grab the fondue and Fresca, and we'll get down to some serious card playing. Harry and me against you and Lewis."

As she moved to the kitchen Lewis leaned close. "Let's kick some butt."

He didn't sound like any churchgoing man Vanessa had ever met—which, all things considered, was a good thing.

⸻

Vanessa screamed. Then she high-fived Lewis over the table.

"We are the champions!" Lewis jumped out of his chair and did a *Rocky* victory dance. Then he came around the table and pulled Vanessa up to join him. She wasn't used to such exuberance, but gave it a shot.

Lewis clapped. "All right, Vanessa! Get down!"

She stopped her dance and felt herself redden. But it was a good blush. She liked Lewis's approval. In fact, she liked everything about him. Of course, what wasn't to like? He was charming, funny, intelligent, and had a smile that could melt a brick. And eyes. . . When he looked at her, she was torn between wanting to look right back and be drawn into a wonderfully soft place, or look away in case he saw too much of who she really was.

Harry tossed his cards into the center pile. “That should have been our victory dance, Dorian. I shouldn’t have played that jack. I should’ve played the queen.”

“Yup,” said Mother. “I hereby declare it all your fault.”

Vanessa laughed and loved the *real* feeling it gave her. As if tonight she’d finally awakened from a long bout of sleepwalking.

“Who wants tea?”

“I’ll help,” Harry said.

“I’m going to the little boys’ room,” Lewis said.

Vanessa was left alone in her mother’s dining room. It was as different from the dining room in the Pruitt home as Frankie’s Café was to Tavern on the Green. And though the lack of wealth had initially hit her as a negative, after spending time within its walls it seemed an attribute. There was no china cabinet displaying silver and crystal, no twelve intricately carved chairs sitting on a hand-tied oriental rug. None of those lovely things that screamed status but somehow seemed hard to grasp. Even when a crystal goblet was in Vanessa’s hand, it was as if there was a distance between object and holder.

Here, in her mother’s dining room, stood a round oak table with a piece of the veneer missing on the side and four straight-lined chairs with yellow polka-dotted cushions. Instead of a buffet or cabinet, there was a bookshelf stuffed with books. Vanessa let her fingers walk across the covers. Shakespeare, John Jakes, Jane Austen, C. S. Lewis, Tolkien, Solzhenitsyn. She remembered her mother reading books to her at bedtime. Vanessa couldn’t say she’d read many since. She didn’t have time.

She shook her head at the lie. She had time; she chose not to read. Why was that?

She looked at the avocado-colored fondue pot on the table and gathered up the crumpled napkins and plates. Her father never would allow such fare. Vanessa had become an expert at setting a proper table: a brocade tablecloth complete with a padded liner to protect the tabletop, cloth napkins, china on gold chargers, Grandmother Pruitt's sterling flatware, water goblets, wine glasses, and bread-and-butter plates. Luckily—after one disastrous dinner when Vanessa had burned the cordon bleu—her father began to hire in a cook. Vanessa was left to the hostess duties, which entailed looking pretty, offering second helpings, and being the foil for her father's conversation. She was an expert at nodding and smiling.

Quite a contrast to tonight: clinking fondue forks together to commemorate the beginning of the card game, catching the drips of cheese with their fingers, drinking Fresca from the bottle, and Harry pointing a fork at her mother, saying, "*En garde*!" making her mother laugh.

Her mother's laughter was another surprise. Each time Vanessa heard it, her mind zoomed back to other times, old times, when Dorian Pruitt and daughter used to play Go Fish or swing in the park. *"Higher, Mommy, higher!"*

When had "Mommy" changed to "Mother"?

At the question, the image of her father's face intruded. A stern face. A proper face with his eyebrows drooped toward a center point marked by a deep vertical line. Eyes that could change from disapproving to plaintive in a single moment.

Vanessa couldn't remember when the laughter had started to fade, but snippets of harsh words and slammed doors populated the time between Go Fish and her mother's going away.

Sent away.

She clutched the napkins to her chest. A huge lie. How

many other lies had she clung to as truth? Daddy's version of truth?

She noticed a cross-stitched sampler on the wall: *Bless This House.*

She nodded and gathered some plates for the kitchen.

Amen to that.

Saying good-bye at the door, Lewis kissed Vanessa's cheek. "Why don't you come to church with your mother on Sunday? We'll save you a place. It starts at ten thirty."

She imagined herself sitting next to him in a pew, his hand straying to the space between them, taking hold of hers. . . It was a pleasant image. But a bold one considering the white-black thing. "I'll think about it."

" 'Night then." He left with a wave and one more killer smile. When Vanessa turned around to make her own good-byes to her mother, she found her in Harry's arms. Kissing.

When Mother opened her eyes and saw Vanessa looking, she blushed and pushed him away. "See you tomorrow, Harry."

He kissed her once more on the cheek and pointed a finger at Vanessa. "You come back soon. We demand a rematch."

She nodded, but her mind was not on cards. She hung back so he would leave first. Her mother stood by the opened door, waiting for her to go, but Vanessa closed it.

"You're *seeing* him?"

"Harry?"

"Yes, Harry. The man who had you lip-to-lip."

She smiled. "He's a great kisser."

"Mother!"

She put her hands on her hips. "Why are you objecting? I thought you liked him."

"I do. But I didn't know he was your. . .what is he to you?"

Her grin was like a schoolgirl's. "Actually, dear daughter, he's my fiancé. We're getting married July Fourth. We figured it was a good way to celebrate the Bicentennial. The country doesn't know it, but all the fireworks will be for us."

"But. . .but Daddy didn't remarry!" Lame. Very lame.

Her mother placed both hands on Vanessa's shoulders, looking her straight in the eyes. "Your father and I have been divorced nearly five years. I am way beyond the age of consent. And in spite of what you may think, I'm a relatively young woman. Do you actually want me to be alone for the rest of my life?"

Vanessa knew her feelings were petty, but they came out anyway. "Daddy doesn't even have a girlfriend."

At this, Mother dropped her arms, gave a bitter laugh, and led Vanessa to the couch. "I really don't like taking on the position of bubble-burster, but here goes another one." She fueled herself with a deep breath. "Your father has always had girlfriends, even when it wasn't proper for him to have girlfriends—if you get my drift."

Vanessa scanned her memories for evidence. "I've never seen—"

"He's always been discreet, I will give him that."

"But if he had, *has* girlfriends. . .now that he's single, why doesn't he bring them around?"

"Ask him. I stopped trying to figure out the psyche of Yardley Pruitt a long time ago."

Vanessa's mind zeroed in on a cruise her father had taken last year. She'd asked to go along, but he'd told her she couldn't, telling her it was a business trip.

Mother stroked Vanessa's hair. "It's late. You've had a lot sprung on you the last two days. Why don't you stay here tonight?" She patted the couch cushion.

Why not?

Vanessa let her mother take care of her.

Dawson—1987

Lane grabbed a lukewarm Pop-Tart along with her jacket and hugged Grandma Nellie from behind. "Am I forgiven?"

Grandma patted her arm. "It's your life, chickie. Far be it from me to tell you how to live it."

Lane's mother laughed. "Far be it." She poured a cup of coffee before heading off for her shift at the soybean plant. The pungent smell of the processed beans was always present—on her person and in the town.

"Maybe I should just keep quiet. Is that what you all want?"

Lane whispered in Grandma's ear, "Never." She kissed her cheek and gathered her things for school. She purposely didn't tell them she was trying out for the school play today. Let it be a surprise when she told them she was Juliet.

Toby honked out front. "I'll be late coming home. I have something after—" Her backpack was upstairs. "Oops. Forgot something."

She ran and got it, but as she was on the landing coming back down she heard her mother say, ". . .seems to have recovered well."

"It'll hit her," Grandma said. "One of these days she'll realize she passed up the chance of a lifetime, and we'll have to scrape her up off the floor."

The air went out of her. But then Toby honked a second time.

She ran to him.

Lane pushed her lunch tray toward Toby so he could finish her goulash. "So you don't object to me trying out?"

He shrugged. "I'm not going to be the one to hold you back."

"But. . . ?" There were things unsaid.

He draped his arm over her shoulder and leaned his head against hers. "Those plays take a ton of time. Time we could spend together." He tried to feed her a bite of garlic bread. She pushed it away, so he ate it himself. "Of course, if you don't want to spend time with me. . ."

She scoped for a teacher and seeing none, kissed him on the lips. "Of course I do."

"Then it's a no-brainer." He stood, taking his tray. "Gotta get to gym. See ya in history."

Yeah. See ya.

She pulled her tray back and nibbled on the leftovers. Why did he have to pull the guilt trip on her? Yet she'd expected as much. Which is why she hadn't told him her intentions until lunch. If only she hadn't told him at all, just tried out, gotten the part, and *then* told him.

"Hi, Lane." Melissa Peterson sat beside her, her shirt slanted off the shoulder like Jennifer Beals's in *Flashdance*. That was the only similarity.

Lane would rather have sat next to Freddie Krueger. She concentrated on what was left of her lunch.

"Fine," Melissa said. "Don't talk to me. That's just like you, you know. Being a stuck-up snob, thinking you're too good for

Dawson." She laughed. "As if you could ever make it in Hollywood."

Lane stood. "I don't need this."

Melissa grabbed her sleeve, pulling her back down. "And we don't need you—especially not at the auditions."

"Who's *we*?"

Melissa swept a hand around the lunchroom. "You see anybody who isn't turned off by your better-than attitude? Acting like we're nothing. Like our plays are nothing."

"I never—"

She stood to leave. "My advice to you? Don't try out after school. Let the rest of us who love Dawson get the parts. Frankly, Lane, you're not that good."

She was gone before Lane could even think of a comeback.

Lane noticed the girls at the next table talking behind their hands, looking at her.

She got up, taking her tray—

Dropping her tray.

Laughter all around.

It was not a good day.

After school, Lane slammed her locker shut.

"Well?" Toby said. "What'll it be? Me or Romeo?"

She shrugged. She still wasn't sure what to do.

He walked his fingers up her arm. "I'm real. He's not."

Good point.

Lane spotted Melissa Peterson walking by with two other girls. They looked at her, Melissa said something under her breath, and they all giggled. She waited for Toby to come to her defense—yell at Melissa and tell her to back off.

But he didn't. "Surely you don't want to spend the next six weeks with her," he said. "Not when you could spend it with me." He pulled her close for a kiss.

The vice principal cleared his throat as he passed by. They separated. Toby took her hand. "Come on. Come with me. I have a surprise for you."

Lane looked down the hall toward the drama room.

"I'll make it worth your while," he said.

Why not? She was tired of thinking about it. She let him lead her toward the door.

"How much farther?" Lane asked.

"Not much. Keep your eyes closed." He had his hands on her waist, pushing her. The ground was uneven and she stumbled often, but he kept her safe.

Finally, he let her stop and positioned her just so. "Okay. Open your eyes."

They were on the crest of a hill and could see for miles. The trees were still weeks away from budding and the ground was splotched with snow, but the view of open fields and groves of trees stirred her.

"It's gorgeous."

He pulled her back against him. "Just like you."

"Where are we?"

"It's my grandpa's land."

"I didn't know your grandpa owned land."

"Neither did I, until recently. I heard him and Dad talking about Grandpa's retirement. He bought this land back in the fifties and has been holding on to it ever since."

"What for? Farming's bad now." *We had to sell our land.*

She felt him shrug. " 'Maybe nothing, maybe something' was what I heard him tell Dad."

"Is he going to sell it?"

He hugged her tighter still. His voice was soft. "Maybe."

Volumes were said with that one word. She turned her face, trying to see his.

He smiled. "I talked to Grandpa about it. About selling it. Or part of it."

She turned all the way around. She didn't want to presume, but she desperately wanted him to say. . .

"It could be our land, Lane. Yours and mine together. We could build a house here."

She squealed and wrapped her arms around his neck, surprised by her own enthusiasm. She'd never thought much about having a house, having a home. Just the usual teenage thoughts. But to actually be here and see the view that her house—their house. . . It changed everything.

He took her hands. Then he got down on one knee. "Lane Holloway, will you marry me?"

How could she say no?

She didn't.

Lane and Toby sat in his car in front of her house. She pulled away from him. "I need to go in."

His eyes narrowed as he snuggled into her neck. "But we're engaged. Let's celebrate. Really celebrate."

Before she was forced to think of another excuse, the porch light blinked on, then off. "The porch light. . ."

He glanced up, then returned to her neck, pulling aside the edge of her shirt. "So?"

She found the door handle and opened it. “I’d better go.” She got out.

He reached, as if to pull her back, but she was on the grass. “Laney!”

“The porch light. I gotta go.”

“But we’re engaged. Can’t they cut us some slack?”

She leaned down to look at him. “But they don’t know we’re engaged.”

“Then—”

She blew him a kiss and shut the door. “See you tomorrow.” She ran up the front walk and inside—where Grandma waited.

“It’s late.”

Lane pushed the door shut until it clicked. “I know.”

“You spend way too much time with that boy and I—”

Lane slipped past her and took the stairs two at a time. “I have homework. ’Night, Grandma.”

She didn’t feel safe until she was behind the locked door of her room. Only when she found herself leaning her forehead against it did she realize her heart was pounding. It was as if she’d escaped from the boogeyman. *What’s with that?*

Suddenly, her strength evaporated. She turned around and let the door guide her to the floor. Tears followed, confusing her even more.

She was just tired. Everything would be all right in the morning.

It would.

⁂

The phone woke her. Lane’s arm got caught in the covers, so by the time she answered it, her father had, too.

“Hello?” he said.

"Hello?" she said.

"Laney. . ." It was Brandy. She was crying.

Lane sat up. "Dad, I've got it. It's Brandy."

John Holloway's voice gained strength. "Brandy? Are you all right?"

"I'm sorry to call so late, Mr. Holloway. I—"

They heard a crash in the background.

"You okay?" Lane asked.

"Can I come over? She's drunk again."

Lane's dad took over. "Meet us outside. We'll come get you."

By the time Lane and her dad got back from collecting Brandy, Lane's mom had made hot chocolate. Somehow at two in the morning her teal zip-up robe looked doubly bright against the white kitchen cabinets.

Dad helped Brandy off with her coat, hanging it on the back hall tree under his own. Protective. *You can't get to her unless you go through me.*

"Would you like marshmallows, Brandy?"

She nodded and sat at the kitchen table, pulling the sleeves of her sweater over her hands.

Lane sat across from her, with her father to her left. Her mother served steaming mugs, then took the remaining seat. They all blew across their drinks, taking sips.

Only then did Lane's father say, "I thought she was getting better."

"She was."

"She needs to go to AA."

Brandy shook her head. "She won't." She looked up from her cocoa, her smile bitter. "She's got it under control. Can't you tell?"

"Did she hit you?" he asked.

"No." Brandy looked between them. "But she's bought a gun. I saw it in her dresser. She says it's for protection 'cause she works late at Moby's."

Lane's mother shook her head. "A drunk serving drunks." She slapped a hand to her mouth. "Oh. I'm sorry, Brandy."

"It's okay. It's true. Actually, she doesn't get drunk on the nights she works. It's the other times. . ."

Lane's dad reached over and patted her hand. "You stay here as long as you want."

Brandy nodded, her eyes filling with fresh tears. "Thanks, Mr. Holloway. I appreciate it."

Lane's mother stood. "I'll go put out some fresh towels in the bathroom."

Sometimes Lane really loved her family.

Lane and Brandy lay in bed, looking at the ceiling. The shadows of branches played in the moonlight. "You going to be okay?" Lane asked.

Brandy nodded. "You realize how lucky you are, don't you?"

She hadn't thought about it much. "Sure."

"Good. Because not everybody has what you have." Brandy turned over on her side, snuggling deeper in the covers. "I'm glad you didn't go to that audition. I don't know what I'd do if you left Dawson."

Bangor—1958

David was going crazy. Ever since the wedding-dress fiasco the day before, he'd left Millie alone, certain she'd call. But she didn't. And she wasn't answering the phone either. That in itself was strange. Millie lived with her parents. Her mother didn't work. Millie didn't really work—except part-time at the hospital gift shop. There was always someone at the Reynolds' home.

Dina knocked on the doorjamb of his office. "Excuse me, Mr. Stancowsky, but Mr. Reynolds wanted you to have these bids for the school estimate."

He motioned her inside and she set a stack of subcontractor bids on his desk. She took a step to leave, then stopped. "Is everything all right?"

For some reason, he really saw her for the first time. Though she'd been working as his secretary a month, he hadn't had time to take notice. Besides, the best secretaries were the ones who were invisible, there when you needed them, but otherwise, a part of the furniture. She wasn't pretty like Millie, though she was pleasant looking. She wore her dishwater hair in a french roll, making her look older than she probably was. "How old are you, Miss Edmonds?"

She blushed. "Twenty-eight."

"Hmm," David said. "Same as me. So you're married?"

She looked down. "No, I'm afraid not."

"Why not?"

"I. . .I haven't fallen in love."

"Ah."

"Ah?"

"You're one of those romantic types," he said.

She opened her mouth, then closed it. Finally, she said, "I suppose I am."

"Have you met my fiancée?"

"Yes, I have. She's lovely. Her father has a picture of her on his desk." Her eyes strayed to his desk, where there was no such picture.

"Thank you for the estimates, Miss Edmonds."

⸻

David didn't crave food when it was time for lunch—he craved information. He was stopped at an intersection a half a block from the Reynolds' home when he spotted Millie hurrying to her car, her arms full of books and notebooks. She hesitated where the walk met the driveway and turned to say something to her mother, who stood at the door. So she *had* been home when he'd last called? He didn't like the implication. And where was she going? He knew her schedule. Today was *not* one of her days to work at the hospital.

She got in the family car, pulled out of the driveway, and drove away from him. Without making a conscious decision, he found himself following her, hanging back, not letting her see. His mind swam with possibilities. She occasionally tutored, so maybe she was heading to a student's home, some fifth-grade textbook in hand.

But maybe not.

It was the *not* that made his stomach pull. Millie was a beautiful woman. Desirable in every way. Wavy chestnut hair that kissed her jawline; brown eyes; a smile that had grown more wistful of late, but was still stunning. And though he was no slouch in the looks department either, he'd seen other men look at her. Want her.

She surprised him by turning into the parking lot of the community center. He'd driven by the building often but had never been inside. What did he need with knitting or tango lessons? He didn't dare pull in behind her, so he went around the block. When he came back, she was already inside. He would have followed her, but the building was small and she'd certainly see him. So he cruised the length of the parking lot, peering in the windows. He spotted her in the next-to-the-last room. A half dozen people were there, some seated at desks, some talking. Millie stood next to a man at the front of the class, her notebook and books held close to her chest, her face serious, her free hand gesturing. He was nice looking in a burly sort of way and had curly red hair—

The voice of Mrs. Stephens from the bed-and-breakfast infiltrated his thoughts: *"A handsome man with curly red hair. Midtwenties."*

Could this be the same man who'd brought Millie a note with her earring?

No. That was absurd. Bar Harbor was an hour away. Why would a man who worked at a gift shop there be here?

The man stepped away from Millie and she took a seat. He stood in front of the group like a teacher.

And it was clear. His Millie was taking a class.

Without telling him.

His first inclination was to storm inside and confront her right there in front of her classmates. He wouldn't mind getting a better look at the redheaded teacher. And yet. . .knowledge was power. And the advantage always went to the one who owned the element of surprise.

Which would be him.

⁂

Millie's mother opened the door. "David." Her eyes skirted his.

Oh, yes indeed, something was up.

"May I come in?"

"Uh. . .Millie's not here."

"I know. I came to see you."

Rhonda Reynolds fingered the collar of her dress. "Well, then. Come in." She led him into the living room of the two-story Victorian. "Would you like some coffee? Or a sandwich? I was just making some lunch for Millie when she gets—" She put a hand to her mouth.

The perfect opening. "How is Millie liking her class?"

Her eyebrows rose. "You know about that?"

"Of course."

He sat on the couch and she took a seat in a rocker. One hand found the other as she rested them in her lap. "She likes it fine. She's a very good writer."

A writing class? Why? "What's the teacher's name again?"

"Uh. . .I'm not sure."

She was lying. "Is he from around here?"

"Well, I don't know. I assume so."

"Because we saw a man up in Bar Harbor who looked like him."

"Oh. Really?" Her surprise was pulled. She knew something. "Must have been a coincidence." She stood. "Are you sure you wouldn't like a sandwich?"

"No, thank you." He stood to leave. There was one more thing to clear up. "I tried calling all morning. Were you both out?"

Mrs. Reynolds sat back down. "No. We were here."

"Then why didn't you answer the phone?"

She looked at her hands. "Millie told me about the wedding dress. She didn't want to talk. . . ." She glanced at him, then down again. "Last night, Ray spoke to me about staying out of it. I don't want to be a bother, David."

"You won't be, I'm sure."

"But. . ."

"Yes?"

"I hate to see Millie so upset. A girl only gets one wedding."

"Which is why some guidance is needed to make it perfect."

Her voice was so soft he could barely hear her. "Perhaps perfection shouldn't be the goal?"

He stood in front of her and took one of her hands in his. "The Reynolds name means something in Bangor. Mariner Construction is a well-respected business here. In some ways I'm a newcomer, an outsider. I am very honored to be a part of this family, and I wish to continue the legacy." He smiled. "Aren't you eager for grandchildren?"

"Of course."

He gave her hand a pat before letting it go. "Then let me do what I need to do for the future legacy of the Reynolds line. Let me honor you and your family with the perfect wedding."

She hesitated, then nodded.

Case closed.

The call from Millie came an hour after he returned from visiting her mother. "Hello, David."

He took the offensive. "So. You decide to make contact again? It's been an entire day, Millie."

"Mom said you came by."

"When were you going to tell me about the class?"

"It's nothing. Just a creative-writing class. Adult ed. Two mornings a week."

"Since when do you write?"

"I've always enjoyed writing. I took some classes at Beal College—"

"You dropped out."

"Because Father wanted me to work at Mariner. I'd still be working at Mariner. . ."

"If it weren't for me. I told you. I want to be the provider of the family. There's no need for you to work beyond a little part-time diversion."

"But I want to work more. I need something to do, David. I can't sit around all day twiddling my thumbs. I have a brain. I'm smart. I have something to offer the world besides. . .oh, never mind."

"So being my wife isn't enough for you?"

"I didn't say that."

"You implied it."

He heard her sigh. "I just look at my mother, at how she thinks little about anything beyond this house. I'm interested in the whole world, David. Eisenhower, de Gaulle, the threat of communism, the space race, desegregation."

"You get out. You work at the hospital."

"In the gift shop. That doesn't change anyone's life."

He laughed. "You want to change people's lives?"

"Don't laugh at me, David."

He had to be careful. A woman's ego was fragile. "You're going to change my life, dear one. You're going to make me the happiest man in the world."

"So you say."

He sat forward in his chair. "What's that supposed to mean?"

There was a pause. "I'm just tired. I need to know if you're going to give me a hard time about the class."

"And if I do?"

"It's not hurting anything, David. It's not taking one minute away from my time with you."

"I assume you have homework?"

"Yes. . .but I'll do it during the day, before you come home. I promise. It won't affect you in any—"

"What was your teacher doing in Bar Harbor?"

Silence.

"Millie? I asked you a question."

"I believe my teacher's aunt is the one who owns the gift store where I lost my earring."

"Yesterday you said the man was probably the proprietor's son. You acted like you didn't know him."

Silence again. Then she said, "He mentioned it to me today. When his aunt asked him to return the earring to the hotel, he recognized my name. I didn't know it was him until he said something."

"Why didn't he just wait and give you the earring in class?"

She cleared her throat. "Are you going to stop by for dinner tonight? Mom and I were going to make meat loaf, your favorite."

"Count on it."

This wasn't over.

The lot is cast into the lap,
but its every decision is from the LORD.
PROVERBS 16:33

Bangor—1958

Dina placed a stack of three files before him. "You seem very tense today, Mr. Stancowsky."

He put down his pencil and rubbed his forehead. Before he could even open his eyes, she was behind him, kneading his shoulders.

"This is what you need. My brothers used to say I give the best back rubs."

It wasn't bad. He closed his eyes and let himself enjoy it. For such a small woman, she had strong hands. He wondered if Millie was good at back rubs. . . .

"Well, what have we here?"

David's eyes shot open. Millie stood in the doorway. Dina pulled her hands away, but none too fast. She retrieved a letter from the desk and walked toward the door, but it was blocked by Millie.

"May I get by, please?" Dina asked.

Millie glared at her, not moving an inch.

"Millie, let her pass." He hoped he wasn't blushing.

She stepped to the side. "Oh, I think your secretary knows all about passes."

Dina left the room and Millie started to close the door behind her.

"Leave it open. I have nothing to hide."

She pushed it open, raising her hands. "Fine. Let your girlfriend hear."

"Jealousy does not become you, Millie."

"And infidelity does not become you."

This was ridiculous. "Sit down."

"I prefer to stand."

What had happened to his old Millie?

"Why did you ask me here, David?" she asked, standing behind a chair. "I have to get to the gift shop. You mentioned some kind of opportunity?"

He sat back, trying to focus. "I thought it would be nice if we had a dinner party for a few of Mariner's biggest accounts. At my place. With you acting as hostess."

"Why don't you have it at our house? After all, my father *is* still the president of the company."

He didn't like the challenge in her tone but decided to ignore it. For now. "I've talked this over with Ray, and he agrees that my idea would be a good first step to establish the two of us as a team."

She laughed. "Us? A team?"

"You? Cook?"

That shut her up. But when she turned to leave, he was afraid he'd gone too far. He really needed her to cooperate in this for the good of the business. He hurried after her, taking hold of her upper arms. "Millie, please. I'm sorry."

She looked down, her head shaking back and forth. "You want a perfect wife, David. You deserve a perfect wife. I just don't think I'm her."

He pulled her close, enveloping her. "Don't say that. We'll work on the menu for the dinner together. That's why I asked you to come over." He led her back to her chair. "We'll work on it together."

Millie had been no help with the menu, just sitting there like a zombie. He'd finally told her to go to the hospital and he'd bring the menu by over lunch—for her approval.

She was impossible to understand. One minute she chastised him for making all the decisions, and the next—when he asked for her input—she threw everything back in his lap.

He sat with a legal pad before him. He knew the kind of food he'd like for the dinner, but the difficulty was choosing something that was impressive *and* that Millie could make. If Rhonda had done her job and taught her daughter to cook, he wouldn't be in this mess.

He looked up when Dina appeared at the door. "Yes, Miss Edmonds?"

She stepped into the office. "I just wanted to apologize for causing any conflict between you and your fiancée."

He flipped her concern away with a hand. "Don't worry about it."

She nodded once but did not leave. "You look pensive," she said. "Is there anything I can do to help?"

Actually. . . "Are you a good cook?"

She looked almost pretty when she smiled. "An excellent cook, sir."

"How are you at planning executive dinners?"

When David came into the hospital gift shop, Millie was helping a man buy a vase of carnations. A mother and a little girl were looking at the stuffed animals. The girl sang a song and made a teddy bear dance. She was adorable in a plaid dress under a red wool coat. While he was waiting for Millie, he moved close. "Your bear is a good dancer," he told her.

She looked up at him with the most amazing brown eyes. *Their* children would have such eyes. . . .

"Thank you," she said.

The mother, who was wearing a beret that reminded David of the ones beatniks wore, chimed in. "All Nessa's animals are very talented."

"Nessa?"

"Vanessa."

He smiled down at her. "What a pretty name. How old are you?"

With some work, the girl held up four fingers.

"My, my. Four years old. You're a big girl."

She nodded.

He noticed Millie watching him. Good. She would see how good he was with children. "Millie, come meet this darling child."

She came out from behind the counter. "May I help you?" she asked the woman.

"We're visiting from Atlanta. My sister just had a baby, and we—"

A perfect opening. David dove in. He put an arm around Millie's shoulders, speaking to the mother. "This is my fiancée. We hope to have our own babies as soon as possible."

He was shocked when she shrugged his arm away. "Children are a long way off."

David looked at the woman, who seemed to be studying Millie's face. Why was Millie intent on embarrassing him today?

But instead of being on his side, the woman put a hand on Millie's arm. "Here's my philosophy on such things: Just because you can doesn't mean you should."

"Pardon me?" David said.

He saw Millie's eyes brighten. "I like that," she told the woman. She looked down at the little girl, who was taking it all in, and put a hand on her head. "I do love children. But I'm in no hurry. The time has to be right." She glanced at David.

The subject had gotten out of hand. David pulled out the menu he and Dina had created for the dinner. "Can we go to lunch? I'd like to go over this."

"If you'll excuse us?" Millie stepped away from the customer. "That was rude."

"Don't talk to me about rude. How dare you act like you don't want my children?"

Millie kept her voice low. "That's not what I said. But the woman's comment was a good one. 'Just because you can—' "

He'd had enough. He shoved the menu against her chest. "Forget lunch. I'm not hungry. Look at the menu and bring it back to the office with any changes." *If you dare make any.*

He walked out before she could object.

Decatur—1976

Vanessa flushed the toilet and sat back on her haunches. The tile of her mother's bathroom floor was cold on her bare feet.

A tap on the door. "You okay, Nessa?"

No, I'm not okay! I'm pregnant! "I'm fine," she said.

"I'll get you some crackers and Fresca. That'll make you feel better."

She hated Fresca.

She scooted back against the wall, letting her head be cushioned by the orange bath towel hanging from a bar. Last night had been so nice, she'd actually forgotten she was pregnant. Yet it hadn't been without its own crises. She'd learned that her father had secret girlfriends, he had been unfaithful when he'd been married to her mother, and he'd been the one to kick her out of their lives. Those three revelations were enough to mess up any person's life, much less waking up only to race to the bathroom to barf.

What was with morning sickness anyway? What purpose did it serve?

It reminds you what a fool you were to sleep with Bruce, that you've totally screwed up your life.

Then she remembered it was Saturday—she wasn't home, at her father's. She couldn't remember the last time she hadn't gone home for the weekend. *He'll make me feel so guilty. . . .*

Her mother interrupted her thoughts. "I have those crackers, Nessa. Come out and greet the world."

A few cuss words came to mind, but she kept them to herself. She got to her feet and opened the door.

Mother held out a saltine. "You look awful."

She grabbed the cracker and shoved it in her mouth as she

headed for the living room. "I gotta go."

Her mother trailed after her. "But it's Saturday. You don't have class. I thought we'd spend the day together."

Vanessa folded the crocheted afghan that had kept her warm on the couch. "Thanks for the offer, but no thanks."

"But Harry and I were thinking of going to a movie—that *One Flew Over the Cuckoo Clock*. We'd love to have you join us."

"It's 'Cuckoo's Nest,' but no thanks." She sat on the edge of a cushion to put on her sandals.

"I'll call you later and we can do dinner."

She grabbed her purse and made for the door. "I won't be here."

Her mother strong-armed the door, preventing her from opening it. "Where will you be?"

It was easier just to tell the truth. "I know you don't approve, but I need to go into Atlanta. Daddy's having a dinner party tonight. He wants me to be hostess."

"But you're a college student with your own life. He shouldn't expect—"

"It's okay. I want to do it."

"You baby him. He's a big boy."

"He needs me."

Her mother shook her head. "Are you going to tell him about seeing me?"

"No!" She hadn't meant to be so adamant. "At least I don't think so."

"You should, Nessa. It would be a big step."

"I don't know. . . ."

Her mother sighed deeply. "There you go, choosing him again."

"I'm not choosing—"

"Sure you are." She stepped away from the door, giving Vanessa access. "I should have known you'd go running back to your old life. I despise the control he has over you, the way he uses guilt to manipulate you."

"He doesn't manipulate me. But I made a commitment to help and I need to follow through." Her father's past words haunted her: *"You're weak in that department, Vanessa. You have a tendency to fall short, to bow out of the final goal."*

Mother opened the door. "Whatever. Go ahead."

Although Vanessa didn't feel up to arguing, there was no way she could leave. She closed the door. "What's got into you? You take care of me last night, but this morning you're all over me."

"I thought we were starting something here—you and me. I didn't think you'd run back to the status quo so quickly. I thought at this point in your life you might choose me. Choose us."

"It's not about choosing."

"Of course it is. Life's about choosing. When we divorced, when the judge asked your opinion, you chose your father because he always gave in to you, bailed you out of every trouble you had, then made you feel guilty if you didn't pay him back with undying servitude. You didn't choose me because I'm independent and strong, and I'd make you work for your dreams. Life isn't worth much without work, Nessa. A life without work makes dreams null and void."

"I'm not going home to get Daddy to bail me out of anything. I'm helping him with a dinner party."

Mother took a step away from the door. "You know what? I'll share a life lesson with you. All in all, the divorce was a good thing. It forced me to find myself. That's what I want you to do. Divorce yourself from your daddy's influence and find the true Vanessa that he keeps under wraps. Don't blindly accept who your father thinks you are—or who he wants you to be. He's pulling the same trick on you that he did on me. He tried to change me into *his* image of a corporate wife. Since that didn't work, he's trying to change you into being the perfect corporate daughter."

"I like being hostess."

She made a face. "And I like going to the dentist."

Vanessa couldn't think of anything else to say. Her mother put a hand on her arm. "Yardley Pruitt is not the father you should be following, Nessa. Don't let him mold you to his image. There's a heavenly Father who deserves that job, and with Him being molded is a privilege."

The last thing Vanessa wanted was a Jesus speech. She kissed her mother's cheek. "I'll call you tomorrow."

"Stand up to him, Nessa. Stand up for yourself."

Atlanta

During the twenty-minute drive from her mother's house to her father's home in the Buckhead section of Atlanta, Vanessa tried to rehearse her excuses for not coming home the night before. Her thoughts couldn't settle on one lie, much less a believable string of them.

And lies were needed because her father would never accept the truth that she'd spent the evening with his ex-wife, *her* fiancé, and a black man with a to-die-for smile whom his daughter felt an attraction to that went beyond friend.

But what about all *his* lies? Should she confront him? The idea of calling down Yardley Pruitt was not pleasant. She knew he'd flip anything she said until the conversation was about her faults, her sins.

Sins. Maybe she was being too hard on him. Maybe he'd told the lies to protect her. Maybe he hadn't strayed that far from what any loving father would do.

She finally turned on the radio, dialed past "Philadelphia Freedom" and "Fifty Ways to Leave Your Lover" and landed on "My Eyes Adored You."

"Though I never laid a hand on you. . ."

Interesting how Lewis's eyes came to mind.

Vanessa turned off her car and headed up the front walk. Yardley Pruitt met her at the door, his baby blue leisure suit making her think of Easter eggs. He tapped his watch. "We have a lot to do."

She was more than willing to focus on his "to-do" list, hoping it would keep him from asking questions she couldn't answer. She reached the threshold and kissed his cheek. "How many are coming for dinner?"

He moved to the living room, toward a piece of paper on the desk. "Just one. The owner of a construction company who's going to be the general contractor for the bank's new building."

Vanessa couldn't imagine her father hobnobbing with any construction guy. Especially not if he was hiring him. Daddy socialized with his peers—or better. Not with worker men. She chose her words carefully. "If you've already hired him, then why are we trying to impress him?"

He slapped the list on his hand. "He's not just any contractor, he's one of the best. He's been on many best-contractor lists and has won awards."

Whoop-de-doo.

"Remember this, Vanessa. If you want someone to do a good job for you, then pull out all the stops to show him who you are and what you expect. Make them want to do your bidding. Make them want your respect."

It sounded reasonable.

"Besides, if he does a good job on the bank, then I'd like to team up with him on a few other projects I have brewing."

Ah. She knew the truth would come out eventually. Daddy had a need and had found a way to fill it.

The phone rang and he answered it. But the way he gave Vanessa a quick glance and then turned his back on her made her radar scream.

"No. No. That's not a good idea. . . . I don't care what you think."

His nasty tone. The attempt at secrecy. Suddenly Vanessa listened with new ears. She tapped him on the shoulder, and when he turned around, she took the phone away from him.

"Vanessa? What are you—?"

She put the phone to her ear. "Hello?"

"Nessa?"

"Mother?"

"Yes, it's me. I needed to call, to let him know that we—"

Daddy tried to regain control of the phone, but with a turn of her body, Vanessa managed to keep it. "Hold on." She covered the receiver with a hand and felt a surge of energy. "Daddy, I want to take this call. If you'll excuse me a minute?"

She had never, ever seen her father's jaw drop and wasn't sure she liked seeing it now. Frankly, it made him look way too human. And when his hands clenched and his feet fidgeted, she realized he truly didn't know what to do.

She turned her attention back to the phone. "Yes, Mother, I'm here. What did you say?"

"I wanted to apologize for giving you a hard time this morning—not that anything I said wasn't true, but I refuse to turn into a demanding parent. You have one of those and one is enough."

She had that right. Her father had discarded his shocked look and was glaring at her, arms crossed. "I appreciate that, Mother."

"And as for telling your father about us. . .sorry. I just couldn't risk you *not* telling him. I've got you back in my life and I'm not going to let you go, and the only way for that to happen is to shove it out in the open. You're too important to me, honey."

She turned her back so her father couldn't see the tears in her eyes. "Me, too."

"As far as the other decisions in your life. . .you're a big girl and you'll have to make your own choices, but I beg you to keep your eyes open. You know more truth now than you did the last time you were home. Don't let your father pull a veil over your eyes. See things clearly. That's all I ask."

Realizing the fact that someone truly trusted her decisions was a new experience.

Daddy tapped his watch again.

"I have to go, Mom."

"Mom. Not Mother. I like that."

Vanessa hadn't consciously made the change. But she liked it, too.

"One last thing. Will you be coming to church with us in the morning? I know Lewis would love to see you."

The feeling was mutual. But the logistics of being up late with the dinner party, then driving home early. . . "We'll see."

"Your choice, dear girl."

Dear girl.

Her father's jaw had tightened to the point of stone. "I have to go. Thanks, Mom."

"I love you, Nessa."

"Me, too."

She hung up and faced her father. She could feel her heart in her chest.

"How dare you! How long has this been going on?" he asked.

She wished she could have said years. *Let's see how he likes secrets.* But instead she said, "I ran into her the other day." She swallowed. "We've had some nice talks."

Was that a flicker of fear she saw or was she only hoping? Then without warning, he covered his eyes with a hand. His shoulders slumped. "I can't believe you'd betray me like this."

"I'm not be—"

He stumbled to the couch, putting his head in his hands. "After all I've done for you. After all we are to each other."

She sat beside him, a hand on his back. "None of that has changed, Daddy. I'm still here, aren't I? Just because I talk to Mom now and then doesn't mean anything has changed between us." It was a lie.

He turned and stared at her. "What's gotten into you?"

Two words popped out. "The truth." Had she actually said that?

The tears were replaced with a snicker, and he stood. "My, my. A few days in the presence of Dorian and you're corrupted. Why am I not surprised?"

The word *corrupted* pushed her button. Her mother was probably the most uncorrupt person she'd ever met. She pulled a needlepoint pillow into her lap. "Why did you tell me *she* left *us*?"

"She did."

"Only because you kicked her out."

"I do not *kick* anyone."

"You forced her out. Because she was too much of a free spirit for your corporate-climbing agenda, because she wouldn't let you stifle who she was. Because. . .because she wouldn't wear that awful orange dress with the flower pin."

"What orange dress?"

Vanessa wished she hadn't mentioned it. "Forget the dress."

His smile was victorious. "No, no. Obviously the dress is the key to all your mother's grievances against me."

"Daddy. . ."

He began to pace in the space between them. "I think it's important we deal with this dress issue. I have always been a wonderful provider, and during our last year together I was rising to an even greater position which would bring your mother more money, more orange dresses, and more jewelry. Yet she complains because I wanted her to be a part of my journey?"

"She. . .you wanted her to change."

"Change back into the woman I married. Talk about betrayal. . .your mother betrayed what we had when she became a beatnik, a—"

"Beatnik?"

"Precursor to the hippies. Out of the blue she became my enemy, treating me as if I was a horrible person because I liked money, didn't want to grow my hair long, and wouldn't go to some sit-in for whales in Antarctica. She was ruining everything we had, so—"

"You kicked her out."

"I gave her the option of changing and staying, or holding

on to her flower-child lifestyle and leaving. It was her choice."

Vanessa bit the tip of the pillow. How could he make black white, and white black? She thought of another point. "She's been trying to contact me for years. She called; she sent letters. I don't know how you did it, but you've intercepted every one. Why? And why have you always told me she wanted nothing to do with me; she didn't love me?"

He sat beside her. "There, there. It was for your own good. And see? I was right. Contact with your mother has done nothing but stir you up. Where's the good in that?" He pulled her under his arm. "You were a confused teenager. You didn't need the complication of a divisive maternal influence in your life. You needed me and I needed you. The two of us are enough for each other, aren't we?"

At the same time she accepted his hug, she found that his words made her want to break free of all contact. It's not that they weren't the right words—they were exactly the right words. That was the problem. As usual, no matter what the subject, no matter what the argument, Yardley Pruitt was able to turn the situation around to suit himself, to make himself the victor or victim, whichever suited the moment.

He pulled her head to his cheek. "Enough of this. Let's let the past die and move into the present. Into the future. Besides, we really need to get going with the tasks of the day." He sat back to look at her, still holding the list, smiling his best smile. "How about I let you use my Corvette for the errands?"

That would be cool. He never let her use—

She sat up. "No!"

"You don't want to use the Corvette?"

She ran a hand across her face. "No, I mean yes, I'd love to use your car, but that's not the point."

He stood. "You're right. The point is that time is getting away from us, but if we both get going and work hard—"

The thought became words. "What about the women?"

He froze. "Excuse me?"

She stood but didn't move closer. "You were unfaithful to Mom. And you have girlfriends now. Girlfriends I know nothing about."

"That's none of your business, Vanessa."

She realized he hadn't denied it. Any of it. If her mother was right about this, maybe she was right about all of it—no matter what smooth patter her father handed out.

She took a chance. "Why doesn't your girlfriend handle the hostess duties? Why do you make me come home every weekend?"

"Oh, that's right," he snickered. "You have better things to do at college. Like get pregnant and ruin both our lives."

She couldn't move. Couldn't talk. She'd been defeated by a master. She had no power at all.

He came close and lifted her chin. "You made a huge mistake—I've even made a few myself—but the key is to do what you can to make the mistakes go away."

Make the baby go away.

He kissed her forehead. "You can take care of that particular mistake on Monday. Today, we have other items on our list."

Her breath left her. An abortion lowered to the position of groceries and booze on a "to-do" list?

He put his arm around her and led her toward the kitchen, talking all the way. She hadn't the strength to break free of his control.

But she wanted to. She really wanted to.

And that was progress.

Vanessa knew she wasn't being a very good hostess. Not that the table wasn't set to perfection. Not that she didn't remove the plates from the left and serve from the right. Her lack of perfection came in regard to the conversation. No matter how hard she tried, she couldn't concentrate on what her father and this contractor, this David Stancowsky, were saying.

Actually, most of the time she wasn't expected to. When they talked of her father's bank building, she knew she was free to let her mind wander. But not too far. At any moment she might be asked a question, and if she wasn't careful she would look as dumb as she often did in class when a teacher interrupted a daydream. It had happened once already when her father had asked her to serve more coffee. From the tight look on his face, she knew it wasn't the first time he'd asked.

When she finished pouring and offering Mr. Stancowsky the cream and sugar, he drew her into the conversation. "And how is college going, Miss Pruitt?"

She glanced at her father, hoping he wouldn't share her academic failings.

No such luck.

"Vanessa has trouble reaching her full potential."

She felt herself blush but was relieved when Mr. Stancowsky said, "A common problem, I'm afraid. Myself included."

He smiled at her. She smiled back, vowing to pay attention to every word this man said. Then, out of nowhere, she said, "Actually, I was thinking of quitting school."

Her father choked on his coffee.

A surge of pleasure flowed through her and she knew what

it was: power. So this is how her father felt when he dropped a bombshell, when he took over a conversation.

His face was red. "No daughter of mine is going to quit school. If you need me to go to the dean, to your teachers, I'll go. I'll fix it like I've always fixed it, but you will not—I repeat—will not quit school. You can't."

"I can." And with those words she knew it was true. She had choices—in regard to all her life. Not just school.

David patted the table between them. His voice was a calm ripple compared to her father's roar. "A long time ago, I heard a woman say this, and for some reason it's stuck with me: 'Just because you can doesn't mean you should.' "

She was stunned. "That's my mother's favorite saying."

Her father harrumphed. "Baloney to that. Those who can should."

She let the two men discuss the semantics and let her mind apply the wisdom of it. The words had been an elixir to her confusion. The point was she *could* quit. She *could* have the baby. She *could* have a relationship with her mother. And even Lewis. . . Life was suddenly full of possibilities. The question was, should she take them?

Her father sat back in his chair, shaking his head. "Forgive me, David, but I don't think that's the kind of advice you should be giving to an ignorant child."

"I'm not a child, Father."

David smiled. "No indeed. And I can see she's far from ignorant." He fingered the handle of his coffee cup, giving her his eyes. "Don't give up on school, Vanessa. Figure out what's wrong and fix it."

Her father put his napkin on the table. "That's what I said. I'll go fix—"

"No!" That one word took all her air. She took a fresh breath. "I'll fix it." She stood, half expecting her legs to buckle. When they did not, she said, "Would you like me to freshen your coffee, Mr. Stancowsky?"

He winked at her. "That would be nice."

When her father and David withdrew to the den to go over blueprints, Vanessa quickly cleared the table, settled things with the cook, and escaped upstairs to bed. At eleven fifteen she heard a tap on her bedroom door. She did not answer it. And when the door opened and her father peered in, she pretended she was asleep.

There was only so much courage a girl could display in one day.

Dawson—1987

Lane and Brandy stood side by side at the bathroom sink. Lane leaned toward the mirror, her mouth open as she put on mascara, while Brandy tried to tame her hair. "It's hopeless," she said.

Lane returned the wand to the tube. "What's hopeless?"

"My hair, my makeup, my everything." She took Lane by the shoulders and stood behind her, glaring into the mirror. "Look at you. Against my advice you get yourself a tomboy cut in the land of long permed curls and big bangs, and you look magnificent. My hair looks like I put my finger in a light socket."

"Next time you'll have to go to a salon for a perm. It's partly my fault. I'm not very good at rolling."

"Sure, next time I have an extra thirty bucks sitting around, I'll splurge." She leaned her chin on Lane's shoulder, looking at both their reflections. "Life's not fair."

Lane hated when Brandy was pessimistic, but couldn't argue. Her friend *did* seem to get more than her share of bad breaks. Lane tried to do what she could to even things out. Luckily, Brandy had moved beyond fighting the charity of it, accepting it as an act of sisterhood.

Lane rummaged through her makeup bag. "Want to try this new lip gloss? Toby says it tastes like watermelon."

"And who, in my case, will care?"

Never mind.

They put the makeup away. "I did notice Simon Blalock looking at me funny the other day," Brandy said. "I think he wants me."

"Yuck."

"Hey, beggars can't be choosers."

"Don't put yourself down. You know I hate that. Someday you'll find the perfect man who will adore you, you'll have tons of kids, and be ecstatically happy."

Brandy ran the water, cleaning out the sink. "I doubt it. I is what I is, Lane."

"You're beautiful—to me. And you're my very best friend."

Brandy put the hairspray under the sink. "That I am. Are you ready? The world awaits."

Lane guessed it wasn't a good time to bring up the fact that she was engaged. . . .

⊶

Lane was just settling into her desk in German class when Brandy stormed in, slammed her backpack onto her seat, and faced her. "How could you?"

Lane glanced around the room and was really glad Herr Schallert wasn't around yet. "Shh! How could I what?"

"Get engaged without telling me!"

"You're engaged?" Laurie Baker asked from two rows away.

"Uh. . .yes, but—" Within moments, Lane was surrounded by the girls in the room. The boys faced forward.

"When are you getting married?"

"How did Toby ask you?"

But before Lane could answer, Brandy grabbed her backpack. "I'm outta here."

"Brandy. . ." Lane had no choice but to follow.

She ran into the teacher on his way in. "Where are you going, Fraulein Holloway?"

Brandy turned the corner at the end of the hall. Lane had to hurry. "Emergency, Herr Schallert. I'm sorry. I'll come in after school and talk to you." She didn't wait for him to argue with her.

Lane heard the push bar of the front door and saw Brandy running down the steps. She ran after her. "Brandy! Stop!"

Brandy turned and walked backward. "Why should I?"

"Because you owe me."

That stopped her. Brandy set her jaw and strode toward her. "Don't worry. I'll never impose on your family—"

Lane took her arm. "Stop. Please. I'm sorry. I didn't mean it like that."

"How did you mean it?"

Good question. "You're my best friend. We owe it to each other to listen to each other."

Brandy pointed a finger in her face. "We owe it to each other to share important events firsthand and not hear them from a third party. A sixth, seventh, eighth party."

"Who told you?"

"Lyla Jenkins."

"Who's that?"

She spread her hands. "My point is made."

Lane let her backpack fall to the ground. "Toby must be telling everybody."

"Wasn't he supposed to?"

"I. . .I don't know. We didn't talk about how to tell people."

"Or *if* you should tell people, in my case."

"I would've. But when you came last night, and then this morning. . .it didn't seem the right time." Brandy eyed her in that knowing way she had. "Don't look at me like that."

Brandy slipped her hand through Lane's arm. "I know what we need."

Every time Lane saw the sign for Olson's Ice Cream Shoppe, she was bothered by the two *p*'s. She realized they were there to make it sound old and quaint, but considering the oldest thing in the place was Mr. Olson—and he was more quirky than quaint—it seemed fake. Put on. As an actress she was all for pretending, but she also knew that in order for the illusion to be a success, it had to *seem* real. Olson's soda-fountain equipment and white ice-cream tables and chairs tried too hard.

But the ice cream was super, and the shop was a favorite spot of farmers and local families, plus the occasional stranger passing through on the way to the Twin Cities.

Since it was only ten o'clock, the place had just opened. A family of three sat at a table; the daughter of five or six was pouting with folded arms and a big lip, even though she had a dish of ice cream in front of her.

Mr. Olson was refilling the chocolate-sauce container. "Shouldn't you girls be in class?"

"Study hall," Brandy said. "French vanilla in a sugar cone, please."

Lane had to laugh. "Dozens of flavors and you choose vanilla?"

"French vanilla."

Mr. Olson looked up from his scooping. "It's one of the top choices. What'll you have, Lane?"

She looked through the glass at the tubs. "You got a new one. Cookies and Cream. I'll try that."

They got their cones and sat at a table by the window. Once they'd taken their first bites, Brandy asked, "So tell me why you don't want to marry Toby."

Lane got some ice cream on the tip of her nose. "Brandy!"

She shrugged. "That's the only explanation I can figure for you not telling me, not calling me the minute after it happened, gushing with the news."

"You're way off. Of course I want to marry him. I've always wanted to marry him."

"Even if you shouldn't?"

"Don't start. Mom and Dad love him."

"More'n you."

"That's not true."

Lane saw the woman at the other table glance at them. The father was arguing with the daughter, who still refused to eat. But the woman appeared to be listening—to the girls.

"Your mom and dad would love anyone who's *known.* And they've known Toby's family forever. Your dad plays Whist with his dad. If you marry Toby they know you'll stick around

Dawson. That's their goal."

"And what's yours?"

Brandy took a swipe around her entire cone before leaning forward to answer. "I want to sit in a theater and see Lane Holloway on a screen twenty feet tall. I want to see you at the award shows wearing long sparkly gowns, posing for the cameras. I want you to have the chance to kiss Richard Gere and Sly Stallone, not just Toby Bjornson."

It sounded good to Lane, too. "But you said you didn't know what you'd do if I left town."

Brandy bit into her cone. A piece fell onto her lap. "Small-town life is great. But for some people, it's not enough. It's not enough for you."

Suddenly, the little girl at the other table flung her bowl of ice cream across the room. It narrowly missed Lane's shoulder, landing on the floor between her and Brandy.

"Rachel Lynn Caldwell!" The father grabbed the girl by the arm and marched her outside.

The mother sped toward the mess. "I'm so sorry, so sorry. . . ."

Mr. Olson came to the rescue with towels. When he took the debris away, the woman stood, wiping her hands on a napkin. "I've asked you to forgive my daughter, but I need to ask you to forgive me on another count. For eavesdropping. Did I hear that you are engaged?"

"Just."

"Aren't you. . .kind of young?"

Lane sat up straighter, as if that made her look older. "We're both seniors."

Brandy chimed in. "She shouldn't marry him. She's a great actress. She needs to go to Hollywood."

The woman glanced out the window, where the girl was getting a scolding from her dad. When she looked back, she nodded at Brandy. "You said life in a small town is great, but for some people it isn't enough?"

"Yeah, that's right," Brandy said.

"Though I haven't thought about it in a long time, I remember my mother saying, 'Just because you can doesn't mean you should.' Not that I've heeded that advice much. . ." She looked out at her family again, and her face suddenly looked weary and old. She looked back. "Nothing wrong with marriage and family and staying put in your hometown. But do it for the right reasons."

There was a tap on the window. The husband crooked a finger at his wife. They could barely make out his words. "Vanessa? Come on."

"I have to go. Good luck, girls."

Brandy and Lane watched the family walk down the sidewalk.

"Whoa," Brandy said. "That was cool."

Lane licked a drip off her hand. "Weird."

"But right. That lady was right on. Just because you *can* marry Toby doesn't mean you should. Unlike some of us, you've got options."

"There you go again, putting yourself down."

"There I go again, talking sense. Hey, I know the limitations of my life. I accept them—unless you got an extra miracle lying around."

"Sorry. Fresh out."

Brandy evened off the top of the cone. "Just think about the marriage thing. No need to rush. Now I really wish you'd gone to that audition in the Cities."

"Me, too."

Brandy wiped off a drip on the table. "At least you've got *Romeo and Juliet*. You're a shoo-in for that part."

Oh dear. That was the other thing she hadn't told Brandy.

"You did try out, didn't you?"

Lane ate her cone.

"Why not?"

It was going to sound lame. "Toby wanted me to spend more time with him, and then Melissa Peterson—"

"I'll skip the first reason and zoom to the second. Nothing Melissa Peterson says should have any bearing on life as we know it." She stood and tossed her cone in the trash. "We're going back right now and you're going to talk to Mr. Dobbins, and try out, and—"

"It's too late. The cast list is supposed to go up today."

Brandy snatched Lane's cone and tossed it after hers. "Then we'd better hurry."

The lips of the righteous nourish many,
but fools die for lack of judgment.
PROVERBS 10:21

Present-Day Kansas City

Mac closed the door to his office. He wished it had a lock. He didn't want to talk to anybody. He just wanted to be left alone.

He hadn't meant to say it. And the ironic thing was that it wasn't the truth. But yesterday morning the answer had slipped out after he'd spent the night worrying about the effects of Cheryl's "He's my boyfriend" statement.

When the reporter had caught him at his car and had asked, "Are you and Dr. Nickolby involved romantically?" he'd said, "No. We're just friends."

No wonder Cheryl had not returned his calls. His pages at the hospital. His E-mails. His knocks on her door. It had been thirty-six hours since he'd seen her, talked to her, touched her. He was in pain.

And how was he supposed to answer his son when Andrew continued to ask where Cheryl was? The boy loved her. *He* loved her. He wanted to marry her. Why had he been such a wimp?

It didn't help that Wriggens was mad at him. His boss didn't care about the truth, he was just concerned with what the press *perceived* as the truth. And his comment to Mac, "Why couldn't you keep your hormones in check?" was an insult to what he and Cheryl had.

Had? Past tense?

The by-product of his personal upheaval was that he truly didn't care what happened on the Toby-Yardley-Dina front. Let the whole world talk to the press. What did he care? And yet, handling this was his job.

He turned on the television, hoping some world crisis had usurped any Time Lottery coverage. Unfortunately, the world had behaved itself. Toby Bjornson was on yet another talk show. How many was this? He'd been working on his fifteen minutes of fame for three days now. What else could the man possibly say? He was far from eloquent. "Uh, yeah" seemed to be his credo.

The interviewer leaned close to Toby, crossing her legs. "I would really like your reaction to the latest news regarding your Laney."

News? Mac felt as confused as Toby looked. He turned up the volume.

"Uh, sure. What news?"

"We've heard that Ms. Holloway's true reason for going back to Dawson, Minnesota, in 1987 is not to rekindle her relationship with you, but to explore what would have happened if she had not gone to the national audition that landed her the part of Bess in *Empty Promises*, the part that made her a star."

Toby's jaw hung low.

"You didn't know?"

He shook his head.

Mac slapped the credenza. "No!"

The reporter feigned concern, touching Toby's knee. "I'm so sorry. I know this must be a blow."

Toby's head was shaking like a dog in a car window. "It can't be true. She loves me."

The reporter broke for a commercial. Chicken.

Mac slapped the TV into silence. How had the information leaked? He was glad he hadn't told Cheryl. He didn't want to deal with that kind of suspicion on top of their other problems.

Only three people knew Lane's secret: Mac, Dr. Rodriguez, and—

Mac nearly upset his chair on his way out of his office.

"How could you?"

Wriggens was on the phone. "I'll call you back." He hung up and faced Mac. "I suggest you calm down and lower your voice."

Mac closed the door—which would take care of only one of Wriggens's concerns. He stood at his desk. "Why did you tell the press Lane's secret? And don't you dare deny it."

Wriggens sat back in his chair, the epitome of nonchalance. "Why would I deny it? It's a stroke of marketing genius—if I do say so myself."

"Genius? I gave Lane my word."

"Conditions changed. Your word was no longer applicable."

"Applicable? Since when is a promise applicable?"

"Since that moron Toby has managed to stay in the news."

"But Lane didn't want the world to know she is exploring a

life devoid of fame. She didn't want them to think she doesn't appreciate the success that *they* have made possible."

"Yes, yes, she *will* have to deal with that *if* she comes back, but I decided she'd rather deal with that than a lovesick nobody who might prove to be a menace. That guy's trouble. I can feel it. He had to be stopped."

"At the expense of Lane's career."

Wriggens flipped a hand. "Oh please. If she can't handle a few questions about her motives for going back to 1987, then she's not as good an actress as we thought."

Mac was sick of the whole thing. And he was especially sick of dealing with Wriggens. The man was ruthless. "What if I arranged my own leak? A leak about a leak?"

Wriggens sat forward. "We have an arrangement, Mac. You deal with me as chief administrator—and all that entails—and I let you stay on indefinitely. Of course, if you're tired of your cushy job, feel free to leak away."

Mac loved his job. He was meant for this job. He wanted to keep this job. But he couldn't continue to do it with Wriggens in charge. The TTC deserved better.

"By the way. . ."—Wriggens had a horrible smile on his face—"I wouldn't push things if I were you. You haven't been the essence of ethics yourself. Sleeping with one of the winners?" He shook his head and made a *tsk-tsk* sound. "What got into you, Mac?"

There was nothing he could say about his relationship with Cheryl that this man wouldn't turn into something dirty. It didn't matter that all they'd ever done was kiss.

"I rest my case." Wriggens stood. "Now, if you'll excuse me?"

Mac let himself out.

This wasn't over. Somehow. Some way. . .

Santa Monica, California

Randy turned toward Brandy but pointed at the TV. "I hate the press. Hate them. Why can't they leave Lane alone?"

"This whole thing is a mess." Brandy pulled her feet onto the couch and tucked an afghan around them.

The phone rang and she picked up. It was a reporter. "As Ms. Holloway's personal assistant, what do you think about the latest news that she went back to give up her fame? How long has she been feeling this way?"

"No comment."

"But certainly she told you and those close to her of her true intention?"

"None of this is anybody's business. When I bought her the ticket—" Oops.

"You bought her the Time Lottery ticket?"

"Sure."

"Why did you think she needed a ticket?"

"I. . ." She looked to Randy. He mimed for her to hang up the phone. She was within a few seconds of doing so when she had the thought that maybe she could be of some help. After all, who knew Lane better than she? If she could word things right. . . "I bought the ticket for her wanting her to take another look at a past man in her life—and it wasn't Toby Bjornson."

"Who then?"

She saw a dark crevasse open before her. *Never mind.* She'd already said too much. So much for helping. "Uh-uh. I've changed my mind. You're not getting me to say. No comment."

"Then how about this question: Is it true that your life will be ruined if Lane doesn't come back? You've lived off her for seventeen years. You depend on her for your livelihood."

Brandy tossed the afghan aside, plenty warm now. "I've been her best friend since high school. I've been happy to work as her personal assistant—and be her friend—ever since she left Dawson. If she chooses not to come back, I will miss her terribly, but my life will not be ruined." She looked at Randy, who was shaking his head no, making a turn-the-key motion in front of his mouth. "I just so happen to be married to a wonderful man who—"

"Is it true your mother was a drunk and beat you?"

All breath left her. She hung up.

Vipers. All of them.

Long Island, New York

Millie watched the reporter on TV. Her name wasn't Millie anymore. Hadn't been for forty-six years. But suddenly, that name had come to life. And it scared her to death.

The TV reporter sat next to her father, Ray Reynolds, in a nursing home, holding a microphone toward the elderly man. Her father looked so frail. . . . "Yes, it's true my daughter, Millie, was headstrong. But no one loved her more than David. He would have made the perfect husband. He was so attentive and caring."

"She sounds like a handful. Hardly the perfect wife?" said the reporter.

"My Millie was strong-willed, and it often took both David and myself to make her see how things should be."

"Such as?"

Millie's mother, Rhonda Reynolds Grayson, pointed a

craggy finger at the screen. "How can you tolerate that, Tracy? It's a bunch of lies!"

Millie—who'd changed her name to Tracy a lifetime ago—shrugged, but in truth, it was starting to get to her. It had not been easy seeing David again as the winner of the Time Lottery, and it had almost made her skin crawl when he'd told the world he was going back to 1958 to stop the crash that had killed her.

Killed Millie Reynolds.

The crash that had borne Tracy Osgood Cummins.

She was shocked to discover that he had never married and was still pining for her. Yet it was proof that her initial desire to escape from David's obsessive, all-encompassing domain had been a wise one.

"They're making him out to be a legend," Millie's mother said. "It's sickening."

"He *was* a good man," Millie said. "He had the makings of a great businessman. That was never the issue."

"Freedom was the issue. For you—and for me."

Millie moved to her mother and hugged her from behind. She never could have pulled off her "death" had it not been for her mother's cooperation. Rhonda was the perfect coconspirator, because back in 1958 no one ever would have suspected Rhonda Reynolds of having a rebellious bone in her body. In public she'd appeared to be the obedient, complacent fifties wife. June Cleaver had nothing on Rhonda. Even Millie had believed the image—until her father and David had teamed up to make Millie his wife.

At first she *had* loved David—or at least been interested in him, though now, in hindsight, she realized her interest initially had stemmed from his. David had been intently responsive to all that encompassed Millie's life. He was different from any man she'd known. She'd been flattered, until she recognized his interest for what it truly was: controlling interference. The organizational, detail-oriented, totalitarian attributes that made David such an asset at Mariner Construction made him unbearable as a fiancé and future spouse. But to be fair, now Millie blamed part of her suffocation on the times. Being a woman of independent nature did not suit the complacent role of a woman in 1958.

And her father had to take his share of the blame. He and David had all but conspired to make her David's wife. They didn't care about her feelings as much as they cared about the business. It was as close to an arranged marriage as one could have in the twentieth century. And Millie would have rather died than go through with it.

Hence, her "death."

It had been quite a thrill when she'd pushed David's brand-new 1958 Pontiac Bonneville Sport Coupe with the "Wonderbar" a.m. radio; a sliding Plexiglas sun visor; a "Memo-Matic" power memory seat; Rochester "TriPower" triple, two-barrel carbure—

Why do I remember those details?

Because David had repeated them so many times. He was always well versed on all the details of his possessions.

Including me.

She shivered and forced her thoughts back to the car. Her revenge. Her escape. She'd taken great pleasure in pushing the car off the cliff, into the ocean. The fact they'd never found her body was a detail that was more easily accepted in the unsuspicious aura of that innocent time. And getting a new identity had been fairly simple without the added security of photo IDs and computers.

Her mother zapped the TV picture to oblivion and turned to face her. "You can't let them get away with this. You can't."

Millie looked at the blackened television. "Is this because of what's being said about me, or the fact that you saw Father again?"

Her mother also looked at the television, as if Ray's face were still on the screen. "Divorcing him was the best thing I ever did. I had thirty-two good years with Connor."

Her stepfather had died two years previous, but her mother still wore his picture in a locket. Theirs had been a sacrificial, giving love.

"I'm not sure what it will prove if I come forward," Millie said.

"It will prove that you were a strong woman who was willing to give up everything to escape a bad relationship. A huge step, considering the era. You'll be an inspiration to woman all over the world."

"I don't want to encourage other women to fake their deaths."

She shrugged. "It was the only way out. We both knew that."

"But what will David say if he comes back and hears the truth?" Millie asked.

"He's not coming back, honey. He jumped into 1958 to prevent your crash. Unless you managed to pull it off at a later date, he's thrilled and happy there."

"And I'm miserable. As his wife."

"Don't worry about that," she said. "It's his Alternity, not yours. You've had a wonderful life with Deke. And I wouldn't trade my redheaded grandchildren for anything."

Millie and Deke Cummins had two sons and a daughter, and now three granddaughters. Which reminded her. . . She looked at the clock. Deke and her son-in-law would be back any minute from golfing. It took snow or ice to keep those two from the course. And New York had plenty of both in January.

Her mother started to get up from the chair and Millie hurried to help her. "I'm going down for a nap, honey. You think about coming forward, all right?"

How could she do anything else?

Peachtree City

Yardley Pruitt shut off the television and threw the remote on the floor. "That's it! I can't take any more."

Vanessa's husband, Dudley, returned the remote to the coffee table. "It's best not to overreact. The press exaggerates."

Yardley began to pace in the Caldwell living room. "Any minute now, my dear ex-wife will get the Nobel Peace Prize. I think they've set a record in finding her past students and colleagues. I even saw the requisite neighbor 'She was such a nice person' interview."

His granddaughter, Rachel, looked up from the book she was reading on the outskirts of the room. "My grandmother sounds like a very nice person."

Yardley turned toward her. Honestly, he'd forgotten she was there. "The press can make anybody sound better than they were. Like that David Stancowsky. I wouldn't be surprised to hear he's up for some award, too."

She cocked her head. "They were pretty hard on Lane Holloway's ex. And one of the Time Lottery higher-ups is in trouble for having an affair with last year's winner."

She was missing the point. "Yes, yes. The press can do

that, too. They can do whatever they want, create their own form of the truth. But I could tell them a thing or two about Dorian—and even David Stancowsky."

Dudley straightened a pile of magazines. "You know him?"

"Mariner Construction built a bank building for me back in the seventies. At first I didn't get the connection, I was so wrapped up in the fact that Vanessa had won."

"Small world."

"Cruel world." Yardley resumed his pacing. "David Stancowsky is not the king of the business world. If I remember correctly, he didn't do that great a job. In fact, I don't think we even paid him in full because of it. The world should hear *that. That* would balance out the Saint David talk. I'm just as good a businessman as he is."

"Are you thinking about giving an interview?"

Yardley stopped near the phone. "I was thinking about it."

"You'd better be careful, Yardley. It's hard to be interviewed and have things come out as you plan. And afterward, the interviewer can put a spin on things and make—"

"Yes, yes. Are you implying they're smarter than I am?"

Yardley saw his son-in-law and granddaughter exchange a look. Then Dudley said, "Just be careful. And don't let them rile you."

"I assure you, I'll be the essence of restraint."

Rachel Caldwell retreated to her bedroom, glad to escape the presence of her father and grandfather. She could hardly wait until semester break was over and she could return to college. To independence. To *away*.

Usually dinners with Grandfather were a non-event. She'd

gotten the meek-and-mild routine down so well that they rarely asked her a question and most of the time truly forgot she was even there. But tonight, she'd been forced out of her cocoon by her grandfather's stupid ranting about the press. She didn't care about his connection with David Stancowsky, but for him to disparage the good press her grandmother was getting was petty.

She sprawled on the bed, getting comfortable on the blue-and-green comforter. When Rachel had first heard the glowing accounts of her grandmother's life she'd been skeptical. The new information was a complete one-eighty to everything she'd heard about Dorian Pruitt. Surely the press was wrong. But when the reports continued and intensified. . .her grandmother seemed like a cool lady. A woman of spunk and independence, brains and creativity. And people liked her, genuinely liked her. Rachel would have liked to meet her.

Now it was too late. She was dead. And Rachel would never know her.

But her mother would.

It wasn't fair. Right this minute her mother was back in the past, back to the time when *she* was twenty-one, Rachel's age. She was getting to spend time with Dorian.

Which meant there was no way Rachel's mother would come back to the future. No way she'd come back to *this* life, with her boring volunteer activities, and her boring family, with their boring dinners.

Mother and daughter were spending time together in the past.

Mother and daughter were *not* spending time together here in the present.

Never had.

Rachel turned onto her side. She couldn't remember the last time she and her mother had actually talked about anything important. Though, in truth, it was more her fault than her mother's. Rachel had embraced the frumpy, silent wallflower persona years ago. As her mother got more and more frenzied in her quest to become the matriarch of the volunteer-fundraiser set—or at the very least Saint Vanessa, doer of all good things—Rachel had vowed never to need anything, including any attention. Whatever people needed, her mother was intent on supplying. In response, Rachel became the opposite: a reverse-doer. Whatever her family wanted, she gave them the opposite. She wouldn't sacrifice any part of her life for them. It was her life.

What her family didn't know was that her wallflower image was only put on for their benefit—and their discomfort. Rachel knew how to wear makeup to perfection, had a stash of stylish clothes in the car, and had dozens of friends at school. She even had a boyfriend, though she was far from being to the point of wanting him to meet her family. Maybe, if the time became right, they'd elope. That would send her family into a proper tizzy. Like mother, like daughter.

Rachel suddenly noticed the pile of letters on her dresser, all nicely strapped with a rubber band. She'd found them the day her mom had left for her Alternity but had been so angry at her for leaving that she'd never looked at them. The fact her mother had *wanted* her to look was a sure way to make her *not* look.

But things had changed. As the positive information about her grandmother had come to light, Rachel's anger had been redirected at her grandfather. And since there were only a few more days before her mother came home—or didn't come home. . .

Rachel retrieved the letters and sat on the bed.

Atlanta

Yardley was impressed at how quickly the interview was arranged. After all his elusive "no comment" statements, he assumed the media was ripe, ready to be squeezed into a wine of his own creation. And there had to be an advantage to being interviewed after the crowd of wannabes, knowing what everyone else had said, getting the chance to counter it.

He *was* disappointed that the interviewer and the cameraman didn't take his suggestion of having the interview in front of the fireplace in his home, but moved him to a chair in his den—one he never sat in, near the window. But he was willing to let them have their way on that detail. As long as he could control the rest of the interview.

They were just about to start when Yardley heard the front door open and heard Rachel's voice: "Grandfather?"

Great. He did not need his dowdy granddaughter to be seen by the news crew. If for some bizarre reason they wanted to interview her, he'd be mortified and humiliated. Rachel had the personality and presence of a chair. An old, threadbare chair.

She came into the den. At least he assumed it was Rachel. Her hair was styled, she was wearing makeup, and she sported a black blazer over a black turtleneck and slacks. "Rachel? What have you done to yourself?"

She ignored his question. "I see you didn't waste any time setting up your rebuttal."

The reporter—Jack Shamblin or Shandren?—looked up from his last-minute preparations. "And who is this?"

"This is my grand—"

"I'm Rachel Caldwell. I'm Vanessa Caldwell's daughter and Dorian Pruitt Cleese's granddaughter." She looked right at

Yardley. "Though *I* never had the pleasure of knowing her," she lifted a pack of letters, "until recently."

What does she mean by that?

Jack looked from Rachel to Yardley, then back. "Perhaps we should include you in the interview with your grandfather."

"No!" Yardley found himself standing and calmed himself. "No, thank you. I'd rather do this solo."

Jack looked at his watch. "I understand that, but we *would* like to hear from the daughter, and in the interest of time. . ." He motioned to a crew hand to bring another chair over. Within seconds, Rachel was ensconced next to her grandfather. She set the stack of envelopes she'd been carrying on the floor beside her.

The way she was smiling so smugly. . .Yardley wanted to call a time-out. Something wasn't right. Something was up. Every instinct told him it wasn't good. But he couldn't back out now, not when he'd made such a fuss to get this interview.

"Well then," Jack said, settling into the chair near Yardley. "Why don't we begin?" He turned to the camera, gave a signal, then smiled. "We're here today with Yardley Pruitt, the father of Time Lottery winner Vanessa Caldwell, and Rachel Caldwell, her daughter."

Yardley tried to ignore Rachel's presence and smiled into the camera. "I'm also the president of Fidelity Mutual Bank, a very successful regional institution. Perhaps you've heard our slogan: 'Fidelity Mutual Bank: We've Got Your Number.' We have a dozen branch—"

"Thank you, Mr. Pruitt. Your standing in the business community is well known. But today, what we'd really like to know is, when did you first realize you knew David Stancowsky?"

How rude. "When I kept hearing the name of his company over and over," he sighed, "and *over* on the news."

"Mr. Stancowsky is the CEO of Mariner Construction, an international, multibillion-dollar—"

Yardley's nerves were already on edge and this statement. . . "Yes, yes. We could all recite that in our sleep by now."

Jack's eyebrows rose. "So how do you know Mr. Stancowsky?"

"He built a bank building for me back in the seventies. Did a shoddy job of it, too. If memory serves, we ended up withholding money from him because of the workmanship."

"Perhaps we'll ask Mr. Stancowsky about it if he comes back."

"I could tell you more. I believe it had something to do with faulty concrete work in the parking lot."

Jack cleared his throat. "Let's move on and let you tell us about your ex-wife, Dorian Pruitt Cleese, the woman your daughter has traveled back in time to see. She sounds like an interesting woman."

Yardley did not let himself look at Rachel but let a snicker escape. "She was amazing all right. Amazingly stubborn. The empress of the hippies, she had absolutely no sense of propriety and decorum."

Another raised eyebrow. "How so?"

Yardley hadn't planned on citing any specific incidents and racked his brain for one. Rachel was leaning slightly forward as if she wanted to hear, too. "There was this one important dinner party at our home where she decided to go all organic. All natural. And she had on some weird folk music. Judy somebody and—"

"Judy Collins?"

"Whatever. The point is, by the end of the evening, she and the clients were all singing along to the record, drinking wine, having a grand old time."

"It sounds nice. What was the problem?"

They didn't include me. "Uh. . .it wasn't. . .appropriate."

Jack gave Yardley another incredulous look, causing him to quickly add more information. "No matter what I said to her, no matter how often I pleaded with her, Dorian would not do things my way, the proper way. She had a strange manner of looking at things, of approaching life."

"She won numerous teaching awards for her strange manner of looking at things, of approaching life. She was also active in many environmental causes."

This was not going well. He had to think of something else. . . . "Dorian left us to pursue her hippie lifestyle. She left Vanessa—who was a needy teenager—and me. And she showed absolutely no interest in us again."

"She never made contact?"

"Never." He put on his best pained expression. "It was tough raising a teenager alone."

He noticed Rachel open her mouth to speak. Jack must have, too, because he turned his attention her way. "Ms. Caldwell. Did you ever have a chance to meet your grandmother?"

"No, I didn't. At least not exactly." Rachel collected the stack of envelopes, placing them in her lap. She had the address side turned downward so Yardley couldn't see what they were. They looked like letters. What letters could have any bearing on this particular moment in—

With difficulty, he pried his hands off the armrests of the chair and placed them on his thighs.

"What have you brought with you?" Jack asked.

She slapped the pile. "These letters prove that my grandmother did not leave my mother willingly." She nodded toward Yardley. "*He* divorced *her*. And he kept my grandmother from having any contact with her daughter."

"And those letters are from whom?"

Yardley broke in. "I really don't see how this has any relevance—"

Rachel continued. "They are from my grandmother to my mother." She turned the stack over and showed the camera the addressed side. "See? 'Return to sender.' " She nodded toward Yardley. "He sent them all back. He was the one who kept mother and daughter apart. On purpose. He intercepted all phone calls, all visits. . . ."

Jack turned to him. "Is this true, Mr. Pruitt?"

He wanted to grab the letters away, throw them in the garbage. "There were extenuating circumstances."

"Such as?"

He couldn't think of any and had only repeated the line because he'd heard it said often—though he *did* have the uneasy feeling it was usually used by guilty parties when they were put on the spot. He stood. "This interview is over." He walked away, but his lapel mike pulled him back. He ripped it off.

Once in the hall, he realized he had no place to go. This was his house. These people were intruders. He should go back in the den and order them out.

But he stopped when he heard Jack continue the interview. "How did you get possession of these letters, Ms. Caldwell?"

He was doomed. He hurried upstairs and locked himself in his bedroom. They'd all pay for this. They could count on that.

It was unfortunate that the windows in Yardley Pruitt's bedroom faced the back of the house. He'd heard commotion downstairs—doors opening and closing, people coming and going. He'd heard the sound of car engines. He put his ear to the door. Had everyone finally gone?

Had Rachel gone?

He never wanted to see her again. Only grandchild or no only grandchild, she'd sealed her fate with her betrayal. He'd call his lawyer in the morning and have his will changed.

But wait. He needed to see if Vanessa came back before he did that. Who knew if there would be *any* Caldwell women listed in Yardley Pruitt's will?

Actually, he hoped Vanessa *did* come back. It would prove that life with Mommy dearest wasn't what it was cracked up to be. It would prove that she chose him, that life here was ideal and better than anything science could create. It would prove he was a good father.

He leaned against the door. Scratch that.

He was a horrible father. Or at least that's what the world would think. He didn't know why he'd returned all Dorian's letters or why he hadn't let Vanessa see her. But when the first letter had come, he'd impulsively sent it back, which had started a pattern that he hadn't been able to break. Because to suddenly let the two of them communicate would have allowed them to compare notes, and Vanessa would have found out the truth about who left whom.

The truth he'd kept hidden for over thirty years.

He thought he heard a sound. He whipped open the door. "Rachel?"

He moved to the railing overlooking the stately foyer and perked up his ears. Nothing but silence—and the faint ticking of the grandfather clock marking the passing of time.

Bangor

Dina Edmonds stirred the spaghetti sauce and watched the news. But as soon as she heard what Yardley Pruitt said about David. . .

"Liar!" She shook the spoon at him, making sauce splatter across her cupboards.

The mess didn't matter. She couldn't let this go unchallenged. She grabbed her coat and purse.

⁂

Dina chastised herself for not remembering sooner that Mariner Construction had done work for Yardley Pruitt. Until now. Until this. She usually was so good at remembering jobs, even dates and contract amounts.

She hoped it wasn't because she was getting old.

Yet the details *had* streamed back as soon as she'd heard Yardley's interview. The number $52,384 came to mind. . .

She set her purse and coat on a waiting-room chair and made a beeline for the old file cabinets in the storeroom. The file drawers were in chronological order. She thought the job was 1974 or 1976.

1976.

She took the file back to her desk. It had been a bank building in Atlanta. One of Mariner's first buildings outside the Northeast region. Dorian seemed to remember David or Ray Reynolds mentioning that the head of Fidelity Mutual was the friend of a friend of a friend who liked the idea of using someone out of state. Dina remembered thinking how odd it was that people often looked far away for experts when there often were some right next door. What was that pithy definition? *"A professional is someone who carries a briefcase and lives at least forty miles away."* Or a dozen states away. . .

She flipped through the yellowed pages, her mind skipping back over three decades. Pruitt had said he'd withheld money due to shoddy workmanship. Mariner did not do shoddy workman—

Her finger pegged an amount. $52,384. The money *had* been withheld by Fidelity Mutual. However, it wasn't withheld for any workmanship issue but because Yardley Pruitt had said he didn't want to pay extra for five change orders he'd requested. Five upgrades in finishes.

"We threatened to take him to court," Dina told the room. She flipped a few pages and found further correspondence. Because they had signed change orders in their possession, Pruitt's lawyer had wisely gotten him to back down—after Pruitt tried to get out of paying by making the shoddy workmanship claim. Dina held up a check stub for the payment. In full. Proof Yardley Pruitt was a liar. Proof her David ran a respectable business.

But what should she do with the information? David would be back in a few days—at least she prayed he'd be back. What would *he* do to make things right?

Though David wasn't a vindictive man, and though his reputation spoke for him, he would not let the lie pass. He would issue a simple statement—worded ever so succinctly—that would prove Pruitt was mistaken. He *would* take care of it. *If* he came back.

Yet with the uproar over the three winners' return, would such a statement get lost in the media hype?

She stood, taking the check stub with her. She'd take care of it. It was her duty as David's most loyal employee. Most loyal friend. She wouldn't let him down. Now. Or ever.

Long Island

Millie had no idea how to go about breaking the news. She wasn't a public person. She'd never sought attention. And she wouldn't be doing this now if it weren't for Deke's support—she wouldn't be anything if it weren't for him. He'd saved her in 1958 and had continued to do so every day of their lives.

He sat beside her now on the couch, with the phone sitting in her lap. She was calmed by the way his arm and leg touched hers. A simple presence, never wavering.

"You don't have to do this, you know."

She looked at him. "I don't?"

He put his hand on hers. "Of course not."

"But Mom—"

"I love your mom to death, but she has an I-beam on her shoulder in regard to your father and David. I've always admired you because you don't."

"You admire me?"

He pulled her hand to his lips. "I adore you, Tracy. Millie."

She let her head tilt until it met with his. The past was past. Who cared what people thought about Millie Reynolds? She was dead.

Tracy Osgood Cummins was alive.

Tracy set the phone on the end table and turned her attention to the man beside her. Where it belonged.

Rhonda closed the door to her bedroom. She couldn't believe it! Her daughter wasn't going to call the press and tell them she was alive? Without that truth coming out, David and Ray would get away with the lies, with pretending they were attentive, loving, grieving men. Pretending they had a heart.

Rhonda knew better. David and her ex-husband didn't own a heart but shared a communal, stubborn, egotistical will that overshadowed and smothered anyone who came within their sphere. Rhonda had remained silent for forty-six years mainly because she'd been lovingly held in the kind embrace of Connor Grayson.

But now that her dear husband was gone, now that David Stancowsky and Ray Reynolds had burst onto the public scene, all her bitterness and hatred came flooding back. In the last few days, the thought of eking out a bit of revenge filled her up and made her come alive in a way she found both invigorating and disturbing. At age eighty-four, it was quite exciting.

She couldn't let Millie take that away from her. David might be coming back in a few days, and the chance would be lost. Or at least complicated. Best to do it now, before he came into the picture.

She looked at the phone on her bed stand. It called to her.

She answered.

When she was confronted with the reporter's question, Rhonda's mouth went dry.

"Ma'am? You said you had some information about David Stancowsky?"

Rhonda cleared her throat. "Actually, I have information about his fiancée." The words gained momentum. "Millie Reynolds, the woman he went back to 1958 to save from a car—"

"Crash. Yes. What about her?"

Here goes. "She's alive."

Silence.

Rhonda tried again. "Did you hear me? Millie Reynolds is alive. She never died in that crash. It was all faked so David would leave her alone. She didn't want to marry him, but he was so possessive he wouldn't let her go."

"And how do you know all this?"

"I'm her mother."

So there.

Somewhere over the Midwest

"Can I get you anything to drink, sir?" asked the stewardess.

Toby knew they weren't called stewardesses anymore, but he couldn't remember the politically correct term. "No thanks. But I'd like a blanket and pillow."

Toby's seatmate poked him with an elbow. "Hey, drink up, man. You're a celebrity now. Certainly someone else is paying?"

Toby nodded, then shook his head. He'd done plenty of drinking and eating on someone else's tab the last few days. He couldn't believe the prices room service charged for a simple burger and fries, but the TV stations *had* told him to enjoy himself.

He was having some fun now.

The man next to him lowered his tray, ready for his drink and pretzels. "Bad break on that one interview. You know, the one where—"

"I know the one." He'd never forget the interview that had ruined his life and shattered all his hopes against a brick wall.

"Weird how Lane Holloway told the media she was

going back for you when she was really going back to *not* be famous. What's with that? It's my ten bucks at the movie theater that pays for her lifestyle, that helps her get twenty million per movie. And she wants a shot at *not* being famous?" He laughed and spread his hands, palms up. "Hey, welcome to my world." Another poke in the side. "Hey, yours, too now, right?"

Right.

"Don't feel bad for giving it a shot. I woulda done the same. But it might be hard going home. You think reporters are going to be camped out at your house?"

"I hope not." It was his biggest fear.

"I'd brace myself if I were you. You've opened Pandora's box, and there's no way you can close it up again."

Toby had no idea what Pandora's box was, but he got the gist of it.

And it wasn't good.

The stewardess brought his blanket and pillow. He turned his body toward the window and pulled a blanket over his shoulder—though he really wanted to pull it over his head.

"Hey, I getcha, man. I don't blame you for not feeling like talking. You have a right to be depressed, so have at it."

Don't mind if I do.

Long Island

Millie pulled the living-room curtain aside. "Deke. . ."

He was on the phone. "No comment!" He hung up and joined her at the window. "I don't know how they found out, but they did."

She pressed her fingers to her temples trying to think. No one knew her secret. No one.

She dropped her hands when a thought took hold: *Except Mom.*

She walked toward the hall leading to the bedrooms. "Mother!"

Rhonda came out of her room, the essence of innocence. "You called?"

Millie tried to be calm but found it impossible. "We have a yard full of reporters and we're getting calls. Somehow, they know I am David's Millie and I didn't die. How do they know that, Mom? How?"

Deke had slipped in behind her, and Millie saw her mother look in his direction, too. Gauging how united they were? Millie reached back and took her husband's hand. "Deke and I agreed it was best to let this go."

"I know. I heard. And I disagreed."

It took Millie a moment to let it sink in. "So you *did* call them? You *are* the leak?"

She took hold of the doorjamb leading to her room. "I most certainly am. It had to be told. The truth had to come out."

"It did not! Both of us—all of us—have lived happy lives without that particular truth ever being public knowledge."

"Speak for yourself."

"Mom!"

She rolled her eyes. "Fine, fine. I'll admit I've had a lovely life, but it galled me to hear Ray say you were strong-willed and headstrong—"

"I was."

"You still are. But they're making David out to be this attentive, grieving lover. They're making it sound like you caused your own death because of some character flaw, not because *he* forced you to do it to gain your freedom." She stepped toward Millie and placed a hand under her chin. "You were a hero to me, honey. So strong, so brave. You saved me as much as you saved yourself. I will always be grateful. Can I help it if I want the world to know what an amazing daughter I have?"

"Oh, Mom. . ." Millie hugged her, and they held each other until Deke brought them back to the present.

"What's done is done," he said. "I think you need to make a statement."

She looked toward the door. "Go out there?"

"I'll go with you," her mother said.

"Me, too," Deke said.

It was the only way. "Let's get it over with."

They moved to the front door. Deke put his hand on the knob. "Do you know what you're going to say?"

"Not a clue." She kissed him on the cheek. "Open it."

Bangor

Dina popped off the couch and loomed over her television.

Millie was alive?

One of the reporters asked, "But why would you fake your death and live under an assumed name for over forty years?"

Millie looked at the man next to her, who'd been introduced as her husband. They held hands. "David was a good man, but he was obsessive, insisting on having a say about every tiny aspect of my life from what perfume I wore to how I spent my free time. Though I loved him at first, I found myself being smothered by him."

"Then why not just call the marriage off?"

"You don't understand. . . . David worked for my father. They became close and my father, Ray Reynolds, who has also been interviewed lately, was intent on handing his business down to David. After all, I was unworthy of the task—being female and all. The best way to do that was to have David marry me."

"So the marriage was arranged for a business connection?"

"It certainly wasn't a love connection. Not on my part, and though he'd never admit it, not on David's part either. Obsession and possession do not equal love. The point was, with my father and David showing a united front. . .and considering the limited power of women in 1958, I felt I had no choice but to take drastic action."

"Would you do it again?"

She did not hesitate. "Yes, yes, I would."

"What are you going to do if David Stancowsky comes back?"

Dina wondered the same thing.

Millie looked at her mother, then her husband. "I will let him live his life and hope that he will give me the same courtesy." She turned right to the camera. "Now, if you'll excuse us, we'd appreciate your leaving us alone."

Dina turned off the set and sank onto the couch. Millie was alive. She'd said she didn't want any contact with David, yet. . .if he came back. . . What Millie said was correct. David was obsessed. He'd insist on making contact. She would become his focus now as she was then.

Which meant Dina didn't have a chance.

She shook a fist at the television. "It's not fair! Why did you have to come forward?"

Then she remembered that she was scheduled to be interviewed tomorrow to clear up the Yardley Pruitt allegations.

But why should I?

It was a good question. She sank lower into the cushions, raked her hands through her hair, and let them sit on top of her head. She didn't owe David anything beyond being a good employee. She didn't need to go this extra mile for him, defending his reputation—especially when everyone else seemed intent on cutting him down.

Especially when he was going to come home, find Millie alive, and have tunnel vision in her direction. He wouldn't even notice Dina. What chances she'd had were used up. Over. Gone.

Was it really time to move on and let him go?

She laughed at herself. At age seventy-four she was finally realizing this? How pitiful was that?

She sat upright. "I won't go to the interview. Let David deal with it. I don't owe him anything."

It sounded good. But Dina, more than anyone, knew that old habits died hard.

13

Listen to advice and accept instruction,
and in the end you will be wise.
Many are the plans in a man's heart,
but it is the LORD*'s purpose that prevails.*
PROVERBS 19:20–21

Atlanta—1976

Vanessa's plan was to get up very early, sneak out of her father's house, and head back to campus so they couldn't argue anymore. So he wouldn't be able to yell at her for being insubordinate in front of their dinner guest, Mr. Stancowsky. But her plans were ruined when her father woke her at eight.

"We'll be leaving for church in a half hour, Vanessa. Hurry up."

She turned onto her back. Great. If only she hadn't overslept.

You could still leave.

She shook her head. To leave now would be a blatant, walk-the-plank mutiny.

"Vanessa? Did you hear?"

"I heard." She sat up and swung her legs over the side of the bed.

He opened the door. "We can't be late. My name's going to be in the bulletin as one of the top three benefactors of the new wing, and I need you to be there with me."

To hear the accolades. To play the part of the proud daughter.

"Gimme a half—" She was suddenly overcome by morning sickness and bolted past him toward the bathroom down the hall. She barely made it.

He appeared in the doorway. "Aren't you glad that tomorrow you'll be done with that?"

A second wave took her body captive.

"How long does it usually last?"

She sat back on her heels and pulled a towel off the rack to wipe her mouth. "An hour or so. Crackers sometimes help."

"Good. You can grab some on our way out."

And he was gone. And she was alone.

So be it.

She did *not* want to be in the car with her father all the way to church, so she made the excuse that she needed to drive separately so she could go back to school right after the service. She lied and said she had a test to study for. Hey, life was a test. She just hoped she didn't fail.

She stood by her father in the narthex, looking pretty and proud while he accepted the accolades of some of the elders and deacons. One man with a shock of Elvis hair and an awful avocado tie, slapped her father on the back but winked at her. "Yes indeed, this church owes a lot to your father, Vanessa."

"I know." Then, out of nowhere, she was assaulted with

a new bout of queasiness.

Elvis's wife touched her arm. "Are you all right? You look a bit pale."

Her father flipped a hand. "She's fine. She's just—"

"Pregnant. If you'll excuse me."

She ran to the restroom.

When Vanessa came out of the restroom, her father was not in the narthex. Obviously, the truth of her condition was not an appropriate topic of conversation when Yardley Pruitt held court.

She looked toward the exit. Now would be an excellent time to leave. He had to be furious. Today's faux pas, added to yesterday's rebellion. . .

As the prelude sounded on the organ, she walked toward the door but was intercepted by Reverend Mennard, ready to make his entrance. "Vanessa?"

"Good morning, Reverend."

He looked into the sanctuary. "I see your father's already inside. Go ahead and join him. I'll wait."

With Reverend Mennard blocking her escape, she slipped into the pew beside her father. He did not even look at her but kept his face forward. His jaw was set, his arms crossed.

A sure sign that she'd pay. Dearly.

Vanessa went through the service by rote. She stood when it was time to stand, read aloud when it was time to read aloud. She heard little and felt nothing.

Nothing in regard to church, that is.

Her heart ached. Her mind throbbed. Her stomach churned. In the past few days, she had systematically chopped away at the one piece of stability she had in her life. Daddy. Father.

And there *had* been a change in his title. Just as she'd progressed to calling her mother "Mom," Yardley Pruitt no longer deserved the "Daddy" title of endearment. He was Father now. Yet oddly, it wasn't because of anything new *he'd* done. The change in his status had occurred solely because of something new inside herself.

But what was this new something? What was different in her now that hadn't been there a few days previous?

Suddenly, Reverend Mennard's voice broke into her thoughts. "Our Scripture reading today is from Galatians 5:1. 'It is for freedom that Christ has set us free. Stand firm, then, and do not let yourselves be burdened again by a yoke of slavery.' "

Freedom! That was it! That's what she was feeling. Ever since her mother had re-entered her life, she'd been teased with the offer of freedom. Not from her troubles—she still had many at the moment—but from the burden of thinking she didn't have a choice. The truth was, she didn't have to do things her father's way. She could think for herself. She *should* think for herself.

The organ was playing again, and Vanessa noticed ushers in the aisles, passing collection plates. Out of habit, her hand found her purse on the pew. But then, unbidden, it found a new purpose, one that shocked her so much she rested her wrist on top of the purse a moment to let the thought fully form.

No, I couldn't. . . .

Oh yes. You can. You must!

She must.

She opened her purse and pulled out some specific bills, so

neatly folded in half. She kept them hidden in her palm. Her father glanced her way but couldn't see. No indeed, he couldn't see what she was doing. Not until it was done.

The offering plate approached from her right. She took the folded bills and placed them on top. The hundred-dollar bills nodded at her decision.

She passed the plate to her father.

He saw them.

He touched them, then looked at her.

Her heart pounded and she wanted to look away, but she forced herself to meet his gaze. *Yes, Father. It's exactly what you think. And I dare you to snatch that money out of the offering plate in front of the world. I dare you.*

He suddenly glanced to his left. The woman on his other side had her arm extended, ready. He put his own offering envelope on top and passed the plate along. Away.

The money was gone. Vanessa was free of it. Free of the decision the money bought.

Free of him.

Almost.

When the congregation stood for the doxology, she sidled out of the pew and left the church—and all that was inside.

Vanessa didn't drive to her mother's house in Decatur; she coasted on adrenaline. The contrast between yesterday's trip *toward* her father's world and this trip *away* from it was the difference between hiking a mountain trail with a forty-pound pack and running barefoot through a field of wildflowers. How long had she been carrying that pack? Five years? Or even longer? At least the weight of it hadn't permanently stooped her shoulders.

It was 10:05. Hadn't Harry said their church service started at 10:30? She hoped they hadn't left yet, because she had no idea which church was theirs. *Please, make them still be there.*

As soon as she turned onto the right street, she craned her neck to see if her mother's Volkswagen was in the driveway. It was.

She pulled behind it, cutting over the curb. The front door was open and she caught a glimpse of red pass by. Then a face in the window. Then the door pulled wide just for her.

"Nessa! You're here!"

She put a hand to her belly. "We're both here."

Before her mother could respond, Vanessa ran into her arms. They rocked, right there on the stoop. Sentences were exchanged without a word, and five years evaporated into the all-important moment of *now.*

It was just as she'd imagined: sitting in a pew, her mother on one side and Lewis on the other. It was as if she'd come home.

And Lewis's voice. . .it was everything her mother had said it was. When they stood to sing the hymns, she had to force herself not to stare at him. They shared a hymnal, yet he never looked at the page. His face was raised and his eyes were closed. It was as if he was singing for an audience of One. And Vanessa knew—she knew—that God heard his voice and was pleased. Though her own voice was more curdle than cream, she gave an extra effort because of her seatmate. Did God appreciate her song, too?

The minister was the opposite of Reverend Mennard at her father's church. Pastor Bill smiled. He made people laugh. And when he read verses from the Bible, his eyes got all excited like he'd burst if he didn't share this very cool thing he'd just discovered. Reverend Mennard preached *at* them. Pastor Bill spoke *with* them.

And he wasn't the only one talking. The first time the old lady at the end of the row said, "Amen!" Vanessa looked at her mother, embarrassed, only to find her mother nodding as if she could easily say it out loud, too. As things got going there was an "Alleluia," three "Praise the Lords," and even a few soft calls of "Thank You, Jesus!" No one, but no one would dare interrupt Reverend Mennard's monologue with such comments, no matter how heartfelt.

But that was the point. Vanessa couldn't imagine anyone who heard her father's preacher being moved to exclaim anything—except maybe a muffled "Thank heaven, that's over" when the benediction was finally pronounced.

The clincher was that Vanessa found *herself* nodding a few times when Pastor Bill talked about people feeling helpless and hopeless as they dealt with complicated lives. He said Jesus was the way through all that. Jesus was the answer. Vanessa didn't know about that but was willing to listen. What could it hurt?

However, the highlight of the service was not the sermon or even the music. It happened during the singing of the final hymn, "Holy, Holy, Holy." It happened when Lewis wrapped his arm around her shoulders and pulled her close. Vanessa noticed that with their hands sharing the hymnal, their bodies created a circle. Unbroken. She heard a song in her head. The Nitty Gritty Dirt Band singing, "Will the circle be unbroken? By and by, Lord, by and by. . ."

The thing was she didn't want this circle to be broken. Not ever.

At that moment, Lewis turned his head and looked at her.

His smile was her amen.

"You're practically glowing. What happened?"

This question was posed by both Vanessa's mother and Lewis after church—and at various times throughout lunch. And though she would have liked to explain it to them, she couldn't. Because she couldn't explain it to herself.

Her transition from wimpy child to free woman had been swift; yet it had been brought about by so many different emotions and incidents intertwining that it was hard to pinpoint event from sentiment. Action from reaction.

And as the day wore on and she spent more time with these two wonderful people, she realized that maybe knowing the why and how wasn't essential to enjoying her new self. As the day wore on, she realized it was okay to just accept the changes as real and good. On faith.

Amen. Alleluia. Thank You, Jesus!

Dawson—1987

By the time Lane and Brandy got back to school from their outing to Olson's Ice Cream Shoppe, it was lunchtime. The halls were busy, and no hall more so than the one in front of the drama room.

Lane pulled up short. "We're too late. The list is up."

She heard Melissa Peterson squeal. "I got it!"

From the faces of some of those grouped around the list, it was clear not many thought this was good news.

Melissa spotted Lane and hurried toward her. Lane was

appalled when Melissa actually took her hand. "Oh, Lane, I'm so sorry you didn't try out."

Lane didn't know what to say.

Brandy did. She pushed Melissa's hand away. "Get away from her, you witch."

The group moved closer to the real drama being acted out right in front of them. It was surreal and all Lane could think was, *No, this isn't happening.*

But it was.

Melissa pushed Brandy so she nearly fell. "Don't call me names, you frizzy freak."

Brandy attacked with a push of her own. Within seconds Lane was engulfed by the crowd—who loudly egged them on. How had this happened?

Mr. Dobbins burst out of his classroom and broke it up. He finally stood between the two girls, his arms holding them apart. "Talk to me, girls."

Melissa pointed a finger at Lane. "She's jealous because I got the part of Juliet."

Mr. Dobbins's bushy eyebrows dipped. "I don't see Lane fighting."

Brandy rallied her entire five-foot-two frame. "I'm fighting *for* her."

Lane hated being on the receiving end of Mr. Dobbins's disappointed look. She put a hand to her chest. "I'm okay about Melissa getting the part. Really. I didn't even try out."

Mr. Dobbins opened his mouth to say one thing but seemed to change his mind and say something else. "All right people, move on. Get to class, lunch, wherever you're supposed to be. This show's over."

The hall emptied of all but the three girls and the teacher.

Mr. Dobbins looked at Melissa, then at Brandy. "Shall we go to the principal's office?"

Right on cue, Melissa started to cry. "Please no, Mr. Dobbins. My parents will kill me. I'm sorry. I blew it." She looked imploringly at Brandy. "Can't we just forget this ever happened?"

Brandy's mouth was in its *aghast* mode. Then she rolled her eyes and applauded. "Bravo! There's Oscar written all over that performance."

Melissa's torso flinched, as if she wanted to pounce.

Mr. Dobbins sighed. "Go on. Get outta here. And behave yourself."

Lane started to leave, but Mr. Dobbins said, "Lane? Got a minute?"

"Sure." She and Brandy exchanged a glance, then Lane followed her teacher through the drama room, into his cluttered office. He moved a pile of scripts from a chair, and she sat across from his desk.

He fell into his own chair and ran a hand through his hair, which was as frizzy as Brandy's.

"I'm really sorry, Mr. Dobbins. I never asked Brandy to defend—"

He raised a hand, dismissing her comments. "I take it your audition in Minneapolis went well?"

It took her a moment to change mental gears. "Uh. . .I didn't go."

He gave her an extended blink. "When you didn't try out for Juliet, I assumed your movie audition had gone well."

Lane let her backpack slip to the floor. Right then she felt her energy level drop. She leaned forward on her thighs, covering her face with her hands. "I've really blown it. All around."

"You only get so many chances, Lane. What do I repeatedly tell you kids?"

" 'Always audition. There's everything to gain.' "

He rocked in his chair. "Hollywood casting directors don't come this far that often. You had nothing to lose."

She could barely get out the words. "I know."

"As for our little production? It's cast, Lane. I had to go with the best of the kids who tried out."

"Melissa."

He shrugged.

"I'm too late."

" 'For though we sleep or wake, or roam, or ride, ay fleeth the time, it nil no man abide.' "

"Huh?"

"Chaucer. *Canterbury Tales*. Time waits for no man. Or woman."

"Don't I know it."

"You know it now."

Now that it was too late.

He sat forward. "Why? Why didn't—?" He sat back. "No. Don't tell me. Because there are always a thousand reasons not to do anything. It all comes down to your passion. Do you want it enough to step over the obstacles, move through them? Obviously you didn't."

She pushed her hands on her eyes, trying to keep the tears in. "I don't know what I want. I thought I did, but—"

The bell rang, ending lunch. Ending further discussion.

Ending so many things.

Though Lane certainly knew two wrongs didn't make a right,

after her discussion with Mr. Dobbins about how she'd messed up by not trying out for the movie or the school production, there was no way she could go to any classes.

She walked home. If she got in trouble, she'd deal with it—one of the advantages of being a good girl was having adults cut her a bit of slack once in a while. Today she needed all the slack she could get.

She was glad both her parents worked. The house was empty—except for Grandma. But that was okay. Sure, Grandma would give her a hard time and slip some advice into the mix. But whatever it was would be better than her own messed-up thoughts.

Lane didn't even try to be quiet, afraid of scaring Grandma by slipping in unannounced. She closed the door with a solid *click.* "Grandma?"

She came out of the kitchen, a bottle of mustard in her hand. " 'Lantic Ocean, child. What are you doing home? You sick?"

Lane pointed to the mustard. "Whatcha making?"

"Bologna sandwiches. Want one?"

"Two would be good."

Grandma raised an eyebrow. "Since when does the bird eat two sandwiches?"

"Messing up my life makes me hungry."

"Then two it is."

Lane helped make sandwiches, peel bananas, and pour milk. Grandma didn't ask any questions until they sat down and took a bite.

"There. Fuel in. Now information out. What's going on?"

Lane told her all about Brandy's fight with Melissa and the talk with Mr. Dobbins. "I blew it. I gave up two auditions for nothing."

"Not for nothing. For that good-for-nothing boyfriend of yours."

Oh no. Grandma didn't know about the engagement.

"Uh-oh. Your face looks guilty as a politician on the news." The old woman pointed a banana at her. "Spill it. What's Toby done now?"

The words came out in a rush. "He asked me to marry him. His grandpa has some land south of town, and it has trees and a great view and Toby says we can have it, and he'll build me a house and we'll live—"

"He bribed you with land?"

"No!" *Kinda. Sorta.*

Grandma shook her head. "What is it with women and land? First Scarlett O'Hara messes up her life for Tara, then I marry your granddad for a cracker box on the edge of town, now you."

Lane hadn't heard this story. "What cracker box? You lived in a nice house."

"Yeah, well. . .it took me sixteen years to get from the cracker box to the house you knew—a decent house. But it served me right for marrying the wrong man for the wrong reasons."

Lane wasn't sure she wanted to hear this. "Didn't you love Granddad?"

"Eventually. Sure. Enough, I suppose."

"What's enough?"

"Enough to get by." She put the uneaten banana on her plate. "Don't settle, child. Not with marriage, not with your dreams, not with your life. If you do, you'll end up like me."

Lane didn't know what to say. "Aren't you happy?"

She shrugged and ran a finger along the curve of the banana. "A person learns to make do, find their happiness where it's sitting." She looked up at Lane. "But that doesn't mean it's the happiness that could've been. 'Course, we'll never know that for sure. Not unless somebody comes up with a way to go back and try things a second time. And I'm not holding my breath for that one."

Lane pushed her plate away. "The trouble is, I really love Toby. And I know he loves me. He's a wonderful guy."

"I know."

It was Lane's turn to raise an eyebrow. "You know? You act like you hate him."

"Hate's a strong word, better left for the Hitlers of the world. Toby *is* a good guy. As for him loving you and you him? No way for a third party like me to judge such a thing. Love's a bigger gamble than cards."

"Then why don't you like him?"

"Because he's making you waver like a centerline painted over a bump. If you don't know what you want to do with your life, you can't get hooked up with someone else who doesn't know either. Both halves of a couple need to be strong and look out for each other's best interests. If they don't, then you'll live life like a chicken with its head cut off, bouncing around, getting nowhere, 'til you fall down from exhaustion, ready to die."

Lane laughed nervously. "That's a little dramatic, don't you think?"

"Hey. Life can be pretty dramatic—and not in a good way either."

Lane tore the edge off a piece of bologna that had strayed

past the bread. "So what do I do?"

"About the engagement or your talent?"

"Both."

"Be engaged. I don't care. Just take it slow and don't be rushed into any plans until you're ready. As for your talent? I'd like to be all sympathetic, comforting and tell you not to worry, there's always another audition; but that isn't true. Some doors are opened only once."

"That's depressing."

She shrugged. "I can't make gold from brass no matter how hard I try. Let it go. Move on." She flicked the tip of Lane's nose. "And don't miss another chance."

"I won't."

"Promise?"

"I promise."

"Good. Now eat your bologna, child."

The doorbell rang and Lane knew who it would be.

As soon as the door opened, Brandy stormed in. Toby was right behind her. "What happened? Why did you leave school?"

In light of Brandy's brawl with Melissa it seemed a dumb question, but Lane led them up to her room to answer it. Once Brandy was settled on the bed and Toby in the rocker by the window, she stood between them and told them about Mr. Dobbins.

"So he won't let you have the part of Juliet?" Brandy asked. "Because everyone knows you're the best."

"You are," Toby said. "I may pretend otherwise, but you are."

Suddenly all the tears she'd held in while with her teacher and Grandma Nellie burst out. "You guys are super. I'm this mixed-up mess, yet you stick by me."

Brandy let out a breath. "Oh dear."

"What?"

She rolled her eyes. "I feel a group hug coming up."

Brandy was right.

⸻

Brandy went home, and Toby and Lane stood on the porch, saying their good-byes. But after a dozen kisses, Lane's mother drove in the driveway, home from work, and Lane pushed away from Toby's embrace.

He pulled her back. "Surely we can kiss in front of your mom. We're engaged."

Lane heard her mother go in the kitchen door. "I'd better go inside."

Toby stared at her. "You haven't told them, have you?"

"I. . ." There was no way out. "No. Not yet."

He backed away from her. "I tell everyone at school, I tell my parents, I'm ready to yell it from the rooftops. . . . Who *have* you told?"

She was going to say Brandy, but even that wasn't true. Then she remembered. "Grandma knows."

The air left him. "I'm sure she's thrilled."

Lane sidled up next to him, taking his hand. "She said it was fine to be engaged but suggested we take it slow. Not rush into anything."

"Don't you want a summer wedding?"

Not this summer. "We'll see."

"My mom was going to call your mom because she wants to help with the planning."

Lane placed her palm against his. "That can still happen.

Let's just let *us* get used to the idea first."

He pulled his hand away. "Get used to it? I've wanted to marry you for months. I thought you felt the same."

"I. . .I do."

He shoved his hands in his pockets and walked down the steps. "I'll talk to you tomorrow."

"Toby. . ."

She watched him drive away.

Bangor—1958

It was quitting time and David had gotten little accomplished. He'd been consumed with thoughts of Millie—anger at Millie. Why was she being so difficult? He'd tried to think of some incident, some starting point that might have spurred her to change from loving and cooperative into this argumentative, difficult woman, but he could not. It seemed to have come on one snide comment at a time, gaining strength as she put into practice this absurd assertiveness. She was slipping out of his control. Out of his world.

The newest infraction was the menu—or rather the lack of the menu. He'd told her to bring it by after she was through at the hospital. That had been hours ago. No menu. No Millie.

But then. . . Hope surfaced as he remembered he had been gone for an hour. Maybe she'd brought it by and left it with Dina. He buzzed her on the intercom. "Come in here a moment, please."

Within seconds, she was at the door. "Yes, sir?"

"Did Millie bring a menu by while I was gone?"

"Our menu?"

He didn't like her presumption. "Actually, it's my menu. For my dinner."

She blushed. "No, sir. I haven't seen a thing. Though I *was* in the file room a good portion of time."

"Never mind. Thank you."

He shoved himself away from the desk, shut off his adding machine, and put on his coat.

He had to nip this in the bud. Now.

Rhonda Reynolds answered the door. "Hello, David. Were we expecting you for dinner?"

"No, no, you weren't." He looked past her into the house. "I need to talk to Millie."

"Is something wrong?"

Millie came out of the kitchen. "David. I didn't expect you—"

He strode past Rhonda. "How dare you defy me!"

Millie pulled up. "What are you talking about?"

He hated when she acted innocent. She was far from innocent. With each new day that was becoming stunningly clear.

Rhonda sidled past them, moving toward the kitchen. "If you'll excuse me."

He took Millie by the arm and pulled her into the parlor.

"Let go of me!"

"Then tell me why you didn't bring the menu by the office like I asked you to."

"I did bring it by. I left it on your desk."

He laughed, incredulous. "The fact you can stand there and lie to my face. . ."

"I'm not lying. I brought it in. Right after I left work. Just like you asked."

"There was no menu on my desk."

She paced between him and the piano. "Your secretary wasn't at her desk, so I put it right where you could see it."

He shook his head. There had been no menu. "Why are you lying to me?"

She faced him. "Why would I lie?" Her eyes lit up. "Maybe your girlfriend took it."

"Why would Miss Edmonds take a menu?" That had come out wrong. "I mean—"

She made a massaging motion with her fingers. "I can think of ten reasons why. She's after you."

"Don't be absurd."

"Don't you be absurd. And don't be blind. That woman has her sights set on you." She stepped closer. "Think about it. Wouldn't it be to her advantage to cause trouble between us?"

The front door opened and Ray came in. "What's going on? I could hear you from the driveway."

David jumped in, taking the offensive. "Your daughter continues to defy me at every turn."

Millie's jaw dropped. "That's not true."

Ray turned to his daughter. "I thought I told you to behave, to accept David's generous direction as he takes time away from the hard work he already does for the company to help give you the best wedding you—"

"This has nothing to do with the wedding, Father. And David's wrong. He asked me to do something and I did it."

"Then where's the menu?" David asked.

She threw her hands in the air. "I don't know! Like I said, ask your precious Miss Edmonds where it is."

"What does Miss Edmonds have to do with this?"

Millie's look was smug. "I caught her giving David a back massage. She likes him—way more than an employee should like a boss."

Ray shook his head. "I can't believe that. Miss Edmonds is a sweet girl. She's hardly the aggressive type. You must be mistaken."

"Why must *I* be mistaken?" Millie yelled. "I'm your daughter. Why can't you support me? Believe me?"

"Calm down, Millie. You're being irrational."

She stood between them, then suddenly sucked in a breath. She pressed her fingertips to her forehead. "I can't stand this. The two of you are suffocating me."

"Don't be ridiculous," her father said. He put a hand on her shoulder. "Now be a good girl, apologize to David, give him the menu—or whatever it is he needs—and then go tell your mother I'll be ready for dinner in five minutes. I'm going to change."

He went upstairs. It was nice to have Ray on his side. David took a seat in the wing chair by the window. "So?"

Millie just stood there in the middle of the room. Her head shook back and forth like a pendulum. It was as if she was in a daze. What was wrong with her?

"I'm waiting."

After a moment's hesitation, she marched to the front door, grabbing her jacket off the rack as she passed. Her purse toppled to the floor, spilling its contents, but it was as if she didn't see. Or care. She stepped over it and opened the front door. "I'm going for a walk."

David was content to let her go. Good riddance. She was being impossible. And if she wouldn't even obey her father. . .

But he did get up to pick up the mess of the purse. As he

was putting the items back, he saw an odd key. It was small and had a plastic numbered bobble on it: *24*.

He heard Ray at the top of the stairs. He pocketed the key and hung up the purse.

Take your evil deeds out of my sight!
Stop doing wrong, learn to do right!
ISAIAH 1:16–17

Athens—1976

On Monday morning, Vanessa tried to be as quiet as she could getting dressed. She knew Connie didn't have a class until ten thirty. She, herself, didn't have a class for hours. The sun was just starting to come up.

She accidentally dropped her brush on the floor.

Connie stirred and opened one eye, saw Vanessa, then checked her clock. "What are you doing? It's not even seven."

Vanessa took advantage of her roommate being awake and put her makeup away in its tray. "I have some errands to run." She gathered her books and purse before Connie could ask more. "Go back to sleep."

Connie pulled the blanket over her shoulder and complied.

It had taken Vanessa forty-five minutes to weave her way around campus to the office of each of her professors. She taped the final note on the final door.

There. Step one completed.

She heard footsteps and turned to see Professor Harler approach. "Miss Pruitt?"

She pulled the note from the door. "Good morning, Professor. I was just leaving you a note."

"Then come inside and give it to me personally." He put a key in the lock and went in.

Vanessa hesitated, her resolve weakening. Step one, distributing notes to each of her teachers, asking for a meeting, was hard enough. But to suddenly zoom on to step two, the actual meeting, without the proper psyching herself up for it. . .

Professor Harler settled in at his desk. "Sit, Miss Pruitt." He extended a hand. "The note, please?"

"Actually, the note isn't necessary now that you're here. I was wanting to schedule a meeting with you."

"Concerning. . . ?"

He wasn't going to make this easy. Yet maybe it served her right. "I haven't been doing very well in your class."

"Why is that?"

She heard her own teeth click together.

He leaned forward, resting his forearms on the desk. "Here are the reasons for a student doing poorly." He used his fingers to count off. "One: The student is dumb. Two: The student is lazy. Three: The student is distracted. Four: The student doesn't care." He kept his four fingers on display. "Which one are you?"

Any excuses she might have used broke away like a magnet yanked from its bond.

The professor rocked back in his chair. He clasped his hands across his torso and smiled. "Gotcha, didn't I?"

It felt good to smile. "Yes, you did."

"Let's dissect this a bit." He held up the four fingers again. "One: stupidity. The truth is very few people are incapable of learning. True, it's harder for some, but stupidity is usually an excuse used by those who should be claiming reason number two: laziness. A person can achieve most anything through work. Nothing can be achieved through laziness, and dreams die. 'The sluggard craves and gets nothing, but the desires of the diligent are fully satisfied.' "

Vanessa's mother had mentioned the necessity for work. About dreams being null and void without it.

"Reason number three: distraction. Distractions are as inevitable as death and taxes. There is always something else to do, someone else needing your attention. The pull of the world can be defined by its distractions. Handle it."

He balanced an index finger on his pinky finger. "Finally, four: apathy. The most insidious of the four deadly excuses. Indifference is a cancer that will spread from one corner of your life to another. Apathy is the essence of stupidity and produces laziness, which makes you too weak to fend off a total immersion in distractions until they nibble away at what's left of your life, making you curl into a ball and die." He lifted his hands and let gravity drop them into his lap. "There you have it. The fate of a person who offers excuses."

The room fell silent. Professor Harler was looking at her. Waiting. "I. . .I don't know what to say."

"Excellent."

"What?"

"If I've rendered you mute then I've stated my case well, because there are no acceptable excuses for your grades, Miss Pruitt. Your grades are your choice. How you attain the grade you want will vary from teacher to teacher, but the point is, *you* are in control, and sink or swim, it's your responsibility." He leveled her with a look. "No one else's."

The insinuation made her wonder if her father had contacted him before.

His voice softened. "Here's the key to doing well in my class, in college, and in life: 'Be strong and do the work.' Actually, there *are* enough assignments and tests left to turn this thing around—though it's best to remember this is not always the case. Time *can* run out." He stood. "Will there be anything else, Miss Pruitt?"

That about covered it.

The door to the dorm room swung open and Connie and a girlfriend burst inside, dancing and singing "Jive Talking." Two hustle steps in and they pulled up short. "Vanessa, what are you doing?"

Vanessa turned around in the desk chair. "I'm studying."

Connie looked at her friend and burst out laughing. Vanessa knew she deserved it. "What brought this on?"

The friend—was her name Suzy?—started doing a hustle step in between the beds. "I don't want to hear about studying. We're going dancing at Uncle Sam's."

"Wanna come?" Connie opened her tiny closet and changed into a yellow knit top that hugged her curves. "It's time to boogie down, Vanessa."

"I can't boogie down." She tapped a notebook with a pencil. "I need to buckle down."

Connie moved her hips. "Let's party."

The perfect answer came to mind. "Just because you can doesn't mean you should."

Connie hesitated a moment, then rushed to Vanessa's side, putting a hand to her forehead. "Are you sure you're feeling okay?"

Vanessa laughed. "I'm fine. Go on. Have fun."

They left her alone.

There. Distraction handled. That wasn't so hard.

Vanessa snuggled into the covers and stared at the phone. Her father hadn't called once since she'd left him in the church, since she'd donated her abortion money to charity. Since she'd decided to keep the baby.

She shook her head. "Keep" was the wrong word. She hadn't decided to keep the baby, but she had decided to *have* the baby. Big difference.

Big decision.

A decision for another day.

Dawson—1987

Lane was at her locker when her teacher approached.

"Hey, Mr. Dobbins."

He was grinning. "I have a proposition for you this morning, Lane. You interested?"

"Of course." Her first thought was that Melissa Peterson had fallen off the face of the earth. Fat chance.

Mr. Dobbins stepped away from prying ears. "As you know, I cast Molly Perkins in the part of the nurse—it's a good part, a comedic part, the most important female part after Juliet."

Why is he telling me this?

He shook his head as if clearing his thoughts. “Anyway, Molly called last night. Her dad’s been transferred to Denver. They’ll be moving in a month. She can’t take the part, so I’m offering it to you.”

Her thoughts collided, but one word emerged from the rubble: “Sure.”

His eyebrows rose. “Really?”

Second thoughts pounced. “Well, maybe.”

“No, no. I take your ‘sure’ as a definite yes. I’m thrilled. I was hoping, but I thought since it’s a smaller. . .” He shrugged. “I’m proud of you, Lane. Practice starts after school.”

She had a hard time swallowing. “I’ll be there.”

Mr. Dobbins walked away and was immediately replaced by Brandy. “What did Dobbins want?”

Lane was not at all sure how Brandy would react. “Molly Perkins is moving to Denver. He offered me her part. The part of the nurse.”

“The nurse doesn’t even have a name.”

“It’s a good part, Brandy. A funny part.”

“But it’s not *the* part.”

“Unfortunately, Melissa’s not moving anywhere.”

Brandy sighed dramatically, and once again Lane wondered why *she* didn’t get involved in theater. “I suppose it’s doable.”

“At least I’ll be in it.”

“Yeah, well. . .”

They started walking to class. “I don’t deserve the main part, Brand.”

“Actually, you do. But hey, if you’re happy, I’m happy.”

“You’re too good to me.”

"Go figure. I guess this means I should work backstage."

Cool. Very cool. Maybe things would work out after all.

The cast of *Romeo and Juliet* sat in a circle for the first read-through. From experience, Lane knew it wasn't a time to *act*, it was a time to get to know the words, the rhythm. A necessity, especially with Shakespeare.

Unfortunately, no one had filled Melissa Peterson in on this fact. It was painful to hear her say every line as if it was the climax of a soliloquy. Overacting 101.

And it wasn't just Lane's opinion. One by one, the other cast members' faces contorted in varied levels of pain. If Mr. Dobbins had said, "Tone it down, Melissa," a dozen times, he'd said it a hundred. How had she ever gotten the part in the first place?

When they took a break, Jason, who'd gotten the part of Romeo, cornered Lane by the water fountain. "Do you hear her? There's no way I can play against *that*."

Music to Lane's ears. She took a sip of water, then wiped her mouth. "Can't help you there, Jas."

"Why, oh why, didn't you try out?" It wasn't a question as much as a scolding.

"Sorry," she said.

"Maybe we can stage a mutiny? Maybe if we all go to Dobbins and tell him how we feel, he'll fire Melissa and—"

"You can't fire someone who isn't getting paid."

"Kick her out, then. Anything."

She'd like nothing better. But no, it wasn't possible. It was absurd. It—

Jason nodded toward the guys playing Tybalt and Mercutio.

"I can get them to join us—as soon as rehearsal is over."

"No, Jason. Don't do that." There was no conviction in her voice.

Mr. Dobbins came into the hall. "Come back, people. There's work to do."

And a mutiny to attend.

Jason threw his script to the floor. "Come on, Melissa, cut it out."

Melissa looked genuinely shocked. "What are you talking about?"

"We're not doing a melodrama. Take it down a notch."

Tybalt chimed in. "With a Juliet like that, Romeo would kill himself to be away from her."

The others laughed.

Melissa turned to their teacher. "Mr. Dobbins, don't let them say such things."

"Come on, boys. This is just the first read-through. Everyone needs work."

"Overworked."

"Overplayed."

"Overdone."

Melissa popped out of her chair, her face red. "If that's what you think. . ." She ran from the room.

Lane felt bad but also experienced a warm satisfaction. What next? If they were going to have a mutiny, it was now or never. But no way would she start it. No way.

She didn't have to. Jason leaned toward the center of the circle of chairs, keeping his voice low. "Actually, Mr. Dobbins, a bunch of us were talking and we wondered if you could let

Melissa go. Now that Lane's with us, let her have the part and let Melissa do the nurse or something."

Tybalt spoke. "Or let her shine our swords. That would be good."

Lane watched Mr. Dobbins's face. With each word, his jaw moved from a twitch to a tight rock. He shook his head. He looked to the floor. Then he looked in her direction. She looked away.

If only they could replay the last few minutes. . . This was a mistake. A huge mistake.

Jason continued. "We all want what's best for the play. And we all agree Lane would make the best Juliet."

With a sigh, Mr. Dobbins stood. She felt his eyes. "Lane, do you agree with them?"

At that moment, walking the plank sounded like a good alternative. "I. . .I'm not going to say a thing."

Jason stood and pointed at her. "But you said, out in the hall. . . You agreed with us."

Lane had a sudden urge to leave. Escape. She stood and gently set her script on her chair. "I'm sorry. I didn't mean to cause trouble. I'm sorry." She ran from the room and, not knowing exactly where she should go, took solace in the rest room.

There, standing at a sink, was Melissa with mascara streaking her cheeks. She whipped her body toward Lane. "You! You arranged all this!"

"No. No, I didn't." But she had. If she hadn't been the one to instigate it, she'd certainly gone along. She *was* guilty. She took a step toward her, but the girl moved away, wetting a paper towel for her cheeks.

"Why did you have to come back? Why couldn't you just stay away and let someone else have a chance? Ever since the eighth grade you've gotten every good part. If Lane Holloway tries out, the rest of the girls don't need to show up. Or if we do, we know we'll get the part of the shopkeeper, or the maid, or the best friend. But never the lead. Not until this time. And now you're trying to take this part away from me, when I won it fair and square."

Lane had no idea what to say. It was all true.

When she didn't speak, Melissa flipped a hand at her. "Go on. Go back to the read-through and take my part. Make everybody happy."

With difficulty, Lane held her ground. She scuffed a shoe against a bobby pin on the floor. "I don't want the part this way."

Melissa snickered. "Why didn't you go to the movie audition? Get that part."

"I didn't have a chance at that part."

"Sure you did. You're good. Too good for Dawson."

"Uh. . .thank you."

Melissa shrugged and threw away the paper towel. She stood close enough for Lane to see that the eyeliner on her right eye was half gone. When Melissa spoke, her voice was soft. "I want to be a good actress, too."

"You are good." *Kinda.*

Melissa shook her head. "I try too hard."

Lane could tell her another lie or. . . "Good acting flows. Right this minute, neither one of us has to think about acting mad or frustrated or sad, or whatever else we're feeling. It just *is.* That's what acting needs to be. You have to lose yourself, forget about what *you* feel at the moment, and let the character feel through you."

"You make it sound so easy. Like you can flip a switch and turn yourself off."

"That's nearly true. You have to flip 'Melissa' off, and turn 'Juliet' on."

"But how?"

How did Lane do it? She'd never had to dissect it before. Then she thought of something that might help. "You get to know her. You study Juliet and find out why she does the things she does, why she feels the way she does. And as you do that, you'll find similar places in yourself. That's what you draw on, the places where you and Juliet intertwine."

Melissa was looking past her, deep in thought. Finally, she said, "Thanks. That helped a lot."

"You're welcome." She sidestepped to the door. "Shall we?"

Back in the drama room everyone was leaving. Lane hung back until Mr. Dobbins was free.

He saw her, then started putting the chairs back in rows. "Can I help you?"

She felt relief that he wasn't yelling at her, but also shame. Her sin was laid out between them. Separating them. And she couldn't have that. Not with her mentor. "I want to apologize."

"Want?"

"Need."

"Better. And yes, you do."

"It was just so hard to hear her—"

"Tough."

She fumbled over a chair and it toppled.

Dobbins helped her put it right. "The trouble with people who have extraordinary talent is that things come easily for them. Not that you don't work at your acting—I know you do.

But there's something inherently present within a person of talent." He indicated she should sit and took a seat himself.

"Does Melissa have talent?" she asked.

"That's of no concern to you. She's been chosen. This is her part, her slice of time to shine or fade."

Lane looked at her hands, then up at him. "She and I talked. We're okay."

"That's good, but actually it doesn't matter. There are going to be people you work with whom you don't like. Despise even. To be a success you have to work beyond what is and find out what could be. And you, Lane Holloway, could be great."

She covered her mouth with a hand. "Really?"

He leaned forward and patted her knee. "Really." Then he sat back with an expressive sigh. "What you've just learned here, during this situation, is a lesson you *had* to learn. You're probably lucky to have learned it early rather than late. Here rather than on some movie set."

He'd lost her. "And the lesson is. . . ?"

"Humility. You didn't get the part you wanted. You are not the star of this production. But you *do* have a part—a good one. And so you need to be the best nurse you can be. Learn your craft through all parts, all participation. Put your heart and soul into the small opportunities, and the big ones will fall at your feet."

Her stomach stirred with excitement.

He looked at his watch. "We both need to get home to our families. Life goes on without us." They stood and finished the chairs. "There's just one more thing I want to leave with you."

"What's that?"

"A very famous man named Thomas à Kempis once said,

'Lord, give me the willingness to be obscure.' " He put a hand on her shoulder. "Think about it, Lane."

She would. She would.

⊶

Lane hung up the phone. Her insides pulled.

"What's wrong?" her dad asked from his recliner. The opening strains of *Dallas* came from the TV.

"It's Friday. Brandy and I were supposed to go out like we always do. She's late, but I got sidetracked going over my lines, and now she's really late. And no one answers." She got her coat from the front closet. "I'm going over there."

Her dad stood. "You want me to come with you?"

She was already out the door.

⊶

At Brandy's house, the porch light was off, but there was a lamp shining from the living room. Lane's shoes sounded too loud on the wood porch. She opened the screen door and knocked softly, then listened.

She knocked a little louder.

She heard rustling inside and felt the slight tremor of footfalls. The curtain on the door was pulled aside. Brandy opened the door a crack, but Lane pushed her way inside. "Where have you been? I've been worried."

Brandy was looking at the floor, her head tilted oddly. Lane took hold of her chin and turned her face into full view. Her cheek was swollen. "Who?"

But she knew who, even before Brandy looked up the stairs leading to the bedrooms.

Lane grabbed Brandy's coat from the hall tree and held it

open for her arms. "You have to get out of here. You can't stay and let her hurt—"

Brandy took the coat but did not put it on. "She didn't mean to hurt me."

"That's what you always say."

Brandy touched her cheek, wincing. "She did get me good this time. She was talking big and swung the bottle, and. . ." Her smile was full of sarcasm. "My face got in the way."

Lane took a step toward the door. "Come on. Come home with me. Now."

Brandy shook her head. Her forehead wrinkled and her eyebrows nearly touched as she tried to get herself under control. "I need to get far away, Lane. Way far away. I can't stay with you, with anybody here in Dawson. It's too close, plus. . . I'm not a charity case."

They'd had this discussion before. "You're not—"

"I am." Brandy looked up the stairs a second time.

"Is she passed out?"

She nodded. "Finally." She sank onto the bottom step. "I wish I were brave enough to leave. For good."

Lane put an arm around her friend. "You're the bravest person I know."

They sat in silence a moment.

"I'm so glad you're here, Lane."

Though the lure of Hollywood still pulled, Lane discovered the feeling was mutual. Maybe everything *had* worked out for the best.

Bangor—1958

It was all Millie's fault.

The same file sat in front of David, showing the same empty page. His mug of coffee was full and cold. And no matter where he tried to look, his eyes kept returning to the key sitting on top of his flip calendar. Luring him. Mocking him. Holding secrets he desperately wanted—

"Mr. Stancowsky?"

He looked up and saw Dina standing in front of his desk holding a plate. How long had she been there, watching him watch the key with a 24 on it?

He sat back, putting distance between him and this taunter. "Yes, Miss Edmonds?"

She set the plate on his desk. On it was a piece of cake. "I made this for you," she said. "It's carrot cake. Yesterday when we were talking about menus, you mentioned how much you like it, saying it had been a long time. . ."

"How nice of you."

She glanced at his coffee. "Would you like me to freshen that for you?"

"That would be great." He moved the file to the side and zeroed in on the cake. Maybe some sugar would give him a jump start. Dina returned with a steaming mug. "You're too good to me, Miss Edmonds."

"Nonsense. You make it easy. I'm very happy to be here, to be of some help."

He was reminded of her short tenure. What was it now? A month? "So you like working here?"

"I like working for you."

The distinction was slight, but it created an awkward

silence—and a blush on her part. "I'm here to stay, Mr. Stancowsky. I'm very loyal to those I respect and admire."

Surely he was imagining the undertone of her words. She was his secretary. She wasn't even that pretty. Besides, he was engaged—to the boss's daughter.

"Is that a locker key?" she asked, pointing to the key sitting on the calendar.

Locker key? He picked it up, looking at it with new eyes. "I don't know. Is it? I. . .I found it."

"May I?" He handed it over. "It looks like the keys they have for the lockers at the bus station. I used one once when I first moved here and needed a place to keep my suitcases for a bit."

She handed it back, and he turned the 24 over and over. . . .

"If you'd like me to go over there and turn it in, I'd be happy—"

"No. Thank you." He set the key down and took up his fork. "But thank you for the cake. It's very good. That will be all."

He didn't look at her face to see if she looked disappointed. He had enough to think about.

David had never been in the Bangor bus station. There'd been no need. One did not drive a new Bonneville and take public transportation.

He spotted a band of lockers against a wall. His heart pounded as he closed in on number 24.

It was a large locker. Large enough to hold a piece of luggage. His hand shook as he aimed the key at the lock, and he was tempted to stop and walk away. Ignorance was bliss.

Ignorance is stupidity.

Call him many things, but never stupid.

He turned the key and opened the door. Inside was a medium-sized suitcase, marbleized ivory in color, along with a matching overnight case. They each had luggage tags. He looked at one of them. The name was Tracy Osgood, and the only address was a post office box in New York City.

Why would Millie have the key to a locker containing a New York woman's suitcases?

He was about to shut the locker, when an awful, niggling feeling came over him. He removed the overnight case and set it on a bench nearby. It was unlocked. The contents were not unexpected. In the top removable tray were a pink plastic hairbrush, comb, and mirror; toiletries; some pins and matching earrings; and makeup. Underneath were lingerie and some hair curlers.

Then it happened. When he put the tray back he noticed the compact. It was gold with an initial on it.

Not a *T* for Tracy but an *M*.

He sank onto the bench and pulled the case to his lap. He rummaged through it roughly, looking for more. More what, he wasn't sure. He didn't recognize the lingerie, but that wasn't surprising considering the limits Millie had set on their relationship.

But in a small pocket on the side he found a wad of money: $280. And within the folds of the bills was a driver's license issued to Tracy Osgood: five-foot-four, one hundred twelve pounds, brown hair, brown eyes.

No. No.

He shoved the case aside and yanked out the big suitcase, opening it right there on the floor. Inside was a blue sweater set he'd given Millie for her birthday, a red plaid dress he'd seen her wear a thousand times. . .clothes he knew. Clothes he had felt against his hands as he'd held her. He pulled the sweater to his face and inhaled. "Evening in Paris." Millie's scent.

He closed his eyes, nearly sick with the smell.

An old man carrying a broom came close. "You okay, mister?"

"Leave me alone!"

David's voice echoed in the large room. People looked at him. They whispered behind their hands. He looked at the man, who'd backed away. "Sorry. I'm fine."

The man nodded but looked unconvinced.

David had to finish this—whatever *this* was. He tore through the rest of the belongings. He found a metal music box, whose lid came off revealing a dusting of powder and a pink powder puff; two books: *Gone with the Wind* and *Wuthering Heights*; and a small photo album.

He opened it, only to find pictures of Millie and her parents. Millie and her friends. A picture of the Reynolds' house. Her high school. Her favorite park. Old pictures of grandparents long gone. Noticeably absent were any pictures of David. He kept flipping the pages, hoping the chronology of her life would place him at the back, on the final page. The climax.

But when he got to the back page, there was a snapshot of Millie with another man. Her teacher with the red curly hair. Smiling. His arm around her waist, and hers around his.

He ripped the photo from its corner mounts and started to tear it in two. A half inch in, he stopped. No. This was evidence. He put it in the inner pocket of his suit coat. Then he closed the suitcases and returned them to their hiding place. He strode from the station, the determination of his stride echoing in the hall.

It was a hollow, empty, lonely sound.

David was within a block of the Reynolds home when he slammed on the brakes, mirroring the abrupt stop of his thoughts.

Yes, he desperately wanted to confront Millie with her betrayal. Demand answers. But. . .

This was bigger than Millie. Bigger than a wedding. His entire future was at stake. If the wedding was off, then his position as the favored son-in-law was off. There was a chance—business talent or no business talent—that he'd be just another employee. Could Ray Reynolds ignore his daughter's personal life even if it would be best for Mariner Construction?

Maybe. Yet who knew the true power of a heartbroken child on her parents? Suddenly, his future was based on emotion, which made David uncomfortable. In the business world, one plus one always equaled two. Not so with women, love, marriage, and family.

David needed time to think. He turned right and headed out of town. North. Going nowhere in particular.

Going nowhere fast.

David hadn't meant to end up at the Rocky Ledge bed-and-breakfast near Bar Harbor and didn't really realize what he was doing until he saw his own hand on the doorknob of the entrance. Before he could assimilate the thought, *Stop! What are you doing?* he'd stepped inside. There was still a chance to leave.

Until Mrs. Stephens appeared. "Welcome! Wel—" She stopped. Her eyebrows rose. "Oh. Mr. Stancowsky. What. . . how are you today?"

He moved to the check-in desk, putting his hands upon it. He needed it for support. "I have to cancel our reservations for May."

"For your honeymoon?"

The next words didn't want to come out. To be said out loud would make them real.

She gently put a hand on his. "Did you two have a spat?"

If only they had. A spat could be repaired. A hidden suitcase packed for flight, a driver's license with a new name. . . Those things were not fixed with an "I'm sorry." Or even a "Forgive me." There was no forgiveness for betrayal.

He slapped a hand on the counter, making her jump. "Just cancel it!" He walked out.

"Of course, Mr. Stancowsky. But I hope things work out. . . ."

He slammed the door.

It was over. It was really over.

David sat in the dark of his house, his hands clamped on the armrests of the chair, his feet flat on the floor. For the ninth time the phone rang. For the ninth time David didn't answer it. It didn't matter who it was. Ray, wondering where he'd been all afternoon. Dina, pledging her undying loyalty. Or Millie, wondering—

Wondering what? Had she even missed him when he hadn't called all day? All evening? When he hadn't shown up at the Reynolds' door like a puppy panting for its mistress, had she worried and wondered why? Or had she felt nothing but relief? *Good. I have some time without him.*

His heart flipped at the knock on the door. He pushed a hand against his chest. He wished he could look out and see who it was without being seen. But that was impossible. Who'd missed him? Who'd been worried? Who'd come to see if he was okay?

Or was it the Fuller Brush man, wanting to sell him a new toilet brush? He stifled a snicker.

The knock repeated itself. A pattern of five instead of three. Then the female voice: "David? Are you in there?"

He said nothing but slowly leaned forward, covered his face with his hands, and waited for Dina Edmonds to go away.

15

Find rest, O my soul, in God alone;
my hope comes from him.
He alone is my rock and my salvation;
he is my fortress, I will not be shaken.
PSALM 62:5–6

Present-Day Bangor

So much for Dina's resolve to leave things alone.

Even with the cameras running, with the TV lights bright in her eyes, with the interviewer asking her questions, Dina Edmonds chastised herself for being a chump. Loyal beyond all logic.

But it was too late now. Although this was just a local television station, they'd told her that the network wanted clips of the interview. By the end of the day, the entire nation would know that Mariner Construction did not do shoddy work and Yardley Pruitt was a liar. David would come back the day after tomorrow with his reputation intact.

And his Millie alive.

If he came back at all.

Dina gave her thoughts a mental shake. She couldn't think

about that. Especially not while on TV as the interviewer, Lynn Daniels, was asking her *the* question that would bring out the truth.

"Ms. Edmonds, you contacted us because of some comments that Yardley Pruitt made regarding your boss, David Stancowsky, and his company, Mariner Construction." The woman looked at her notes. "Mr. Pruitt stated that David Stancowsky—and I quote—'built a bank building for me back in the seventies. Did a shoddy job of it, too. If memory serves, we ended up withholding money from him because of the workmanship.' " She looked up. "What would you like to say in regard to Mr. Pruitt's comments?"

"I have proof that Mr. Pruitt's memory is faulty. Mariner Construction did an exemplary job on the building, and the money withheld had nothing to do with workmanship. Mr. Pruitt didn't want to pay for some change orders—that he'd approved. Back in 1976, the issue was handled by our lawyer, Mr. Pruitt realized his error, and he paid us in full."

"Nineteen seventy-six is a long time ago. You must have had to do a lot of digging for that information."

"Not really. Though I didn't initially remember the connection our company had with Mr. Pruitt, as soon as he said something, I remembered—"

"You remembered?"

Dina straightened her spine. "I've worked for Mariner Construction for forty-six years, since 1958. I've been Mr. Stancowsky's secretary, office manager, and assistant for that entire time."

"Your longevity is amazing, Ms. Edmonds. Very few people can make such a claim of loyalty."

Or is it gullibility and false hopes?

"You must really enjoy working for him."

Dina was appalled to feel a blush. She looked at her lap. "I do. He's a good man." She quickly added, "A good boss."

The interviewer hesitated the slightest moment. "Are you married, Ms. Edmonds?"

Dina's radar flipped its ON switch. "No, I'm not. I've never been married."

"And neither has Mr. Stancowsky, correct?"

No, he was obsessed with Millie. She shook her head.

"You've been loyal only to each other all these years?"

Suddenly, Dina saw herself on national television with commentators focusing on a sordid love relationship between herself and David, all reports of his company's reputation pushed aside. She had to stop this. Now.

She sat forward on her chair. "Excuse me, Ms. Daniels, but I resent your implications. There is not, and never has been, any love connection between myself and my employer. For over four decades we have enjoyed a relationship based on hard work, respect, and friendship. I will not have you implying anything more to gain ratings. I will not have Mr. Stancowsky come back to anything hinting of the unsavory."

Ms. Daniels's eyes had widened. But she recovered quickly. "What do you think about his ex-fiancée coming forward, saying that she faked her death to get away from him? Since you worked for him back in 1958, did you know Millie?"

Were you jealous of Millie even then?

"Yes, I knew her."

Ms. Daniels leaned closer. "So you were there when she supposedly died?"

Dina didn't want to get into all this. "Yes, but—"

"Did you have any inclination that she *hadn't* died? Were

there any clues? Did you ever suspect?"

"I. . .I think these are questions you need to ask Mr. Stancowsky when he gets back."

"If he comes back. You do realize there is a good chance he may not come back. Especially considering that he traveled back to 1958 to save Millie's life."

Dina managed to swallow. "Of course I realize that."

"How do you feel about it?"

Dina wanted to get back to the office. She'd had enough celebrity. "If Mr. Stancowsky decides to stay in his Alternity, then I will mourn his absence, but I will find joy in knowing that he obviously has found new happiness in the past."

Now leave me alone.

Ms. Daniels nodded. "I'd say he's lucky to call you a friend." She looked at the camera. "Lynn Daniels, Breaking News, in Bangor."

Atlanta

The intercom in Yardley Pruitt's office buzzed. "There's a reporter on line one, Mr. Pruitt. Would you like—?"

"No reporters! No calls!"

The line went dead. He turned his chair toward the window that looked out over downtown Atlanta. If only he'd stuck with the "No comment" answer. Why had he felt the need to cash in on David Stancowsky's name? He was the father of a Time Lottery winner; why hadn't that been enough?

Because you're an egotistical, arrogant, manipulative—

Yes, yes, he was all that and more. He wasn't blind. He was an intelligent man who recognized his weaknesses.

No.

Weaknesses was not the correct term. Because having an ego and being arrogant *did* have their place, especially in the business world. They *could* be a strength—as could be the art of manipulation.

But not this time. He'd blown it. And not out of ego or arrogance. He honestly hadn't remembered the David incident correctly. Now, reminded, he seemed to remember the threat of a lawsuit on Mariner's part and his lawyer telling him, "You have to pay this, Yardley. They're legitimate change orders that you approved."

He remembered this now but hadn't at the time. And that fact bothered him. A lot. He was seventy-seven years old. Up until now, he'd rejected all suggestion that he should retire or pass the reigns of the bank to someone younger.

More able?

He turned his chair away from the expanse of the city and noticed a picture of Vanessa and her family on his desk. He picked it up, really looking at his daughter for the first time in years. She was not a pretty woman anymore. Her hair had thinned and was cut in a nondescript short shag. She had bags under her eyes. And even though she was smiling, there was no joy there.

Joy. What was that?

Yardley tried to remember a time he'd felt true joy. Decades rewound without stopping until an image appeared, that of a little Vanessa, sitting on his lap at another office desk in another bank building. He had his arm around her, pulling her close as he showed her how to use an adding machine. *Ca-chunk, ca-chunk.*

"This is fun, Daddy."

And it had been. One moment of joy in a life filled with. . .what?

He touched Vanessa's photo-cheek but only felt the cold of the glass. He sucked in a breath, breaking the moment. "She'll be home day after tomorrow."

But the words fell flat. They had no substance. They had no bearing or truth. For in his heart, he knew she wouldn't be coming back. She was with her mother now—lively, exasperating, but loving Dorian. She was having her baby. The past held love for her. Promise.

The present held. . .no such thing.

He pulled the photo to his chest and cried.

Peachtree City

Rachel Caldwell sat on the window seat of her childhood room and looked outside but saw nothing. Apparently heard nothing either, because when she finally realized her father, Dudley, was outside the door, it was clear it was not his first knock, or the first time he'd called her name.

"Rachel? Are you okay in there?"

She let her feet find the floor. "Yes, Dad, I'm fine. Just a minute." She unlocked the door and opened it. "Sorry."

"You know I hate a locked door."

"I know. Again, I'm sorry."

He looked past her as if looking for clues. "Want something for dinner?"

"No, thanks. I'm not hungry."

"Me, neither." He looked pitiful standing there with his hands in his pockets. "I. . .I really like your new hair. And the clothes. You look very pretty, Rachel."

She touched her hair. "Thanks." She thought about telling her father this is the way she always looked away from the Pruitt-Caldwell sphere, but saw no reason to be mean. "Want to sit down?"

He looked warily into the room. Had he ever come in and talked? "Sure," he said, and took her place on the window seat but faced toward the room. He didn't say anything. It was awkward.

She sat at the foot of the bed and pulled her legs beneath her, trying to give a casual tone to the scene—however false. "I'm sorry to embarrass the family with that interview. Going against Grandfather and all. . ."

"It needed to be said."

Really? "Have you heard from him?"

Her father hesitated. "No."

"Should we call him?"

He slid his hands beneath his thighs. "You did what the rest of us should have done a long time ago."

She let her jaw drop.

He laughed. "It was wrong keeping Dorian from Vanessa. If I would have known. . ." He shook his head. "Who's kidding whom? I honestly can't say I would have done anything to intervene."

"Why not?"

He looked past her and shrugged. "Habit mostly. Your mother and I have been guilty of letting Yardley use us. We've always been at his beck and call. When we were first married I didn't like it much but eventually jumped into the flow of it. It was easier to go along than fight."

A question popped out. "Did you and Mother ever really love each other?"

She could tell by his quick breath that he was going to say, "Of course," but he stopped himself. She suspected—and hoped—what would come out next would be the truth. "We loved each other at first. At least I did. And I love your mother still, I really do."

"But?"

"But there are different kinds of love. We shouldn't have married. I think we both got cheated. If she comes back, I'll try to do better. Be a better husband."

Silence hung between them.

"I don't think she'll come back, Dad."

He nodded and his forehead crumbled. Then he abruptly stood. "Are you sure you don't want something to eat? I make a mean omelet."

"Sure. That would be nice."

Kansas City

Andrew ran up the stairs and slammed his bedroom door.

Mac called up to him. "Andrew! You come back here this minute!"

He wasn't surprised when nothing happened, and he didn't feel like being a consistent father by pushing the matter. Andrew's anger was Mac's fault. Andrew wanted to see Cheryl and at age six didn't understand that it wasn't as simple as a phone call. Cheryl had to actually answer the phone for it to do any good.

And so far she hadn't.

Mac sat on the stairs and leaned his head against the railing. He was out of energy, both physically and emotionally. Yet in two days, when the winners returned from their pasts—or stayed behind—he had to be *on* and be in charge. The thought of dealing with the press and being the essence of charm was like asking him to climb Mt. Everest. He needed someone to carry him. Pull him along.

I'm here.

He nodded at the inner words. God was here. Yes, that did make it better. More doable. He whispered into the railing. "I want her back, Lord. I'm so sorry for hurting her. Bring her back to me. To us. I won't take her for granted anymore. I pro—"

The doorbell rang. Reporters? Maybe if he remained perfectly still they'd go away.

Then there was a knock. But not just any knock. A rhythmic knock Mac had come to know.

He ran down the rest of the stairs and flung open the door, halting the action of her wrist as it readied itself to repeat the pattern. "Hey," she said.

His chin quivered. "Oh, Cheryl. . .I'm so sorry."

She took his hand. "May I come in?"

"Of course."

They went inside and closed the door. In the entry, she pulled their clasped hands upward between them, adding her other hand to the mix. "It *is* all your fault, you know," she said.

"I know. I should have owned up to our relationship."

"True, but that's not what I'm talking about. All this is your fault because you made me love you. I can't stay away. I can't stay mad. I'm afraid you're stuck with me."

He pulled her into his arms where she belonged.

A door upstairs opened. "Cheryl!" Andrew hurtled down the stairs. He jumped off the last few steps, barreled into them, and made them lose their balance. They fell onto the floor, a tangle of arms and legs. Oblivious, Andrew crawled over whatever was in the way and wrapped his arms around her neck. "I missed you!"

She hugged him back. "I missed you too, bud."

Andrew got to his feet and stood between them, casting one arm around his father and the other around Cheryl. "Are you getting married now or what?"

Mac looked at Cheryl and they laughed. "Remember how I told you when I got around to proposing you'd know it?"

"I do."

"So. . . ?"

She got to her knees and leaned toward him, giving him a proper kiss. Andrew's applause made everything perfect.

Montebello

When all the press attention started, Toby had hoped to go back to work as a conquering hero. He'd even daydreamed about quitting his job. After all, as the love of Lane Holloway's life there was no need for him to work.

Daydreams. Pipe dreams. Dead dreams.

Reality won. There were bills to pay. And ribbing to take.

As Toby drove to work, his dread was as heavy as his foot was light. He'd called in sick yesterday but couldn't push it, even though he *was* going to be way late. He tried to brace himself for the heckling and the jokes. He'd even come up with a decent comeback line that might fend them off, "Hey, it was worth a shot."

If only he didn't feel so weary. His extra day off hadn't

brought him rest. Reporters were still camped outside his apartment, though the numbers *were* down. He'd taken the phone off the hook. What did they want him to say anyway? He'd come forward based on the lie that Laney still wanted him. It was her lie. None of this was his fault. In fact, he should sue the Time Lottery for. . .what did they call it? Pain and suffering? Mental cruelty? A friend of his had a brother-in-law who was a lawyer. . . .

He went through McDonald's and got lunch and then stopped for gas. But finally, he couldn't put it off any longer. A Big Mac seemed like a very bad idea when he pulled up to the job site and saw his coworkers strapping on their tool belts after their lunch break, when he saw them point at him. Lean close together. Laugh.

Keep driving. You don't need this. You don't need them.

But he did. He really needed things to get back to normal so he could forget any of this happened.

He got out of his truck, grabbed his toolbox and belt from the back, and walked toward them.

Their words pummeled him and he froze in place.

"Decided to lower yourself to our level, Bjornson?"

"Dumped in the past, dumped in the present, eh, Tobe?"

"Getting the shaft in two lifetimes. Isn't that a new world record?"

"You were real smooth on TV. *'Uh. . .duh.'* Oh yeah, you're in Lane Holloway's league all right."

"Maybe you *could* go change her lightbulbs or unclog her toilet."

"Once a loser, always a loser. Ain't that right, Tobe?"

"You thought you were hot stuff, didn't you?"

"You fizzled big-time. On national TV, too."

"Hey, can I have your autograph?"

His confidence evaporated and the muscles in his arm tensed.

One of them shoved his shoulder. "What's the matter, Tobe? Can't take the heat?"

In one sweeping motion of his arm, Toby's toolbox landed against the left side of the guy's head.

They jumped him.

⁂

Toby couldn't see out of his left eye. He suspected some bones in his hand were broken. It was hard to breathe. Did he have a cracked rib?

He managed to drive away from his beating and knew he should go to an ER. But that would mean more publicity. He could imagine seeing a shot of himself all swollen and bloody on the front page and as the lead story of every network: *"Lane Holloway's Ex Bloodied in Brawl. News at eleven."*

He couldn't go home. Not with the piranhas lurking. He couldn't go to any public place. Even if people didn't recognize him, his current appearance would freak them out. Someone would call the police.

Every moment led him deeper. Deeper into the dark.

He needed somewhere to hide out. If only he knew someone who had a place in the mountains or by the ocean. Somewhere he could crash for a few days.

Then he laughed. He *did* know someone who had a place at the ocean.

And at the moment no one was home.

Malibu

Toby parked two blocks away and walked. Once outside Lane's house, he hesitated. There were no cars in the driveway. It was his for the asking. And oh, was he asking. Begging. He was out of options. The gun in his pocket was proof of that. He'd bought it ages ago and kept it under the seat in his truck. He'd never used it and didn't want to use it now, but. . .

Then, just as he was about to cup his hand against a window, his mind cleared and found logic. This was a fancy house, and fancy houses had alarm systems. He looked around for a sign from a security company and found one near a bush by the walk. *Great.* He had to assume it was on. Meaning there was no way he could break in without bringing down the cops. Not an option. Gun or no gun.

But neither was leaving—and the reasons went beyond his desperate need for rest. As he'd driven over, he'd gotten a funny feeling that his destiny was here. At Lane's home. Everything that had happened the past few weeks was leading him to this place, to this point. She would be back in two days and he would be here to meet her. Greet her. Beg her to give him another chance. If not as a boyfriend, as a fellow human being whose entire life had gotten messed up because of her. She owed him.

He cautiously walked around the side of the house, glancing at the neighbor's windows. The sound of the waves got louder. Even though he'd lived in L.A. for years, he'd never spent much time at the ocean. It held a force that scared him. He'd only had to feel the undertow once to make him stay away.

He felt an undertow now, threatening to drown him. But it would pass. He just needed rest. Sleep. Everything would be all right in a couple of days. When his Laney came back to him.

He slipped behind a bush, waiting for a jogger to pass. As soon as it was safe, he made a beeline for the stairs leading to her deck. That would be an acceptable place to wait—as if he had a choice. With each step he took, his ribs screamed, and he had to lean on the railing. When he spotted a cushioned lounger. . .

He fell into it and slept.

Santa Monica

Randy Lopez got himself a bowl of what Brandy called his *Law and Order* ice cream—Randy always liked a bowl of butter pecan while he watched his favorite program. He licked the spoon. "Are you sure you don't want a bowl?"

Brandy rifled through her purse. *Where is my list? I just had it.* "No thanks. I really want to go to Lane's and get things perfect for her return." She swung at him with a pointed finger. "And don't remind me she might not be coming back."

He shrugged. "Don't be gone long."

She found the list and was on the way out when she had the oddest feeling of unease. She'd been out alone at night before. She'd been at Lane's alone at night before. *What gives?*

She backtracked and hugged Randy from behind. "Wait up for me?"

"As always, doll-face. As always."

Malibu

As Brandy put the key into the door, she was assailed by the scent of the bouquet in her arms. Pink roses. She drew the flowers closer, drinking them in. The pink against the newly painted yellow walls of Lane's bedroom would be lovely.

It would be a grand homecoming. This evening, Brandy planned to make a batch of brownies with extra-thick frosting, and earlier today she'd stocked the fridge with all Lane's favorites. She'd even tied a half dozen Mylar balloons to her bar stools. *Welcome Home! We Missed You!*

She got the door open and heard the high-pitched tone of the security system. She flipped on the foyer light, punched the proper buttons into the key pad, and the house returned to silence.

She moved into the kitchen and got a vase for the roses. She arranged them nicely and took them into the bedroom. The room still smelled of fresh paint. A good smell. And the roses made it perfect.

Speaking of plants, she really should water Lane's. In two days, things would be crazy busy.

Brandy got a pitcher and filled it with water. She'd get the ones on the deck first.

A light woke him. It took a moment for Toby to remember where he was. But as soon as the thought *I'm on Laney's deck* took hold, a door from the house came open. A woman came out, carrying a pitcher.

He didn't know what to—

She saw him and squealed. Then she threw the water at him and ran for the door.

He wiped his wet face with one hand and fumbled for the gun in the other. "Hold it right there!"

He was surprised when she followed his direction. She

froze in the doorway and raised her hands. "Don't hurt me! I'll give you whatever you want."

He stumbled to his feet and held the gun on her. He didn't know how to answer her. He didn't want to hurt her and he didn't want any *thing*.

"My purse is inside. Take it. There's a stereo, a TV. . .have at it. Just don't—"

"Shut up, just shut up!"

Then, to his surprise, he saw a shift in her eyes, almost a softening. Her body actually relaxed as if the fear had left her. What was going on?

She studied him a moment, then began shaking her head. "Toby? Toby Bjornson? Is that you?"

All words left him. Surely he wasn't *that* famous?

She took a step toward him as if the gun wasn't even there. "Oh my. . . Toby, it's me, Brandy. Brandy Mayer from Dawson—though it's Brandy Lopez now." She made a face. "You look terrible. What happened?"

No. This wasn't happening. He waved the gun at her. "Get inside. Now!"

He followed her inside, closed the door, locked it, and adjusted the blinds.

Brandy started walking toward a hallway. "Let me get something for your cuts and—"

"No! Stay right here!" He shook the gun toward the floor and had to remind himself to be more careful; it was not an extension of his finger.

She dug a fist into her hip. "Fine. You want to call the shots, you call the shots. I was just trying to help."

He had no idea what to do next. His ribs really hurt. He needed to sit, which meant he needed her to. . . "Sit."

She hesitated, then pointed to the kitchen. "You want something to eat?"

He did. He hadn't eaten anything since his Big Mac. But he shook his head. "I'm not going to let you go to the kitchen and use the phone to call someone."

"Then come with me. Want a cup of tea?"

He snickered.

She motioned for him to follow her. "Not a tea man, eh? How about a Coke?"

Her banter was absurd. He had the gun. He was holding her hostage and she was offering him a Coke like an old friend visiting? And yet, that's exactly what they were. Old, old friends.

She pulled out a bar stool and patted it, making a bunch of *Welcome Home* balloons gyrate. She got him a Coke, popped the tab, and set it on the counter in front of the chair. "Crackers and cheese sound good?"

"Sure." He half sat, half leaned against the stool and downed the Coke. He rested the gun on the counter.

"So, Tobe. What are you doing here, sleeping on Lane's deck, all beat up?"

The brick of cheese she was slicing looked good. "I'm waiting for Laney."

"She may not be back."

He bonked the nearest balloon, making them all dance. "You obviously think she will."

"Well, yeah. Wishful thinking. She's still my best friend." She placed the plate of food in front of him. "And I'm her personal assistant. Have been since we left Dawson."

He popped a slice of cheese in his mouth. "You're a mooch. The pretty one gets famous and the dumpy one hangs on."

"You're one to talk about looks. What happened?"

He lifted his chin, trying to find some dignity. "I was defending my honor." He wiped a cracker crumb off his chin.

She laughed, then stopped herself. "I don't really blame you for coming forward, you know."

"Laney started it when she mentioned me. When she lied."

"Yeah, I saw your interview. Bummer."

He sat on the stool. "I'll never live it down."

Brandy stopped with a cheese-topped cracker halfway to her mouth. "So that's what caused. . . ?" She nodded to his injuries.

"Becoming a somebody then being thrown back to being a nobody. It's cruel, man. Real cruel."

"Yes, it is. The media is. Lane has to deal with them all the time. She can't even go to the store without one of them hounding her, trying to get a picture of her without makeup, or so they can critique her clothes. Who dresses up to get a gallon of milk? That's why she has me."

"You're a gofer. An errand girl."

She got herself a Diet Coke. "Part of the time, sure. But I don't mind." She traced the top of the can. "I owe her. She saved me."

Toby remembered now. A drunken mom. Bruises. "Your mom still in Dawson?"

"She died five years ago."

"Sorry."

Brandy shrugged. "You still got family there?"

Toby didn't answer as a wave of dizziness hit him. He grabbed for the edge of the counter, toppling his can of Coke.

"You okay?"

He shook his head, making it hurt worse. “I gotta lie down.” He got off the stool and headed for the couch, then backtracked and grabbed the gun.

“Here, let me help—”

He pushed her away—into an end table. The lamp toppled. They reached for it. He tripped.

The gun went off.

16

But you, O LORD, be not far off;
O my Strength, come quickly to help me.
PSALM 22:19

Present-Day Kansas City

Mac woke up smiling. And why not? He was engaged to an amazing woman, the world knew about their relationship so there was no need to hide, and tomorrow was the day the Time Lottery winners would be coming home.

Or not.

Either way was fine. Either way was good. Either way the winners had gained more knowledge and more insight into their life and their purpose. Knowing a little more about the "Why am I here?" question was a plus in anyone's life.

Mac glanced at the clock. He didn't have to wake Andrew for a half hour, so he reached for the remote and bathed the room in the bluish light of the television. Might as well see what had happened in the world during the night.

A reporter stood in front of a house, but police could be seen going in and out of the door behind her. ". . .Lane

Holloway's home, which was the site of a shooting last night."

Mac sprang to a sitting position, upping the volume. "Toby Bjornson, a high-school boyfriend of Time Lottery winner and movie star Lane Holloway, was the object of recent reports and interviews concerning their relationship. Bjornson was shot last night in the presence of Ms. Holloway's personal assistant, Brandy Lopez. Ms. Lopez was not hurt, and Mr. Bjornson was taken to the hospital. His condition is not known at this time. Police are calling the incident accidental, though there are still questions about what Bjornson and Lopez were doing in Ms. Holloway's Malibu home. As a winner of the Time Lottery, Lane Holloway is due back tomorrow from her adventure into her Alternity. Ms. Holloway returned to 1987 under the auspices of renewing her relationship with Mr. Bjornson. . . ."

Mac hit the MUTE button and pulled the phone into his lap. As he was doing so, it rang. "Hello?"

He was glad to hear Cheryl's voice and not Wriggens's. "Mac! Did you see it? Did you hear?"

"I heard."

"Do you think it was a suicide attempt?"

He let out a breath. "I never thought of that."

"You should. Public humiliation does wonders for undermining self-esteem. Especially when it's fragile to begin with."

Mac saw his bedroom door move. Andrew appeared in the gap. He motioned him to the bed. "I should call the hospital, but they didn't say which one." He pulled aside the covers, giving Andrew access. The little boy snuggled into a pillow.

"Let me see what I can do. Surely my hospital has connections. I'll let you know what I find out."

Mac stroked his son's rumpled hair. "Thanks, luv."

"Anytime. I'm surprised Wriggens hasn't called."

"He doesn't get up this early."

"Hey, I have an idea. Why don't *you* wake *him* up for once?"

It was tempting. But then Andrew pulled on his arm. "Daddy, I'm hungry."

Fatherhood called. The rest could wait.

Malibu

Brandy leaned her head against her husband's cheek, though the armchairs in the hospital waiting room prevented the close contact she craved. It was six a.m. but she hadn't slept. Between calling 911, pressing a towel to Toby's side. . . police. . .questioning. . . Sometime in there she'd called Randy. They'd come to the hospital together to wait for news about Toby. The check-in attendant had asked Brandy for information about the patient, assuming they were close, but Brandy hadn't even been able to give an address. And was there family? A wife?

No, not a wife. Toby wouldn't have been on those talk shows proclaiming his love for Lane if there'd been a wife. Though even that was uncertain. Kids? She hoped they were taken care of someplace. She'd never felt so helpless.

And so at fault. If she hadn't tried to help Toby to the couch, she wouldn't have spooked him, he wouldn't have pushed her. . . She'd had trouble telling the police exactly what had happened. The few seconds that had transpired from point A to point B were a blur. Only the sound of the gunshot was clear. And Toby's scream. And the blood.

She looked at her jeans and spread a hand across her thigh,

trying to cover the stain. If only it were so easy.

Toby had come out of surgery okay. The doctor had told them that much. He'd be in recovery awhile. They could go home. But Brandy wanted to see him, really see him. She wanted to tell him how sorry she was. She didn't want him to be in a hospital room hurting, scared, and alone.

Nobody deserved to be alone at a time like this—though with her four kids, Brandy wouldn't have minded a bit more solo time. Yet such time *would* come. Soon enough or too soon? Either way, she was well aware that the chaos of motherhood was temporary and should be cherished.

Yeah, right.

She glanced at her watch. Six-thirty. She'd left thirteen-year-old Marianne in charge of things and was totally confident in her sibling-sitting abilities. But today was show-and-tell for Emmanuel, and the twins were out of lunch money, and—

Brandy pulled away from the comfort of Randy's arm. He startled awake. "What?"

Oops. She'd kept him here when he should have been home sleeping. He had to go to work today.

Enough. She stood and pulled him up with her. "Go home. The kids need you."

He tucked his shirt in the back of his pants while checking his watch. "Did the doctor come out again?"

"No. So I'll stay. I've come this far."

"But you need sleep, too."

"I'll sleep later. I have to talk to Toby. For him and for Laney. She'll have enough to deal with later. I need to know firsthand how he is."

"But your car's at her house. . . . How will you get home?"

"I'll take a cab. Bus." She pushed him toward the door.

"Don't worry about me. I'll find my way home. I always do."

Toby heard snoring.

He opened his eyes and saw a woman slumped in a chair close by. He blinked a few times to focus. It was Brandy.

Then he remembered the gun. The shot. The pain.

He moaned as the memory of the pain proved to be more than memory.

In one motion, Brandy opened her eyes and sat upright. "Toby!" She rushed to his bedside and touched his arm.

He didn't know what to ask first: Why was she here? How was *he* doing? What happened? or—

"The bullet hit a kidney. You had surgery," she said. "The doctor doesn't know how you ever managed to shoot yourself at that angle, and even the police had a hard time understanding how it happened, but—"

"The police?"

"Shootings attract police, Tobe."

"Am I going to be arrested?"

She hesitated. "When I talked to them I tried to downplay what happened, but you *did* hold me at gunpoint."

"Only when you scared me by coming out of the house."

"To find you sleeping on Laney's deck. All bloody and beat up."

"Because she humiliated me in front of the entire country."

Her hand found her hip. "And how did *she* do that? She wasn't even here."

His mind was too fuzzy for this conversation. He closed his eyes and let a moan escape. What had started as a ploy had turned into reality. He wasn't sure what hurt worse, the gunshot surgery or the beating.

"Oh, Tobe. I'm so sorry. I shouldn't have argued with you. The truth is, I don't know what's going to happen."

"I just wanted to see her one more time. Talk to her."

"Me, too. And tomorrow's the day she might come back."

Whatever. What did it matter? Everything was ruined. "I'm tired."

She touched his shoulder. "I'll leave you alone then." She hooked her purse on her shoulder. "I'll try to come back tomorrow."

"No." He sounded more certain than he felt.

"But—"

"No. It's over and done, Brandy. Let it die."

With a nod, she left. He was sorry to see her go.

His fifteen minutes of fame was over. Fade to black. Cut.

Santa Monica

Brandy was wiped out. She was glad the kids were at school, and even glad Randy was at work. It made the house quiet for sleeping—though the boxes of Trix and Captain Crunch on the counter, and the coloring books and crayons spread over the table, were proof that in spite of shootings and Time Lotteries, life went on.

Her purse hit the kitchen counter, and her shoes were off by the time she crossed the threshold of the master bedroom. She had her top pulled over her head before she reached the dresser. The pants came next, then the nightshirt went over her head. Door to bed in twenty seconds, tops.

Speaking of bed, she noticed Randy had pulled down the

covers on her side. What a sweet—

There was something on her pillow. It was a single sheet of paper with a sticky-note on it. The note said,

Go. Be there for Lane. The Time Lottery people know you're coming—I called them.
I love you through all *time, Randy*

She peeled the note away and saw that the paper was a computer printout of an e-ticket to Kansas City, including hotel reservations for two nights. She knew what a financial stretch this was for them, and yet. . .

She held the ticket to her chest. "I love you, too, Randy."

She looked at the departure time. She had four hours.

Where was that suitcase?

Kansas City

Mac finished making a statement regarding Toby Bjornson in the Time Lottery auditorium. He dreaded saying the last two words but said them anyway. "Any questions?"

Feeding frenzy.

"Was Toby Bjornson stalking Ms. Holloway?"

"Will he be arrested?"

"Will this incident change Time Lottery policy?"

Insipid questions that could be handled with a sprinkling of common sense. He let it go on for a generous amount of time before saying, "I'll allow one more question, then I have work to do. After all, tomorrow is the day the winners return."

But the final question pushed his hot button. "Why do you think this year's Time Lottery has been plagued with such conflict among the people the winners left behind, as well as leaks, and—"

Because of you! Mac raised a hand, stopping the rest of the question. He was tempted to give them a lecture, tempted to tell them it was Wriggens who'd leaked the Toby story, tempted to yell at them for keeping him and Cheryl apart one moment. Yet he knew that to explain and defend would feed the frenzy even more. But what could he say? Should he say? *Give me the words.*

He scanned the room, waiting until he had every eye. "The essence of the Time Lottery is based on emotion, wanting to change a negative to a positive, a sadness to happiness, a failure to success. Change elicits more emotion. As does the threat of being left behind. And that is what drives the family and acquaintances of the winners into the limelight. Fear and worry that they are going to be left behind, that their loved one is not coming back. And as the day of that climax is imminent, emotions run high."

Good segue, Mac! Good segue.

"Which leads me to this moment. By the end of tomorrow, all three winners of the Time Lottery will have made a decision that will change their lives—and the lives of their family and friends—forever. Who will come back? Who will stay in their Alternity? I think in light of these life-changing moments and choices, our little intrigues will pale." He leveled them with a look. "Don't you?"

He could tell that a few of them wanted to say more, but he left before they could sully the moment.

Bangor

Dina stared at her empty desk. She knew she should offer to help one of the other secretaries. Mariner Construction was busy, even if Dina was not. Yet in her current mental and emotional condition, *doing* was difficult.

"Hello? Earth to Dina." Linda, the head estimator, stood in front of her desk.

"Sorry," Dina said. "Did you need something?"

Linda looked to the right, then the left. Then she leaned on Dina's desk. "I need you to stop playing the martyr."

Dina straightened her flip calendar so its edge was parallel with the desk. "What are you talking about?"

"I'm talking about you pining for David for over half your life and continuing to pine for him now."

"I do not pine."

"Semantics. He comes back tomorrow."

"Perhaps."

"And you need to be there."

"There?"

"In Kansas City. Sitting beside his bed."

"I would never sit beside Mr. Stancowsky's bed."

Linda leaned even closer, her voice soft but full of power. "You need to be sitting next to his bed at that Time Lottery place so that when he wakes up and opens his eyes, the first person he sees is you—the woman who loves him."

If anyone else had talked to her that way, Dina would have objected. But Linda had guessed the truth a long time ago. She was the only one who knew the state of Dina's heart.

"I wasn't invited."

Linda straightened. "That's your problem. After all these

years, if you're waiting for David Stancowsky to invite you to be anything but his slave, you haven't learned a thing. You aren't *getting* an invitation."

"I can't push myself on him."

"You're not. If the man comes back it means his dearly departed Millie was not the woman of his dreams. Hey, she's made her true feelings pretty clear in this time zone, so I wouldn't doubt she did it back in his second pass through '58. Which means he'll have a broken heart that needs mending. He'll need the comforting arms of a good woman." She raised and lowered her eyebrows as a hint.

Dina's pulse rate had doubled. She'd always assumed David would continue to pursue Millie no matter where he was. Linda had brought new insight into the matter. "Do you really think. . . ?"

Linda came around the desk and nudged herself in front of Dina's computer. "Move over." She commandeered the mouse and clicked away.

"What are you doing?"

"Getting you an airplane ticket to Kansas City."

"But. . ." Dina stopped herself with a nod. "Okay."

"Now we're talking."

Kansas City

Rachel looked out the window of the airplane as they made their descent into Kansas City. It was odd to come back for her mother's return when her mother might *not* return.

Yet how could she not be there to say welcome back—or good-bye.

Rachel looked at her father in the aisle seat. His hands were clasped across his middle, his eyes closed. She thought he was sleeping, until his forehead tightened and his eyebrows dipped. He took a deep breath and she realized he was fighting off tears. Nearly thirty years of marriage was not something easily discarded, especially in this bizarre manner. If her mother didn't come back, it was final. She would be dead to them; in fact, her body *would* die. There would be no second chance to say what should have been said. To hug. To kiss. To hold.

Rachel drew in her own breath and put her fingers over her eyes against the tears. Then she felt a touch on her arm. She turned and found her father's hand reaching toward her.

They held hands across the empty seat.

In his heart a man plans his course,
but the Lord determines his steps.
PROVERBS 16:9

Dawson—1987

Lane, as Juliet's nurse, put her hands on Melissa's shoulders, sending the girl off to meet the man she was to marry. " 'Go, girl, seek happy nights to happy days.' "

Mr. Dobbins clapped. "Excellent! That's the way. Let's take ten, then come back and start on act one, scene four—the street scene."

Lane spotted Toby sitting in the back of the auditorium. She waved and went to see him. She leaned down and kissed him before sitting beside him. "What a nice surprise."

He shrugged but didn't say anything.

"What's wrong?"

He rested his elbows on the armrests and clasped his hands. He studied his fingers, seeming to avoid her eyes. "You're amazing. You're good. Really good."

It was rare praise indeed, because Toby never said much about her acting, usually giving her compliments in bland three-word bursts, such as "That was nice," or "I liked it."

Yet there was something about his tone that made her long for the bland comments. "Why do you make it sound like a bad thing?"

He looked toward the stage, where the crew was messing with a backdrop of Juliet's garden. "I lied to you before."

"Which before are you talking about?"

"When I told you not to go to the movie audition because I didn't want you to be hurt. That was a lie."

"What's the truth?"

He finally looked at her, turned toward her, taking her hand. "Watching you up there. . .the whole world can see how good you are. And those Hollywood people would see it, too, which is why I didn't want you to go."

"Because I can act?"

"Because you'd win the part. I was afraid. I knew you had a shot and I didn't want to lose you. I was being totally selfish."

It was easy to zip over the selfish part and zero in on the fact that Toby believed in her. He believed in her talent.

She slipped her hand around his arm and leaned close enough to kiss him again. And again.

She felt good. She'd made the right choice. For how could she ever leave this marvelous boy? Her destiny was here. With him.

After Toby left, Lane remained at the back of the auditorium. The actors onstage were deep in the street scene when she felt a tap on her shoulder from the row behind.

"Grandma!" She lowered her voice when Mr. Dobbins turned around. "What are you doing here?"

Grandma crooked a finger at her and they went into the hall. "Is everything all right?"

" 'Lantic Ocean, child. Can't a grandmother come see her talented granddaughter at work?"

"You can, but you haven't before this."

"That's because I have a surprise. You and I are going on a trip."

"A trip? Where?"

"Chicago."

"Why?"

Grandma pulled a piece of paper from her purse. It was a fax from the Hollywood casting company that was handling the *Empty Promises* auditions. There was a list of towns.

Grandma pointed at the word *Chicago*. "There's an audition in Chicago tomorrow. And we're going. I'm driving you."

Lane stared at the sheet. "I'd never thought of going to another town in another state."

"Well, I did. And you're going." She held her chin. "You *will* do this. You *will* know. You *will* have no regrets. Not if I can help it."

Lane hugged her. "I can't believe you thought of—" She pulled back. "I can't go. I have rehearsal."

Grandma pointed toward the auditorium. "I took care of it. Had a nice chat with your Mr. Dobbins this morning. He says you can go. He wants you to go."

This couldn't be real. People didn't get second chances like this.

Then her elation was brought up short when she thought of Toby.

"Toby doesn't have anything to say about this," Grandma said.

Lane hadn't realized she'd said his name aloud. Hadn't she just decided he was her destiny? Now destiny's door had been flung open and everything could change. Everything.

Grandma slipped her hand through her arm. "You quit thinking of Dawson, child. You quit thinking about life here at all. Though this life is wonderful, it's not for everyone. It's not for you. You belong in Hollywood or on Broadway. Movies, TV, the stage. Who knows? You will. Because you will have taken every chance to get there. God likes hard work, and He appreciates people who use the gifts He's given them. That's all you're doing, Lane. Making God proud." She smiled. "And me, too. Me, too."

Lane pulled Grandma into another hug. "You're too good to me."

"I know. And you owe me at least two lemon cakes and a batch of molasses cookies."

"The doctor says you're not supposed to have sweets."

"What does he know?" She popped Lane on the behind. "Now get back to your rehearsal, but get home as soon as you can. You need a good night's sleep. We're leaving early."

Brandy plopped onto Lane's bed, pulling the teal teddy bear into her lap. "I wish I could go with you."

"Me, too." Lane stood at her closet. She pulled out a red top and a green one and held them for Brandy to inspect. "Which one should I wear? The character I'm auditioning for is innocent, yet pretends to be sleazy because that's what people expect of her."

"The red, definitely the red. But try it on so I can see for sure."

Lane put on the top, pairing it with black pants. She

looked in the mirror. It looked nice. It made her look—

Suddenly she remembered the image she'd had a few days ago. The image of herself, in a red top—

"What's wrong?" Brandy asked. "I think it looks perfect."

Lane pulled it over her head. "I can't wear it."

"Can't?"

She put on the green shirt.

"I repeat: can't?"

"I had a vision of myself crying in front of judges, wearing a red shirt."

"Good crying or bad crying?"

"What?"

Brandy tossed aside the teddy bear. "Were you crying because you'd blown it or because they'd just said you had the part?"

Lane sat at the foot of the bed. "I don't know."

"Have you ever messed up an audition? Ever?"

"Well. . .no."

"Then you need to wear the red shirt so you can cry your tears of joy when they offer you the part."

"Always the optimist. Always thinking—"

Suddenly Lane saw a new flash, and the image of frizzy-haired Brandy pulsed and merged with the memory of another Brandy: a heavier Brandy with short Dutch-boy hair.

She whipped her head around, seeing her bedroom as if for the first time. The teal and fuchsia bedspread, the teddy bear Toby had won for her at the state fair, her homework sitting on the desk by the window.

Homework? She hadn't done homework in over fifteen years.

"Lane? You zoning out on me again?"

She turned back to Brandy. It was like being on the set of

a movie. Real, but not real. Only there were no cameras. No special lights. No director to yell, "Cut!" This was real.

This was her Alternity! She'd just entered the state of Dual Consciousness that Mr. MacMillan had told her about. She took a few moments to let the knowledge sink in. What an amazing feeling to see both times, know both times. . .

Then she remembered one important fact. She had only an hour to make a decision—*the* decision of her life.

She put a hand to her forehead, not having to fake exhaustion. Though she hated to see Brandy go, she had no choice. "I need to get to bed. Do you mind?"

Brandy stood. "Of course not." She pulled Lane into a hug. "I'll be thinking of you every second tomorrow. Praying for you, too, if you want. You'll do great. I feel it."

Lane let Brandy find her own way out. She locked the door of her room and leaned against it. Why did the colors seem more vivid, the items more distinct?

She covered her eyes. She couldn't focus on *things.* She had to think.

She slipped to the floor and leaned her arms on her raised knees. Then she realized something: The Dual Consciousness had kicked in *before* her audition! How could she ever make an informed decision when she would never know for sure if this Chicago audition would get her the part of Bess? As a professional actress, she knew how fickle auditions could be. Talent played into the decision, but so did luck, and the quirkiness of human nature. What if one of the judges had a migraine? What if one of the judges who *had* chosen her the first time through this situation was sick and was replaced by someone who wasn't impressed by her performance? What if the whole lot of them were hungry and impatient, wanting lunch?

Now, with this new audition, in a different town, there was no guarantee she would get the part.

"So what?"

She pushed her fingers through her hair. The pearl promise ring Toby had given her last Christmas caught in a strand and pulled.

Toby. Marriage. Family. Land.

If she stayed behind, if she didn't get the part, she would have a nice life in Dawson. She'd have the family that had eluded her as a movie star. The first time around she'd left town before Toby proposed. It had been hard leaving him, but the audition had been before he'd asked her to marry him. There hadn't been that final act of commitment. But this time they were engaged. If they got married, there would be no string of live-in lovers who broke her heart and tried her patience. She might have two or three kids by now. Kids in school who would need sack lunches, who would need to be reminded to zip up their coats, who would need to be cuddled and tucked in at night.

She wanted to be a mother. Or did she only *want* to want to be a mother? Did the reason she'd dragged her feet about announcing the engagement have deep roots?

You're thirty-four.

Oh no, she wasn't. At this moment she was eighteen. She got to her feet and moved to the mirror. She touched her hair and face like a blind woman seeing. Yet oddly enough, after a few moments, she realized she liked her thirty-four-year-old face better. She'd taken care of herself. Her older self had a face rich with character. With characters.

If she stayed behind, there might not be any more characters. Sure, she could continue to act in local productions. Maybe she could even be instrumental in starting a community theater here. But maybe not. And as Grandma had said, would she be using her God-given gift to her greatest ability here? It was kind of odd—but nice—to think that God had anything to do with her acting ability. Maybe she should actually contact Him more often. Consult Him. Thank Him. It would be the least she could do.

Well, then. Family or fame. That was the choice.

Lane picked up the teddy bear Brandy had been holding and set it in its proper place by the pillows. Brandy. . .

Lane sighed, grabbed the bear for her own comfort, and sat on the bed. The first time around, when Lane had been awarded the part of Bess and had headed to Hollywood, she'd gotten Brandy to go with her. Lane's success had given her best friend a means of escape from an abusive mother. They'd been together ever since.

If Lane stayed behind. . .

Her mind left Brandy and swam with memories of the Cannes Film Festival, the house on the ocean, filming in places like Rome and London, calling famous people "friends." She led a glamorous life. She'd had experiences that never could be duplicated here in Dawson.

Yet Dawson could hold experiences never duplicated in Hollywood. Night-and-day differences, each good in its own right. And it wasn't the money. Wealth was a perk but not a driving force in her life. She could be happy in a two-bedroom house on a hill. With Toby. With their kids. With Mom, Dad, and Grandma Nellie close by. . .

She twirled Toby's ring on her finger. This wasn't just about her. Her decision would affect others. She loved Toby and wanted what was best for him. *Which means* stay.

But she also loved Brandy. *Which means* go.

Which was the stronger love?

Who needed her more?

She turned over on her back, covering her face with the teddy bear's paws. Toby was a sweet guy. He'd find another girl to love. And maybe if she went back to her movie-star life, she could look him up. Now, wouldn't that be a Hollywood ending: *Movie Star Finds Old Love.*

But Brandy. . .without the escape route that went with Lane's success, Brandy might stick around Dawson her entire life. If her mom didn't kill her first. If she didn't run away.

Lane got off the bed, her decision made. Yet before the time got too close, there was something she had to do.

She opened her bedroom door and descended the stairs, letting the sounds, smells, and sights of her childhood fill her up. At the bottom of the steps, she turned toward the living room. Her father chuckled to a joke Mike Seaver made on *Growing Pains*; her mother sat on the Wedgwood blue and mauve couch, doing a counted cross-stitch of a goose. Grandma sat at the small table by the window, playing Solitaire and eating a Rice Krispie treat.

Grandma looked up first. "Hey, child. You all ready for tomorrow?"

"I think so." *Hope so.* Tomorrow was so very far away. . . .

"Want to play gin?"

"Sorry, Grandma. I need to take a walk." Lane bent over and gave her a hug. "I love you."

"Well. . .I love you, too."

Her mother had turned around to see. "What's made you all sentimental tonight, Lane?"

"Nothing. I just appreciate you guys." And even though it might make them suspicious—even though she would not be around to witness their suspicions—Lane hugged her mother and father, too, and told them she loved them.

"My, my," her dad said.

She went to the door. "I'm going for a walk now." *I have to be able to concentrate on the future. I can't be here with you. I can't.*

"Don't be gone long," Mom said.

"See you later," Grandma added.

Much later.

Athens—1976

Over the next three days, one by one, Vanessa met with her teachers. And though Professor Harler was by far the most eloquent, their message was the same: Be strong and do the work.

Duh.

And oddly enough, it wasn't that hard. Once she made that decision she actually caught herself listening and (gasp!) taking notes. She'd even found Russian History rather interesting.

After finishing that class, she went back to the dorm with a plan to grab her other textbooks and head to the library to study. She almost didn't see the answering-machine light flashing. . . .

She pushed the button to listen and heard her father's voice: "I called to tell you that I'm granting your wish. You want nothing to do with me or my advice, then I won't burden you with them. If you're selfish enough not to care about anyone but yourself, so be it. You are on your own. Completely. There will be no more checks unless you come to your senses and offer me the apology that's due me. And you *will* be back. I know it. Father *does* know best."

The machine clicked off. She shivered.

She hated that her first thoughts were about the money, not the relationship. Did that prove she was just as cold as he was?

The back of her legs found the bed and she sat. What was she going to do?

Get a job.

No way would a part-time job give her enough money for tuition and board.

Apply for a scholarship.

Based on what? Grades?

Then give in to your father. Maybe he does know best.

Did he?

No. He wanted her to get an abortion. He wanted her to stay away from her mother. He wanted her to stay tethered to *him.* And, though she'd never really thought much about it, he wanted her to get a degree in business so she could help him with *his* business. Had he ever once asked her what she was interested in or what she wanted to be when she grew up?

What do *you want to be?*

Too many questions. Not enough answers. She needed sound advice.

She left her books behind and set out to get it.

Decatur

It had not occurred to Vanessa—until she was nearly at Eastridge School—that her mother was working and couldn't leave her second-graders and have a powwow with her daughter to figure out her life.

She looked at her watch. It was after eleven. Was there a lunch break soon? Since she'd come this far, she didn't turn

back but hoped for the best. She checked in at the school office, introducing herself as Dorian's daughter.

The secretary was nice and led Vanessa down to her mother's classroom. She knocked on the doorjamb. "Excuse me, Mrs. Pruitt?"

Her mother looked up from the book she was reading aloud to a gaggle of children seated on the floor. She jumped out of her too-small chair. "Vanessa!"

Twenty-some heads turned in her direction.

Her mother came toward her. "Thank you, Miss Green. Nessa, come in, come in. Come meet my wonderful students."

Vanessa was led to the front of the group like she was a prized possession for show-and-tell.

"Children, I would like you to meet my daughter, Vanessa. Can you say hello?"

In unison they said, "Hello, Vanessa."

They were incredibly cute, all squirming on the floor in their brightly colored outfits, with their eager eyes.

"Would you like Vanessa to finish reading the book to you before we go to lunch?"

"Yes!"

Her mother handed her *Green Eggs and Ham*, opened to the right page, and held the pint-sized chair for her. "You'll pay for this," Vanessa whispered as she sat down. She took a breath and looked at her audience. They were waiting. For her. As if she was the most important person in the world.

Not a bad feeling.

"How do you like your mac and cheese?"

Vanessa finished chewing. "It's surprisingly yummy."

Her mother took a bite of her fruit cocktail. "Yet I take it you did not come here to partake of the cuisine?"

Vanessa set her fork down. "Daddy has cut me off."

"Not surprising. He never did tolerate independence well. He's just mad. He'll come around for his darling daughter."

"I don't think so. I've been more rebellious in the past week than I've been in twenty-one years."

"You could recant."

Vanessa was shocked. "You want me to go back to the way things were?"

Her mother put a hand on hers. "Of course not. I want you to be all you can be. But I want it to be your choice, not mine. Not his. Yours. Ultimately, you're the one who has to live with it, Nessa."

"I need a job."

"Then get one."

"The dorm's paid through the semester, but then I'll need a place to stay."

"Then get one."

Her mother was exasperating. "It's not that easy."

"Sure it is. You apply for a job and take it. It may not be the job of the century, but it will pay the bills. Then you find a place to stay. Believe it or not, Nessa, struggling when you're on the road to achieving a dream can make the blood flow in a most invigorating manner."

"The struggling part is right, but the dream? I don't have one."

"Sure you do."

"No, I don't."

Her mother slapped a hand on the table. "Then you'd better get one!"

"You make it sound so simple, like I'm shopping for a new blouse."

"Simple it's not. But it's not impossible either. Here's the key: Life is not random, dear girl. Each one of us has been created with a unique purpose. The trick is to find out what it is."

"Some trick."

Dorian took a sip of milk. "Hey, God's aching to tell us. We just need to be open to the information."

Vanessa laughed softly, then spread her arms. "So I just say, 'Here I am, God! Show me your plan,' and I'll know?"

"Pretty much."

"Mom. . ."

"Hey, what have you got to lose? And though He usually doesn't show us all the details up front, if you open yourself up to a little divine direction, it *will* happen. You *will* get it. And suddenly you'll start noticing all sorts of hints and pieces of the puzzle."

If only it were true.

Her mother took a bite of brownie and flicked a crumb off her lip. "Here's a question for you: Are you truly interested in business, or are you getting a business degree because your father wants you to?"

Vanessa stopped pulling her fork through the mac and cheese. "I just had that same thought this morning."

"Great minds. . ."

She looked away, trying to think it through. "Business *is* kind of interesting."

"But it doesn't float your boat, does it?"

She smiled. "No. Probably not."

"Then what does?"

"I. . .I don't know." She put her fork down. "And shouldn't

I? If we each have this unique purpose, shouldn't it be right out there, smacking us in the face?"

"Sometimes it is, and sometimes it isn't. Or it's been covered up so long we have a hard time seeing what's what. Sometimes it's a mystery and we have to put together the clues." She dabbed her mouth with a napkin but kept her eyes on Vanessa, as though if she looked hard enough, she'd see purpose written on her daughter's face. "Mmm. Here's a thought. You *were* good with my students. They really like you."

"I really like them."

"Remember how you used to spend hours playing school?"

"That's because you were a teacher."

Her mother shook her head. "There was more to it than that."

Vanessa thought back to all the imaginary schools she'd created in their basement, complete with seating charts, lesson plans, bulletin boards, and tests. And what had she requested for birthday and Christmas presents? School supplies. There was nothing more comforting and exciting than a new box of crayons and a fresh pad of paper.

Her mother was nodding. She waved a finger at Vanessa's face. "I see your brain working. He answered fast, didn't He?"

"Didn't who?"

"God." She mimicked Vanessa's previous arms-out stance. "You asked, He answered."

"I asked in jest."

"Tough. God'll take any 'in' He can get."

Vanessa felt her heart pumping. The idea of being a teacher. . .it was interesting.

Then reality hit. "But I'm a junior in Business. I've been taking all the wrong classes."

"*Some* of the wrong classes. I bet a lot of them would transfer. And so what if it takes an extra year? A teaching degree would open the door to your talents, your purpose. Isn't that the real goal?"

"But—"

Suddenly, there was a flash of light, and it was as if Vanessa had been fed a dose of new thoughts. Her already confused mind was inundated. Full. She looked across the table at her mother and marveled at how young she looked.

Why, she's younger than I am.

What?

I'm fifty.

"Nessa? Are you all right?"

Vanessa looked down at her hands. They were unwrinkled, smooth. She noticed her blouse. It was a cheap knit with an orange-and-lime diagonal pattern. She wore green double-knit pants.

"I hate these clothes!"

Her mother laughed. "You could do with a makeover. I blame your father for making you a fuddy-duddy at twenty-one."

Twenty-one. She was twenty-one!

It's the Dual Consciousness!

She stood up from the bench, nearly toppling her tray of food. "I have to go!"

Children turned their heads. Teachers looked in her direction.

Her mother whispered. "Nessa! Sit down and tell me what's—"

"I can't. I have to go!"

"Just a minute and I'll go with you."

"No!"

She was acting like a crazy person. She forced herself to take a breath and managed a smile as she motioned toward her mother to remain seated. "Sit. Finish your lunch. I'm sorry to act so strange, but you've just given me a lot to think about. I need to be alone for a while."

Her mother looked doubtful. "Are you sure?"

"I'm sure." Then she realized this might be the last time she would ever see her mother. If she went back to the future, Dorian Pruitt was—

Dead? No!

She couldn't think about that now. She had to get her thoughts organized.

Vanessa went around the table and gave her mom an awkward hug. "Thank you for all you've done. I love you."

"I love you, too, Nessa. And I'll continue to help you. Any time, any place. I'm not going anywhere."

But I might be.

She hurried from the building.

Vanessa ran a hand around the huge steering wheel of her car. She couldn't believe she was driving her 1973 Gremlin again. She'd loved this car. It had been a high-school graduation present from her father. Looking at it now, comparing it to the BMW she and Dudley drove around—

Dudley! She was married! They had a daughter. *Rachel!*

And you have a child here. Now. In this time. She put a protective hand on her abdomen. "I didn't have the abortion! The baby is still alive."

A car honked and Vanessa swerved back to her own lane.

Too close. How horrible would it be for her to die just minutes from making the decision of a lifetime.

Two lifetimes.

I need to stop. I need to think.

But where? Sitting in her car on the side of the road seemed anticlimactic. But where could she go to be alone?

She spotted her mother's church a block ahead.

Perfect.

She hesitantly entered the sanctuary, hoping she wasn't disturbing anyone, but she was alone. She walked up the center aisle to the second row of pews and slid in. The afternoon sunlight lit the stained-glass windows that flanked the wooden cross hanging up front on a wall of stone. She'd felt something here before. . . .

"I need help," she whispered.

The room answered with silence—not that she expected anything verbal, but it would have been nice.

She ran her hands through her hair, expecting to find it short, but it was long and silky again. This was so incredibly odd. To have the mind of a fifty-year-old in a twenty-one-year-old body. Actually, it was ideal. To find the wisdom of age present in a body that had many years left to live. Only a handful of people would ever experience that phenomenon. Only a handful of people would have this chance.

She dare not blow it.

The thing was, her present combination of wisdom and youth wouldn't last. In less than an hour she would choose either wisdom and age, or ignorance and youth. Which would it be?

She leaned forward on the pew in front of her and rested her forehead on her folded hands. "I want to make the right decision. Please help." She hoped God didn't expect her to be eloquent, because at this moment it wasn't possible. It was a time to get down to basics. Look at the facts.

Which were. . .

She had to sort out her two lives, figure the pros and cons of each. First the future. The pros: It was known. She'd lived through the hard part of life. In spite of all the jokes about being over-the-hill at fifty, there was also freedom in that age. She'd already traveled through many difficult times. Her life was established. It was time to enjoy the fruits of her labor.

Which were. . .

"I'm married." As soon as she said the words, she was tempted to take them back and put them in the "con" column. It's not that she didn't love Dudley. He was a good man, a good provider, and an okay father. But what was the phrase her mother had used? He didn't float her boat.

Not that she expected mad, passionate living at age fifty. Yet shouldn't there be *some* passion? And for that matter, when had she ever experienced any passion?

She snickered. The only ardor she'd encountered in either life was with Bruce, her crud of a boyfriend who'd left her the moment he found out she was pregnant.

Once again her hands covered her unborn child.

The first time around she'd suffered through an abortion *and* the subsequent depression that had caused her to flunk out. Back in 1976 doctors hadn't recognized the mental and emotional aftereffects of abortion like they did now. They'd been too caught up in just being able to do it that they hadn't considered much about if they should. *Just because you can doesn't mean you should.*

Her mind flashed to the man who'd recently given her

that quote: David Stancowsky.

David Stancowsky?

She sucked in a breath as she realized he was one of the other winners! The phrase "small world" was not adequate.

So this is what the first Time Lottery winners had meant when they'd talked about a link and mentioned meeting each other in their pasts. How interesting. . .

She shook her head against the diversionary thought. "Focus, Vanessa, focus."

The baby was here in 1976, but there also was a child in the future: Rachel. If Vanessa had been a fuddy-duddy at age twenty-one in 1976, Rachel was following suit during her own twenty-first year. She was old before her time. Vanessa could blame her father for her own staid stuffiness, but what was Rachel's excuse? Were Dudley and herself to blame? Or. . . could she blame her father for this, too? For Yardley Pruitt was still highly involved in their lives. Had he succeeded in stifling a third generation of Pruitt women?

If Vanessa stayed in the past, she would never see Rachel again. Never be able to inspire her toward independence. She had her own mother to thank for that experience.

But in the future Mom is dead.

Tears came. Tears of regret. To think she'd spent thirty-four years of her life without her mother. Never knowing what their relationship really meant to both of them. Never knowing the truth and basing her entire life on lies.

If she went back, she might be able to undo some of the damage her father's deception had caused. Some. But the fact was, most moments were irretrievable. And only through the memories that she would retain from this visit into the past would she ever know her mother. She'd never be able to see the complete life that could have been lived under her influence, with her love. In the future, that life was gone.

She lifted her head and circled back to her first point. "But the future is established. It's known."

That *was* a plus. She was a successful community volunteer, she lived in a lovely home, she wanted for no material possession. She knew who she was and what she was. People respected her.

But for what? For raising the act of do-gooding to the level of a divine appointment? For making everyone around her feel inferior because they weren't as good, weren't as giving, weren't a saint like she was? Oh, the pride she'd taken in being needed. Her need to be needed.

But was that really a bad thing? Wasn't that a common human trait?

Not to the point of obsession.

She ran her fingers through her hair, trying to get back on task. If she went back to the future there was one perk she hadn't acknowledged. She'd have the chance to call her father on all his past lies. Face-to-face. There would be satisfaction in that. Revenge could be sweet.

But what would it prove? What good would come of it? Most likely she would end up being estranged from him then, as she was estranged from him here in 1976.

"I'll start over in the future."

That was an option. Fifty wasn't *that* old. After telling her father off, she could rid herself of all the mediocrity of her life. She could quit her obsessive community work, quit her marriage, get an apartment of her own, and start fresh. *But isn't that what you're doing here?*

She raised a fist to the cross. "I'm confused!"

Another voice sounded behind her. "I'm sorry to hear that."

She turned around to see Lewis standing in the middle aisle. "What are you doing here?" she asked.

"I could ask you the same question."

She let out a puff of air. There was no way she could ever explain Dual Consciousness to a 1976 man who didn't even know about PCs, CDs, or DVDs, much less Alternities, Serums, and Loops. "I have a big decision to make, Lewis, and I—"

He slid in beside her on the pew. "Can I help?"

"If only you could."

"I'm a good sounding board. Talk. Let your ideas bounce off me."

It was a stupid idea, and yet. . .maybe a brilliant one. As her thoughts needed to turn to why she should stay in 1976, they might benefit from the compassionate heart of this man who would certainly be a part of her life here.

But how to word it? She took a moment and looked at the calm assurance evident in his face. There was compassion there. Acceptance. Understanding. She found words to start. "I'm experiencing an upheaval in my life."

"The baby."

It was a good place to begin. "I'm having it. I've gotten that far in my decision. But I'm not sure beyond that. I don't think I'm ready to be a mother."

His eyes lit up and he put a hand on her knee. "There's a couple in church here. . . They've just started to talk about adopting a child. They can't have any of their own and have been praying for a baby for years. Maybe you're an answer to their prayers."

Vanessa's hand moved to her chest. "I can't imagine being an answer to anyone's prayers."

Lewis smiled at her. "Oh, really?"

She bumped against him, shoulder to shoulder. She liked him. A lot. The possibilities of a relationship with Lewis O'Neal were definitely intriguing. Yet she couldn't ignore the fact he was black. Though that didn't mean as much in the future, back in 1976 it was still an issue. A relationship with him would involve more than just the usual man-woman concerns.

"What else?" Lewis asked.

She glanced at her watch. She was glad he was spurring her on. She had only a short time left before the Dual Consciousness would fade and she would be stuck here.

There were worse fates.

She tried once again to focus. "Mom thinks I should change majors. I don't really like Business."

"Pursuing that degree is the result of your father's influence, right?"

"My entire life is the result of my father's influence." She looked at the cross, remembering the offering incident in her father's church. "He's mad at me."

"I'm sorry to hear that."

"I'm not sure we'll talk again. Ever."

"That's a little drastic."

"All these changes I'm talking about. . .he doesn't—or won't—approve of any of them."

"Do you need his approval?"

"I've always had it."

"Have you?"

His question stopped her cold. Had she? Even when she'd done what her father wanted her to do, in his eyes it was never done well enough, and *his* needs always took precedence. Perhaps there was no way to truly please him.

So why try?

She thought of more practical matters. "He's cut me off financially."

Lewis extended his hand and waited for her to shake it. "Welcome to membership in the Just-Getting-By Club."

She tucked her hand under her thigh. "I'm sorry to admit I'm used to having money."

"Nothing wrong with that. We all want money. We need money to survive. It's an unfortunate fact. But there *is* a certain satisfaction in working hard to get it."

If she was going to be involved with Lewis there was another question she had to ask. "Do you like being a maintenance man?"

He looked toward the cross a moment, then back at her. "I have a college degree."

She let her jaw drop. "You do? Then why—?"

"Why do I work as a glorified janitor?"

She nodded.

"Right out of college, I had an office job and used my accounting degree."

"What happened?"

"It didn't suit me. I found it hard to focus."

"You find focus in being a janitor?" She hated the way it sounded.

He put a hand on her knee. "I've discovered that the jobs I enjoy most are the ones where I find worship in the work. A way to offer it all up to Him. Attitude is everything, Vanessa. A paycheck is frosting. Though no one else may understand it, I find worship in my work here."

"Wow."

He laughed. "Don't get me wrong; when I'm fixing a toilet

or cleaning the carpet where some kindergartner spilled grape juice, I can complain with the best of them. It takes work to find worship in everything we do. But it's possible. It's a goal."

She found herself tearing up. "I've never met a man like you, Lewis."

"Yeah, well. . ."

"Excuse me? Lewis?"

They both turned around to see a woman in the doorway leading to the narthex. "Can you come help in the office? A shelf just broke and all Pastor Bill's books are on the floor."

"I'll be right there."

Lewis turned back to Vanessa. "Sorry. I have to go."

"Go to it. Go worship in the work."

He laughed. "I'll do my best." He stood and put a hand on the back of her head. "You going to be okay?"

She nodded. "Thanks for listening."

"Anytime. I'll see you later, okay?"

"Okay." And as she said the word she knew it was true. Nineteen seventy-six was full of uncertainties, of hard times ahead—both personally and in the world—and of big decisions yet to be made. There was nothing luxurious or easy about living a life here. And yet that was exciting. A breadth of possibilities lay before her. Would she make better decisions this time around?

Sometimes, and sometimes not. It was inevitable. But the fact that she had friends here, good friends, would help. And her mother was here. She looked back at the cross.

She also had Jesus here. Not the Jesus of ceremonies, fancy buildings, and business connections, but a God of the heart. A God who had created her with a unique purpose that He'd help her discover.

She'd wasted so many years in so many ways. There were only two parts of the future she would miss.

Dudley and Rachel.

There *was* a chance she'd end up marrying Dudley again. And maybe they'd have Rachel again.

She shook her head with a certainty that it would never happen. Their marriage had been an emotional reaction to the abortion she was *not* going to have. Her chances of even meeting Dudley Caldwell were slim. And if she never met Dudley, Rachel would not exist in this Alternity.

But if you go back to the future, your baby will not exist.

She pressed her hands against her face. In a way she was being forced to choose one child's life over another. It wasn't fair.

Life isn't fair.

She thought of the couple Lewis mentioned, the one who'd been praying for a baby. Her baby? If she stayed behind, another family could be created. That was a good thing, wasn't it?

Or what about the creation of a new family consisting of the baby, myself, and Lewis?

She removed her hands, letting herself breathe. Then she raised her face to the ceiling, and repeated the words she'd said in the cafeteria. "Here I am, God! Show me Your plan."

There was no direct answer. No overwhelming peace. And Vanessa realized there was no surefire way to know whether the decision she wanted to make was the one God wanted her to make. If her experience this second time around had taught her anything, it was that some decisions weren't simply black or white. Gray prevailed. The best she could do was try to follow Him, try to think of the bigger picture, and then move forward. The peace came in knowing God would be with her either way.

Time was up. She left the sanctuary to find Lewis.

Bangor—1958

Showing up at the Reynolds' home at breakfast would be considered strange, if not inappropriate—two traits David Stancowsky usually abhorred but today embraced. After spending the night *not* sleeping in the chair in his living room, he had little use for convention, logic, or even manners. Even the risk of dire consequences had faded from neon red to a dull gray in his consciousness. Whatever happened, happened. With the discovery of Millie's luggage in the locker, life had changed without his permission. So what good did it do to worry about some final meeting when it would all be wrapped up like stinking fish in a newspaper to be tossed in the trash?

The sound of his feet on the porch steps was too loud, offensive, but he was unable to do anything about it. And why should he? Shouldn't Millie hear him coming? Him, a soldier marching toward battle? Didn't ancient warriors utilize such an ominous sound against their enemy? The sound of impending disaster, marching ever closer. *Hear me, Millie? Hear me coming to do battle? To take the upper hand?*

The front door opened before he could knock. Rhonda was in a white housedress dotted with red rosebuds. She pulled the high collar together at her neck, as if it was a plunging décolletage. "David! I thought I heard someone out here."

"May I come in?"

She eyed him oddly and stepped aside. "Of course."

They stood awkwardly in the foyer. He hoped she would forgo the "Where were you yesterday" questions.

"May I take your hat and coat?"

His hat! He couldn't remember the last time he'd entered a building without removing it.

She took his things, hanging them on the coat rack. "Millie's making coffee for her father, and I was just going to make some eggs. Would you like to join us?"

"No, thank you. But could you ask Millie to come out here? I need to speak with her."

He felt himself being studied. Rhonda put her hand on his arm. "We were worried about you, David. Yesterday. When you disappeared. Is everything all right?"

He glared at her, causing her to remove her hand. "If you'll get Millie. . ." He moved to the parlor, leaving Rhonda to do as he asked.

A few moments later, Millie came into the room in a rush. "David! Where have you been?"

"What do you care?"

She blinked twice. "What's going on?"

He pulled the locker key from his pocket. He tossed it at her. She caught it with both hands. She looked at it.

Then she headed into the foyer and took her coat from the hook. "Let's go somewhere where we can be—"

His laugh sounded foreign to him. Removed. "You want to go somewhere? Yes, indeed, I think that's the problem. How's New York sound?"

She clutched the coat against her chest. Her eyes strayed to the kitchen. "Please, David. I don't want my father to hear."

He stood, and with a sweeping hand, encompassed the room. "But I want them to hear. Ray? Rhonda? Would you come in here, please?"

Millie rushed toward him, her hands trying to press down his words. "Shh. Please."

Ray and Rhonda appeared in the doorway. "Ah. Too late. Our audience is assembled." He led Rhonda to the rocker, and

Ray took a seat on the couch.

"What's this about?" Ray asked.

"It's about deceit. Betrayal. And don't ask me; ask your daughter."

Rhonda's hand once again found her collar.

"Millie? What have you done?" Ray asked.

Millie's eyes filled with tears, and she flung the coat across the room. "What have *I* done? I've tried to survive. No one can fault me for that."

Ray turned to David. "What is she talking about?"

Millie laughed. "See? You've just proven everything, Father. You don't ask me to explain myself; you ask David to do it for me." She moved to the edge of the coffee table, which divided them. "Between you and David planning my life, planning my wedding. . ."

"Don't use that tone with me, young lady."

She raised both hands in surrender, took a step back, then kowtowed. "Forgive me, almighty father, for daring to express my own thoughts."

He got to his feet, pointing at her. "You *will* show me respect!"

"You don't want respect, you want servitude." She crossed to her mother, putting a hand on the back of the rocker. "You want me to be another silent, obedient, meek woman like you've made Mom, never daring to confront, to question, to express herself."

Rhonda's eyes flitted between her husband and David. Her mouth moved, but she said nothing.

"You leave your mother alone." Ray offered his wife a hand, pulled her from the rocker, and deposited her on the couch beside him.

"Mom, do something. Say something. Stick up for yourself." Millie started crying. "Don't let him beat you down. We've talked about this. You agree with me. Show him some of the spark you've shown me."

Rhonda looked at Millie with panic in her eyes. Then Ray put his hand on her knee. Silencing her. Which was fine with David. This had nothing to do with Rhonda Reynolds.

"Can we get back on track, please?" David turned to Millie. "I want you to explain to your parents—to all of us—why you have a suitcase full of clothes and nearly three hundred dollars in a locker at the bus station."

Oddly, Rhonda looked at her hands, while Ray said, "A locker? Where were you planning to go?"

Millie raised her chin defiantly. "Anywhere that's away from both of you."

Her father shook his head. "This doesn't make sense. You're getting married. You're planning the wedding."

"No, you're planning the wedding. David's planning the wedding. Mom and I are merely supposed to agree and marvel at your brilliance."

"I'm putting up a lot of money for this affair, Millie," Ray said. "I'm doing it for you. It doesn't matter to me if you have a big to-do—"

"Of course it does. The president of Mariner Construction can't allow his daughter's wedding to be small and nondescript."

"You're making it sound as if I have an ego problem—and I don't. I'm as humble as the next man."

She laughed as if he'd told a joke. "You two know nothing about how a real man should behave. A loving, kind, generous. . .never mind."

Since she'd brought him up. . . David pulled the snapshot

from his pocket. “Were you leaving town with this man?”

Millie didn’t touch the picture.

Ray held out his hand. “Let me see.” He looked at it. “Who’s this?”

“My teacher.”

“He’s more than that,” David said. “Look at the way his arm is around your shoulders. Plus, I’ve seen the two of you talk while you’re in class. It’s more than normal student-to-teacher—”

Millie tossed her hands in the air. “Who needs a husband when one can have a spy? You see why I have to leave?”

David moved close, his voice low. “I’d find you. I’d come after you.”

Her chin quivered, then firmed. “But you wouldn’t have found me. Because Millie Reynolds would be no more.”

He remembered the driver’s license. “You’d change your name. So what? There are still ways to find you. I’d find ways.”

“Not if you thought I was dead.”

No one moved.

Millie straightened her shoulders. “You didn’t know it, David, but you foiled the plan last weekend in Bar Harbor.”

His brain wasn’t functioning. “What are you talking about?”

“When you stopped me from driving away in your precious car, in the rain. Just a few seconds more. . .if only I hadn’t flooded the thing, I would have been on the road, driving away from you, driving to a particularly steep, curvy point in Acadia Park.” She smiled at him proudly. “I must admit it was going to be an added bonus to let your car be involved in my plan. I was going to take great pleasure in seeing your 1958 Calypso and Burma green Pontiac Bonneville Sports Coupe with the sliding Plexiglas sun visor and the 'Memory-maniac' power memory seat destroyed."

The "Memo-Matic" *power memory seat.* "What were you going to do to my car?"

She strolled past him, pulling a finger under his chin. "I thought it was *our* car, darling."

"Millie, enough!" her father said. "What were you going to do with David's car?"

She closed her eyes and raised her face to the ceiling. "You two. With every word you confirm my choice. You are the two most unfeeling, possessive, controlling, arrogant—"

Without warning, Rhonda stood up. "She was going to fake her death by letting the car drive over a cliff into the ocean! She was going to take her new identity, run away, and start over with a man who truly loves her and who doesn't feel the need to control her."

After her outburst, Rhonda hurried to Millie's side, taking refuge under her arm. "Thank you, Mom."

"You knew about this, Rhonda?" Ray asked.

"I encouraged it. I helped plan it."

All David could say was, "Why?"

She smiled at her daughter. "I was not about to risk having Millie live the same broken, weak, beaten-down life I've lived. I want her to be happy."

How simplistic. It sounded like Rhonda. She was not a bright woman. Anyone who thought in terms of happy or sad was—

All of a sudden David saw a pop of light like someone had taken a flash picture. But when his eyes cleared, no one was standing before him with a camera. In fact, they were all looking at him oddly.

"David?" Ray pointed at his face. "Are you all right? You jerked like you'd been shocked."

David wanted to say he was fine, but it wasn't the truth, or wasn't quite the truth. Physically he did feel fine, but mentally. . .it was as though his mind was a video, fast-forwarding.

Video. Fast-forward. *There is no such thing.*

And then he knew. Knew everything. This was the Dual Consciousness! He knew all about the David Stancowsky in 1958 but also about the David Stancowsky of the future. He caught a glimpse of himself in a wall mirror and rushed to see. He was young again! Twenty-eight. He ran his hands over his face. There were only hints of wrinkles on his forehead and at the corners of his eyes. It would be years before the lines became the permanent fissures that marked his age.

He looked down at his body. Though he'd taken good care of himself his entire life, he felt a strength now that had been absent too long. He flexed his biceps. Muscles. Power.

"David, what's gotten into you?"

He turned toward Millie and his breath left him. She was stunning. She was alive! He rushed toward her, taking her face in his hands. "Millie!"

She tried to push him away. "Let go!"

Rhonda looked to her husband. "Ray. . ."

He realized how strange his actions must seem. And there was no way he could explain it to them, to these people who thought television was a modern marvel, these people who'd never heard of computers, microwaves, the Vietnam and Gulf Wars, or that there'd been a man on the moon. The Berlin Wall hadn't been built yet—nor torn down. They only knew of Nikita Khrushchev, Sputnik, and forty-eight states. Elvis was a GI, *West Side Story* was a new show on Broadway, and Buddy

Holly was still singing "Peggy Sue"—live.

David felt Ray's hand on his arm. "Let her go, David. I don't know what's gotten into you, but—"

David raised his hands, setting Millie free. She moved to the other side of the room. He couldn't blame her.

But then he remembered that she'd wanted to move farther than that away from him. She'd planned to run away with another man. She'd planned to wreck his car. . . . That's where they'd left off when the Dual Consciousness had kicked in. He finally said what had not been said. "You were going to fake your death."

Millie and her mother exchanged a look. Then she said, "Yes."

"You hated me that much."

She let out a breath. "I don't hate you, David. I just need to be free of you. Free of my father. Free of the past. Free to have a future."

He nearly laughed. Wasn't that the point of the Time Lottery? "But faking. . .you didn't have to go to that extreme." He wished his thoughts would calm. He needed to think clearly. "I'm just glad you're alive. I'm just glad I stopped you from driving off the—"

His mind skipped the here and now, and landed on the there and then. The first time through 1958 he hadn't stopped her. She'd driven off in the rain and wrecked the car and—

Died?

He sucked in a breath, nearly losing his balance. "You didn't die? You never died!"

"What?"

His chest was tight. Was he having a heart attack? "I have to sit."

He found a chair. "I'll get you some water," Rhonda said.

He shook his head in total disbelief. "You never died!" Everything he'd known. Everything he'd believed. Everything he'd based his life upon was false.

Ray put a hand on his shoulder. "David, you need to calm down."

They didn't understand. They couldn't. He bolted from the chair, shoving their attention away. "I need to go. I need to be alone." He grabbed his coat and made for the door.

"Stop, David. You shouldn't be alone when you're like this."

He yanked open the door and pointed a finger in Millie's face. "You've been alive the whole time! I mourned for you. My entire life was spent mourning for you."

She took a step back into the waiting arms of her mother. "You're talking like a madman."

Oh, yes, indeed. A *mad* man. That's what he was. He ran to his car and drove away. He was assailed by its new smell. Repulsed by how much it had meant to him. He would drive it off a cliff himself if it meant he didn't have to know this awful truth.

A car honked. He'd missed a stop sign. He was speeding.

Speeding toward what?

He pulled to the curb and shut off the car. He had to calm down and think. *If only I didn't have to think. It hurts to think. It hurts to know.*

He slammed his hands onto the steering wheel. "Enough! I have only an hour to decide whether I want to stay or go back. Be logical. Think it through."

He forced himself to take some deep breaths and was relieved his chest no longer hurt. Wouldn't that have been laughable? To have a heart attack and get stuck in 1958 forever?

But would that be so bad?

A little girl came down the sidewalk on roller skates. Roller skates, not Rollerblades; the kind worn over shoes and tightened with a key. She wore a dress and saddle shoes.

A milk truck pulled across the street, and the milkman tipped his cap to David when he got out. He took two glass bottles of milk to the back door, put them in a milk box, and retrieved two empties.

It was a simpler time. Innocent. A better time? The calm before the storm of an assassinated president, Vietnam, civil unrest, shuttle disasters, and 9/11. There was so much history to suffer through. Why would he ever choose to do it again?

He closed his eyes, blocking out this time and place. What if he did stay here? What would he be leaving behind?

The first time around, when he'd thought Millie had died, he'd found comfort from Ray—and comforted Ray. His father-in-law-never-to-be had decided to ignore that technicality and had taken him into the business as a son. David had found great satisfaction turning Mariner Construction into a megacorporation. If he stayed here and started over, would he be able to duplicate that same success? There was no grief to bond him and Millie's father. There was no guarantee he'd even have a job.

And yet. . .wouldn't that be exciting? To truly start over fresh? Over the years he *had* occasionally wondered what he would have done if he hadn't teamed up with Ray. But it was a risk. Though he'd be the first to ring his own bell, if he stayed here, he might not rise to his former height. And would he be content as a middle-class business owner, struggling to make the payroll each week? So much of his identity was enmeshed with what he did.

That's because you didn't have a family.

Ah. Family. Why hadn't he ever settled down? Sure, there had been a few women, but never a relationship. He'd always held back, content to mourn Millie.

"She's alive!" His words echoed through the car.

Back in the future Millie was alive! She'd been alive these forty-some years, living another life with a man with curly red hair. Was there a Tracy Osgood alive and well and living in. . .

He had the sudden urge to find her. Demand to know—

Know what? Right here in 1958 he'd discovered why she'd gone to such lengths. "I picked out her wedding dress."

At the sound of his own words, he cringed. It just wasn't done. Not in 1958. Not ever. What had he been thinking? Sure, Ray had condoned it, even egged him on. But that didn't make it right. Two controlling men, controlling their women. Being *too* involved.

A snicker escaped. After Millie's "death," Rhonda had found her freedom, too, though in a less dramatic way. Soon after the crash she'd divorced Ray. It had been a totally uncharacteristic act of gumption. But now, knowing the plan, it made sense. Rhonda was in on it. Rhonda knew where Millie-Tracy was going to live. So for the past four decades, they'd been having the last laugh on the men in their lives. Living free. Being happy.

He leaned his head back but found his usual Mercedes headrest missing. He'd made fun of Rhonda's desire for happiness, and yet. . .had *he* been happy the first time around? He'd found success. He'd found recognition. He'd found wealth. But happiness? Purpose?

He covered his face in his hands, ashamed at what he'd ignored. How could he have lived an entire life seeking what didn't matter and ignoring what did? What a waste of time.

Time!

He looked at his watch. When the Dual Consciousness had first come upon him, he hadn't checked the time, so he had no clear idea of how much of the hour he had left.

He pressed his fingers against his temples. "Concentrate!"

What were the rules? If he wanted to go back to the future, he needed to focus on it, and an hour after the Dual Consciousness kicked in, his own mind would lead him back. He would awake in the Sphere.

But if he wanted to stay in the past, all he had to do was continue on. The Dual Consciousness would fade, and he would forget about the future life that once was but would be no more. He would live life fresh and new from this point on.

Fresh and new. That was appealing.

Without Millie. That was not.

He felt out of control and didn't like the feeling.

Good.

He blinked at the thought. Good?

Then suddenly, David suffered a shiver, and with it a knowing that he was not alone. There was another power at work here. One he had ignored too long.

Oh God, help me.

Had he just prayed? Had the great David Stancowsky finally realized that he was not in control?

How ironic to come into the past in order to be broken. In the future he'd never felt like this, had never felt out of control. He'd wrapped his entire being around the memory of Millie and the quest to make the business great. But what had it gotten him? A life of loneliness and possessions. All in all, quite pitiful.

Look at what you have. Here.

If he stayed here, he would be alone. He might not even have a job. A man with no connections. No loyalties.

Dina's voice rang in his head. *"I'm very loyal to those I respect and admire."* There was more implied than business loyalty. The cake, the neck massage, the other comments. . . Plus, she'd come to the door of his home, worried about him.

She cares for me!

He pulled a breath through his teeth. Dina Edmonds. His secretary in the future was his secretary in 1958. She'd been with him all these years. She'd never married. Had she cared for him all that time? Had she been waiting for him to notice her beyond duty? Had she spent her life pining for him as he had pined for Millie? How tragic for both of them.

A wave of regret nearly drowned him. Had he made her suffer all this time? She was the epitome of loyalty, all right. And he was the epitome of blindness.

He'd known Dina Edmonds her entire adult life. He knew the kind of woman she was. Had become. And here she was in 1958, close by, young and eager. And willing to love him if only he let her. Could he love her back? Was this possibility of love enough to start a life?

He laughed at the thought of it. He started the car and headed toward the offices of Mariner Construction. Though it went against his very nature and made little sense, he was going to let someone else make his decision for him.

But he had to hurry.

"Good morning, Mr. Stancowsky," Dina said.

He had no time for small talk. He placed his arms on her

desk and leaned toward her. "I've sensed that you're attracted to me, Dina."

She blushed. "Sir, I. . ."

He realized he'd omitted an important fact. "Millie and I are no longer engaged. No longer dating."

"Oh. I'm so sorry."

"Are you?"

She fumbled for words. He stopped her efforts with a raised hand. "I know I'm being presumptuous and forward, but trust me, I have my reasons and time is of the essence. I just need to know if you're interested in me as a man."

Her eyebrows rose. "Uh. Yes?"

"You didn't sound very positive."

She cleared her throat. "Yes. Yes. I am interested in you, David. As a man."

He stood. "Good. Because I like you, too. And I think we should go out to dinner tonight. To get to know each other better."

She put a hand to her lips, stifling a laugh. "I don't understand what brought this on, but I'd love to go to dinner with you."

He made another decision. He shut off her adding machine, then went around the side of her desk and extended a hand. "Let's make it brunch."

18

Understanding is a fountain of life to those who have it,
but folly brings punishment to fools.
PROVERBS 16:22

Present-Day Kansas City

"You can sit over here, Mrs. Lopez."

"Thank you, Mr. MacMillan." Brandy took a seat on the perimeter of what they called the Sphere. It was like being inside a huge ball and was painted blue so it looked like the sky. It reminded her of a ride at Epcot. And seemed just as unreal.

She looked across the room at Lane. She was in a hospital bed with a curved contraption wrapped around the top portion of her head. Tubes and monitors kept her alive while she was mentally in 1987. Oh yeah. This was Epcot-ish, all right.

Directly across the Sphere, sitting along the opposite edge, was an elderly woman. She was Dina Edmonds, the secretary to Stancowsky. To Brandy's left sat the Caldwell family—the husband and a daughter. The grandfather who'd made a fool of himself with the press was absent. Poor man. Brandy had gotten to meet the other three for a few minutes right before they'd all come inside to take up their waiting positions. They were an odd bunch, instantly bonded by the desire to see their loved ones again.

Loved ones. Though the world had only seen Dina acting as Stancowsky's secretary, her feelings were obviously deeper. Maybe that was natural after working together for decades. It wasn't anything the woman had said, but there was a level of concern that showed in her eyes and in the way she couldn't sit still.

Brandy felt sorry for the Caldwells. They didn't just have a friend at stake, they had a wife and mother. Yet certainly Vanessa Caldwell would be coming back. Brandy couldn't imagine ever choosing to leave her own family forever and ever. A few days was hard enough.

She watched the doctors and technicians hover around the three sleeping winners. Alexander MacMillan and some other bossy man hovered, flitting from one to the other, getting updates. Brandy and the others had been told there was no set time for the Dual Consciousness to wear off. They'd been told to be patient.

Not Brandy's strong suit. But she'd do it. For Lane she'd do anything.

Come back to me, Laney-girl. Please come back. I miss you so—

"She's waking up!"

Brandy popped to her feet as people converged on Lane. She wasn't sure if she was allowed to go closer but didn't wait to be asked.

"Not too close," said the bossy one, barring her way.

Mr. MacMillan took her hand. "It won't be long now."

Lane stirred, her body moving in short spasms as if it was waking up one nerve ending at a time. Her eyelids fluttered.

"Come on, Laney-girl, you can do it," Brandy whispered. Mr. MacMillan smiled, but the bossy guy gave her a dirty look.

Lane opened her eyes once, then closed them. Brandy gasped. "No! Wake up!"

Mr. MacMillan patted her hand. "She's fine. Just give her a minute."

After a few more attempts, Lane opened her eyes for real and left them open. *Yes!* Brandy began to cry. She hugged Mr. MacMillan. "She's back! She's back!"

The doctor and nurse talked quietly to Lane and took her vitals. Brandy couldn't hear what was being said but felt her heart burst with excitement. The doctor gave a thumbs-up. *Oh yeah. It's a thumbs-up, all right!*

In no time at all, Lane was helped to sitting. She dangled her feet over the side of the bed. Brandy looked to Mr. MacMillan. "Can I?"

Before he had a chance to answer, Lane saw her and held out her arms. "Brandy. . ."

Brandy wanted to fling herself at her friend but hugged her gingerly. "Oh, Laney, I'm so glad you're back. I missed you so much."

They pulled apart and Lane smiled. "I didn't miss you. You were with me. With me all the way—as always."

The doctor stood close. "How are you feeling, Ms. Holloway?"

Lane ran a hand across her forehead where the machine had been. "I feel fine. A bit like I've awakened from a long nap, but fine."

Mr. MacMillan stepped forward. "If you're up to it. . . would you ladies like to withdraw to a private room for a bit?"

"Love to." With help, Lane got off the table and tested her

legs. Brandy was right there supporting her.

The bossy guy came close. "There will be a debriefing soon. And then a press conference tomorrow."

Mr. MacMillan seemed to ignore the man, giving his full attention to the two friends. He gave them a wink and a smile as he led them out of the Sphere. "Don't worry about that. For now, you have time."

Lane folded the scrubs into a neat pile after changing into her street clothes in one of the waiting rooms near the Sphere.

"So you don't know if you got the part of Bess at the *Empty Promises* audition?" Brandy asked.

"Not for sure. The Dual Consciousness kicked in before I even went to it."

"But we can assume. . ."

Lane shook her head. Her memories of the past were vivid, for they truly *had* just happened yesterday. "I don't think we can assume anything. As Mr. Dobbins reminded me, auditions aren't a science. They're subjective from the judges' end and iffy on the actor's end. I was really on when I went to the original audition. Who knows if I would have done as well in Chicago?"

"But surely. . ." Brandy shrugged her shoulders as she looked at Lane. "I mean, you're *you*."

Lane laughed. "I always appreciate your support, Brand, but I had no clout then. I was just a skinny teenager taking a shot."

Brandy straddled a chair, leaning against its back. "But if you chose the fame back then and have the fame now, why didn't you stay? Wouldn't it be fun to do it all over again?"

Lane realized now more than ever how natural it was to

think that the grass was always greener. Natural and dangerous. "It might have been fun. But if this Time Lottery taught me anything, it's that one choice can change everything. Winning the Bess audition was the first of many steps. The only way I got to this point in my career was to make a series of distinct choices. If I did it over again, chances are I would choose differently at least once, and then I wouldn't be here." She took a breath. "Does that make any sense?"

Brandy wriggled her hands by her ears and mimicked the theme to *Twilight Zone.* "Doo-do-do-do."

Lane reached over and took Brandy's hand. "Forget the audition and the fame a moment. One of the reasons I came back was you. After being around your mom again—"

"You saw my mom?"

"In all her glory."

Brandy looked down. "Oh."

"I saw how crucial it was to the life you have now with Randy and the kids that you got away from her. Though we didn't think about it so bluntly at the time, I truly think she would have killed you, Brandy." When Brandy didn't respond, Lane feared she'd gone too far. "Hey, I'm sorry. I have no right to—"

Brandy looked up. "You're right. Following you to Hollywood didn't just get me a fun job and a new life; it gave me life—period."

"Of course, we'll never know for sure."

"I know." Brandy patted her heart. "I know." She stood, whipping the chair around forward. "But you know the best thing about you coming back?"

"What?"

"I don't have to look for another job!"

Lane loved the way Brandy made her laugh. She stood. "I suppose I should go debrief; do my duty."

Brandy put a hand on her arm. "Just a minute. There's something you need to know."

By the look on Brandy's face, Lane feared something had happened to Randy or the kids. But no. . .surely she would have told her that right off. Surely Lane would have read it in her face. "What's wrong?"

"Toby Bjornson came forward."

"My Toby?"

"The very one." Brandy told her about Toby and the media attention, and how the leak had changed everything, climaxing with the shooting.

"A shooting—in my house?"

"I broke a lamp."

"No, no. I don't care about the house, but to think he had you in there, by yourself, with a gun. You must have been petrified."

"Actually, I wasn't. It was Toby. And though he *was* desperate, it was a sad desperation more than a dangerous one. I felt sorry for him. I feel sorry for him." She looked around the room. "I really should call the hospital and check on him."

No, I should call the hospital. "It's all my fault."

"Stop that! The leak caused the problem. In the initial press conference, you had a right to tell the media what seemed best at the time. There was no way for you to know it would go wrong. It wasn't any of their business if you wanted to go into the past to see Toby or try—"

"No." Lane turned away. "I'm talking about Toby turning out the way he did, having the life he did. He loved me and I left him. Twice. That *is* my fault."

Brandy rubbed her back. "He wasn't the one for you, Laney-girl. You just proved that. As for the way his life turned out, that's due to his choices, not yours. Besides, this last week when he *chose* to step into the limelight—your limelight, I might add—it sounds like he had a good-enough life. He worked construction, had an okay place to live."

"Is he married?"

"I don't think so."

"That's too bad." She sighed. "And yet. . ."

"And yet what?"

Lane had to walk away from her. Brandy, Mrs. Susie Homemaker, would not understand what she was about to say. "Did you ever think that maybe some people are not supposed to be married and have children?"

"You're just saying that because you're manless at the moment."

Lane faced her. "I don't think so. Back in the past, I met up with a woman who said something that stuck with me: 'Just because you can doesn't mean you should.' "

"That could apply to a lot of things."

"Including getting married and having children. The thing is, Brandy, I'm not sure it's possible to have it all. And by coming back here, I made my choice. Acting is my talent—my God-given talent if I want to give credit where it's due. The fame and opportunities I've been given shouldn't be tossed away. They were too hard-fought. Giving them up wouldn't be fair."

"Fair to whom?"

The next word didn't come easily for Lane. She'd never been one to talk about God much. But with Grandma Nellie's voice still fresh in her head, she said it. "It wouldn't be fair to God."

Brandy's eyebrow raised. "Since when do you mention the *G*-word?"

"Don't act like I'm some heathen. I believe in God."

"Good, 'cause He believes in you."

"Really?" She hated the way her voice sounded. So needy. Like a child desperate for approval.

"Cross my heart."

There was a knock, then Alexander MacMillan popped his head in. "Ms. Holloway? Can I interrupt your reunion for some Time Lottery business? Just a short debriefing. Then you can meet up with Mrs. Lopez again."

"Of course." She gave Brandy a hug. "Later, friend."

"I'll be here."

When Lane reached the hall she looked toward the Sphere. "Has anyone else come back yet?"

"Not yet."

Mac led Lane into another room. Wriggens was supposed to be there waiting for them. Now he was making them wait. Mac suspected it was on purpose. That man.

Mac pulled out a chair for Lane. "Chief Administrator John Wriggens will be joining us in a moment."

"Actually, I'm glad for the chance to get to talk to you alone."

"Oh?"

"My friend Brandy said there was a leak to the media regarding my true motives for visiting 1987."

"Yes, I'm afraid—"

"And that leak caused Toby Bjornson to be humiliated, which caused him to be beat up, which caused him to be in a situation where he was shot?"

Mac was taken aback. She certainly got to the point. "Yes, I suppose one led to the other."

"How many people knew about my true motives?"

Uh-oh. "Three."

"You, the doctor who got me there, and. . . ?"

Mac glanced at the door, hoping Wriggens wouldn't choose this moment to enter. He considered some double-talk, stating that anybody could have found out.

"The truth, Mr. MacMillan. At the moment I hold truth in the highest regard."

"John Wriggens was the only other person who knew."

"The man we're waiting for?"

Mac nodded.

"Are you the leak?"

"No!"

"Do you think the doctor did it?"

"I would trust Dr. Rodriguez with my life—with your life."

"Which leaves John Wriggens."

"There is no proof, Ms. Holloway. And I assure you the TTC is a highly respected—"

She stopped his defense with a raised hand. "The TTC organization is a prize to *be* prized. But it doesn't necessarily follow that every employee is above reproach."

What could he say?

She leaned toward him across the table. "Do you, Alexander MacMillan, think John Wriggens leaked the information?"

"I. . ."

The door opened and Wriggens entered. "Well, well, here you are. Finally. Did you have a nice trip?"

"Yes, I did. But if you'll excuse me a moment." She turned

back to Mac. "Regarding that particular piece of information, I just want you to know that I'll take care of it. I'll take care of everything."

Wriggens pulled out a chair at the head of the table. "Everything? What's this? What did I miss?"

Everything.

Lane patted Wriggens's hand and smiled her Hollywood smile. "Now, Mr. Wriggens, would you like to hear about my experience?"

Mac sat back in awe—of her charm, her acting ability, and her integrity.

He could hardly wait to see how this turned out.

Dina watched as Mr. MacMillan led the Caldwell family out of the Sphere to take them to their hotel. Like David, Vanessa hadn't come back yet, and it might be tomorrow before they knew for sure what was happening. As it was, it was nearly tomorrow now: 11:45. They'd been waiting in the Sphere for nearly twelve hours. And it had been a good ten hours since Lane Holloway had awakened.

The VIPs had left their balcony perch, and the team of doctors and technicians had been relieved. Only Dina stayed behind. Only Dina stayed loyal to the end.

The end. Was that what she was waiting for? The end of David's life—as he knew it. *Which would mean the end of my life as I know it.*

She stood by his bed for the umpteenth time. As the hours had passed, they'd allowed her to move her chair from the perimeter to his side. Though they hadn't said anything, and though she hadn't asked, she knew it was an act of sympathy.

Let the grieving loved ones move close for the final hours.

She lifted his hand and linked her fingers through his. How many times had she longed to hold this hand, to feel his skin against hers? The only contact they'd ever made had been perfunctory, yet in her dreams. . .

Those dreams were dead now. She'd been such a fool. Pining after a man for nearly fifty years. *Hope springs eternal.* Wasn't it Shakespeare who'd said, "Lord, what fools these mortals be"? And wasn't she being a fool now, staying deep into the night beside a man who had never loved her? A man who'd chosen to stay in his past with a woman who hated him enough to die *because* of him, rather than return to a woman who would willingly die *for* him.

She swiped away a tear, not sure if it was a tear of sorrow or anger. Probably both. Her lifetime spent on the periphery of David's life had always elicited conflicting emotions.

There was a sudden flurry by the computer console. "He's going."

Going? The doctor and nurse moved close and Dina took a step back, giving them room. They checked his vitals. Then the doctor looked at her. "He *is* dying, Ms. Edmonds. Dying here, that is. He must have decided to stay in his past."

Must have.

Then, without consciously deciding, Dina found herself walking to the exit.

"But don't you want to stay—?"

No, thank you. She'd finally had enough.

For you, O God, tested us; you refined us like silver.
PSALM 66:10

Present-Day Kansas City

The phone woke her.

Rachel reached to the left, then realized she wasn't at home. She was in a hotel and the phone was to her right. "Yes?"

"It's Dad, honey. Mom's gone."

The words did not compute, and she sat up and found a light switch. "What?"

"I got a call from Mr. MacMillan. Your mother just passed away."

"We weren't there? We weren't there!"

His voice took on an edge. "Neither was she, honey. She stayed in the past. She chose not to come back to us."

Though they'd expected this might happen, to have it be over. . .

"MacMillan says we'll need to make arrangements for the funeral. But there's no need to hurry over there unless we want to."

She shook her head. "I don't want to go back there. Ever."

"I know. Me neither. Do you want me to come to your room?"

"No. I'm fine. I just want to be alone."

His voice caught. "Yeah. Me, too. I'll call you in a little while, okay?"

She hung up, not wanting to hear his tears. She was surprised to find none of her own. The closeness she'd felt toward her mother—since her mother had left for the past—suddenly seemed contrived. And way too late. However, the closeness she'd felt for her father since then. . .

She looked in the direction of his room. Why did that seem more real?

Because he's real. He's here. You still have time with him. A lifetime with him.

A second chance with him. One she didn't intend to waste.

She got dressed.

Alexander MacMillan stood before the media, ready to make his statement. Lane Holloway—the only winner to return—stood in the wings. They began peppering him with questions, but he held out his arms, quieting them. "Thank you for coming to this post–Time Lottery press conference. I know you're eager to know who stayed in their Alternity and who returned. So here's the answer to that question: Vanessa Caldwell and David Stancowsky did not return."

"Do we get to talk to their families?"

"Not at this time. As you can imagine, they are in mourning and need to be afforded the respect that goes with their grief."

"And their $250,000 in life insurance."

Their laughter aggravated Mac. Though the life insurance policy was a necessary accoutrement to the Time Lottery, there always seemed to be someone who focused on the money rather than on the experience. He moved on. "However, as you have deduced, since I have mentioned the two who stayed behind, that means one has returned to us and is thus able to share her experiences." The applause started before he said her name. "I give to you Lane Holloway."

As soon as Lane heard the applause, she knew she'd made the right decision to come back. Her soul was like a sponge, soaking in the life-sustaining refreshment. She strode across the stage, waving to the audience, and took her position beside Mr. MacMillan.

As soon as the applause died, she spread her arms and said, "I'm back!" More applause. Hoots and hollers, too. "Thank you for that wonderful welcome home. And I *am* glad to be home. Though it was an interesting experience returning to my childhood roots, I came to realize that the blessings I've been given through acting opportunities in this lifetime are not to be thrown away without cause and—"

The back door of the auditorium opened and a man rushed in. "Toby Bjornson is dead! He died!"

Bedlam. Lane felt her knees buckle. She was glad Mr. MacMillan was there to steady her. "Is it true?" she whispered to him.

"I don't know. But I'll find out." He motioned for the man who'd run in with the news to come toward the stage. They conferred a few minutes, then Mr. MacMillan returned to his place beside her, giving her the slightest of nods before speaking. "I am sad to report that it's true. Though Mr. Bjornson's condition was thought to be stable, he took a turn for the worse this morning and died."

"Oh, Laney!" Lane turned toward Brandy's voice calling from the wings. She wanted to go to her but could not. Not now. For inside her, besides the sorrow and shock, a fierce anger brewed. One that could not be denied. One whose time had come.

Questions were tossed in her direction, but she ignored them. She left Mr. MacMillan, moved to the edge of the stage, raised her hands, and waited for them to be quiet. She needed their full attention.

Finally, she had it. "I am deeply saddened to hear that Toby has died. Although I had not seen him since 1987, I wished him no harm. Obviously, in my absence I was unaware of all that has transpired this past week with him coming forward and receiving media attention—and humiliation. I cringe at the pain he must have gone through that led directly to his death." She pointed to her chest. "I am partly responsible." She pointed to them. "But so are you. We all are. This obsessed fascination we have with so-called news, with butting into the private lives of others to fulfill some kind of sick need. . ."

She heard a stirring but quieted it with a hand. "I've chosen a life of fame and celebrity. The media is a necessary part of my life. I need you. In part, you have made me what I am. But there has to be a balance. We each have public and private parts of our lives. And when the private is shoved into the public domain. . .could your own lives survive such scrutiny?

"I am partly to blame for Toby's humiliation because I lied about my true motivation for visiting the past. I didn't want the bad press that would surely come out of my choice to explore a life without fame. And so I lied and offered you a choice I hoped would satisfy yet keep my reputation intact. The choice of young love. For whatever reason, Toby latched onto my words and stepped into your path—and was run down because of it. More specifically, because of a leak of information."

She looked at Mr. MacMillan. It was payback time. "Although the wisdom of my initial lie is questionable, it was never meant to hurt anyone, and it never *would* have hurt anyone if the truth would have remained secret. But without me here to explain and soften my true choice, the leak created havoc—and now death." She shifted her weight to the other foot. "I can only assume that the person who created the leak did so out of a sick need for scandal and publicity. Unfortunately, I have discovered that the person responsible for the leak is the chief administrator of the TTC, John Wriggens."

The audience responded with shouted questions. She gave them a nod, said thank you, and left the stage.

She grabbed Brandy's hand. "Let's go home."

Mac fell into his office chair. He had not seen Wriggens since the press conference. The press conference room had been chaos after Lane had left the stage. But chaos that he had enjoyed handling. If the Time Lottery caught a little heat, so be it. Fire refined silver and made it stronger.

For now it could be stronger without John Wriggens at the helm. And though Mac hadn't heard anything from the higher-ups, he couldn't imagine them allowing Wriggens to keep his job. Of course, there was a possibility that Mac's job was in jeopardy. If so, he would make the sacrifice. For the good of the Time Lottery.

"Busy day at the office, hon?"

He looked up to see Cheryl in the doorway. "You could say that."

She came in and closed the door. "Is he gone?"

"I don't know."

"Lane did a boffo job. You couldn't have planned it better yourself." She looked at him through her lashes. "Unless. . . ?"

"She'd told me she was going to handle it. But I didn't know how. I didn't know she'd accuse him in front of the world."

Cheryl took a seat in the guest chair. "He deserves whatever he gets. After he took that bribe from Phoebe's husband last year, we all knew he was working on borrowed time."

Mac cleared off his desk, ready to leave, to go with her anywhere. "You know what's odd? I feel sorry for him."

She laughed. "You're way too godly for me, Mac. For the world."

Not at all. "He's a bitter man. The only time I've ever seen him joyful is when he got one up on someone."

She stood. "You ready to go?"

"You mean am I ready to surrender myself into your capable hands?"

She pulled him close. "You have no idea."

At the last second, Mac backtracked to Wriggens's office, feeling the responsibility to check on him, offer some word, some comfort. But it was dark. He flipped on the lights. The desk was cleared. There was a bare space on the wall where a modern art reproduction used to hang.

"He's gone," Cheryl whispered.

That he is. Thank You, God, for large favors.

Mac shut off the light and closed the door.

epilogue

And we know that in all things
God works for the good of those who love him,
who have been called according to his purpose.
ROMANS 8:28

Present-Day Buckhead—Two Weeks Later

Yardley Pruitt sat in the leather wing chair by the fireplace. The fire had grown cold.

When?

He'd lost track. He pulled the afghan around his shoulders, causing his feet on the ottoman to stick out the other end. He was missing one slipper. He reached to find it and saw that his glass of milk had tipped over on the side table, making a gooey mess of the crackers there. It smelled bad.

He smelled bad.

He felt bad.

He felt tipped over, missing, and cold. Extinguished.

He had no idea what day it was. All he knew was that it was post–Vanessa. She hadn't come back. She'd chosen a life with her mother rather than come back to him. Never again would he see her smiling face or put his arms around her to tell her he loved her.

Not that she'd smiled much. Not that he'd ever hugged her or told her how much he cared. And now it was too late.

He ran a hand over his face and found days' worth of stubble. He felt old. He *was* old. Too old to start over without her. He put a hand to his chest. His heart ached. Could a person die of a broken heart? He closed his eyes, willing to glide into that place of nonbeing. Maybe if he slowed his breathing enough his body would allow him to slip away. He started when he heard a key in the front door. *Who—?*

Then Rachel's voice. "Look at all these newspapers, Dad. I know there's something wrong. I know it."

They came inside and saw him. Ran to him.

"Yardley, what's happened to you?"

Rachel knelt at his side. "Are you all right? We've been calling and calling and—"

"Here's the problem." Dudley picked up the phone's receiver, which was making an odd pulsing sound. "How long have you had it off the hook?"

To admit he didn't know would admit too much. "I don't want to talk to anyone." He lifted his chin. "And no one wants to talk to me either."

Rachel moved to the ottoman, nudging his legs to the side. "We missed you last week at Mom's funeral."

"She didn't think about me when she stayed in the past; why should I think of her?"

Rachel put a hand on his. "But isn't that exactly what you've been doing? Thinking of her?" She looked at her father. "We have. It's going to take awhile to move forward." She looked back at him. "But it will be much easier with us helping each other. I took a semester off to do just that."

Her words were like a slap, forcing him into the moment, into reality. He sat forward, putting his feet on the floor. "You quit school? You can't do that. I need you to finish, young lady, and not throw away all the opportunities I can offer—"

Her laughter stopped him. Then Dudley joined in.

"What *are* you laughing at?"

Rachel cupped a hand around her mouth and pretended to whisper to her father, "He's back."

And Yardley realized she was right. It was as though he could actually feel the blood flow through his veins, as if each breath of air had power behind it, filling up his deflated shell. He held out a hand. "Help me up, girl. We have work to do."

She pulled him to standing. "I don't like the sounds of this."

He headed for the kitchen. "Of course you do. We have your future to plan, but first, I need a sandwich."

She and Dudley followed him. "Don't I have any say in this?"

He faced her, putting a hand on her shoulder. He looked at her seriously. "Of course you do, Rachel. Turkey or bologna?"

It was good to be back.

Malibu

"Well?" Brandy asked.

Lane closed the book and set her hands on top of it. "It's wonderful."

Brandy burst out of her chair and pumped a fist. "I told you! I told you *The Seat Beside Me* is the movie you need to make, the story you need to tell."

Lane nodded, admitting it all. Why hadn't she read it before now? Brandy had been after her to read this book for months.

Yet she knew the answer. Before the Time Lottery, she'd been so concerned with which movie was Oscar material that she hadn't had time for more obscure screenplays. Or books.

But now. . .it was as if she felt a responsibility to create meaningful movies, movies that moved people to change in positive ways. Which meant no nude scenes. No gratuitous violence or language. In the past two weeks she'd watched dozens of classic movies, reacquainting herself with the joys and talents of Jimmy Stewart, Grace Kelly, Cary Grant, Deborah Kerr. . . Good stories that entertained and lifted up. Stories that made people happy.

Her agent had not taken her new outlook well. He thought she was crazy for turning down the movie role they'd been discussing before her trek into her Alternity. "You turn down this part, someone else will win the Oscar for it. Mark my words."

At his pronouncement, her heart had skipped a beat and she had nearly wavered. But then she remembered how blessed she was to have gotten the chance to go back in time, to be reassured that her life was on the right path. She was supposed to be an actress. Now it was her responsibility to be a great one. In ways beyond awards and box-office statistics.

Brandy returned to her seat nearby. "You know who I think would make a perfect Anthony Thurgood in the movie?"

"Who?"

"Denzel Washington."

Brandy was right, and Lane added another thought. "He's directing now. What about getting him to direct the movie?"

Brandy left the chair and returned with a phone. "Call him."

"Now?"

"There's no time like the present."

Long Island

Millie pulled aside the front curtains and gasped.

"What's wrong?" her mother asked.

"There's no one out there."

Millie felt her mother's chin on her shoulder. "It's been two weeks. It's over, honey. It's finally over."

She nodded and felt an odd hint of disappointment. She'd spent over forty years with David in the back of her mind, with the lurking fear her real identity would be discovered.

"Do you wish you hadn't come forward?" her mother asked.

"It's okay. Actually it felt good to let people know the truth."

"Are you disappointed he didn't come back?"

Now, there was a question whose answer didn't make sense. She'd been nervous about David finding out the truth of her existence, yet now that he was gone and she was truly free, she missed him.

"Honey?"

"I would have liked to talk to him one more time—on neutral ground."

"Do you think, back in David's Alternity, that you married him?"

Millie shook her head vehemently. "If I wouldn't have faked my death that day, I would have found a way to do it on another day. There is no chance I would have allowed David to be my husband."

"Would *you* have liked a chance to go back and change something?"

Millie heard Deke humming in the kitchen. "I loved Deke then; I love him now. I don't need an Alternity. Unlike some people, I got it right the first time around."

Shipboard—The Caribbean

Dina sat on the deck chair and looked out over the aqua water. Other than a faint slice of land on the horizon, there were only miles and miles of deep blue sea.

How long had she been staring at nothing?

What did it matter? Her time was her own. And this cruise was hers to enjoy in whatever way she wished. If she wanted to spend the entire day napping, reading, and staring across the water, that was her business. She was a retired woman with no responsibilities whatsoever except to see the world that had been going on without her. And when she was done seeing the Caribbean, she had plans to hop on a plane to see Rome and Venice. St. Peter's and the Bridge of Sighs would no longer be places in a book, but would be claimed as her own.

So there.

She put on her reading glasses and went back to her book, a biography of Abigail Adams. Now *there* was a resourceful woman of intellect and gumption.

"Interesting book?"

She looked up, shading her eyes to see the speaker, but he was in silhouette.

"Oh, excuse me." He moved to the side so she wouldn't have to look right into the sun. "That better?"

"Much." In all ways. He was a handsome man with sophisticated gray hair, wearing a jaunty red-and-yellow tropical shirt. "And yes, the book is quite good. I enjoy biographies."

"So do I," he said. "They prove that ordinary people can do extraordinary things." His smile was kind. "It's never too late, you know."

She found herself blushing. She thought she'd forgotten how.

He motioned to the chair beside her. "Is this seat taken?"

"Not anymore."

Kansas City

Mac stood before his dresser mirror and combed his hair. Today was his wedding day. He set the comb down in order to adjust his tie, and his eyes locked onto the photo that had held this place of honor for nearly three years. A photo of Holly, smiling bashfully back at him, one hand waving at the camera.

He picked it up and touched her face. Lovely, sweet Holly who'd been taken too soon. He closed his eyes and could almost smell her scent and feel her hand on his cheek.

He forced away the memories. Today was the day he was truly starting over. With a new wife. Creating new memories.

Cheryl was nothing like Holly. Tall to Holly's petite. Blond to Holly's dark. Exuberant to Holly's quiet shyness. A career woman to Holly's domesticity. Would the two women have liked each other? Probably. Yet it was unlikely they would have been good friends. So why had each of them found a place in his heart?

It didn't matter. They had, and he thanked God for them both. Two different women for two different seasons of his life.

Andrew burst into the room, making a final jump into place before him. "How do I look?"

"Exactly like a best man."

Andrew lifted his toes. "My shoes are shiny."

Mac pointed to his own. "We're twins."

The doorbell rang and Andrew bolted. "She's here!"

Yes, she was. His new wife-to-be had arrived, and it was time to go to the church to get married. Time to appreciate the here and now and let the past go.

Alexander MacMillian went downstairs to open the door.

There is a time for everything,
and a season for every activity under heaven.
ECCLESIASTES 3:1

About the Author

Nancy Moser is the best-selling author of eleven novels and three books of inspirational humor including *The Seat Beside Me*, *The Ultimatum*, and the Sister Circle series coauthored with Vonette Bright. Her book *Time Lottery* was the recipient of a 2002 Christy Award for best novel in its genre. *Second Time Around* is its sequel.

If you enjoyed

Second Time Around,

check out Nancy Moser's

TIME LOTTERY

What if you have a chance to relive one life-changing moment? Three "lucky" people find out with the Time Lottery. Winner of the 2002 Christy Award in the futuristic category.

ISBN 1-58660-587-9

384 pages

$8.97